WHEN THE WOOD IS DRY

WHEN THE WOOD IS DRY

An Edgy Catholic Thriller

by

JOSEPH CILLO, JR.

Infornuity Publishing, LLC

Infornuity Publishing, LLC

Flemington, NJ 08822

EBook ISBN: 978-1-942590-20-0

Hardcover ISBN: 978-1-942590-28-6

Paperback ISBN: 978-1-942590-27-9

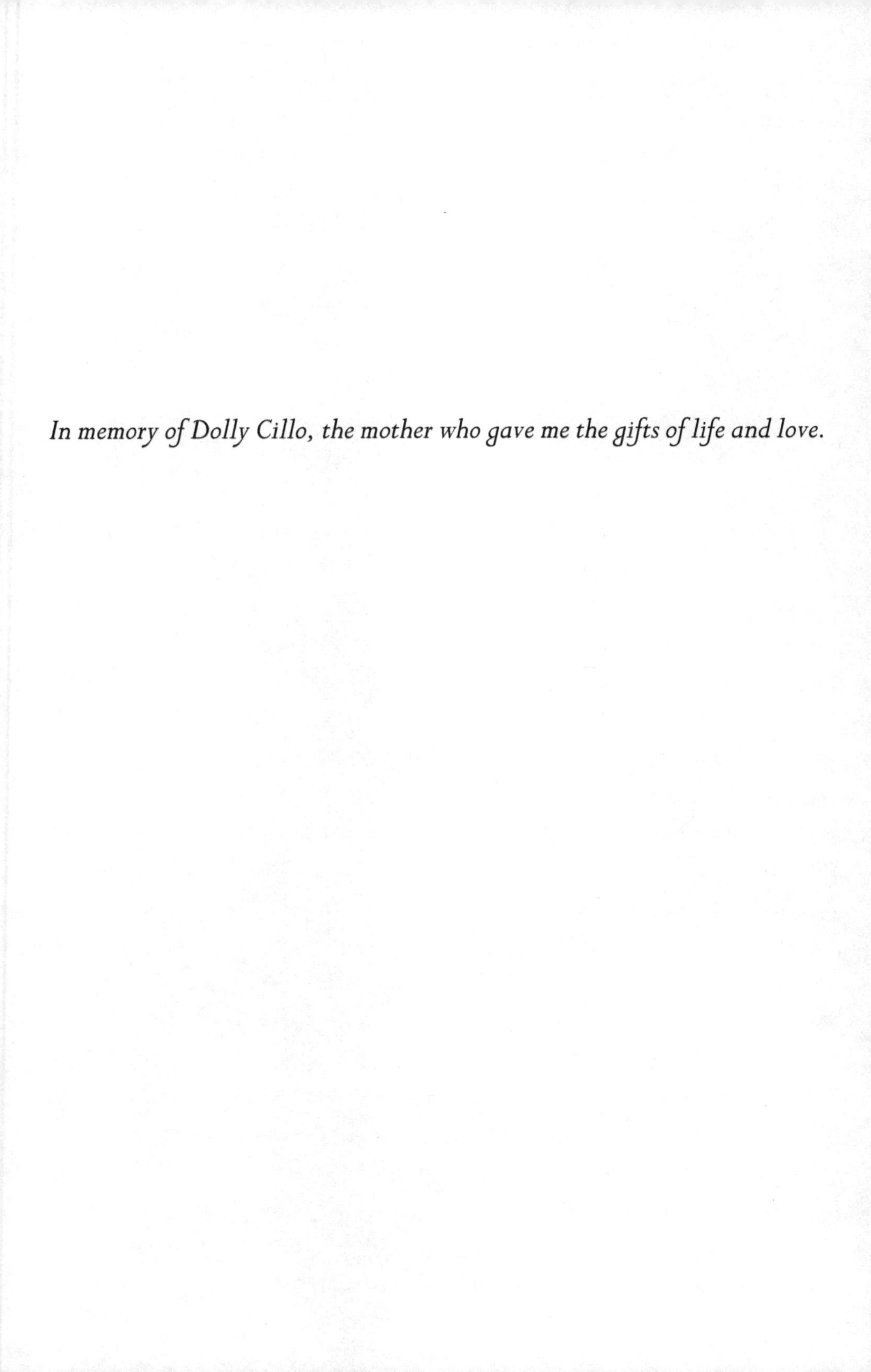

In memory of Dolly Cillo, the mother who gave me the gifts of life and love.

Jesus turned to them and said, "Daughters of Jerusalem, do not weep for me; weep instead for yourselves and for your children...For if these things are done when the wood is green, what will happen when it is dry?"

Luke 23:28,31

WHEN THE WOOD IS DRY

An Edgy Catholic Thriller

I

*Call of
the Innocent*

JOSEPH CILLO, JR.

I

Call of the Innocent

Do all things without grumbling or questioning, that you may be blameless and innocent, children of God without blemish in the midst of a crooked and perverse generation, among whom you shine as lights in the world.

Philippians 2:14-15

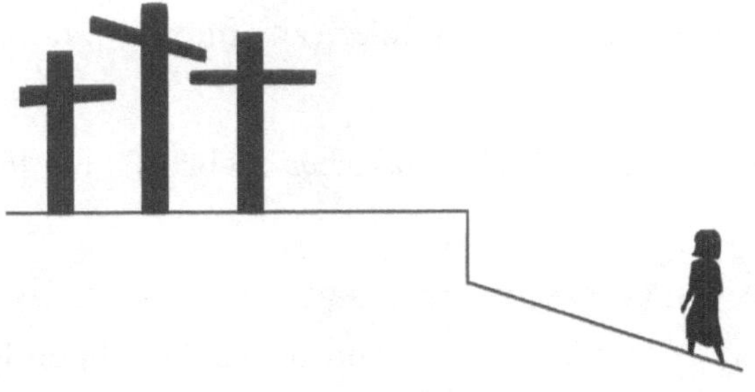

1

Lali

LALI LOVES TO SPIN. Leaning her head back, gazing into the clear blue sky, a lonely cloud circles as her long dark hair whips round and round until she falls laughing on the ground. Giggling, she scrambles back to her feet, the world swirling in her dizziness, and there He is, again. In a white tunic, bearded, dark curls of hair bounce on His shoulders. He smiles and laughs, His eyes bluer and more intense than the spinning sky. He opens His arms invitingly. She staggers toward Him, the red blotches on His palms awhirl as she struggles to steady her focus, to see them more clearly. As she draws closer, the light peeks through the wounds, twisting and turning in her disoriented field of vision.

He bends down as she approaches. His eyes now on her level, He grins and extends His hands toward her with His palms up, the red circles of dried blood more visible now, as her vision steadies. The holes become more distinct, like peepholes into another world, a glimpse of the other side before deciding to open a door. Her heart fills with empathy, sharing the pain of the wounds. She takes His right hand in her little hands. She traces the wound with her finger and looks quizzically into his piercing, yet gentle, blue eyes.

"Does it hurt?" She tilts her head, and raises her eyebrows, her long hair lightly dancing in the gentle breeze.

"Not anymore. But sometimes we must suffer if we are to save souls." Jesus takes her little hand in His own and traces a circle on her palm. "I will be with you when your time comes."

The world spins. She falls through space and time in an endless swirl, and then, for just a startled second, she hears angels singing and giving glory to God.

Lali awoke and looked at the clock just as the alarm rang and quickly silenced it. Why that dream again? She turned her body and sat up on the bed. Lali cocked her head and glanced at the statuette of the Sacred Heart of Jesus on the dresser. The man from her dream pointed to His heart wrapped in the crown of thorns, rays of light streaming from the wounded source of love and mercy. Her heart warmed but not so much as to remove her sense of foreboding. Twelve years, and now that dream again.

The memories of when she first had the dream that she never told anyone about swirled in her mind. It was Him, He who hung from the great cross in the front of the church, his hands and feet nailed and bloody, the great wound in His side. It was Him! Her five-year-old heart had swelled with joy. But what did it mean, "Sometimes we must suffer?"

And then Papa had told her. Mama was dying and to pray for a miracle. And she had prayed. And they had suffered.

Lali started from the swirling flood of twelve-year-old memories, caressing the Miraculous Medal her mother had given her, and focused on the clock. It was late. She would have to hurry. She quickly put on her Catholic school uniform, a plaid skirt and white blouse, and the navy sweater with the school's insignia, *St. Mary's High School.* She hurried down the stairs. The familiar aroma of burnt bacon amplified the mix of emotions from the memories inspired by her dream, the loss of her mother, the consoling love of her father. Papa was at it again, trying to make breakfast. Lali chuckled to herself as she entered the kitchen. He stood over the frying pan, an apron over his police uniform, his jacket hung over the back of one of the kitchen chairs.

"Good morning, Officer Russo," Lali said cheerfully, coming up to him from behind, smoothing the shoulders of his pressed shirt, not that they needed any smoothing. "You look quite dashing, today!"

Papa scraped some runny eggs and burnt bacon, a sticky mess clinging to the pan, onto a plate.

"I've made some bacon and eggs for breakfast." She followed his eyes to the mess now moved to the plate. "I know I'm not much of a cook, but I try."

Lali smiled. "Thank you, Papa. You know I love you more than anyone in the whole world!" She kissed him on the cheek.

"Even Rodrigo?" Papa raised a suspicious eyebrow.

"Yes, most certainly, even Rodrigo." She rolled her eyes. "I don't love Rodrigo, at least not like that. I'm just spending some time with him. We enjoy each other's company. You should really give him a chance. He's really smart, you know. He's taking all honors classes."

The heat of his glare forced her to look away. She dropped her gaze downward, to where the wall met the floor. She had given him an opportunity for his favorite lecture.

"He's in with a bad crowd, Lali," She sensed his searching eyes but avoided them. "A very bad crowd. That gang he's with, that *La Hermandad,* we're investigating them for dealing drugs. Lord knows what else they may be into. He's a bad influence on you."

Lali regained his eyes and struggled to smile, but her exasperation grew. "You always say that! Do you ever think that maybe *I'm* a good influence on *him?*"

"I really don't care about him. I'm trying to protect you. You're all I have since your mother died, you know."

There it was, again. The bubble of protection, promising a place where all would be safe. But how could she live, if she was always in the bubble and safe? She huffed, then raised her head.

"Yes, I know. But you have to let me live, Papa."

"I know, Lali." He turned to put the pan in the sink. "But it's hard. You're so innocent, and I've seen so much evil. You can't know all the bad things there are out there. I just want to protect you."

Perhaps she had won a little victory? At least he knew he needed to let her live, and she could not always be safe. She reached beneath her blouse for the miraculous medal and pulled it out to show him. She pointed to the image of the Blessed Mother, the tarnished silver allowing only a slight glint of reflection, weathered as it was from years of wear. She brimmed with confidence, holding up the medal with the figure of the lady in long robes, arms extended, palms up, and the words around the image, O MARY CONCEIVED WITHOUT SIN, PRAY FOR US WHO HAVE RECOURSE TO THEE. *Mother Mary will always be with me. She'll never let any harm come to me!*

"Don't worry, she'll protect me."

"She didn't protect your mother so well." Papa looked away, resentment and hurt in his voice.

"Oh, but she did!" Lali pulled the medal back and forth on its chain. "I believe Mama is with her right now. Safe as can be."

Lali tilted her head and raised her eyebrows. He had lost his faith. It was so sad. *Mother Mary, pray for him!*

Her father shook his head. She was waiting with a smile when he raised his chin.

"You're so sweet, Lali," he said, then his expression turned more serious. "But I'm telling you, you want to stay away from Rodrigo and his crowd. They're bad news."

Lali replaced the medal under her blouse and kissed her father on the cheek. Then she changed the subject.

"I'll be stopping by the unwed mothers' home to help with the kids after I pray at the abortion clinic. I'll call you for a ride about seven."

Papa let out an exasperated sigh and glanced down at the runny eggs on the plate. "I really wish you would stay away from that abortion clinic. That's a very bad place too, you know."

Lali closed her eyes for a moment. The words from her dream rang in her ears, *sometimes we must suffer…* And then the gospel message, *your light must shine before others, that they may see your good deeds and glorify your heavenly Father.* And finally, the commandment, *honor your father and your mother.* The messages crashed against each other like confused currents roiling against the rocks. Her way forward seemed to spin like a faulty compass, pointing one way and then as quickly the other. To dispel the confusion, she would need his permission, or at least, his tacit acceptance.

"Yes, I know it's a bad place." Lali stabbed a piece of burnt bacon with her fork but thought better of eating it. She pushed the blackened meat into the runny yellow of the egg. "That's why I go there and pray for them, and for the babies that will never be born. You know, there are people in there who are doing these things, and they really don't know what they are doing." She turned and faced her father. "They need our prayers. And, they need to know we are praying for them. We have to be there for them."

He closed his eyes, then glanced back at her. Lali noticed the softening of his eyes, the hint of resignation in his voice. "Just be careful, Lali. The world can be a very hard place."

"But maybe we can make it a little softer if we are there, present to those who are caught in hard places. If we always just stay safe, won't the world become even harder?"

And then there it was, the glint of a tear in his eye, the sigh, the slumping of his shoulders, and the pensive smile.

"Well, we'd better get you off to church." He cleared the plates and placed them in the sink, then grabbed his jacket from the chair. "Or you'll miss the readings again. We don't want any trouble with Father Fernandez."

Lali considered her father's concerns as his squad car wound its way through the mountain roads along the familiar route into the town of Santa Inés. *It will be hard on him, Lord, if I must suffer, if that is my calling.* It was so hard on him when Mama died. *Be with Him, Lord, even if he has lost faith.* Lali glanced at her father as the car pulled over to the curb and stopped in front of St. Sebastian's Church. She was lucky to have a father like this, who loved her and would always protect her, but what about his soul? *Lord, help him to regain his faith.* Lali leaned over and kissed him.

"You know, you could come with me?" She raised her eyebrows hopefully, as she grabbed her backpack. "It might help you to stop worrying and trust God if you came to Mass in the morning before work."

Papa's features tightened as if she had poked some hidden wound. He closed his eyes and turned his head, looking forward through the windshield.

"You know I can't, Lali. I tried all that praying when your mom was sick. Didn't help anything. I love that you believe and have such faith, but I've lost mine."

Lali paused, then turned to her father and kissed him, again. "I'll pray for you, Papa. I'll pray that you regain your faith."

Lali opened the door and slid out of the car. After a few steps, she glanced back over her shoulder. The morning light seemed to glimmer on her father's face as if a tear had caught the light at just the right angle. She hesitated a moment and closed her eyes. *No, if it is a tear, it is something I am not meant to see.* She turned and trotted toward the church.

Lali approached the chapel at St. Sebastian's Church, where morning Mass would be offered. The chapel lay in the shadow of the main church, that towered over the street, a neo-gothic facade strangely out of place in the quaint northern California town. Lali breathed in the familiar scent of stale incense and candle wax that clung to the air in the chapel like an old, familiar song, unheard and yet always present, and she knew in the depth of her soul that she was home. Some twenty older men and women were gathered for morning Mass, no one else under fifty years old. Those not absorbed in prayer glanced at Lali and smiled. Lali returned the gesture, then knelt facing the tabernacle to pray. An indescribable peace settled in her soul and she recalled His touch, gently tracing the circle on her palm. She opened and closed her hand.

She prayed for her father and Rodrigo, for the workers at the abortion clinic and their clients, for the souls of the babies never to be born, and for the girls at the unwed mothers' home. And then, remembering her dream, she prayed, *Oh, Lord, please help me to bear the sufferings that may come my way with grace and dignity. Let me never lose my faith, and always be with me, my sweet Lord Jesus, in my times of trial, just as you promised in my dream. Amen.*

Father Fernandez, an elder Hispanic priest, dressed in the green flowing robes of ordinary time, with the golden chi-rho cross on the front, rang the bell and progressed up the middle aisle to the altar. Lali, lost in her prayer and meditation, stood when she heard the bell and realized Mass was starting. Her mind wandered, and her thoughts drifted to the meaning of last night's dream as the familiar liturgy progressed. That dream, again! Was another trial coming? Last time, Mama was dying. Would something happen to Papa? *Oh, I just couldn't bear it, if something happened to Papa!* She clutched her rosary beads to her breast and began to pray again for her father. Her mind meandered past specific prayer, and more into a conceptual reverie. Men like her father, they stood for honor and bravely answered the call to protect and serve. They willingly placed their lives on the line each day, the last line of defense against the darkness of humanity. How necessary but how futile. And how dangerous! The last line of defense. Surely, it was not the best line. But for men like Papa, it was the only way they knew.

Mass progressed with the standard liturgy for the day. No saints to commemorate. Just the typical Liturgy of the Word, followed by the Liturgy of the Eucharist and the distribution of Holy Communion, the Bread of Life. Even the feeling of renewal when receiving the blessed sacrament gave little relief to her spiritual disorientation, her sense of being called forward into an unknown and foreboding future. Lali's mind drifted from attention to distraction. The implications of her dream, always present in the depths of her mind, rose and receded from consciousness, as she attempted to maintain her attention on the proceedings of the Mass and on her daily prayer intentions. Why couldn't she focus today? It was that dream again! *I will be with you when your time comes...* The words seemed to haunt her, though their meaning should be a comfort. He would be with her. But what did it mean? *When my time comes?* She looked down at her palm and closed her hand, then stood as Father Fernandez ended Mass with the dismissal rite.

"Go in peace, glorifying the Lord by your life."

A conviction gripped her soul as if it were a command for her to follow. What did it mean? *Glorify the Lord by my life? How do I do that? Was there a deeper call than future marriage and family?* What about the dream? *Sometimes we must suffer if we are to save souls?* Wasn't that what He had said?

The memory of the first time she had that dream flooded her mind. How she had suffered, watching her mother fade and grow thinner. And her mother suffered, the relentless cancer devouring her body, so frail and thin at the end. Her father hunched over the bed, his face wet with tears, seemed to suffer even more. The medal her mother had given her, had dangled on her chest, as she held her mother's lifeless hand in her own and traced a circle around her palm, "Mama's with Jesus now."

Surely, they had suffered. But what souls had been saved? Was it her soul that had been saved through Mama's suffering? And what about Papa? His soul seemed to be lost.

Jesus promised to be with me, so, He'll be with me, whatever may come. She turned her attention to the tabernacle, the Holy of Holies, a golden casing with a cross on top and a door that opened to store the Blessed Sacrament: The Body, Blood, Soul, and Divinity of Jesus.

I will be with you, she heard Him say, as in her dream. A calming peace descended upon her. Renewed and restored, she was certain that she was not alone and would never be alone.

Time to get about the glorifying-the-Lord bit. She chuckled to herself as she rose and made her way to the door. Father Fernandez greeted the people as they left. Lali embraced him.

"Thank you, Father. I'm praying for you and that there will be more men like you willing to sacrifice so much to serve the people and the Church."

Father Fernandez blinked and glanced awkwardly back at the chapel, then refocused back at her.

"Thank you, Lali. I'm praying for you as well."

As Lali strolled the several blocks to St. Mary's High School, she passed a couple of public-school girls wearing jeans and short blouses with exposed midriffs, despite the coming chill in the autumn air. The girls gawked as she passed as if she were some unusual exhibit in a zoo. Lali glanced over her shoulder after they passed and glimpsed them making furtive comments and giggling. The sting of their disapproval made her wince, but she realized she was treading an ancient path toward a narrow gate that most modern folk had abandoned or never knew existed. They would call her old fashioned and defend what they thought of as liberty. But wasn't it just sin? But how could anyone tell them that? If she tried to speak with them, would they see her as an enemy? Or, as their judge?

Lali closed her eyes a moment and pressed her lips together. Would she see these girls one day at the unwed mothers' home? Or worse, at the abortion clinic? If she did, she would never judge them, but would try to help them, as best she could. The world sent these girls terribly mixed messages. How far they were from what the Church taught and what she herself believed. The Church taught that temperance and chastity were virtues, but no one outside of the Church seemed to agree anymore. And worse, they mocked the Church for her beliefs. But at least the Church was consistent. The modesty the Church advised led more naturally to the respect of the entire person. The world encouraged girls to accentuate their sexuality, and then encouraged them even more to express outrage at the injustice when other aspects of their persons were ignored. And, sexuality seemed to be untethered from the natural consequence of motherhood. The message seemed to be that pregnancy was a disease, and mothers were the poor victims who had caught it and not been treated in time. Make love, not children. Wasn't that the message?

But Lali was the oddball on this subject. She accepted the Church's teachings. Most people, even many churchgoers, ridiculed the Church, with its celibate priests, monks, religious sisters, and cloistered nuns, so unfathomable to the modern mind. A relic of a past age of ignorance, they thought it all. The world had outgrown the ancient wisdom of the two-thousand-year-old church, or at least, had left it behind. But had wisdom itself really changed? Or, was the world on a great prodigal journey to some foreign land, squandering an inheritance on loose living? Had science really come up with ways to avoid all the consequences of sin or just the material ones? Was science creating a new morality or enabling an old immorality? Should she have tried to talk to those girls? Wouldn't they just have laughed at her? After all, if anyone had tried to talk the prodigal out of his journey, would he have listened? The prodigal in the parable came to his senses, but only after there was a famine and he was in terrible want. Would the world come to its senses one day? What would have to happen for a whole world to come to its senses? A famine? Some other terrible thing? A sudden gust of wind caught her unprepared and seemed to whisper, *I will be with you...* Lali pulled her sweater closer over her body and listened closely for a moment, but it was only the wind, after all. She trod on toward the school. Would she have the courage to fully commit to all she might be called to do? Glorify the Lord by your life? What did it really mean? *Am I doing it? Should I have tried to talk with them?*

I will do my best to glorify you, Lord, by my life today. Help me to know what it means and how to do it. Lali continued her prayer and contemplation as she approached St. Mary's High School.

Mr. Martinez, the school principal, waited in front of the school doorway greeting students as they arrived. Was he frowning or was it just that big down-turned mustache? Lali could never quite tell, until she heard his voice. He always appeared so serious, even when he was happy. But he was always there each morning welcoming the good and the bad students alike.

"Good morning, Mr. Martinez!" Lali said, brushing a strand of her long dark hair from her face and leaving her hand above her eye to shade it from the morning sun.

"Good morning, Lali," Principal Martinez responded. Lali often took the time to greet the middle-aged principal and felt especially called to do so this morning.

"I'm praying for you."

"Thank you, Lali. I can use all the prayers I can get."

Lali entered the school. The familiar scent of adolescent funk slapped her face, tensing the muscles in her neck. The mix of teenage emotion and turmoil infused the hallway with a kind of forbidding raucousness, most unlike her peaceful entrance into the church for Mass. Kids rushing here and there, lockers slamming, the crowd of muddled voices blending together into a loud, unintelligible hum.

"Hey, give me back my hat," a voice rose above the din.

"Wearing a hat is against school policy!"

A boy scooted past her chasing after Jake Turner, who held a baseball cap high over his head where his smaller victim could not reach it. The boy had no hair. *Oh, my God! The boy's sick; what's wrong with these jerks?* Jake tossed the hat to his buddy, Ted Strickland.

Ted tossed the hat back to Jake. Jake and Ted, those bullies! Well, this was a new low! The two boys adeptly passed the baseball cap between them, easily keeping it from their sick and smaller victim.

The boy bumped into Lali, as he scrambled to pursue his tormentors. "Excuse me!"

"Hey, wait!" Lali called after him.

As the boy turned and caught sight of her, his eyes widened.

"Don't chase after them! That's what they want."

The boy slowly raised his hands to cover his baldness. Tears filled his eyes, then he closed them and looked down. Lali drew near him and put her arms around him.

"You don't need to be ashamed." She held him for a moment, then pulled back to meet his eyes. "What's your name?"

The boy lifted his chin, his mouth falling open.

"Daniel. My friends call me Danny."

"Well, Danny. What period do you have lunch?" She raised her eyebrows.

Daniel cocked his head. "Fourth?" The tone of his voice questioned why she should ask.

Lali clapped her hands with exaggerated glee. "Well, so do I! How would you like to have lunch together?"

Danny eyed her, then squinted. "*You* want to have lunch with *me?*"

"Sure, why wouldn't I?" She put her hands on his shoulders.

Danny lowered his gaze and shuffled his feet. Then, he peeked back up at her. "Well, I'm just a freshman, and...I...uh...uh...oh...you know." Danny stared down at his feet.

Lali nodded. "Yes, I know. I understand if you would rather not, but I would really like to have lunch with you. Won't you join me?"

Danny's glanced at her sidelong. "I guess, if you really want me to."

"Well, okay then. It's a date." Lali beamed.

Danny chuckled. "A date?"

"Yes, Danny, you and I have a date for lunch!" She paused, then tilted her head, "Oh, unless it bothers you to think of it as a date?"

Danny laughed, shaking his head. "No, it doesn't bother me. But maybe it's better to say we're just meeting for lunch… uh… what was your name?"

"Lali, Lali Russo. And I can't wait to meet you for lunch, Danny."

The boys with the hat realized they were no longer being chased and brought the hat back and handed it to Lali.

"Sorry, just having a bit of fun," Jake Turner said.

Lali grabbed the hat from Jake and placed it back on Danny's head. Lali winked at Danny, one hand on each of his shoulders; she met his eyes. "I like you better without it. But I understand why you wear it."

Lali turned to the older boys and shook her head disapprovingly, her lips pressed together, her eyes askance.

"Now, guys. Is this how we are called to treat the sick?"

Jake and Ted avoided her eyes. Ted, a follower, stood quietly, while Jake did the talking.

"We're sorry. We didn't mean any harm. But there is a policy against wearing hats in school."

"Come on, Jake! Who appointed you to enforce the rules? My goodness, when was the last time you cared about the rules? Can't you see the boy is sick, and he just wants to fit in?"

"Yeah, I'm sorry. I guess we got carried away."

"Well, don't apologize to me. This is Daniel. You owe him an apology."

Jake turned to Daniel, with Ted following.

"We're sorry, Daniel. We didn't mean any harm."

The tension seemed to drain out of Danny. "It's okay. I know I look funny with no hair."

She turned to him. "Now, Danny, the Lord said that every hair on your head is counted. You're just making the math easy for Him."

Daniel laughed. "I guess it's easy to count to zero."

Lali chuckled then turned to the older boys, attempting full reconciliation, but knowing it was a stretch. "Well, gentlemen, Danny and I will be having lunch together fourth period. Would you like to join us?"

Jake avoided eye contact and shuffled his feet. "Well, we usually eat with our friends."

"Well, maybe it's time to try something new? Anyway, you're welcome to join us."

The older boys scurried off to class without another word. Would the two boys join them for lunch? Could they all be friends, after such a bad start? Would that be a way to glorify the Lord?

At fourth period lunch, Lali met Danny in line. Most of the other students carried bagged lunches and scuffled by, bypassing the line and entered the cafeteria where the light roar of muddled voices hummed.

"What horrors are hiding beneath the bun today?" Danny quipped.

"Wednesday? Should be a Glorious Mystery." Lali chuckled.

"I always hope for a Glorious or even a Joyful Mystery." Danny grabbed a tray from the rack. "But I guess it's mostly Sorrowful, every day."

"I don't think I'd eat it if it were something Luminous?" Lali picked up a tray and followed Danny in line. "My dad usually makes some kind of burnt offering for breakfast. It's usually more sorrowful than anything here."

They paid for their meals and walked to a table with plenty of room in case the other boys wanted to join them. Suzie Parks and her friends, the clique of pretty juniors, passed by, snickering. Suzie was one of those girls who was a little too popular with the boys in public school, and so had been banished in her sophomore year to St. Mary's.

"Oh, don't worry about them." Lali rolled her eyes. "They're full of themselves."

Danny swallowed a pill with his chocolate milk. Lali changed the subject. "Danny, if you don't mind me asking, how long have you had cancer?" Lali sipped from her water bottle.

Daniel shifted his body. Lali regretted asking. She had made him uncomfortable.

Daniel took a deep breath. "I was diagnosed two months ago. I just came back to school today. The therapy really takes a lot out of you."

"Yes, I know. My mother died of cancer when I was only five years old. I did my best to help care for her, but there wasn't much a five-year-old could do, just be with her, I guess. She loved to tell me stories about when she was growing up, and when she got too weak, I started telling her stories, just made things up. You know, kid stuff. But she really loved it."

Jake and Ted walked by the table. When Lali motioned invitingly, they hesitated, but moved on and sat with their friends.

"I guess they won't be joining us, after all." Lali frowned.

"I don't think I'll miss them." Daniel cut the chicken breast on his plate.

"Well, we have to give people a chance, don't we?" Lali shrugged. "Give them an opportunity to try a different way."

"I guess. But those guys won't change." Daniel shook his head.

"Well, I wouldn't give up on those two just yet. Anyway, I know it's hard being different, Danny, but we are all different in our own way. Those guys stick with their friends, so they don't feel different, but they are. God made all of us unique, yet all in His image. I will pray for you, Danny, and I will pray for those other boys."

Daniel rolled his eyes. "Why would you pray for those bullies?"

"Because they need prayers even more than you do." Lali touched his hand. "You have a sickness of the body. They have a sickness of the soul."

Danny played with his food. "Do you think we could get together after school and talk?" He mindlessly pushed his fork around on his plate. "I don't have many friends."

Lali patted his hand. "I'm going to the abortion clinic to pray after school, then to St. Elizabeth's Home for Unwed Mothers to volunteer there. You're more than welcome to join me."

Daniel glanced up and blinked. "You do that? On your own?"

"Sure," Lali said, blithely. "I go to the clinic and pray the Rosary almost every day. I pray for the women and their babies that will never see the light of day. I pray for the men who pay for abortions. I especially pray for the doctors and nurses, that they may see that what they are doing is so wrong and change their ways."

"Wow! You pray a lot!"

Lali laughed and tugged Danny's hat playfully over his eyes. "I have a lot to pray for!"

Daniel adjusted the hat on his head. He paused a moment as if he were thinking. "Well, I'd like to, but I think my parents would worry about me."

"Honor thy father and thy mother." Lali remembered how her own father had not wanted her to go to the abortion clinic to pray. *Glorify the Lord by your life. Am I doing it? Or should I have done as Papa asked?*

Daniel wiped his mouth with a paper napkin. "I think it's great that you go to the clinic and pray. You must be really committed to this pro-life thing."

Lali tilted her head. "The way I see it, if you believe that life is sacred, you must do all you can to preserve life. But people have freedom, and that includes freedom to sin. All we can really do is make it easier for people to make the right choices, but we can't force them. We all have an obligation to bear the burdens of life. If a pregnant girl sees me praying in front of the clinic, it may help her to make the right decision, remind her of the implications of what she is doing."

Daniel lowered his head, breaking eye contact. "I guess I never really thought about it that way." Danny lifted his gaze, and she found his eyes. Lali laughed, and pulled Danny's hat down, all the way over his eyes.

"Well, think about it, Danny!"

Danny laughed, shaking his head as he adjusted his hat.

Lali became more pensive. "I helped those boys, the bullies who were teasing you, to make the right decision. If you stand tall and unafraid, sometimes you can have an impact." Was this what it meant to *glorify the Lord by your life? Am I actually doing it?*

Danny pensively swirled his fork on his plate. Then he glanced up at Lali. "I really respect you, Lali," Danny looked away quickly when their eyes met, then he finally met her gaze.

"Well, thank you, Danny. I really respect you as well," Lali replied cheerfully, then becoming more serious, she added, "people fight about a great many things, but yours is a fight for survival. And that's the biggest fight of all."

An awkward pause ensued, Danny sighed, and glanced down at his plate again, shifting in his seat. Lali regretted her words, though she had meant them to be encouraging, since they seemed to have caused distress. She changed the subject. "So, how about that hat of yours? The Los Angeles Angels?" She examined the emblem on the hat, the red "A" with the halo above it. "Los Angeles Angels. When you translate it, it's *the Angels Angels?* Isn't that funny?"

"Yeah, it is kind of stupid. Anyway, they stink at baseball, but I like that they are named for the angels."

Lali laughed. "Well, I hope they are good at being angels, these angels angels!"

"You know, the devil started out as an angel, so even some real angels aren't very good at being angels." Daniel's tone turned abruptly sober, as he made his deeper philosophical point.

Lali worried that she had led the conversation to a difficult place for Danny. Not even changing the subject to angels seemed to have helped. She reached over and jostled the hat on her friend's head. "Well, aren't you the gloomy one!"

Danny cracked a grin. "I try to keep my spirits up, but I guess I can be gloomy sometimes."

The bell rang, signaling the end of fourth period.

"Well, I guess it's back to the fight for survival." Danny packed up his tray and headed toward the trash cans.

Lali could not help sensing something ominous in Danny's little quip. *Sometimes we must suffer if we are to save souls.* Wasn't that what He had said?

The final bell of the day having rung, Lali gathered her books into her backpack and readied herself for her usual trip to the abortion clinic and then St. Elizabeth's Home for Unwed Mothers. She had been distracted all day by the implications of her dream and confused by the meaning of "glorifying the Lord" by her life. One of the typical Mass dismissals, she had heard it often. Why was it sticking with her? And, what about this business of suffering to save souls? Closing her locker, she headed for the door.

As she exited the school, Principal Martinez stood just outside the doorway, greeting the students as they left. Lali approached him, a brisk confidence in her gait. "I want to thank you, Principal Martinez, for your hard work today."

Principal Martinez's grin almost negated the downward frown of his mustache. "Why, thank you, Lali, for noticing. And, thanks for helping that young boy. It's so hard for the sick ones to fit in. Heck, it's hard for anyone to fit in. But, thank you for reaching out to him. If I had more students like you, I wouldn't have to work so hard."

"I appreciate all you do to keep this school going." Lali adjusted her backpack on her shoulder, then lowered her gaze. "I'm not always proud of my classmates."

Principal Martinez chuckled. "No. Neither am I."

Why had she greeted Principal Martinez this way? How mean the boys this morning had been, teasing Danny. Principal Martinez would be the one who would need to deal with them. If the boys were so unfeeling that they would pick on a kid with cancer, it must really be a difficult job to be principal. *Maybe that's why I thanked him?* Or, maybe, expressing thanks was a way to *glorify God?*

Lali continued musing as she made her way to the abortion clinic. She arrived at an ordinary looking single-family residence with a rundown sign in front identifying it in bold, if weathered, letters as "Dr. Singer's Family Planning Clinic". Were there no sign, it would be just another Tudor style single-family cottage. The sign made all the difference and what happened within its walls. The railing to the brick and concrete stairs had settled over time and was slightly misaligned, the steps making their crooked path to the entrance. Lali retrieved her rosary beads from her backpack, placed the backpack down on the ground next to her, and stood on the sidewalk next to the paving stone walkway leading to the entrance of the clinic, careful not to block the way. She began to pray.

"Lord, give me clarity of thought, as I am present here to you this day. I dedicate this Rosary for the conversion of those in this building, and those everywhere who practice abortion, for the women who seek abortions, and for all those who assist or aid in promoting or procuring abortions."

Lali drew a deep breath and glanced back up at the sign in front of the clinic. Papa was right, this was a very bad place. Lali pursed her lips, then lowered her gaze. *But how can we make bad places better, if we are afraid to go there? I know he doesn't want me here, but isn't this where I need to be? Honor your father and your mother,* the thought came to her again. *Can I honor him and still be present in this place for you, Lord?* Lali shivered as the voice came to her, once more, *I will be with you when your time comes.*

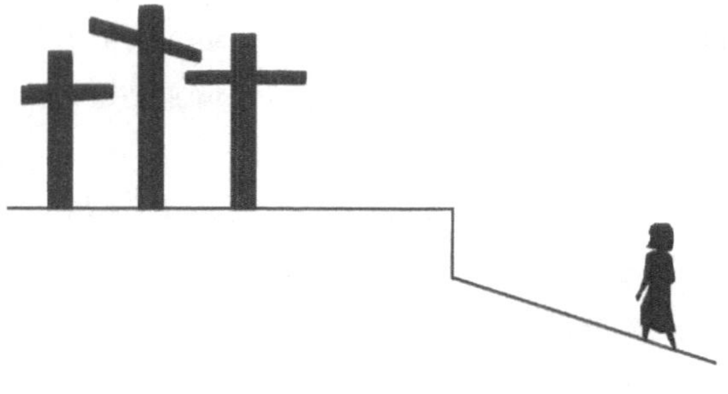

2

Robert

SHOULD I HAVE BEEN MORE FORCEFUL? Sitting in his squad car in front of St. Sebastian's Church, his daughter leaned over and kissed him, pledging she would pray that he regained his faith. Why didn't he just tell her to stay away from that damned place? Robert tightened his lips and closed his eyes. But he couldn't keep her safe by holding her hostage. She was right. He had to let her live. But this faith of hers would get her killed one day, and he wouldn't be able to stop it. Robert shook his head and gritted his teeth. And that stinking medal wouldn't do a bit of good. She would likely die with it around her neck, just like her mother. Robert forced his mind to focus on his mission, his commitment as a police officer: *Protect and serve.* The mantra that directed his mind away from the anxieties and frustrations of his life. His guiding purpose. But the anxieties this time were too great, and the stakes too high to be put off. He couldn't protect her mother. Would he be able to protect her?

Robert watched Lali as she slid from the seat out through the car door. She took a few steps toward the church. Then, she hesitated just a moment as if she had forgotten something. Was it panic that seized him, and almost led him to prayer? *Please, don't let her turn back.* To whom had he made the request? His daughter turned and blithely trotted toward the church, where Father Fernandez waited to begin morning Mass. A tear traced a crooked path down Robert's cheek.

My God, she's just like her mother. Robert took a deep breath, attempting to compose himself, recalling the woman he had married some twenty years earlier, not the frail, hairless remnant she had become at the end. The great loss of his life, when a good part of him had died along with her. How quickly his thoughts turned from his beautiful wife, when they met and married, to that terrible day when he lost her forever. Stolen away by God, Himself.

The day he had lost his faith. Prayers? What good had they done? The long shadows of darkness had spread over all, extending like wispy fingers even into this place of safety, the home he had made with his wife and daughter. Had he not moved them to this remote place of safety? Had he not barred the evil out? Had he not done all a man could do to keep them safe? *Protect and serve,* but how could he protect against this? His wife's body depleted and limp, her bald head lying motionless on the pillow, weakened by the chemotherapy meant to make her well, a desperate chance, the doctors had said. A *Hail Mary.* A miracle, had it worked, they all admitted. Miracles. Doctors depending on miracles. He had watched her take her last gasping breath, as the once vibrant life drained out of what remained of her. And, looking to his daughter at the bedside, he remembered how she traced a little circle on the palm of his dead wife's hand.

"Mommy's with Jesus now," she said with a confidence and innocence that had to be protected. After all, that was his job. To protect and serve.

"Yes, Lali," he had lied, "Mommy's with Jesus, now."

Or, at least, he believed it was a lie. And where exactly was Jesus? Was He there, and did nothing, despite all our prayers? The questions haunted him.

Robert put the squad car in gear and pulled away from the curb in front of the church. As he drove the familiar route to the police station, he forced himself to remember something further back, before his great loss. But his mind hovered on darkness and danger, the inescapable memories, even more horrible than the loss of his wife, more visceral and terrifying than the loss of something as intangible as his faith. He tried to shake himself from it, to think of his wedding, his bride in her white dress, the ring he had slipped onto her delicate finger, but he could not escape the red, the blood of the fallen, the terror of combat. *Semper Fidelis,* Always Faithful, that was his motto then. The Navy Cross for valor, his reward for his bloody rage, or perhaps, not exactly rage. His single-minded focus on vengeance, replacing all empathy and remorse, that saved his men, or most of them, but not the one who had lost his face when the IED had gone off. The red, the blood, where his face used to be. That event he could not prevent, but could only avenge, and accept his award for valor. The distant calls of his comrades to get down, to stay back, to take cover, as he charged forward, his rifle an extension of his being, the killing machine he had become focused on a mission derived from circumstance, not from orders provided by his commanders: *Kill them all!* Turn, look, shoot, turn, look, shoot, turn, look, shoot. Down they fell. His deadly aim never missing. The rounds of his enemies blunted by his body armor, his body staggered with the force of their impact, then one glanced off his helmet. Turn, look, shoot. Turn, look, shoot. Twelve had fallen when he heard the cry from behind him. "*Allahu…*" He turned 180 degrees and looked, and shot, and the boy fell back wounded, the red, the blood. "*Allahu Akbar,*" he had tried to say, Arabic for "God is the greatest," and that was his mistake. "Well, *All hail the back-bar!*" Robert had said, then, as the injured boy foolishly tried to raise his weapon, he fired another round into the boy's face. "If your God is so great, why are you so dead?"

If God is so great, why were we killing each other? Thirteen more martyrs for Allah. He must be running out of virgins for them in heaven.

Robert violently shook his head back and forth, attempting to rid himself of the memory, as he turned into the police station. *That meaningless war really fucked me up!* He parked at the station and took a deep breath, putting his head in his hands. The killing and dying he had seen in war had broken him, and he knew it. Now, he fought a more difficult battle every day to keep the demons at bay. His mind struggled with the senselessness of it all. Fighting an idea with bullets and explosions. The idea that dying for Islam, the distorted view of martyrdom, would bring rewards in the afterlife. As long as those bastards believed they were going to heaven for killing and dying, they were going to keep killing and dying. It was a kind of hellish Valhalla, drawing more good soldiers into meaningless mortal combat for an unattainable end. To end it, beliefs needed to be changed. Was anyone even trying to convince them that there is no heaven for killers? It was just not a battle you could win with a gun.

He couldn't battle cancer with a gun, either. Officer Robert Russo entered the Santa Inés Police Station. *What can you win with a gun?* a thought that was not quite his own rang in his mind. *If I ever kill again, it will be with definite reason and purpose. It will be for family, for honor, for love,* he answered the voice, opening the door to the briefing room, *and if necessary, to uphold the law. To protect and serve.*

Robert made his way to the conference room where Chief Greeley, a stocky man with graying hair and a prodigious belly, and Officer Kincaid, the African American former all-state linebacker, already had begun addressing the disturbing rash of missing person cases that the department had received. Chief Greeley wore plain clothes, a brown blazer over a white golf shirt and khaki slacks. As usual, his golf shirt had come untucked and flapped loosely over his substantial paunch. He was the only member of the Santa Inés Force who did not wear a uniform and acted as lead detective as well as chief. There just was not enough crime in Santa Inés to justify a full-time detective. But that might be changing. The chief nodded to him as he entered, his posture relaxing as if an unseen force had somehow made the room more secure.

Robert chuckled to himself as he noted the slightest of eye rolls from Officer Kincaid. The chief liked to get a variety of perspectives, and he knew that Officer Dennis Kincaid would be cautious and methodical, and Robert would be decisive and more impulsive in his assessment. Officer Kincaid had an imposing, intimidating physical presence, and was well able to handle any kind of trouble, but he was predisposed to avoid it, which Robert figured explained his coming north to Santa Inés, and why the Chief hired him so quickly. A good small-town cop could kick ass if he needed to, but was predisposed not to, unless absolutely necessary. And, that was Officer Kincaid.

The chief stood in the front of the room. Robert recognized the list of names of the missing persons scrawled on the whiteboard. Four local drug dealers, there had only been three yesterday.

"Good-morning, Officer Russo," Chief Greeley greeted him. "I was just discussing a new case with Officer Kincaid, here. Seems another punk drug dealer, Mickey Turnoff, is missing. Somebody seems to be saving us the trouble of investigating and arresting these guys."

"I don't think you should be too happy about that, Chief." Robert took a seat in the briefing room. "I don't think anyone is trying to help us out. It's likely that tougher, more serious players are moving in."

"Santa Inés is hardly a hotbed of drug activity," Officer Kincaid chimed in. "People come here because it is quiet and safe. For the views, the ocean, the mountains, the coastal trail. Why would more hardened players want to come here?"

"For the same reason, Denny," Robert said, "for the quiet. There is little to do and plenty of money to buy drugs in Santa Inés, and not too many people to shoot at you once you've muscled your way in."

"I'm not sure we should jump to any conclusions." Officer Kincaid rolled his eyes.

Robert cocked his head. "I'm just saying it makes sense. You came up from L.A. You know how tough those gangs are. Why slug it out down there, when you can bump off a few minor players up here and live the good life, or at least, a safer, quieter life."

"I guess it's possible, but most of those tough guys *like* the excitement in the city, you know, the party life. They're not looking to go where things are quiet," Officer Kincaid responded.

"In my experience, nobody likes getting shot at, no matter how tough they are." Robert glanced knowingly at Officer Kincaid. He was tough as hell, but here he was, come for the quiet. Not a cop in LA, where he might get shot at. And Denny could be a cop anywhere, without a doubt. Robert respected his friend, Officer Kincaid, but he had his doubts. Would he do what it took when the time came?

"So, Officer Russo, you think there are tougher gangs moving in?" Chief Greeley asked.

"I know there are, Chief. I've seen them on the streets. I think they are eliminating the competition. We've had three long-time drug dealers go missing in the last three months: Johnny Black, Sonny Charles, and Mickey Turnoff, guys with legal pot rackets, dabbling in harder stuff. All white guys, too."

"What about this guy, Juanito Perez?" Chief Greeley circled the name on the whiteboard. "They say he started working the high school about a year ago. He's been missing about three months. He's just a kid, for Christ's sake!"

"They like using kids to deal," Officer Kincaid said, "because they don't get in as much trouble if they get caught."

"They're pushing into the high school. They're gonna use kids." Robert tightened his lips, thinking about his daughter and Rodrigo. "It's a hard business for a kid to get messed up with. Wasn't Juanito in that new gang that moved in, *La Hermandad,* the Brotherhood? My guess is he crossed them somehow. I think that's the gang that's muscling in. Mexicans migrating up from the south, finding it safe and quiet here, and more lucrative, once they get rid of the competition."

Chief Greeley drew an arrow from the circle around Juanito's name and wrote the name *La Hermandad* on the whiteboard. "Oh, geez, I remember when we were lucky to ticket someone for speeding! Now, we got gangs killing each other? We haven't had a missing person's case since the Hennessey girl, and that was almost twenty years ago. Now we have four in three months."

"I know what you mean, Chief." Officer Kincaid sighed. "It's hard to believe. We kinda let those low-level guys go. It would cause more trouble to go after them. But now we got three of the old-timers missing, plus this Juanito guy. If it were just a little drug dealing, as long as it stays quiet, nobody minds much, but it's just hard to think about this kind of serious crime in Santa Inés."

"It's here, Denny. We're going to have to deal with it." Robert removed his revolver from its holster and flipped the cylinder open to make sure it was fully loaded, then flipped it back in place. "We may actually have to use these things one day."

The Chief was awfully jumpy today. Robert tightened his lips as he exited the police station and walked to his car. *And Denny, I'm not sure about Denny.* Denny had come for the quiet like most people in Santa Inéz. But the guy was in love with the idea that this was a quiet, peaceful place, and would always stay that way. Trouble was coming, though. Robert had a sense for it, perhaps even an oversensitivity born from his combat experience. Denny was a tough guy, who surely would have played college football if he had not blown his knee in high school. And he had a good service record in the Military Police, but always stateside, away from trouble. Had he ever fired a shot in anger? Or even at anything other than a target? And, had anyone ever taken a shot at *him?* Robert shook his head. He had seen tough guys with high ideals before. He had seen them change, and he had seen them die. Everything changed when the bullets came toward you, when everything was on the line. And until you faced that moment, you had no idea what it meant to be tough. If you survived your first battle, you learned. But, your first battle, that was when you might get other people killed, even if you survived. *Will his inexperience get me killed one day?*

Robert opened the door to his squad car and got in. *I must keep Lali safe.* That Rodrigo was playing footsy with *La Hermandad* if he wasn't a full member. The grating, then rumbling, sound of the police car starting interrupted Robert's ruminations for a moment. Dealing drugs, perhaps involved in the murder of the gang's rivals? He seemed like a decent kid, his mother seemed fine, but that gang! Did Rodrigo know what he was getting into? The right-hand turn signal chimed as Robert pulled out of the police station. And now, his foolish daughter was hanging with this kid? Rodrigo was smart. He was clever as hell. Could he be involved in these missing person cases? *God, I hope not! For Lali's sake.*

Robert drove the familiar route to Rosie's Dinette. What had happened to his safe little town? The quiet security of its isolated location, so remote and tranquil. And he, more than most, needed that tranquility to put behind him all the killing and death of his combat experience. And now, the darkness seemed to be more than just knocking at the door, but even reaching its fingers into the heart of his home. Would he have to take up arms, again? Robert turned onto Cliffside Drive. *What can you win with a gun?* the voice interrupted his thoughts. The skin on his forehead tightened as he furrowed his brow. *I don't want to use a gun again! Ever! But I will if I have to. To protect and serve.*

Robert noticed unfamiliar motorcycles parked at Rosie's Dinette as he walked toward the door. Not unusual, though it was getting a bit late in the season for bikers. Perhaps there would be some new tales from the cliffs? Opening the door, the usual bells signaled his entrance.

Rosie's Dinette served mostly the locals on the outskirts of Santa Inés, but also the coastal trail hikers. Santa Inés lay near enough to the coastal trail entrance to act as a provisioning station for the hikers on the trail, and even a kind of way station if hikers needed a bed for the night. It was one of the few reliable places to stop along the trail, and Rosie's Dinette earned a reputation as one of the best places to stop for a meal. The dinette was a small and homey place serving simple food with interesting conversations. *The tales from the cliffs*, as Rosie called them, entertained the trail wanderers as they ate their meals and rested their tired feet. Big Foot had often been sighted, and the occasional alien — most likely having to do with the popular use of marijuana by the trail walkers. He always admired how Rosie handled the storytellers. Most often she would curtail any eye-rolling and ask, "Is that a fact? Amazing!" which Robert figured was her way of expressing how amazed she was that people could believe so many crazy stories.

Robert took a seat at the counter. The coffee poured into his cup without the need of a request, as Rosie wiped the counter with her other hand.

"What news from the cliffs?" Robert knew better than to sip his black coffee before it had cooled. He glanced over at the group of bikers at the back table.

"News, Officer Russo?" Rosie snickered. "News is good for business, I say! We got cliff walkers stopping in from all over since that gal Katherine Kelly on Channel 23 did a story about the haunted cliffs. She's one to watch, that one. Sure knows how to spin a yarn!" Rosie rolled her eyes, and in a dramatic fashion, imitated Katherine Kelly, with her breathy voice a hoarse whisper and flipping her imaginary, long red hair from over her eye, in the newscaster's signature move, her real hair up and covered by a hair net, "Or is it, as some say, that the ghost of the lost girl still haunts the cliff walk on nights when the moon is full, and the tide is high?" Rosie laughed, shaking her head, "Amazing, I say!"

Rosie winked as she wiped the counter down once more.

"Well, I guess ghost stories beat what passes for news on those big channels." Robert chuckled. "Like that clown Bob O'Malley always stirring up controversy and getting people riled up, those panelists yelling at each other for an hour."

Rosie winked again. "Well, it's a good thing they keep that stuff mostly in the cities, you know, not out here where it's quiet. What we have here are people who do their best to get along, but there are always little sparks, even here."

Robert glanced back at the men in their leather motorcycle gear. "Getting any sparks from those bikers? They look a little ornery."

"Nah, they're all right. They're Christians, if you can believe it. I was surprised to see them praying over their food. Just making their way back to LA. Those guys rode all the way up to Alaska through Canada, all along the coast. They got nothing to say about the cliffs, just a run-in with a grizzly when they camped up in Canada, or so they say. Amazing, is what I say." Rosie winked, before scooting down to the other end of the counter to fill another cup of coffee.

Lali always insisted that they say grace before meals. His wife had prayed. And he had prayed for his wife, and with her, as she faded away, the cancer eating her body, a little at a time, until there was so little left. The moment she had died; her last words haunted him. "I will pray for you, Robert." The words that did not come out of his mouth echoed in the fathomless never-land of his mind, "I will pray for you, too, Carmela, *Querida.*" He just could not say it. Nor could he do it. Prayer would never do any good.

Rosie returned with Robert's lunch and placed it in front of him. *No prayers before eating for me.*

Robert took a bite of his sandwich. "Any sightings of the *Lost Girl,* or is it all just ghost talk? I mean, they never found a body, so it's still officially a missing person's case." He hoped some conversation would draw his mind away from prayer and the memories of his wife. "The case is still open, too. That's my official excuse for stopping by, investigating, you know." Robert lifted his cup to his lips for a sip, the hot steam close enough to burn his lip, then thought better of it, and placed it back down to give it more time to cool.

"I thought it was my naturally curly hair." Rosie bounced her imaginary curly hair, her straight hair remaining pressed against her head by the hair net. "But we best keep it down a bit."

Rosie glanced toward a booth where a middle-aged man with black plastic glasses was hunched over his coffee, almost seeming to search for something in the bottom of his cup. "He'll be heading for a walk again tonight."

Robert recognized the man immediately. Rosie often referred to him as the father of all cliff walkers, but he really was only father to the most notable cliff walker, the central figure in the seminal *Tale from the Cliffs,* the *Lost Girl.* Mr. Hennessey, the father of Claire Hennessey, missing for some twenty years, the only open cold case in the Santa Inés police files, did not appear to have overheard their conversation. Robert closed his eyes, realizing how callous he had been. "Oh, shoot, Rosie, I feel like a jerk!"

"Don't you get down on yourself, Officer Russo. That girl must have been swept out to sea a long time ago after she fell off that cliff – or jumped, as some say."

"It's just… well, I have a daughter too, you know."

"Yes, I know. You best keep your eye on that one. She's a cliff walker. Those cliffs seem to get into people's heads."

"The cliffs are the least of my worries with her." Robert raised the coffee to his lips, daring to take a sip. "It's the boys I worry about. She's been seeing one that's a little edgy for my taste."

"Edgy? I like that, for a cliff walker." Rosie laughed. "Sounds like a match made in heaven."

"I don't believe in heaven, Rosie, and this one's from the east side, across the tracks, and I'm afraid he's going south."

"From the east side going south? You've got a way with code words, Officer." Rosie chuckled. "So, he's poor and heading for trouble, if I take your meaning."

"Yeah, Rosie, I just can't come right out and say it. It's not bad that he's poor. My wife was poor — and Mexican — like him. He's smart enough to figure out shortcuts, and cocky enough to think he can get away with it and won't get trapped. There are plenty of good folks over on the east side, honest people who mind their business, but there is trouble coming up from the south these days. The trouble most of us came up here to escape."

"We don't get many people from the east side here at Rosie's, but I get you. My family came here from the east, way east, long ago. Go west, young man, they used to say. And my great, great, grandfather, well I'm not actually sure how many greats it should be? But, anyway, he went about as far west as he could, and that's Santa Inés. He came for the gold and stayed for the view, my parents used to say."

Robert laughed softly, swirling his coffee, and taking a sip. "Well, we do have the views, here."

"That is a fact. We do have some great views. So, people come up from the south for the views and the quiet now, like you and Officer Kincaid, good, honest working-class guys. But, also a lot of wealthier people, like Mr. Hennessey over there, made a fortune in computers. And remember that singer, what's her name, who OD'd? She came up here to get off the drugs but didn't quite make it. Now some poorer people are settling on the east side. The town's changing, I can feel it."

"We came for the quiet." Robert rubbed his brow. "But I'm afraid I hear some noise coming now."

And as he drained the last of his coffee, he imagined he heard a rustling in the tall forest trees outside the dinette, something louder than the churning of the waters at the bottom of the cliffs that had swept a young girl out to sea so many years ago. An ill wind from the south, he imagined, carrying gangs and violence, hard men escaping harder men, coming to disturb the peace of his quiet haven. His daughter praying at the abortion clinic, that awful place where their victims went to erase their mistakes. His foolish daughter, armed only with a string of beads and a tarnished medal around her neck, standing in the breach, calling them to a better way, as his wife had once drawn him away, away from that horror of killing and death. Surely, she would be trampled one day by forces she could not possibly understand. *Should I have been more forceful? Should I have commanded her not to go to that damned clinic?*

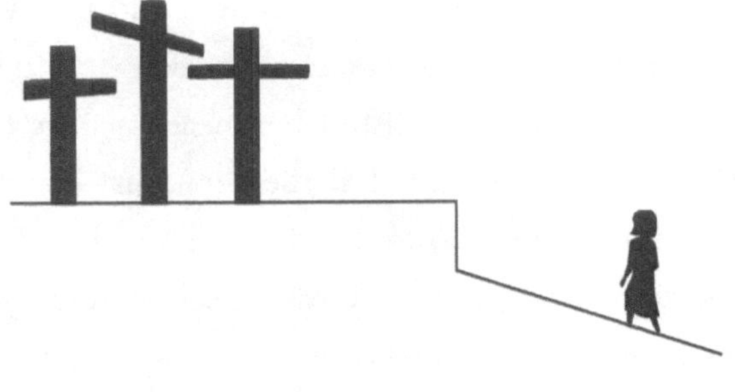

3

Kim

KIM SLOWLY MADE HER WAY to that place of dread, to do as he commanded her to do, what she knew was wrong. One step at a time, and a breath, and a step, along the sidewalk on the east side of Santa Inés. She had passed the place many times in the car or walking by it on the way to town. She never much noticed it, just an old sign in front of an ordinary house, "Dr. Singer's Family Planning Clinic."

There was life inside of her, life she did not want inside her, but a life she did not want to kill. "Get it taken care of, Kim!" he had ordered, with his usual menace and malice. She knew what he meant. *Kill your baby, Kim! That was what he meant. Kill your baby! Be a killer like me!* She shuddered. To kill, the sin beyond all the others, the one she had never committed, and never would have been tempted to commit, if it were not the thing inside of her. The sin he was guilty of. She did not want the thing, but she did not want to kill it. *Maybe I could give it away?* But he would never let her. He would kill her first, for defying him, if nothing else. *I have to get it taken care of.*

Kim, her shoulders slumped, her blond hair windblown and tangled, plodded ahead as if gravity had increased around her causing each step to be heavier and heavier. Finally, she stopped and lifted her head against the seemingly increased gravitational force and stared at the sign. Just beyond the entrance, a girl stood on the sidewalk beside the sign. The girl wore a plaid skirt, white blouse, and navy sweater, surely a Catholic school uniform. Beads dangled from the girl's fingers, and though she in no way physically blocked the way, some invisible force stopped Kim in her tracks.

Was she praying? Kim stood frozen in place, her hands tightened into balls of fingers and knuckles, fear and dread – almost a terror – filled her as she gaped at the girl praying, terror that she might glance up and notice her. *Maybe if I don't move, she'll keep praying and won't see me. Maybe, if I wait, she'll go away.*

Kim could not maintain her frozen posture, and let out a mournful sigh, her shoulders slumping lower as she cringed at the sign in front of the clinic. Terror and rage filled Kim as the girl lifted her eyes, serene and gentle, finding her own. The girl appeared to be able to see through her faded denim jeans and jacket. Could she see her naked body? Or worse, could she peer into the dark abyss that was her soul?

"You don't have to do it, you know." The girl raised her eyebrows and tilted her head. The cross at the end of the beads swayed like a pendulum.

The coldness in Kim's spirit heated up as a defensive anger possessed her, as if she had been falsely accused of a murder she had yet to commit, condemned as guilty before she had done the deed. "What do you know about it? My boyfriend will kill me if I don't." She glanced back at the crooked stairs, the misaligned railing and, at the top, the door of the clinic. She took a deep breath.

"I will pray for you." The girl's eyes warmed with compassion and appeared convicting.

"I don't need prayers!" Kim stiffened her body and squeezed her fingers into bony fists. "I need help! I don't think I can do this. At least not alone."

Kim closed her eyes, holding back tears. *Maybe, if I wasn't alone? Maybe I could do it?* Kim desperately grasped for the courage to do what she had to. "Would you come in with me?"

The girl stepped toward her and opened her arms. What was she doing? *What does she want from me?* Kim cocked her head and stared at the girl for a moment. Stepping forward toward the girl, Kim's shoulders drooped as she staggered for the next step. The girl inched closer and embraced her. Kim let herself fall into the girl's arms. The warmth of the girl's body seemed to dissipate the excess gravity and Kim let herself slump into her arms. All the tension and weight of the decision seemed to float away into the late-afternoon air.

"No, my sweet girl, I cannot help you do this thing." The girl held Kim firmly in her soft embrace. "But if you don't wish to do it, I can help, or I can help you once you have done it."

Kim stepped back and made eye contact with the girl. "I don't want to do it." Like an animal trapped in a maze, Kim sought a way out, but could only find one. The way she did not want to go. She needed this girl to know she was not a killer, that she would not do this thing on her own. That she was not like *him.* "But he will kill me if I don't. You don't know him."

Why did it matter so much what this girl thought of her? But, it did. At this moment, it mattered more than Ralo and his threats, his revolver and his baseball bat, his demeaning commands and his fists. And that meant, it mattered more than her life. Kim shuddered.

A quiet confidence and innocence, a presence Kim could not remember experiencing, stood before her now and confronted her, calling her to a new path. "Before you do this thing, why don't you come with me and meet some of my friends? They help girls like you all the time."

As quickly as she felt the call, the unreasonableness of it overwhelmed Kim. It made no sense. Come with her and meet her friends? *Help girls like me?* How would someone like this even know someone like her? But she just couldn't walk up those steps. Not today. Not with this girl watching and praying. *I just can't do it! But Ralo will kill me! I…just…can't.*

Kim relaxed her shoulders and nodded. As she walked alongside the girl, something stirred deep within her soul, a hidden, long-dormant sensation: hope. Maybe there was another way? *Maybe there are people who help girls like me? Like me?* A pregnant drug user, the girlfriend of a drug dealer, not even sure if he was the father. What was up with these religious people, like this girl, and the God they believed in? God? How could there be a God? *Look at what's happened to me? My own father and now living with Ralo?*

Kim walked onward with the girl, not really knowing where they were going. The girl still had her arm around her as they shuffled along the sidewalk.

"My name is Lali, by the way."

Kim hesitated to give her name but wasn't sure why. She whispered her name as if she were giving away a secret. "Kim."

"How old are you, Kim?"

"Just turned nineteen last month." The questions brought her back to the harsh reality confronting her life. *What a fool I am to think this girl can help me.* But she just couldn't walk up those steps, not alone, not today.

"Oh, I don't know what I'm doing!" Kim's anxiety and fear returned. Her body stiffened, as she stopped and pulled away. "Ralo will kill me if I don't get this taken care of. You don't know him. He's the head of a gang, *La Hermandad,* and a drug dealer. He's a killer."

The girl, Lali, met her eyes with an oblivious innocence. A serenity in the face of danger that made no sense. This girl didn't have a clue. *What am I doing?* Kim winced.

"Well, my boyfriend's in that gang, I think," Lali volunteered. "Rodrigo Alvarez. Maybe he can talk to Ralo?"

Kim's eyes widened in surprise as she pulled back from Lali. "Your boyfriend's Rodrigo? He's Ralo's right-hand man!"

Kim had met Rodrigo. Ralo used him for his mind, not his muscle, but he was still up to his eyeballs in gang activity. Ralo credited Rodrigo with increasing his drug sales tenfold by finding new customers and by coming up with a plan to eliminate the competition. Rodrigo? With this church girl? Praying at an abortion clinic? Did Ralo know? Oh, surely Ralo would not like this! Maybe that was why Rodrigo said no? Kim cringed at how Ralo offered her to his workers as a reward. No one other than Rodrigo had turned down Ralo's offer. If you had a girlfriend like this girl, maybe you didn't just take whatever you could get?

Lali continued talking with that infernal innocence. "Well, sometimes good kids get drawn into gangs, so they feel like they fit in. I think that's what happened with Rodrigo."

Was this girl for real? There were things Kim couldn't talk about, secrets, the law, trouble, but she had to let her know about Rodrigo. But softly, softly.

"Oh, I don't know, Lali. Rodrigo's into some pretty bad stuff with Ralo."

"Yes, I know. I'm praying for Rodrigo, and Ralo as well."

Kim was incredulous but tried not to let it show. She blinked several times. Would this girl still help her if she spilled the beans on her boyfriend? *Can she help me, anyway?*

"I wouldn't waste any prayers on Ralo. He's a killer." Kim shrugged.

"Well, then, he's in most need of prayers."

What planet was she on? Praying for Ralo? *This girl is going to get me killed...*

Lali and Kim approached the gate for St. Elizabeth's Home for Unwed Mothers, an old Victorian-style home, another eclectic anomaly in the Santa Inés landscape, gaily painted pink contrasted with a pastel blue. The path up to the wrap-around porch ascended steps that narrowed toward the top, inviting people to enter. In fact, the basic U shape of the building focused the eye toward the front door in the center. The place looked like something out of a children's book. Kim rolled her eyes. *This is just not for me.* But she did not have the courage to say it out loud, and could not face going back to the dark, forbidding abortion clinic, and what she imagined waited for her inside it. At least, not yet. *Let's just see how goody-goody this place is. They will likely throw me out anyway.*

Lali and Kim entered through the front gate. Kim found herself smiling as she spied a small boy and a girl, likely a bit older, playing on the lawn. On seeing Lali, the children dropped their toys and ran to her. A little something inside Kim's heart began to melt as the excited children dashed toward them with stumbling and frantic steps. The little girl slowed herself, and took the boy's hand, steadying him. Her printed dress danced lightly in the breeze, as her free hand brushed the brown hair from her face. *Those kids are just so cute.* A tear filled her eye as she rubbed her belly. Lali dropped to her knees to be on their level when they arrived. The two children nearly knocked Lali over as they ran up and hugged her.

"Lali!" the boy squealed as he tumbled into her arms. The girl laughed, and hugged Lali from behind the boy, in a kind of loving human sandwich.

"Jerry! How are you, my special pumpkin! And Melissa! How pretty you are in your sundress!" Lali turned and faced Kim.

"This is Kim. I want you to pray for her. Would you do that for me?"

Kim closed her eyes for a moment. *Kids praying for me?* What good would that do? She opened her eyes. The children were nodding in agreement. Lali muffed Jerry's hair a bit and winked at Melissa. Kim's initial pained reaction to prayer faded as she watched the endearing scene.

"Well, you two go back to playing. I'm going to take Kim inside to look around."

The kids raced back to playing on the lawn. Kim could not keep from smiling. Lali turned and faced her.

"It's humbling to think that without this place, these children may never have been born." Lali brushed the hair from her eye.

"Are their mothers staying here?"

"No, their mothers stayed here for a while, but they've moved on. They come back now to donate their time and help out. Most of the girls don't stay very long after they have their children. One of the goals is to help women to be able to support themselves."

As Lali and Kim approached the house, Kim noticed the tall, thin woman, with long dark hair parted on the side, her hair partially covering an ugly scar running down the side of her face. She was keeping an eye out on the children as they played on the lawn. The woman had the long, lean figure and facial features of a runway model, the slight nose, the symmetrical almond-shaped eyes, the full lips. Only the scar marred and distorted her otherwise stunning, if unadorned, appearance. Another, shorter woman with light hair, not quite light enough to be called blond, stepped up behind the taller woman as Lali and Kim ascended the steps to the porch. This shorter woman, more plump and rounded, with a fuller face, had a kind of sad intensity in her eyes, even as she smiled and drew nearer to greet them. The two women appeared to be in their twenties, not much older than Kim.

"Hi Sandra, Hi Molly. This is Kim. I met her at the clinic. I'm going to show her around."

Kim tried not to stare at the scars running down the side of Sandra's face, but a kind of irresistible magnetic force drew her eye to the evidence of hurt and violence from long ago.

"It's okay, Kim, many people are a little shocked when they meet me." Sandra paused. "Melissa's father was a prick who liked to play with knives. But Molly's scars are even worse, though you can't see them."

Molly shook her head and closed her eyes a moment. "Yeah, I guess we all have scars. I'm not sure which one of the bastards that raped me is Jerry's father, but I know Jerry is my son! And he's the best thing that could have happened to me."

As Sandra smiled, the scars made a strange curving shape on her face. "Just wanted to say that the best thing I ever did was to come to this place. Not sure what I would do without my Melissa."

"I don't think I could have made it without this place either," Molly added, "But everything worked out fine."

"I'm very happy for you. Not sure it will work for me, though." Kim twisted her face and avoided eye contact.

"Well, it's not easy, either way." Sandra lowered her gaze, her hair falling to cover more of her disfigured cheek.

Kim was grateful when Lali changed the subject. "Okay, Kim, why don't I show you the nursery, first. Looks like the babies are down for their naps."

Kim and Lali ascended the stairs, then progressed through a short hallway to the nursery. Three babies slept soundly and safely in their cribs. A sense of peace and security enveloped the home, as if nothing could ever go wrong here. She had seen places like this on television, where there were happy homes, and she always just assumed that such things were made up, unreal, propaganda to make people feel better, though everyone knew the real score, the violence, the intimidation, the cruelty of life. But these children slept in peace, without a care. How unlike her own home, where her father had raped her, and her mother had always been drunk and angry, forcing her to escape and move in with Ralo. How could this be real? *What do these people want from me?* She knew what Ralo had wanted.

"Where are their mothers?" Kim rubbed her chin. *Surely, they're nothing like me.* They were probably prim and proper girls from good homes who got themselves knocked-up.

"Their mothers are still at school," Lali said, "completing their homework before they come home. Come on, let's go meet Mrs. Howard in the office. She's the one who runs this place."

Kim and Lali descended the stairs to the office. Mrs. Howard, an African American woman in her mid-fifties, sat behind a desk, doing paperwork.

"Hi, Mrs. Howard. This is Kim. I met her at the clinic."

The woman promptly abandoned her paperwork and stood up to greet her. Kim eyed her suspiciously.

"Nice to meet you, Kim."

Mrs. Howard had a warm twinkle in her eye that sent a shiver through Kim's spine, causing her to wince. Were these people on happy pills or something? "I'm happy to meet you. Yes, you are all so nice." The words awkwardly tumbled from her mouth. She avoided looking at anyone too long. "What is this place anyway?"

Mrs. Howard chuckled, good-naturedly.

"This place?" Mrs. Howard explained, "That's a long story. But the short answer is, this is a place where girls who were not expecting to be mothers quite yet can come and learn how to do it the right way. We help girls to have their babies and then help them to learn how to care for them properly."

Kim pursed her lips together to suppress her skepticism.

"But what do you get out of it?"

"Sometimes I ask myself that!" Mrs. Howard laughed then her tone became somber. "Kim, I had an abortion when I was just sixteen years old. It was legal, and everybody told me it was the right thing to do, so I did it. Then I started getting the dreams. You know, dreams about babies crying, and I was searching for my baby, and I couldn't find her. They all told me I would get over it, but I never really did, even when I got married and had kids of my own. I guess I just don't want no more girls going through what I gone through. I want to help them, so they never are looking for their babies in their dreams. And, there's lots of other people like me who want to help. Like Lali here. She never been in trouble a day in her life, but she wants to help, just for helpin's sake. People really do care, even though sometimes it seems like nobody does."

A warmth filled Kim's soul. The realization of something she may have never known, or had long forgotten, captivated her being beyond just her mind. A coldness in her heart melted. She had hesitated at the clinic because she did not want to be a killer like Ralo. That was a line she never wanted to cross, no matter what other things she had done. She had looked up the steps of the clinic and she could not bring herself to do it. But something was different now. People cared about her, and her child. She in no way wanted to have Ralo's baby and she wasn't even sure if it was Ralo's, the way he passed her around to his friends. But she wanted this warmth, this light. She wanted now something beyond the avoidance of killing. She wanted life, and life for her child.

"So, you just take in girls here who are pregnant, and let them live here for free?" Kim's curiosity nearly outweighed her disbelief.

"Well, if a girl's got no money to pay," Mrs. Howard replied with her same captivating warmth, "then she can help by doing what work she can. Most girls want to earn their keep, so they help care for the other girls' kids, or cook or clean. Or sometimes they find a job, so they can pay something until the time comes to have the baby. We help them to have a safe place, so they can develop themselves and support themselves and their child, so we can make room for the next girl. We are full up, at the moment, but one of the girls will be leaving soon, once her mother is out of the hospital and back on her feet. With her mother being sick, she needed some help is all."

As quickly as the desire for the light and warmth of the place had filled her heart, Kim recoiled from it now. Her cold reality began to reassert itself.

"Oh, well, thank you. But I have a place to stay for now." Kim paused. "I'm staying with my boyfriend. Of course, he wants me to…well, you know."

"Yes, I know," Mrs. Howard said, that warm twinkle again in her eye. "Men often think that will be the best thing, because it's easier for them, and it wasn't something they planned on. But there's a weight that comes with that decision, and it's heavier for the woman. I know. I've been through it. We can help you, if you decide you don't want to go through with it."

"No, I don't think you can." Kim woke from the pleasant warmth of this fantasy of love and help to the bitter coldness of what had always been her reality. "You are all very nice, but Ralo will kill me if I don't..." Kim shrugged, "you know."

"We could help you with Ralo, as well," Mrs. Howard offered. "We have lawyers who could obtain a restraining order for you."

Panic seized Kim. She shook her head violently. "No, No! No piece of paper will keep him away! He'll kill me! I'd be dead before the ink is dry. And he'll probably kill all of you for trying to help me! He's a killer! That's what he does!"

Kim turned and headed for the door, her hand to her mouth as she cried. She ran out of the door, but slowed to a walk on the front lawn, sobbing. Footsteps followed behind her and a gentle hand caressed her back. "Don't worry, Kim," she heard Lali's voice. "It will be all right."

Kim sobbed in her new friend's arms. "No, no, it won't. You don't know him. He will kill you! He kills anyone who doesn't do what he wants!"

4

Ralo

RALO RELEASED THE CYLINDER OF HIS REVOLVER, flipped it open, and ejected the spent shells, letting them clang onto the kitchen table. Keep it clean and keep it ready. Not that there should be an immediate need, now that all the local competition had been eliminated. As he sat, preparing to clean his revolver, he recalled his first handgun. Never had to clean that one. Only used it once. The police had taken it as evidence. Ralo laid his .45 next to his gun cleaning kit on the mat and ran his fingers over the long scar down the left side of his face, the result of a knife fight he had lost. No one dared ask him where the scar came from, and he wasn't volunteering any information. Better let them wonder. *The bastard who give me that scar, he no telling no one.* He had taken a gun to the knife fight rematch, which predictably assured him of victory, and a stay in juvenile detention until he was eighteen years old. He chuckled to himself, thinking of the charges to which he had pled guilty in juvenile court. Unlawful possession of a firearm and negligent discharge of a firearm. *Jes, I so negligent, I kill that cabrón. Oops!*

He snickered, then he double-checked the cylinder to make sure that there were no remaining rounds in it. Fully rehabilitated, that was what they had said. He looked down the barrel the revolver, then pushed the solvent-doused bore brush through making sure not to hit the firing pin, then pulled it back. He glanced down at the toothbrush he would later use in his gun-cleaning procedure and recalled his teeth with their prominent gaps. He ran his hand over his thin, hair. His teeth or his hair might be called *ralo* in Spanish, meaning thin or sparse. *Ralo? is that really me faucking name, or did they just start to call me that as a joke?* He rolled his eyes, then finished cleaning the gun bore, pushing the gun cleaning patches through with the bore rod, as he pondered the sparse details of his childhood compared with the elaborate story he had constructed to intimidate his family. Not his birth family but what he called *La Hermandad,* the Brotherhood, his gang. He picked up the cylinder and began cleaning the chambers that held the ammunition in place. His first gun, the one the cops took, was a semi-automatic, with a spring-loaded magazine. It could fire rounds more rapidly, held more shots and reloaded much faster than his revolver. But a semi-automatic could jam. *No use to have a gun that no shoot.* He opted now for the more reliable revolver. A .45 caliber, no freakin' *pistolita.* And, it had served him well. He traced his finger over his scar, again. He was a survivor. And, sometimes, you had to kill to survive. Sometimes, you had to kill even members of your own family, like that *cabrón,* Juanito.

Having fully cleaned the cylinder chambers, he brushed down the muzzle, the cylinder, and the extractor rod with the toothbrush, as he recalled the day he took care of the "Juanito business". *I bet Mr. Smart-guy Rodrigo no see that coming.* Inventory reconciliation? Who even heard of such a thing? But he sure had taught Mr. Smart-guy a lesson in business that day! Ralo chuckled to himself, allowing the memory to run through his mind. Come up to the cabin, Rodrigo. *I wanna introduce you to the team. Jes, I scare the crap out of him that day!* No more shack duty for Rodrigo! Ralo laughed, as he cleaned and lubricated his revolver, making certain the firing mechanism operated flawlessly. Man, that kid had a head for the business!

Too bad he had no guts. Or maybe that was a good thing? *I'd hate to have to kill him. Maybe one day, I have to.* It made a lot that had happened these last three months. Best to keep an eye on Mr. Smart-guy.

The cabin was located some twenty miles or so from Santa Inés, up in the mountains off the main road, up a driveway — more like a dirt trail — about a mile long. There was almost no way anyone would find the place without knowing where it was. There were no neighbors to see or hear anything. Only the trees might hear and remember what happened there. Or perhaps the ghosts of the men in the unmarked graves in the backyard. But they would not tell anyone. Miles from nowhere. Ralo grinned, and continued rubbing down his fully cleaned revolver, as he recalled with delight his speech to his family. They had gathered inside the small living room of the cabin with its old sofa and coffee table on the weathered area rug, dimly lit, shrouded in a kind of shrieking silence, holding its secrets in the muffled damp of the forest where light struggled to reach, even on the clearest day.

"We family here." Ralo had begun, leaning forward on his baseball bat. "And that's a good thing'. But no' like me real family. You see, me mother, she a whore." Ralo paused to see the reaction of his gang members, just his pushers, the ones who sold drugs for him and brought in the money, Jesús Sanchez, Juanito Perez, and Rodrigo Alvarez, the newest member. Rodrigo did not seem surprised, but he always seemed to keep his cool. That was a good sign, though a kid like Rodrigo with a hardworking single mother might have had some reaction.

"Jes, that is right." Ralo passed his baseball bat from hand to hand. "She a whore in Mexico. Me father, well, no'even me mother know who me father is. Me brother, older brother, he know his father, but that bastard, he went north and left me mother. He make me mother a whore. She have to whore to provide for me brother. But, me, me mother try to kill me before I was even born."

Ralo glared at the members of his self-described family, then raised the bat over his shoulder and paced.

"Ju see, me mother, she have a pimp, Feliz Gonzales, real piece o'chee, this guy! Anyway, Feliz say to me mother, 'Hey, ju can no' be pregnant, nobody pay for ju.' So Feliz, he go to the doctor to, ju know, try to make'er no pregnant no more, I mean, like kill me, really. That what he wanna do. But the doctor, he say, okay, but cost fifty bucks. So Feliz, he say he no gots no fifty bucks, because he gamble it away, and he owes big money to his own family, ju know, who loan him the money. But the doctor say, ju can no pay, he no gonna do it. So Feliz, he say, well, okay, I do it me self. How hard it can be? So, he take me mother back to his place, and he get a coat hanger. And, he start, ju know, working on me mother. And like, right then, just before the piece o'chee kill me, in come his family, and they shoot Feliz dead. Bang, bang, bang, ju know. And, like, there me mamá, with this freakin' hanger sticking out of her. But they no get me."

Ralo looked around at his family members.

"Wow, Ralo," Jesús said, "That's one effed-up story."

"So, I guess the operation was unsuccessful, and the physician didn't survive," Rodrigo quipped.

Ralo laughed, shaking his head.

"Jes, I like that! The operation was no' successful and the physician, that piece o'chee Feliz, no survive! Ju a clever one, Rodrigo."

Ralo laughed again, and his compatriots chuckled nervously along with him. "Can ju believe it? Me own freakin' mother try to kill me! Family! Can ju imagine! So, when I was old enough, I get even. I strangle that beetch with a telephone cord."

Ralo's new family, that is, his gang, were wide-eyed.

Juanito broke the silence, "You strangled your own mother, Ralo?"

Ralo flashed the prominent gaps in his teeth. "Jes, Juanito, me own mother. Ju see, in *mi familia*, ju try to kill me, ju end up dead. Even if ju me mother. Remember that, *mi hermano*."

Juanito shuddered. Jesus was staring at the floor. Rodrigo smiled, coyly. What was he smiling about? Fresh as lettuce! He was a cool bastard, or maybe he just a little too smart for his own good? *I hope he getting the point: No fauck with me!* Ralo cocked his head and squinted at Rodrigo, watching his smile flatten to a look of grim fear. That was better. Ralo shook his head and continued. "And so then, me brother, he come after me. Now I love me brother. He taught me play baseball, ju know. He a good ballplayer, really smart ballplayer. He taught me to bat layfy. Say, ju know, most pitchers, they right-handed, and they throw that curveball, and it's hard to hit right-handed, so is better bat layfy. But I was like, I can hit the ball farther righty. But he say, just shut up and listen to ju brother, is better bat layfy. Me brother! He the only one can talk to me like that, to this day. Nobody talk to me like that! So, I bat layfy. And when he come for me for killing his mother, I beat him to death with his own baseball bat, layf-handed. Maybe it take no so many swings, I bat righty? Always wonder about that."

Ralo stared at the floor. Then he leaned forward on the baseball bat, furrowing his brow, and leered upward at them from his slightly bowed head.

"So ju see," Ralo said, "What we have here, is a family. Me new *familia*. The Brotherhood. *La Hermandad.* When ju mother try to kill ju before ju was born, that no so much of a family. But, ju know, me mother, she got what was coming. If ju try to kill me, well, ju end up dead, even if ju part of me family, a mother, a brother, it no matter."

Ralo drew the baseball bat back onto his shoulder and scowled. He looked at Juanito Perez and smiled. Juanito smiled back nervously, then lowered his head.

Ralo took a practice swing with the baseball bat. "Well, is time to introduce a new member of our family, Rodrigo Alvarez. Rodrigo will work in the high eschool, and I expecting good things from him."

"Hey, cool, Rodrigo," Jesús Sanchez said, bumping fists with Rodrigo. "It will be good to have some new blood."

Juanito squirmed as he stood, facing the floor, shuffling his feet. Ralo stared at Juanito to gauge his reaction. Juanito was currently working the school. Did the cabrón suspect what's coming?

"Welcome, Rodrigo." Juanito glanced furtively at Ralo.

"So, now, one of the things Rodrigo done for me already is look into the books, and see how much money is coming in, and how much stuff is going out. What ju call it, Rodrigo?"

"Reconciling sales with inventory."

"*Sí*, that is it, reconciling sales with inventory!" Ralo swung the bat with one hand and caught it with the other. "Jes, Rodrigo one bright boy!"

Ralo glowered at Juanito, who had begun to visibly shake.

"Reconciling sales with inventory, I like that, makes it sound like a legit beesness." Ralo passed the baseball bat from hand to hand, then he took a step toward Juanito. "And ju know what Rodrigo found, Juanito? This very interesting. What ju call it, Rodrigo?"

"Discrepancies."

Ralo slammed the bat into his left hand. "That is it! Discrepancies! Rodrigo, please, esplain what that mean to Juanito? I no think he understand."

Rodrigo looked a little nervous but continued. "Well, uh, it looks like the decrease in inventory is more than it should be relative to the sales receipts."

Ralo laughed. "I love this guy! The decrease in inventory is more than it should be relative to the sales receipts? Hmmm. Let me translate for ju,

Juanito. What Rodrigo saying is, there should be more money for the amount of stuff go out. Can you esplain how that happen?"

"Uh, Ralo," Juanito stammered, "who is this guy, anyway? What is this all about?"

Ralo shook his head, sneering. "Oh, Juanito, *mi hermano*! What ju think this about? I tell you what I think this about. Is all about ju estealing from me!"

"Calm down, Ralo," Juanito pleaded.

"Juanito, ju know I no like it when people tell me calm down! Especially rats who esteal from me!"

Ralo raised the baseball bat over his head and crashed it down on the coffee table, breaking the table in two. Juanito broke for the door. Ralo dropped the bat and coolly removed the revolver from his pocket.

BANG, BANG, BANG, BANG, BANG, BANG! the shots rang out, the bullets lodging in Juanito's back. Juanito crumpled to the floor with a distinctive, dull thud.

Ralo glanced at Rodrigo, whose mouth fell wide open. The bastard was not smiling anymore. Perhaps, Mr. Smart-guy learned a thing or two today. Ralo looked back toward Juanito's body as the blood began to pool on the floor.

"Ralo!" Rodrigo gasped.

Ralo turned and grinned at Rodrigo. "Good work, *mi hermano*. We bury him out back with the others."

"Others?" Rodrigo's eyes widened.

"Chure." Ralo laughed. "Just what kind of business ju think we in, Rodrigo? When we fire ju, we fire ju!"

Ralo pointed to his gun, laughing, the weapon still warm in his hand.

Rodrigo stared at his feet, then at Juanito's body. *Jes, Mr. Smart-guy learn something, I think? Bet he was no especting this kind of lesson!* Rodrigo's mouth gaped as he stared at the body. Ralo turned to see the object of Rodrigo's horrified fascination, the collapsed body of Juanito on the worn, hardwood floor. They silently watched together the pooling blood slowly spread, certain to reach the rug on which they stood, just a little more, and there, it finally did. Ralo smirked, and turned toward Rodrigo, who closed his eyes then looked up.

"Ralo," he said, "I'll sell your drugs. I'll keep track of the books. Just don't ever make me come here again. I can't be involved in this end of the business."

"Oh, *mi amigo*, ju already involved, involved up to ju eyeballs," Ralo said, holding the business end of his handgun inches from Rodrigo's right eye, "Just remember what ju see here, Mister Smart-Guy, because ju ever think ju so esmart ju can cross me, ju be Mister Dead-Guy."

Rodrigo nodded nervously.

Ralo laughed. "Okay, no more shack duty for Rodrigo. Just the books and the sales. Now, go out and make me lots of money, Mister Smart-Guy."

Jes, that lesson I teach Rodrigo, it sure pay off! Ralo pressed six fresh cartridges into the cylinder chambers, flipped the cylinder into place, and gave it a spin. They would never be where they were without Rodrigo. Rodrigo had sniffed out every competing dealer, and even set up the meetings. Business meetings. *My kind of beesness.* Not much competition remained. *La Hermandad* was way ahead of the game, and the future looked bright. No more struggles just to survive, here in this nice quiet place, where they could flourish. But to maintain their position, they would have to stay sharp. Ralo chuckled as he pulled his machete and sharpening stone out of a drawer in the kitchen.

Ralo made his way to the front porch and sat in the old wicker chair that looked out over the front yard, checking the machete blade for sharpness, then eying down the blade for straightness. As he dragged the stone across the blade, the scraping sound reminded him of the remaining bit of business for the day. Kim. That *puta* had better have got things taken care of!

Ralo glanced up from his blade. *Qué diablos es esto?* Kim dragged herself up the street in her usual slow shuffle, but who was with her? A young girl in a Catholic school uniform, with her shoulders back and head high. Ralo rolled his eyes. Then he dragged the stone across the machete, intentionally making the grating sound louder, without much care for the dulling result on the blade.

Kim slumped and hunched over, like a beaten dog.

"What is this? A Catholic eschool girl?" Ralo slowly dragged the long blade over the stone causing more of the ominous scraping sound and delighted in the cringing reaction beneath the navy sweater, white blouse, and plaid skirt. "So, does this mean ju no get it taken care of?"

Kim shuddered. The girl with her replied, surprisingly undaunted, as if she had found some hidden source of courage. "She didn't kill the baby, if that's what you mean."

Kim's eyes widened. *Jes, Kim. Ju should be escared!*

"No, Lali!" she cried. "He'll kill you!"

"Esmart girl." Ralo smirked, pressing his lips together for a moment. "Ju know me well!"

The girl stepped forward in front of Kim.

"Kim has the right to choose." The girl stood tall, her hands tightened into fists at her sides. "She's chosen today not to have an abortion."

"Oh, is that right? She has the right to choose?" Ralo dragged the large knife over the stone once more. "She has the right to die, as well! Go away, little girl, this is no' ju beesness."

The Catholic school girl stepped back, and glanced side to side, as if looking for help. She blinked a couple times and lowered her head for a moment. *That right, little girl. Ju should be afraid.*

The girl raised her head and spoke with a surprising confidence. "I'm going, Ralo." She paused, as if thinking what to say. "I will pray for you."

Ralo laughed and shook his head. "Jes, *mi cabrona Católica,* ju do that! Prayers! I am well beyond prayers."

The girl paused again, longer this time, blinking a few times. She looked as if she needed something to hold on to or she might lose her balance. "Yes, Ralo, you may believe you are beyond prayers, but I will pray for you anyway."

Ralo laughed, a loud mocking laugh, and shook his head in disbelief.

"Ralo, please," Kim pleaded, "she's just trying to help. She... she doesn't know. She doesn't know anything!"

Then he turned to Kim, staring her down, watching as her shoulders slumped and she looked at the ground.

"Get in the house, Kim," he commanded, then he glared at the girl.

"Mind ju own beesness, little girl." The threat would be clear without being explicit, as he raised the machete and looked coolly once more down the length of the blade, then, once again ran the knife along the stone, making that hideous scraping sound. Ralo's soul filled with a sinister delight, as the Catholic school girl took a step back trembling, then turned and walked away.

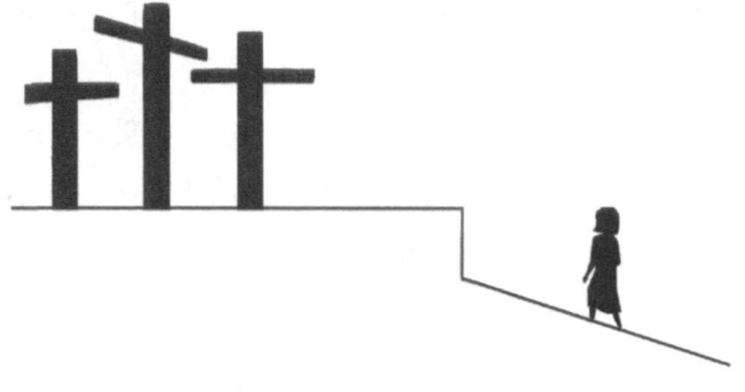

5

Breaking Up

LALI WALKED HALTINGLY BACK THE WAY she came toward the unwed mothers' home from Kim and Ralo's place. The ground seemed unsteady as she sought to take each next step. Was it the chill of the autumn breeze that made her shiver or something else? She pulled her school sweater tighter over the front of her body.

Her knees wobbled as she was slow to recover her composure from the confrontation. Her mind and heart were racing. She said he would kill me. I thought, I thought she was…it was just something people say…And, there he was, sharpening that knife. *I told her Rodrigo could talk to him?* That guy? Rodrigo's gang? *La Hermandad?* The Brotherhood? Lali stopped for a moment and closed her eyes, taking a deep breath, feeling the world spin around her as it had in her dream, though she had done nothing this time to bring on the dizziness. It had sounded almost like a family. A place where boys go to feel like they belong, and not something, so evil…Mind your own business! *I will pray for you? I said that?* To him? He's a killer! Lali took another deep breath, opened her eyes, and staggered ahead. *Glorify the Lord?* Her mind clung to the words like a drowning man clinging to driftwood, not quite buoyant enough to keep his head above the waves. *Glorify the Lord by your life? Sometimes we must suffer?* Suffer? Wasn't that what He said? To save souls? What souls? *Lord, what souls?* Ralo's? He's a killer!

Lali entered the gate at St. Elizabeth's Home for Unwed Mothers. She hesitated at the door, her mind reeling from her experiences with Kim and Ralo. Mrs. Howard met her and invited her in.

"Come in, Lali." She stood at the opened door, her face lined with worry. "Are you okay?"

"Yes, just shaken up, I met Ralo, Kim's boyfriend. It…it…was…terrifying! I think he really *is* a killer."

"What happened? Did he threaten you?" Mrs. Howard covered her mouth.

"He had this big knife. He told me to mind my own business." Lali faltered, her vision blurred, then she met Mrs. Howard's eyes. "I said I would pray for him."

Mrs. Howard closed her eyes for a moment. "You better be careful with that one, Lali. Kim looks like a hard case. She'll have trouble giving up the drugs, and the crowd she's with will have trouble letting her go. Looks like trouble all around."

"Yes, trouble, trouble," Lali stammered. "May I use the phone? I forgot to charge my cell phone again."

Lali fumbled the phone, as Mrs. Howard handed it to her. Lali dialed her father's number, deliberately pushing each button, then took a deep breath.

"Hi, Papa. Would you please pick me up at the unwed mothers' home? Sure. 10 minutes. Great. No, no. I'm okay. I'll be waiting outside. Thanks. Bye."

Lali hung up the phone and stole a glance at Mrs. Howard, a smile creased her lips that failed to cover the lines of worry around her eyes.

"I guess I'll see you tomorrow, Mrs. Howard." Lali stepped outside and waited for her father. The early autumn air had begun to cool as the sun had begun its descent toward the horizon. It would be a beautiful night if it had not been such a difficult day. She recalled tracing her little finger across the hole in Jesus' palm in her dream. "Does it hurt?" she had asked. She chuckled a bit. Does it hurt? *"Not anymore,"* He had said.

As her father's police car approached, winding its way to the unwed mothers' home, the weight of her anxiety lifted. The squad car stopped in front of the house. She tried to cover her distress with a happy expression and approached the car. Opening the car door and sitting beside her father, a sense of security enveloped her. Her father, always the observant policeman, would easily discern that something was wrong.

"What's the matter, Lali?"

"Oh, nothing really, I just had a tough day." Lali struggled to act naturally but was unable to hide the quaver in her voice.

"Why don't you tell me about it?" he asked, more as a father now than a police officer. But he was always the police officer.

Lali squirmed in her seat and took another deep breath.

"I met a girl at the clinic, Kim." Lali looked down at the floor of the cruiser, and leaned her head on her hand, blocking his view of her face. "She doesn't want to have an abortion, but her boyfriend is threatening to kill her if she doesn't. I showed her around the unwed mothers' home. But I'm afraid I've caused her more trouble."

She didn't dare look up. He could read her with a glance. She could feel his eyes probing. Lali heard the turn signal engage as the car slowed, and her body pressed against the door as it turned left. He would know something was wrong and he would worry. She didn't want him to worry. But she didn't think she could hide this from him.

"Why do you say that?" he asked. He knew the kind of trouble she meant! She had to face him. There was no way around it.

Lali turned in her seat and faced her father.

"I met her boyfriend." She shuddered. "I think he may just kill her if she doesn't have an abortion."

Her father sighed deeply, then paused for an awkward moment. "We could get a restraining order?"

"We suggested that, but she said she would be dead before the ink was dry." Lali lowered her head and stared at the dashboard.

He's thinking that he warned me that it was dangerous at the abortion clinic and I should stay away! Lali glanced out the window, turning her body fully away from her father. She realized how hard he had worked to protect her, but now she had stepped into something horrible. He had moved the family way out here to Santa Inéz and sacrificed to send her to Catholic school. Why hadn't she listened to him? Then, she heard the voice again, not quite her own, *I will be with you when your time comes.*

Lali peeked at her father as he signaled for a right turn, the sound of the blinker muffled for a moment behind the sound of his sigh.

"That's a tough one." His hands crossed one over the other as he turned the steering wheel. "We can't do much as police until a crime is committed and then it's too late."

"I know." Lali shook her head. "What's worse is the boyfriend, Ralo, is the boss of Rodrigo's gang. I think you were right about Rodrigo. I don't think I can see him anymore if he stays in that gang."

"Oh, Lali," her father said compassionately and without a hint of the I-told-you-so that she had expected. "I know this will be hard for you, but I really think it's for the best."

"Yes. I know." Lali sighed and turned to peer out the window, leaning against the car door.

Lali breathed a great sigh as she prepared for her date with Rodrigo. She expected that the worst of the day may yet come. She had never broken up with a boy before, and from what she had learned of Rodrigo's activities, he might not take it well. Their relationship had always been chaste, but surely, he would take it as a breakup, and that's how she thought of it. Surely, they were more than just friends. But maybe he would leave that gang? Lali brushed out her long, dark hair, looking into the mirror, just a faint hope in her eyes. After all, wasn't that what she had always thought? That he would grow out of it? That it was a kind of club, where kids, particularly immigrant kids, perhaps from broken families, would feel like they belonged. Especially, boys who often had no fathers in the home. Ralo? That maniac with a machete? A father-figure? *That's what I thought?*

Lali stopped brushing her hair for a moment and studied her reflection. How could Rodrigo be involved with a guy like Ralo? Did she really even know him? Rodrigo had seemed so gentle and nice, and always respectful. Was it all an act? *But he never even tried to kiss me.* If it was all an act, what was he after? Lali bit her lip and began brushing her hair again more confidently. Papa must be right. He must be into a lot of bad things with Ralo. Papa even said the police are investigating them. Why hadn't she listened? She thought she could be a good influence on him? *Pride, Lali! That's pride!* He could be dealing drugs or something even worse. It was clearly not at all like a boys' club. *La Hermandad, The Brotherhood!*

Lali glanced at the statuette of the Sacred Heart of Jesus. Maybe this was what He meant by suffering? Lali rolled her eyes and chuckled at herself. No, the Lord was horribly tortured and crucified. Surely, He meant something more than a silly girl breaking up with a bad boy who had gotten himself onto a very dark path.

Lali changed out of her school uniform and into a pair of jeans and a conservative light blue blouse, topped with a white cardigan sweater. She was trying her best to look reasonably good, but not too good. What were you supposed to wear for a breakup? *I guess something that says I respect you, but it's over, so don't get any other ideas? I think the white sweater will help.* Lali heard the doorbell ring. How would Papa handle Rodrigo? He had training in diffusing tense situations, but he could be over-protective. She knelt beside the bed and prayed. *Lord, give me the strength to handle this situation with Rodrigo tonight. Help Rodrigo to understand that I cannot be involved in this, that he should not be involved in this. And, my father, help him to be patient and understanding with Rodrigo. Maybe Papa could talk some sense into him? Help him to leave that gang! Just, let us all get to a peaceful place, no matter what else happens.*

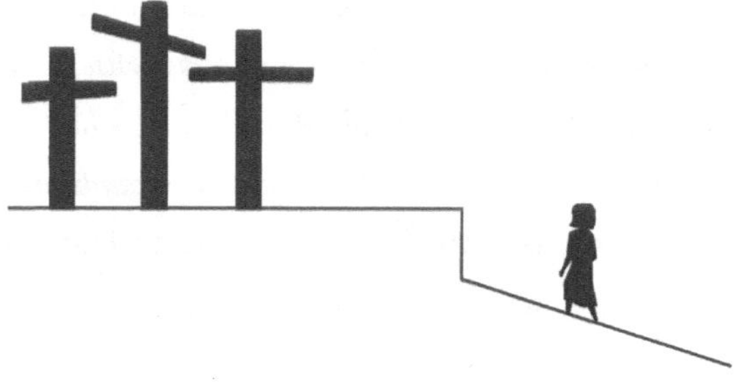

6

Rodrigo

RODRIGO GLANCED IN THE BATHROOM MIRROR as he prepared to shave and wiped off a drop of water that almost looked like a tear in his reflection. Maybe seeing Lali tonight would get his mind off his troubles. Ralo! How had let himself get involved with Ralo? Money. The root of all evil. That was how. He had a mind that was worth money, and his family, his *mother,* not that weird distortion Ralo cooked up, needed money. He had watched his mother slave for the gringos to eke out their meager living, and he knew he could help. He had seized an opportunity. But, why Ralo? He had never even considered other options. Because he was Mexican? Why should that matter, if it was just about money? Now, he was trapped. Ralo would kill him if he didn't do what he wanted. Just like Juanito.

Rodrigo rolled his eyes, Juanito, that *cabrón!* Cheating Ralo? Not smart, not smart at all. Rodrigo would not make that mistake. Rodrigo dragged the razor across his face and nicked himself.

"*Ay! Dios mío!*" He watched the blood from the nick trickle on his face and dabbed it with a tissue. The image of the blood spreading from Juanito's body slowly oozing to the rug on which he had stood filled his mind. Why should this Juanito thing bother him so much? After all, Juanito was a thief, and he was stealing from someone he had to know would kill him if he ever found out. Rodrigo lowered his head, peered into the sink and watched a trickle of his own blood swirl in the water before going down the drain. Juanito was playing a very dangerous game and had lost. Had it really been a full three months ago? *Díos mío, it seems like just yesterday!* That sound! Rodrigo heard in his mind the dull thud of Juanito's body collapsing onto the floor. Why did that subtle sound disturb him more than the gunshots? His ears rang for hours. But it was the sound of Juanito's dying body falling to the floor that haunted his memory. A boy he had known, not so well, but he had heard his voice and knew him to be alive, and then he had fallen to the floor, dead, and now buried in the backyard with the others. *Others.* A chill ran down his spine as he washed the last of the shaving cream from his face and watched it go down the drain.

Mr. Smartguy trapped like a rat! His friends had always marveled at how he could predict events, almost thinking him clairvoyant, but he was just smart enough to recognize the patterns and visualize how things would likely play out. But he envisioned no good way for this to play out, unless…his mind shuddered at the dark conclusion. He would have to kill Ralo. *But I'm not a killer*, his mind protested. As he dried his face on the hand towel, flecks of blood from his nick stained the white of the towel. Or was it his heart that protested? But it was the only way. Or, was it? There had to be another way! *I'm not a killer.* He had been party to murder, several murders, but he had never pulled the trigger. He stepped into his bedroom, grabbed a comb from the top of the dresser, and gazed in the mirror. *Would I be able to pull the trigger and kill Ralo?* Rodrigo took another deep breath and let it out slowly.

"Why should it be so hard? Ralo's an animal. Why should I even think of him as human?" Rodrigo spoke to his reflection in the mirror, leaning with both hands on the bureau.

You're not a killer, a voice that seemed to be not his own spoke in his mind.

"But I have been involved in murders. Many of them. I didn't pull the trigger, but what's the difference?" Only once had he even been there when it happened, only for Juanito. Ralo wanted to eliminate the competition. So, Rodrigo had approached the competition and offered them deals. He acted as go-between. Spoke to their greed. Offered opportunities that they could not resist. Lies with enough complications they had to be true. They all were aware that Ralo was muscling in and wanted to partner with him. To get on his good side. Help him distribute his excess supply. They were small players playing a safe game in a quiet town. They wanted no trouble with a new big fish swimming in their little pond and were eager to deal, especially if they could make a few extra bucks. But Ralo had an entirely different business model in mind. Rodrigo set up the business meetings. And they disappeared. "Business meetings?" Rodrigo sighed. "I bet there's a new grave for each one of those poor bastards in back of the cabin." Rodrigo imagined the new mounds of dirt, the backyard filling up with unmarked graves. "One day, maybe one will be mine."

But it was Juanito's murder that haunted him, even though he was less culpable for that one. "Frigging Ralo, shooting that cabrón in front of me!"

Rodrigo turned from the mirror and sat on the bed hanging his head. His mother, what high hopes she had for him! How happy she had been when he scored so highly on his IQ test.

"Rodrigo!" she said, her eyes so bright, as she glanced at him over the letter, "you escore' a 145! Das in dah top one-quarter of a percent! Dey wanna put ju een dah honors program!"

"Honors program? What's that?"

Some genius! He chuckled. *I didn't even know what a genius was!* He had figured it out, though. He was special. He could see things in ways that others could not, or if they could see it, he could see it much faster. And it meant he would be able to make a good living with his mind eventually, but in the meantime, he had to watch his mother toil to make a living scrubbing floors and toilets, doing whatever menial jobs she could to make extra money. At least she would never be a whore, as Ralo claimed his mother in Mexico had had to become to support her son. Rodrigo didn't believe a word of that crazy story. Or, maybe just the part about Ralo's brother playing baseball. Rodrigo had watched enough detective shows to know that a woman strangled with a phone cord would be hard to miss, and the focus of the investigation would be on the family members. He doubted Ralo could have pulled it off. And, beating his brother with a baseball bat? That would be a bloody mess, if not executed in some hidden location, like the cabin. It was all just bull to scare the crap out of them. Now they were Ralo's *family*. Rodrigo rolled his eyes. But he already had a family. A mother, at least. His poor mother, what would she think of him? He was just trying to help her. *But the things I have done.* That poor woman, slaving for those gringos to make money to support him.

"And that's how I got trapped." Rodrigo pulled on his golf shirt and checked himself in the mirror. No, there was no easy way out, or surely no good way. "Mr. Smartguy." Rodrigo sighed and rolled his eyes. "It doesn't do much good to be a genius when an animal like Ralo is pointing a gun at your head! Your big brain will just make a bigger splatter."

Rodrigo rolled his shoulders and scrutinized himself again. Maybe he could figure a way to set him up? Get someone else to kill him? Or the cops to arrest him? But if he failed, he'd be joining Juanito. "Frigging Juanito, that *cabrón.*" He was just trying to help Ralo out with his inventory control. An accounting discrepancy. *And he shot the bastard right in front of me!* Rodrigo closed his eyes and the oozing blood reached the rug. He could smell the acrid scent of the spent gunpowder. His ears rang from the shots. He heard again Ralo's words, "We bury him out back with the others." *Others.* If only there were a more reasonable person to be in business with! But those reasonable guys were all buried now, in back of that awful cabin. Because he had set them up for Ralo. Rodrigo sighed, and turned away from the mirror.

Rodrigo pulled on his leather jacket over his golf shirt. He hoped to look respectable enough for Lali's father, but to keep a little street credibility. Lali's father, the cop. How would he ever win him over? Officer Russo was suspicious and protective, and trained to sniff out deceptions. One small slip could land him in jail. *If Lali's father knew just a bit of what I'm into, he'd never let me near her. He'd have me in jail.* Rodrigo shook his head and looked down for a moment, then again at his reflection. "Be very careful with Officer Russo. Cover the trail before he gets on it. Give him somewhere to look where there is nothing to find. Just the right lie at just the right time."

Rodrigo sat down on the bed. Lali was lucky to have such a father. "My father, how quickly he left when I was just a baby. I could use a father, right now." But he was on his own. The closest thing he had to a father was Lali's father, who would just as soon see him in jail. *I suppose Ralo thinks he's my father.* Oh, there was a thought. Ralo as a father. Ralo might be a father if Kim did not take care of things. No, Ralo wouldn't be a father. If she didn't get it taken care of, she'd be just another body buried at the cabin. A two-for-one special. What a mess! *At least I know it's not my kid in her belly! I guess it could have been, though.* He cringed at the memory.

"Hey, Rodrigo," Ralo had said, "That was good work with Juanito! Why ju no take Kim for the night?"

Rodrigo had been startled. *Take Kim for the night?* He almost had not understood what Ralo was talking about. After blinking a few times, he had answered, "Oh, that's okay, Ralo, I have a girlfriend, and she wouldn't like it if I did."

Ralo bobbed his head with a surprised smirk, "She no has to know, *mi hermano*? Go ahead. Take Kim. She love to do for the family, don't ju, Kim?"

Kim had cringed and stammered. "Uh, yes, Ralo, yes, uh, I love to do my part, yes, Rodrigo, it's okay." The unmistakable echo of terror rang in her faltering voice.

"See? Kim want to. Ju no wanna disappoint her, do ju?" Ralo had leaned forward.

"No, really, Ralo, I have homework to do, anyway."

Ralo had laughed. "Homework? I offer ju a piece of me girl here, and ju wanna go and do homework?"

"Yes, Ralo, that's right," Rodrigo had said, his spine stiffening, "I'm going home to do my homework now."

An incredulous snigger, and then Ralo had stepped toward him, grabbing his face in his left hand, "That's okay, *mi hermano*, ju no have to if ju no wanna. I just think ju might like to, is all, and ju deserve a reward for helping with that cabrón, Juanito. Ju go do ju homework."

Ralo had given Rodrigo a friendly slap on the cheek.

Maybe it was Juanito's baby inside of Kim? Rodrigo laughed. Wouldn't that be something? Kim having Juanito's baby?

"Son of a *cabrón!*" Rodrigo let his thought audibly escape his lips, louder than his earlier furtive musings.

"What's dah', *Hijo*?" his mother called from the other room.

Rodrigo laughed. "Nothing, Mamá, just talking to myself, like a cabrón!"

"Rodrigo, *mi hijo*, no use dah'word, *por favor!* Ju too *intelligente* for such crude language!"

"*Lo siento, Mamá, no estaba pensando.*"

"Een English, *por favor*. We een America." His mother stepped into his bedroom. He rose from the bed and hugged her, just a whiff of disinfectant reminding him of why he had allowed himself to get into such a dirty business. She stepped back, and he gently held her cracked, dried hands in his as she spoke with a mother's gentle firmness. "Ju too esmar', for no espeakeen' English, no?"

"Si, Mamá, I mean, yes, Mother, I shan't e'er deign to utter such words again!" Rodrigo switched to his best British accent.

"Mees'ah Smar' guy!"

"Mamá, please don't call me that."

Rodrigo hesitated at the door of the Russo home. He imagined he were at the mouth of a dragon's lair, with designs on stealing treasure from some great and dangerous mythical beast. He remembered his first date with Lali, when Officer Russo made a point of showing him his gun.

"As an officer of the law, I carry a sidearm, Rodrigo," Lali's father had said.

"Yes, I am aware of that, Officer Russo."

"I've never had to use it in the line of duty, but we practice all the time. Of course, I also used much more lethal weapons when I was in the service."

"Really, Officer Russo? That must have been a difficult time for you, in the service?"

"Oh, not so bad, Rodrigo. It's kind of a brotherhood, being in the marines. Like you say in Spanish, *una Hermandad.*"

Officer Russo had watched him intently, appearing to watch for the slightest reaction. "The worst part was seeing people you care about get hurt or killed. But, in a way, that makes the awful things you have to do easier. It's not that hard to shoot people who hurt people you love, you know."

But Rodrigo figured it was another line of bull, like Ralo's story, designed to frighten him. Whether or not it was a line of bull, the message was clear: Don't mess with my daughter. Rodrigo did not take it personally. Officer Russo was the best example of a father he had encountered. A father who was present, and who protected his family. He'd do the same if he had a daughter, especially a daughter like Lali.

Rodrigo chuckled and knocked on the door. *Me, with a daughter?* Imagine Ralo with a daughter? Rodrigo rolled his eyes.

Officer Russo answered the door. Rodrigo imagined his stern look as more of a sneer. Rodrigo reconsidered whether his leather jacket was a wise choice. Nothing to be done about it now.

"Hello, Officer Russo," Rodrigo greeted Lali's father pleasantly.

"Hello, Rodrigo," Officer Russo replied, "Lali's upstairs getting ready. Please come in."

This dude was Officer Russo, even at the beach. Never risk any disrespect with him. *The way he looks at me! Like he's a dog and thinks I'm going to take his bone or something.*

Officer Russo directed him to the living room. The living room was dimly lit by a lamp in the corner that cast forbidding shadows, as Officer Russo directed Rodrigo to sit on the divan, while Officer Russo moved to a reclining chair. The living room was modestly decorated, a picture of a woman prominently displayed on the mantel above the stone fireplace. Her eyes were kind and gentle, though they also seemed somehow suspicious and watchful, as though she were somehow aware of all his secrets, every deception, every half-truth. But even in knowing and understanding everything, somehow, she seemed accepting, not accusing. Merciful and forgiving, not condemning, calling him to seek a better way, and to keep her daughter safe. Lali's mother. She looked Mexican, much like his own mother, only prettier. So, Officer *Italiano* married a pretty Mexican, and made an even prettier daughter? She had long, dark hair, just like Lali's. And that same kind look in her eyes. Rodrigo wished she were there, but quickly shut these thoughts out of his mind. He needed first to keep himself safe. Officer Russo was the dragon, and this was his lair.

"Please have a seat, Rodrigo, there's something I would like to talk to you about."

Rodrigo fought hard to suppress an eye-roll as he sat on the sofa.

"You know my Lali," Officer Russo began, "she's all I have. She means the world to me."

"Yes, I know." Rodrigo squirmed on the low sofa. Lali's father stared down at him from the recliner like a lord on his throne, sentencing an accused subject.

"And you know," Officer Russo continued, "she means more to me than my job or anything else."

"Yes, I know."

"So, if anything should happen to her, if anyone should hurt her in any way, you know I would have to deal with that. You understand what I mean, don't you, Rodrigo?" Officer Russo leaned forward.

"Yes, Officer Russo, I understand perfectly." Rodrigo grabbed his own arm across his body. "But I would never hurt Lali. I care for her deeply."

"Yes, Rodrigo, I believe that is true." Officer Russo nodded in agreement, "But I also know that you have some pretty dangerous friends."

"Dangerous?" Rodrigo avoided eye contact and glanced briefly at the picture of Lali's mother. "I'm not sure what you mean?"

Officer Russo shook his head. "Cut the bull, Rodrigo. I know you're in that gang with that punk Ralo, *La Hermandad*. I know you're dealing drugs."

"Dealing drugs is against the law, Officer Russo." Rodrigo feigned innocence as best he could.

"Yes, it is." Officer Russo's eyes burned like lasers, piercing and intense. "And if I catch you dealing drugs, you will go to jail. It won't help you that my daughter cares for you. You understand that, don't you?"

Rodrigo shuffled his feet on the floor as he sat on the sofa. He had not expected such an intense interrogation. He knew any conversation with Officer Russo would be trying and difficult, but this one was so directly threatening, and so pointed at his business dealings with Ralo. Officer Russo seemed to know more than he could possibly know. Or, was he just guessing? Trying to rattle him? Rodrigo glanced again at the picture of Lali's mother.

How like her, she seemed. Calling him, calling him to a better self. *But I'm trapped!* Rodrigo spoke to her in his mind, as if she were there. He glanced down at the floor. *I can't let this guy know anything, or he'll have me in jail. Oh, what would my mother think? I have to find a way out, but I can't be a rat! They'll hunt me down and kill me.*

"Yes, Officer Russo." he kept his eyes down. Then he turned his attention again to the picture of Lali's mother. *I can't just quit the gang.* Rodrigo pleaded in his mind with the picture. *Gang membership doesn't come with a provision for amicable divorce. They'll kill me! I can't go back to being just an honors student in high school. I wish I could.*

Officer Russo leaned even further forward in his chair. "And if you let your drugs anywhere near my daughter, or you let any other harm come to her, you will have to answer to me. And you may have to answer to me as a man, not necessarily as a police officer. You understand what I mean, don't you?"

Lali's father seemed to be right in his face, taunting him, though he was far enough away from him, leaning forward in his chair, glaring down at him. For just a moment Rodrigo's eyes narrowed with a growing resentment. *This gringo bastard, talking to me like that!* No, this was Lali's father, that gave him the right. Rodrigo calmed himself and glanced at the picture of Lali's mother. *But, you see, he'll never help me out of this…*

"Yes, sir. You don't have to worry." Rodrigo's hand moved over his heart without a conscious command from his mind. "I won't let any harm come to Lali. I respect her very much, and I respect you, as a man, and as a police officer."

"Good." Officer Russo sunk back in his chair. "I think we understand each other."

"Yes, sir." Rodrigo's neck and shoulders relaxed. The interrogation had ended.

Rodrigo glanced out of the living room to the stairs as the unbearable silence descended upon him, the police officer's ever-watchful, protecting eyes on him, the woman in the picture's more inviting eyes, calling him to the hope and peril of a better way. Where was Lali? Rodrigo glanced back down at his shoes, then back to the stairway. She descended the stairs like a princess, or, no, like an angel to rescue him from his purgatory. White, it figures she would wear white.

Lali strolled into the living room, her white cardigan sweater over her light blue blouse and gave him a nervous smile. "Hi, Rodrigo," she said, her voice quavering. "So, what have you two guys been talking about?"

Did she know her father would give me the third degree?

"Just a little guy talk." Lali's father gave her a furtive nod.

Rodrigo picked up something in their body language. *Something's up.*

"Yeah, just some guy talk," Rodrigo resisted rolling his eyes. "Are you ready? The movie starts at eight o'clock, so we need to get going."

"Oh, Rodrigo, I'm sorry," Lali said, rubbing her upper arm and shaking her head, "I don't feel up to a movie tonight. Would you mind if we just went for a walk on the cliffs?"

"Oh, really? I thought you really wanted to see that movie about the crime-solving dog? *The K9 Detective*, wasn't that it?"

Lali shuffled her feet. *Oh, something's definitely up!*

"Sure! I want to see it." Lali lifted her chin. "You know I love those silly movies. But just not tonight. I'd rather just go for a walk, if you wouldn't mind?"

"No, I wouldn't mind. It's a nice night for a walk."

"Just be back by eleven." Officer Russo glanced at his watch like he was timing a race.

"Yes, sir. We'll be back by eleven." Rodrigo took care not to let his eyes roll and glanced quickly back at the picture of Lali's mother.

Rodrigo walked with Lali out the front door toward the street. The autumn leaves had begun to fall and swirled in the occasional gust. The sun had just settled below the horizon, and the driveway stretched before them in the twilight. Lali turned on her flashlight, the beam slicing the dimming light, and offering a path forward. Rodrigo noticed Lali shiver in the cool breeze. Or, was it something other than the breeze which caused her to shiver? *Something is up. Just play it cool.* He took her hand once they got to the road. Her hand was soft and warm, but there was a tentativeness in her grip that was unusual. Just a short walk to the coastal trail entrance. They'd gone there often, but something was not quite the same, this time. She loved this place, though. Especially looking down at the water crashing on the rocks and hearing the murmuring sound of the churning sea. He wasn't surprised that she'd want to come here if something were bothering her.

"Wow, sure is a beautiful night." Rodrigo broke the awkward silence. Lali seemed uncharacteristically wistful, almost sullen. She was usually more lively and excited when they were together. Just wait for it. Give her time…

"Yes, it is." Lali's feet shuffled as she walked.

The moon had begun to rise in the east, a great ivory ball peeking through the darkening crimson clouds colored by what was left of the setting sun, and sent out its pale light on a troubled world. A shiver tracked up his spine as he waited patiently to hear the new troubles he sensed were coming.

"Look at that full moon!" Rodrigo pointed at the rising orb behind the colored clouds darkening to violet and blue, knowing that the colors would soon fade and only a brighter white of the moon would remain as the night sky deepened into blue and gray, and finally into the deepest black of night.

Lali didn't respond. Rodrigo sensed the emotional distance Lali was keeping. Something was really wrong, this time. Her father had given him the third degree and all but accused him of dealing drugs and intimated that he might force them on Lali. He would never draw Lali into that part of his life. He wanted out of that business himself. It didn't fit with any of the rest of his life. His relationship with his mother, his studies at school, and certainly not with Lali. He had to find a way out. But he had to find a way that did not get him killed or make him a killer. Or, more of a killer. But now, she was just so distant.

"You know, your father gave me quite a talking to." Rodrigo hoped for a little sympathy. The interrogation had been grueling.

"Oh, is that right?" Lali said flatly. No sympathy, she seemed so indifferent. Almost cold? And Lali was never cold to anyone.

"Yeah, he was afraid I might do something to hurt you." Rodrigo rolled his eyes. "You know I could never do anything to hurt you."

Lali stopped and turned to face him. "Yes, Rodrigo, I believe that." She took both his hands in hers and stared him directly in the eyes. "But that's not really enough."

"What do you mean?" He tilted his head.

"I need to believe that you would not do anything to hurt *anyone*." Lali squeezed his hands gently, then gazed down at the path to the cliffs.

Not hurt anyone? *Was it three or four guys I fingered for Ralo?* He was not in a business where nobody got hurt. Even to get out, Ralo would likely need to be hurt. Probably killed. Even if he were just selling drugs for money, the users would get hurt, at least eventually. She would never understand. But he had to at least try to make her understand the situation, without telling her too much. Without telling her much of anything.

"Well, that's not always so easy when you're a man, Lali." He tried to find her eyes, but she kept her head down. "Men hurt each other, sometimes. Like your father. He would hurt me pretty badly if I hurt you."

Lali met his eyes. He never imagined her capable of such a steely coolness. "Yes, I have no doubt he would."

There was an awkward silence. Rodrigo broke the gaze, and they began walking again. They approached the scenic overlook, where they often sat, looking out over the water, and listening to the surf. As they approached the bench near the split rail fence guarding the cliffs, a shadowy figure loomed in the moonlight, leaning over the fence, anxiously scanning the ledge and the rocks below. The churning tides that formed strong currents along the rocky shore, carrying anything that might fall into the water quickly out to sea, sang mournfully, accompanying the forlorn searcher with its haunting song of loss and regret.

"It's that old dude, again." Rodrigo hoped the familiar sight might diffuse the tension and help them change the subject.

"Mr. Hennessey." Lali pressed her lips together and brushed a long strand of hair from her eye. "He walks three times around the cliffs each night and stops here each time. This is where he lost his daughter about twenty years ago."

"Poor old guy." Rodrigo recalled the steep drop and the water far, far below. The *Lost Girl*. Just let her talk. She likes telling this story.

"She was a cancer patient," Lali continued as if she were telling the story for the first time. "She fell down to the ledge, about ten feet down. Some people think she jumped on purpose. There was no fence back then. Mr. Hennessey ran for help, but by the time he got back, she was gone."

"How do you know so much about it?" Rodrigo was thankful for the change in subject. Just keep her talking, better this again than whatever…

"I talked to him one time." Lali glanced toward the cliff, almost in a trance. "I told him I already have a father, but if it would help, he could think of me as his daughter. I was only ten years old at the time. I didn't know what I was saying."

"You are just the sweetest person, Lali." Rodrigo affectionately brushed back the hair that had fallen back over her eye.

Mr. Hennessey moved away from the railing and walked on, shaking his head, his shoulders slumped and hunched.

"He told me he just couldn't do such a thing." Lali smiled whimsically and shook her head. "What a foolish little girl I was. He told me to leave him alone. I haven't talked to him since then, though I've nodded to him as I passed. He's watched me grow up; I come here so often."

Rodrigo and Lali peered over at the ledge. The jagged rocks gnawed at the waves like the teeth of some shadowy mythical beast far below in the dim autumn moonlight. Why did the rocks, the ledge, the waters, look so foreboding in the moonlight on this particular night? Was it something in Lali's manner, her coolness, her nervous reserve, her distractedness? She was so gloomy tonight. Even this familiar story, there was something different, something heavier about it. They hadn't gotten to whatever was coming yet. Something more was coming. The silly stories of the little girl's ghost haunting the cliffs, so absurd, somehow became plausible here, with the sound of the sea, and the sight of this man. Rodrigo placed no credence in such nonsense, and yet a chill ran through him as he thought of the little girl, and her forlorn father still searching after all these years. If Rodrigo had not seen this man for himself, here, like this, he would have thought it another load of bull.

"Could you imagine?" A sudden chill seemed to catch Lali unprepared, and she tightened her sweater around her. "That little ten-year-old girl down there on that ledge waiting for her father to get help, and knowing she probably only had a couple of months to live anyway? Did she fall, or did she jump? I pray she fell."

"Why do you say that?" Rodrigo shrugged, indifferently.

"Despair is a terrible thing, Rodrigo!" She sprang to life in response, as she turned to face him more directly, and pulled back at the same time. Her eyes widened in shock, more than mere surprise. "A little girl like that?" She glanced back down at the rocks. "I pray she fell."

Lali raised her gaze and regained his eyes, then took a deep breath. *Here it comes. Whatever she's been waiting to say.*

"I met Ralo today."

Rodrigo's head snapped back like she had slapped him in the face. He had been expecting something, but not that. She met Ralo? No wonder she'd been acting so strangely! Who wouldn't act strangely after an encounter with Ralo?

"What? Ralo? How did you meet him?" Rodrigo blinked a few times then widened his eyes. Shock and alarm raced his pulse.

"His girlfriend, Kim, came to the clinic when I was praying." Lali nodded. "I showed her the unwed mothers' home and walked her home."

"You should not have done that!" Rodrigo's worlds were colliding. His mind scrambled for stable ground. It was worse than he could have imagined, even in his genius-level mind. Kim? My God, Kim? No way Lali would ever understand Kim!

Kim was trash, and Ralo treated her like trash. Rodrigo knew lots of trash. Girls who had been so abused, they would do anything as long as you demanded it. You never asked such girls; you took from them. Or you offered them drugs. They would do anything for drugs. Ralo thrived on dominating such girls. The memory of when Ralo offered Kim to him as a reward flashed through his consciousness, as he blinked in stunned silence; Kim's terrified voice echoed in his mind. "Uh, yes, Ralo, yes, uh, I love to do my part, yes, Rodrigo, it's okay."

There were many men who could be the father of Kim's child. But she was Ralo's. It was like he owned her soul, that dead thing inside her that would never be allowed to live.

"Rodrigo, Ralo is a very bad man."

Lali broke Rodrigo's reverie with that innocence that was so attractive, and yet so potentially deadly. It cried out for protection, protection from everything his life had become. It was a thing to die for. It called him. Surely, it would get him killed, and yet it called, an almost irresistible call. Like a siren's song calling a sailor to alter his course, despite the danger of the rocks, he heard it. Would he be able to resist it? Would he be able to steer clear of the danger? Did he want to resist it? He was giving in to it. His own self slipped away. He would die for it, this innocence. *I have to protect her.*

Lali became more animated, as he stood in stunned silence. "He threatened to kill Kim if she didn't get an abortion. And he threatened to kill me if I interfered."

Rodrigo rolled his eyes, "Yes, that sounds like Ralo."

Lali scowled. "You have to get out of that gang, Rodrigo!"

Rodrigo's highly perceptive mind, so adept at discovering patterns and predicting outcomes, had been so distracted and startled by the emotions and memories of the Kim and Ralo drama, and the revelation that Lali had stumbled into this part of his world, that the ultimatum caught him off-guard. He heard his voice become louder without him having willed it. He was losing control, a condition he had seldom known. His calm and his coolness had always been his strength.

"I can't just 'get out!' It's not that simple! Ralo is like a brother."

"He is evil, Rodrigo." Lali's eyes were unwavering, her cool expression chiseled in polished granite.

"Ralo will kill me if I try to get out." Rodrigo waved his hands for emphasis, his anger and frustration welled up, uncontrollably.

"You have to make a choice." The contrast between her coolness and his frustration made Rodrigo physically wince. What was wrong with him? He had to get it back together!

Lali continued, a lecture from an innocent, laying out her demand for death. "You are on a path that will lead to no good. I don't think I can see you anymore if you continue this way."

"Lali, you're not being fair! This isn't something I can just get out of!" Rodrigo's tone was nearly a shout, dying quickly over the sound of the crashing waves at the bottom of the cliff.

"I can't be with someone who is on this path." Lali let his hands go, her arms stiffly at her sides. "I will pray for you."

As Lali turned to leave, Rodrigo grabbed her shoulder and pulled her around. He squeezed her arms. "You little bitch! I've been respectful to you and never even tried to touch you, because…because…I love you, and this is what I get!"

"Rodrigo, let go of me!" Lali shouted back, twisting her arm from his grasp. "Listen to me. I know there is good in you. I know there is. But you are on a path toward evil, and I cannot go there with you."

Rodrigo lifted his hand to strike her but stopped himself.

Lali's eyes flashed anger and defiance. "Would you hit me, Rodrigo? Is that how you show you love me?"

Rodrigo covered his face with his hands and began to sob.

Her arm wrapped around him, her body soft and warm. "You have to leave this path, Rodrigo." Her hand rubbed his back. "Your soul is in danger. Don't do it for me. Do it for yourself, and for God."

"He'll kill me." Rodrigo glanced up at her, his eyes glassy, his voice breaking. And on her lips, a hopeful smile for a hopeless cause, and in her eyes a resoluteness, a commitment to walk a path of ruin, calling him to join her on her fearless and foolish way to self-immolation and death. Calling him to be a better man.

7

My Crazy, Beautiful Girl

LALI LAID HER HAND ON RODRIGO'S SHOULDER, as he sobbed, his eyes pleading with her. Her heart filled with hope that maybe, just maybe, he would leave that awful gang for her. He looked so forlorn and desperate. That confidence, the cool wit and cleverness, lost in grief and hurt. Would he be okay? Had she broken him? And the Gospel verse rang in her head, uninvited, yet not unwelcome. *Father, if you are willing, let this cup pass from me, but not my will but thine be done.* The Lord's acceptance of His passion and suffering, of His self-sacrifice and death. What would they mean for her and for Rodrigo? With a sigh, she turned and left Rodrigo in the cool night, the crashing of the waves fading as she walked on, the shadows in the moonlight long and ominous before her.

Lali lumbered back up the trail toward the road, her head spinning with all the events of her busy day, the beam of the flashlight dancing its morose way before her like some ancient torch in a pagan funeral right. Had she done the right thing? What was best for her and for Rodrigo? Would Ralo really kill him if he tried to leave the gang? Was it unreasonable for her to ask such a thing? *No, I did what I had to, for me and for him.* She pulled her sweater tighter around her body, feeling the cool darkness of the night. What did Papa say to him? He really seemed rattled by that, as well. It was probably good if he was afraid of Papa. *I've hurt him.*

She listened for anything that might distract her mind, but there was little more than the sound of her own breathing, and the light pat of her footfalls on the path, the sound of the surf having faded with the distance. He had raised his hand to strike her, and then held back. What would she have done if he had hit her? The bible verse rang out again in her mind, *turn the other cheek.* She shook her head. Turn the other cheek? *Would I have the strength?* She heard the words from her dream again, *Sometimes, we must suffer.* The beam from her flashlight cut through the forbidding shadows formed in the pale moonlight, then flickered momentarily. She tightened the connection to the batteries, unnerved by even this transient failure of the light.

Lali followed the path to the street and the street to her house, her head bowed, the separation aching her heart. The swirling confusion of events and emotions, the thoughts jumping around in her head, the exhausting process of making sense of things, scrambled her mind, almost like the dizzying spin of her dream. Hadn't she been doing the right thing, praying at the abortion clinic, showing Kim a better choice for her child, even in dating Rodrigo, hoping she could be a positive influence on a kid who was at risk of falling into a difficult life? But there was no reward. Only heartache and confusion. She was happy to be home, to have a home and a father who cared for her. But how could things be going so wrong? And what was this business of the cup? Would it pass? Why had that popped into her head? And God's will. Why should God's will be so ominous and foreboding? Wasn't God a god of love?

As she walked up the steps, Papa opened the door for her. Lali's heart leapt to see him there waiting, aching as she was, to be back in the bubble of protection she had so recently resented. He probably had been really worried. He didn't trust Rodrigo. And he was right to be suspicious. Likely, he was wondering if she had gone through with it, or if there had been any trouble.

"So, it's over then?" Anxiety rang in her father's voice.

Lali nodded. Her father opened his strong, protective arms, and she fell into them.

"I'm so sorry, but it is for the best."

Was it for the best? Was it really over? Something surely was just beginning. She pulled back gently from her father.

"Thank you, Papa." Her voice cracked, then she met his eyes, "I don't know what I would do without you. I need some time to pray now and to think."

Her father recoiled a bit when she mentioned prayer. His face became pensive and sad as if gripped by a painful memory. What had she triggered in him when she mentioned prayer? Would he one day regain his faith? Papa nodded as she slipped from his arms. He scratched his face just under his eye. Was he wiping a tear?

Lali plodded up the stairs to her room, her footfalls heavy under the emotional burdens of her unusual day. Could anything more be demanded of her today? And yet she sensed somehow that there would be more. She knelt by the bed, seeming to collapse under the weight of her heavy heart, and faced the statuette of the Sacred Heart of Jesus. He bore the cross, and yet his heart overflowed with love and mercy. Lali focused on the crown of thorns around the most precious heart of the statue. His very heart wounded by our sins. She was exhausted by so much less! A little anxiety, a little grief, and she struggled to handle it. He said sometimes we must suffer. Would she be able to bear what may come?

Lali meditated on her prayer, shaking off her drifting thoughts, making her petitions. She prayed for herself, for strength to resist sin and temptation, for Ralo and Kim, and Rodrigo, that they would come to the saving knowledge of Christ, for the bullies, Jake and Ted, that they would seek to help those weaker than themselves, and for Danny, that the Lord might heal him and make him strong.

Praying for Danny, Lali's mind drifted. How naked he must feel with his hair gone and looking so unnatural. How alone he must feel? In school, with all those other healthy kids, kids who took their good health for granted, who whined and complained about their homework or doing chores, or some petty slight or insult, and never considered how serious life could be. Her focus turned inward, was she like that as well? How was she any different? Hadn't her thoughts about her breakup with Rodrigo consumed her, and displaced concerns for deeper matters, like life and death? The health of a boy like Danny, mocked for his very affliction, and his attempt to fit in and look a little more normal? How must it feel to be Danny?

Lali stood up and looked in horror at her own long, dark, beautiful hair in the mirror. How was she any different? Wasn't her own health and beauty an affront to those who had neither? Her eyes widened in her reflection with a sudden realization. *No, not my hair!* But the very value she put on it meant it would have to go. *Suffering!* Her eyes widened, then narrowed under her conviction, as the idea solidified into purpose and mission. Didn't he say, "*sometimes we must suffer?*"

Lali grabbed the scissors from the dresser and walked into the bathroom. She considered herself in the mirror for a moment, her long hair positioned between the blades of the scissors. *Suffering! Sometimes, we must suffer!* She closed her eyes and held her breath. She squeezed the scissor blades together. She expected the snipping sound, but the soft sound of the great handful of hair falling onto the floor surprised her. She stared at the pile of her former locks on the bathroom floor, like some dead thing, once beautiful, once a part of her, now lifeless, motionless, gone. And the gospel rang in her ears again: *If your right hand causes you to sin, cut it off and throw it away!* She gazed at herself, scissors in hand, the large gap where her hair used to be. *Cut it off and throw it away!* The scissors opened and closed again and again. The pile on the floor grew larger and larger. What was left, she cropped short and uneven to her head. She grabbed her father's can of shaving cream from the sink and hesitated, closing her eyes. Then, giving it a decisive shake, sprayed some into her hand and lathered her closely, if sloppily, cropped hair. Taking her father's razor in hand, she shaved off what was left of her hair and washed off her head, revealing the smooth, pale skin of her scalp. She ran her hand over her head and gaped, wide-eyed, in horror at herself in the mirror. She sat on the toilet seat and began to weep.

Lali heard her father knocking and tried to catch her breath to stop her sobbing.

"Lali? Are you okay?"

Lali drew a couple deep breaths, trying to get herself together. *What will he think of me? He's going to think I'm crazy! Maybe, I am crazy?* She braced herself with her hands on the sink and gazed at herself in the mirror, her eye makeup leaving tracks as her tears crawled down her face. She had achieved her objective of looking sickly, the dark puffiness around her tear-swollen eyes, the pale baldness of her head. Act as normally as possible for him. Who was she kidding? Nothing about this was normal. She wiped her eyes, sniffled, and stood up. *I can't hide it from him.* She slowly opened the door, listening to it creak, avoiding her father's face. Another deep breath and she raised her head, searching for his eyes, hoping for understanding and love, but uncertain of what might come. Lali managed a crooked, confused sort of smile. Her father's eyes widened in surprise.

"Lali, what have you done to your hair?" His hand moved to cover his mouth.

Grinning sheepishly, Lali lowered her head. "There is a boy at school with cancer." Her voice soft and broken, reverberated against the tiles, her shoulders slumped. "Some of the other kids were making fun of him. He shouldn't be the only one."

Her father's strong arms enveloped her tenderly. His body heaved and sighed against hers. A long, tender moment passed like an eternity. He eased his embrace finally and met her eyes. His rough hands gently wiped the tears from her face. His eyes shimmered in the dim light and as he closed them, a tear wandered down his right cheek and dripped to the floor. Opening his eyes, a wistful smile crossed his lips as he shook his head.

"My crazy, beautiful girl! You've had quite a day."

8

Suffer the Little Ones

LITTLE LALI WANDERS THE DUSTY STREETS of Jerusalem, hoping for just a glimpse of the Master, the great prophet. Curiously bald, even her eyebrows fallen out, she struggles to find her way through the crowd. Like a hound with the scent, she seeks only Him, the one they say heals the sick, the one they say feeds the hungry. Her browless eyes scan ahead for Him, searching, and there, just a glimpse of Him before the crowd closes, and she loses sight again. And, now, finally she scoots between two in the clamoring crowd, and there He is, the same smile, though not a trace of blood on his palms. Lali's eyes widen in joy and recognition at seeing her old friend. But as she steps forward to see Him, perhaps to touch Him, to touch His palm once again, His disciples block her way.

"Go away, little girl!" One of the disciples gives her a shove. "The Master does not have time for you!"

Jesus turns and rebukes the disciple. "Suffer the little ones to come to me, for such are the children of heaven. If anyone should cause one of these little ones to go astray, it would be better for him if a millstone were tied around his neck and he were cast into the sea. Nay, it would be better for him if he had never been born."

Lali woke up, rubbing her shaven head, imagining she heard a cock crow, but there were no roosters around. It was real. She had shaven her head last night. Danny. What would he think when he saw her? She looked around her familiar room and spied the statuette of the Sacred Heart of Jesus on the dresser and chuckled to herself. She walked into the bathroom and stared at her reflection in the mirror. Running her hand over her smooth, hairless head, she recalled the little girl from her dream. *Suffer the little ones?* Wasn't that what He said?

Lali descended the stairs, following the burnt scent of another of her father's sorrowful breakfast mysteries. The unusual lightness of her head on her neck surprised her, as the considerable weight of her missing hair no longer required support. Papa cocked his head and winked, his beard noticeably badly shaven.

"It's going to take a while to get used to this new look." He good-naturedly rubbed his face. "You know, I couldn't get a good shave with that razor."

Lali paused a moment, leaning on the table, then walked over and hugged him.

"Well, I suppose Rodrigo might not be as interested in you now, anyway." Her father shrugged, then raised an eyebrow, closing an eye as he looked at the mess he had made in the frying pan.

"I don't know, Papa." Lali smiled coyly. "I think Rodrigo may have liked a lot more about me than just my hair."

Her father offered her a plate of overcooked eggs with half-cooked bacon.

He stared at the plate. "I just can't seem to get this right."

"It's okay. I'm not very hungry anyway."

Lali could not ignore the concern in her father's eyes as he glanced over at her from the driver's seat of his squad car. He would be worried, and she was anxious herself. How would people react to her new, hairless look? Papa drove the familiar route to the church in an awkward, eerie silence, punctuated by an occasional huff and shake of his head, as if he was about to say something, then thought better of it. The tension of the unverbalized thoughts permeated the safety of the protective bubble of the police car with anxiety. She glanced at him with each little huff, until finally, he broke the silence with words.

"Be careful today, Lali." His cautioning tone made her uneasy. "People will react differently toward you with this new look."

Lali tilted her head, rubbing her hand on her scalp as if she had forgotten that she had no hair. "Yes, I suppose they will." She bit her lip, apprehensively.

"People don't always treat people well, when they appear different." Papa signaled for a left turn, paused, then continued to speak haltingly, apparently choosing his words carefully. "You know, in the cities, lots of people dress…uh…in unusual ways and wear their hair in unusual ways, and…well…uh…nobody would even blink at a girl with a shaved head. But, out here…uh…people will, uh, likely react a bit. You know, maybe, not so well, I think."

Lali chuckled, then considered the point more seriously. "Yes, I think that's why I had to do this." Lali took out from beneath her blouse the Miraculous Medal she wore on the chain around her neck. "Remember the medal Mama used to wear? Don't worry. The Blessed Mother will keep an eye on me."

"I pray she does."

Did he realize the implications of what he had said? Was he regaining his faith? She leaned over and kissed his cheek. "I'll be going to the clinic to pray again after school. Then to the unwed mothers' home to help out. I'll call you for a ride."

"Are you sure you want to do that today, Lali? I mean, with all that happened yesterday, and this new look and all?" His worried look, the wrinkles in his brow, intensified the concern in his voice. "Why don't you take a day off?"

"Oh, I'll be okay, Papa. Just going to pray a little. I think it's where I need to be today." She held up the Miraculous Medal again. "She'll be there to protect me."

He let out an exasperated huff, shaking his head, his shoulders slumping a bit in resignation. "Okay, just be careful. Say your rosary and get out of there. That girl Kim is trouble, Lali. She's in with a very bad crowd. We are investigating several missing drug dealers and we think that gang she's with may be responsible." He pulled his cruiser to the curb in front of St. Sebastian's Church, and moving the gear lever to park, he turned to her. "I won't be there to protect you."

Lali leaned toward him and kissed him again on the cheek. "I love you, Papa. You know that, don't you?" She caressed her Miraculous Medal.

"I love you too." His body heaved with a deep breath, his throat seemed to choke on the words.

Lali waved to her father as he drove off. She glanced down at the sidewalk. Still gently rubbing the Miraculous Medal, the words her father had said, *I pray that she does,* echoed in her mind. Was her father really praying again? Or had he just said something as an expression of hope, with no religious meaning? Or at least intending no religious meaning? Had her modest suffering drawn him closer to faith? Was this what Jesus meant, when he said, *sometimes, we must suffer if we are to save souls?* Was it really Jesus and not just some distant dream of a five-year-old girl, recurring now? Just some trick of the mind in a rudderless universe, wildly random, with no direction or meaning?

Lali looked up from her reverie at the small stone chapel next to the large neo-Gothic church, the place that was more like home than the place her earthly father provided, and pulled the door open. Father Fernandez had already made his way up to his usual place next to the altar and had begun the opening rites. Lali found a pew in the back and lowered the cushioned kneeler that creaked slightly and clanked softly as it hit the floor. She fell to her knees into the well-worn grooves of the kneeler and began to pray, her mind distracted with her own petitions and unable to focus on the proceedings of the Mass.

Oh Lord, please change Ralo's heart, and let him allow Kim to keep her baby. Please guide Rodrigo away from this path of evil he is on. Please give Kim courage to make the right choice. And make Danny well, and guide Principal Martinez in his work at the school, and Mrs. Howard, and the girls at the unwed mother's home, keep them safe.

Mass progressed as usual, but Lali found that she could not keep her mind on the liturgy. The gospel passage for the day rattled like background noise as her mind focused on the agony in the garden and Jesus asking that the cup pass from Him, *but not my will, by thy will be done.* The image from her dream last night, and how the disciples would not let her see Jesus, filled her mind. And, then, her other dream. *That* dream! How she had traced her finger over the wound in His hand. *Sometimes we must suffer if we are to save souls.* She walked up the aisle to receive the Body and Blood of Christ in Communion. *We each must take up our cross and follow.* And follow? Follow where?

She focused on the crucifix as she approached the priest, meditating on the body hanging on the cross, the bloody wounds in His hands, feet, and side. *Sometimes we must suffer...*

Lali bowed her head reverently before the Blessed Sacrament.

"The Body of Christ," the priest said.

"Amen." Lali received His Body on her tongue. Then moving to the Extraordinary Minister holding the cup, she bowed her head once more.

"The Blood of Christ."

"Amen." And then, taking the chalice, she drank His Blood. Lifting her chin, she adored the body of Christ on the cross and in her mouth. *Take up your cross and follow*, the words in her head. Follow where? Lali made her way back to the pew and knelt, thanking the Lord for His presence within her, and asking for His help and guidance. *I will be with you when your time comes,* she heard the words from her dream. Follow where? And then the dismissal again, "Go in peace, glorifying the Lord by your life."

Yes, Lord. But how? How do I glorify you?

I will be with you when your time comes, the voice reassured her, in her mind.

Lali broke from her meditation and realized that she had been tracing a circle on her palm as she prayed. She clenched her fist, then relaxed her fingers again. She exited the pew and genuflected to the tabernacle, stumbling a little as she bent down to touch her knee to the floor and making the sign of the cross. Turning, and proceeding down the aisle, she paused at the door to dip her finger in the holy water and turned once more to face the tabernacle, genuflecting again as she made the sign of the cross. As she exited the church, Father Fernandez greeted her. His eyes widened briefly as she approached, then his face quickly returned to his pleasant smile.

"Good morning, Lali." He extended his hand to her. "This is an interesting new look?"

Lali took his hand then rubbed her head with her other hand. "Just trying to fit in with my new friends."

Father Fernandez chuckled, and shook his head, as she continued on. Lali passed the public-school girls again in their provocative clothes, with multiple piercings in their ears. They did not giggle this time but turned and gaped as she passed. Lali glanced back over her shoulder, smiled and kept walking.

As Lali approached the entrance to St. Mary's High School, Principal Martinez greeted the students as usual. His eyes widened as she approached, and his hand moved up to cover his mouth, his large mustache poked out over the top of his fingers.

"Lali, are you okay?"

"Good-morning, Principal Martinez." Lali smiled pleasantly, as if nothing at all were wrong. "Yes, I'm quite well, thank you."

"What happened to your hair?"

Lali raised her hand and ran it across her bare scalp.

"Oh, that, I thought it would be nice to show solidarity with Danny."

"Lali, we do not help the sick by mimicking their afflictions. The boy may think you are mocking him." His frowning mustache made his critical reaction seem even more stern and severe. Principal Martinez's disapproval stung her through his expression and tone of voice, as well as his words. She was taken off-guard.

"I never thought of it that way." She moved her hand to brush the hair from her eye but found there wasn't any, and rubbed her forehead, instead. "I felt called to it, in a way. I meant no disrespect."

"Well, I'm a little disappointed." He lightened his tone. "This is not what I expected from you."

She lowered her head. "I'm sorry I disappointed you." Lifting her chin, she managed an awkward smile. "I'll pray for you."

Confused by the confrontation with Principal Martinez, she wandered sullenly down the hallway. She spied Danny at his locker, *Well, let's see what he thinks.* She snuck up behind him and snatched the hat off his head. Danny immediately reached up and covered his head with his hand. She smiled affectionately, holding the hat in her hand, her shaven head glimmering in the morning light streaming through the eastern window. Daniel sighed and slumped his shoulders as he grabbed his hat back and placed it on his head, a pained look on his face and a hint of disgust in his actions.

"I didn't think *you* would be making fun of me." His tone was a mix of anger and disappointment.

Lali was crushed. "Oh, I'm sorry, Danny," she stammered. "I wasn't making fun. I just thought you should not be the only one without any hair."

Daniel slammed his locker closed, and looked up at her, with a flash of anger. "I don't want anyone to have to go through what I've been through. Can you be sick like me, too? It's not just my hair that falls out. It's hard for me to keep food down, and I feel weak and sick. I don't want anyone else to be like me; I want to be like other people."

"Oh, I'm so sorry." She covered her mouth with her hand. "I don't know what got into me, but I just felt like I had to."

Daniel paused a moment, which seemed much longer than it actually was. Then he chuckled, shaking his head with a smile and reached his hand up toward her head. She dipped her head down so he could reach it more easily. He ran his hand over her head.

"Pretty nice job, though." Danny studied her handiwork.

"My dad says I ruined his razor."

"I bet you did!"

All seemed to be forgiven. But, how could something she felt called to do be so wrong? She managed an uneasy grin and asked him, "Would you like to meet for lunch again today?"

"Sure." Danny laughed, shaking his head. "I don't think I'll get any better offers, so you don't need to worry."

Lali pulled Danny's hat over his eyes. "You better not get any better offers!"

Danny giggled as he straightened his hat, "Don't you worry, Lali. There are no better offers."

The bell rang for first-period class. Lali made her way through the hallway, hearing the snickers behind her as she passed. She did not turn around but stiffened herself and walked on. So, this was what it was like when people gawked at you for being different? She took her usual seat in

Mr. Trudeau's history class, where they had been studying the Marshall Plan and post-World-War-II France.

Mr. Trudeau was perhaps the most popular history teacher at St. Mary's High School. He managed to make history fun, as well as commanding rapt attention from the students, as they watched intently to see if his remarkable comb-over would fall off the top of his head. C.O. Trudeau, they called him. Poor Mr. Trudeau, when would he just admit he was bald?

Lali heard the snickers and hushed whispers but kept her focus ahead. A sense of anticipation permeated the class, as Mr. Trudeau began his lecture, not seeming to notice the new baldness that captivated her classmates. C.O. Trudeau ran his fingers over his comb-over, almost as if he were checking to make sure it was still there, as if her baldness might somehow be catching.

Lali sat up straight and watched attentively as Mr. Trudeau began his lecture accompanied by appropriate historical slides. The class, once it appeared the shining scalp would have little impact, settled in and began taking notes as his lecture continued, telling of the harshness of the German occupation of France and the French resistance. The slides and commentary advanced, the comb-over properly in place, just another day in class. Mr. Trudeau explained how after the war, the French Resistance took vengeance on those who had cooperated with the German occupation.

"So, one of the things they would do would be to mark the women who were complicit with the Germans by shaving their heads."

Mr. Trudeau advanced the slide and the students gasped as their eyes bounced back and forth from the image on the slide to Lali's remarkably bald head. The slide revealed a picture of a French resistance fighter shaving the head of a woman. Their eyes stared at Lali's gleaming scalp as if she were, in fact, the German sympathizer, in the wake of that horrible war that ended so long ago. She raised her hand. The anticipation grew in the utter silence that followed the initial gasp in the ordinarily active and vibrant class. Lali scanned the class in the awkward hush. No one else dared to raise their hand, not even Tommy Slater, one of the brightest and most active participants in the class. She caught Tommy's eye, but he quickly glanced toward the corner of the room. Not even Tommy wanted to touch this one. Mr. Trudeau would have to call on her. She noticed the slight roll of the eyes when Mr. Trudeau finally acknowledged her with a nod, leaving it to Lali to end the painful silence.

"So, these women did what they needed to do to survive in a time of war? And their countrymen sought vengeance after the war was over by shaming them further?"

"Yes, Lali, that's right." Mr. Trudeau kept his eyes on her eyes. His hand checked his comb-over.

Lali pursed her lips. "Did anyone shave their own heads in sympathy?"

Mr. Trudeau paused. "Not that I'm aware of." His comb-over began to descend closer to his eye.

"That's what I would have done." Lali nodded, with conviction. "The war was over. It's time to move on."

Lali and Danny met for fourth period lunch now seeming to be perfectly matched, united by the unusual feature of teen baldness. Lali drew stares from many students, sensing them turning to gawk as she past. She especially noticed the boys who used to stare at her, now avoiding eye contact when she glanced in their direction. There was a sting in their avoidance and suspected disapproval. She cared less about the girls, some of whom tittered and whispered to their friends. She was accustomed to being noticed but not like this.

"I guess we will be sitting together at the bald table." Danny took off his hat, his face beaming a sly smile. "So, do we let anyone with hair join us? Or is it an exclusive club?"

Lali chuckled. "I say we let anyone who wants to, join. I'd even let those with bad comb-overs like Mr. Trudeau join. I guess we're all bald underneath our hair."

"We're all bald beneath our hair? That's about the stupidest thing I've ever heard."

"Yeah, well, I think that should be our club motto, 'We're all bald beneath our hair!'"

Suzie Parks approached the table looking to join her friends for lunch, having arrived late to the cafeteria. She blinked a few times and covered her mouth; her sparkling blue eyes retained their beauty even as they widened expressing horror. *This should be fun! What will pretty Suzie think?*

"Lali! What happened to that gorgeous hair of yours?"

Lali smirked. "Hi Suzie, I was just discussing that with my friend Daniel here. We both discovered that we are all bald beneath our hair! Isn't that cool?"

Suzie cocked her head, as if trying to understand. "Uh, I'm sorry, uh, I hope you're not sick or anything. I mean, oh, I didn't mean anything by it."

"Suzie, I'm so sorry." Lali's mouth fell open, stuttering, then she lowered her head. "No, I'm not sick. It's just a stupid thing I did to try to be in solidarity with Danny here, who is sick. But we're making the best of it."

"Um, oh, I'm glad you're not sick." Suzie lowered her eyes, as if under conviction of some unconfessed sin. "I know I'm not always, well, good, you know, uh, like you, and, uh, I would feel awful if you were sick or something."

"I'm really sorry about that." Lali motioned toward an empty chair. "Would you like to join us, Suzie?"

"Uh, no, I was supposed to meet Jake, oh, there he is! I'll see you, Lali, really, I hope you're okay. I always loved your hair."

Suzie hurried off to join Jake Turner and a few of her other friends.

"Oh, that pretty girl is with Jake, the bully!" Daniel tossed a roll onto his tray in disgust.

Lali sighed. "Suzie is with a lot of boys, Danny." She lowered her head and closed her eyes for a moment. "You should pray for her, and for Jake, but especially Suzie. Sometimes pretty girls like Suzie, you know, you think they have everything, but they get so much attention, it kind of warps them."

"She's very pretty. I mean, there's something about her eyes." Daniel raised his eyebrows.

"Yes, but she looks a lot older than she is." Lali glanced at Danny. "And she's looked a lot older than she is for a long time, so people treated her like she was a lot older when she was still just a little girl inside. It can be very hard for girls like that. Sometimes I forget that about her, especially because she can be mean and superficial."

"But she's very popular? I mean, isn't she?"

"Yes, but not always in a good way." Lali pressed her lips together. "You see, she has a good heart, though. She really cared if I was sick. I never realized it until now, but I think she looks up to me in a way."

Lali mindlessly stirred her soup. *Why was I being mean like that to Suzie when she thought so well of me?* She shook off her moment of introspection as if she were clearing water that had gotten into her eyes.

She turned her head to the side and glanced back coyly. "But I'll bet she's bald beneath all that beautiful blond hair!"

"Well, now you're just being silly! I don't think there's anything beneath all that blond hair! Just more hair!"

"I say she's welcome in our club anyway!" Lali nodded.

"You know, I think in a way, it helps, you shaving your head. I mean, you're stranger than I am now. Like, I'm bald because I'm sick. You chose to be bald!"

"Yeah, and Mr. Trudeau won't even admit he's bald!"

Danny chuckled, then a brief look of regret wandered across his face. "Hey, I didn't mean to say you were strange."

Lali reached out and grabbed his hand. "Danny, don't go getting all serious on me. Let's just be bald together, okay?"

Danny dropped his head for a moment. Lali twinkled warmly as his eyes raised again to meet hers. Danny chuckled and changed the subject. "So, your name is Lali? Is that like Lollipop?"

Lali laughed. "Nooo, not like lollipop!"

Lali rolled her eyes then met Danny's. She noticed he regained his cheeriness. She loved how their friendship had grown and wished she had been named for a lollipop.

"My full name is Eulalia. I was named after St. Eulalia, the patron saint of sailors. My grandfather was a sailor in World War II. His ship was sunk by a submarine, and he was in the water for several hours with a friend of his who had emigrated from Barcelona, Spain, which is where St. Eulalia was from. They prayed for her intercession and were rescued."

"Wow, that's interesting." Danny dropped his fork on his tray.

"Well, after the war, my grandfather bought a fishing boat and named her, 'Santa Eulalia'. I was born on the day my grandfather died, so they named me Eulalia to honor his wish."

"She must have been a pretty powerful saint to have influenced your grandfather so much."

"St. Eulalia was martyred when she was just thirteen years old during the Diocletian persecution. Diocletian was the last Roman emperor to think it was a good idea to kill and torture Christians back in like the year 300 or so." Her eyes moved past Danny and focused on nothing in particular. "Anyway, she was tortured horribly but never gave up her faith. Oh, some of the things they did to that poor girl! They put her in a barrel, with knives stuck through it and rolled her down a street." She glanced back at Danny. "Can you imagine?"

Lali paused. Daniel blinked a couple of times, his mouth opened, but nothing came out.

"Anyway, they call it now, 'The Descent of St. Eulalia'. But they were only getting started. They say there were thirteen tortures in all. One for each year of her short life. Finally, they cut off her breasts and crucified her. And I guess that wasn't even enough because they ended up cutting her head off!" Lali's view drifted and blurred again. "But she never gave up the faith. They say a dove flew out of her neck after they cut off her head."

Lali paused again, staring past Daniel, her attention drawn into the story of her namesake, and the foreboding portent of her dream. "I pray that I may be so strong."

Danny's blurred figure leaned towards her, in her peripheral vision. "Wow, my patron saint survived the lion's den."

Lali refocused her attention on Danny. "Yes, my brave Daniel. There is a great saint watching over you. 'God Is My Judge', that's what Daniel means in Hebrew. Remember that the next time someone judges you or thinks you're weak or unworthy."

Lali reached over and gently took hold of his hand, "God is your judge, Daniel."

"I never knew that." Danny's mouth fell open.

"Would you like to come with me to pray at the clinic after school?" Lali abruptly changed the subject, her voice almost pleading. "I could use the company."

Daniel hesitated. He lowered his head. "No, my parents would worry too much."

9

Taking Care of Business

KIM LOOKED OUT THE WINDOW of the tan Chrysler sedan, her body turned as far away from Ralo as she could manage and prayed. Not that she believed in God. Only she hoped someone would hear her prayer and answer it. Or, rather, that things would just happen as if her prayer were answered. *Oh God, please don't let that girl be praying when we get there. I won't be able to do this if she is.* And Ralo? What would Ralo do?

Ralo drove in silence. Kim would not look at him. He had made it clear that they were getting this business taken care of today. There would be no more waiting. He would see to it himself. She had no choice. He would kill her if she didn't. He never actually said he would kill her, but she had no doubt that he would. It may not even be his. Kim's hand rubbed her belly.

The right-hand turn signal rang in Kim's ears as they approached the clinic like some strange siren warning of a secret danger, one too terrible to risk alerting everyone but meant only for her. She clenched her fists and closed her eyes. *God, please don't let her be there!*

Kim opened her eyes and there she was. At least she thought it was her. The same Catholic school uniform. The same rosary beads. But what happened to her hair? Kim closed her eyes tightly, crossing her arms, hugging herself closely. *Oh, God, why?* Why did she have to be there? *I can't do it.* Not with her there. *I'm not getting out of the car.*

"Okay, Kim!" Ralo commanded, his tone caustic as he moved the shift lever to park. "Is time to take care of beesness!"

Kim sat silently staring at the car door, not daring to peek out the window again. *I can't do this! I just can't. I'm not a killer! I'm not like Ralo!*

Ralo opened the door and stomped around the front of the car. Kim kept her head down. She had locked the door, but Ralo had the key. There was no avoiding it. He would have to drag her in there. *I'm not going to do it!* Ralo tried the door and found it locked. He shook his head and unlocked the door, flinging it open.

"Come on, Kim! We getting this taken care of!"

Kim grabbed the seat belt and fastened it around her.

"Ju really making me do this, Kim? Ju really making me drag'u out?"

Kim did not say anything. She turned herself toward the inside of the car, away from Ralo, keeping her arms folded against her frail body.

"Okay, we do this the hard way." Ralo reached in and unfastened the safety belt.

"No, Ralo!" Kim squealed. "I don't want to!"

"We getting this taken care of, Kim!"

His strong arms wrapped around her waist and yanked her roughly out of the car door as she shifted all her body weight against him, to no avail. She tumbled out of the door and onto the ground, lifeless as a sack of grain. *He's going to have to drag me in there.* She closed her eyes tightly, squeezing herself in her crossed arms. *God, please! I don't want to do this!*

His rough hands were now under her arms, lifting her up. Finally, she allowed her body to lie limp, not so much struggling against him, but just forcing him to drag her toward the clinic door.

"No, Ralo! I don't want to!" In a sudden struggle to free herself from his grasp, she jostled her body and attempted to twist away. As Ralo tightened his grip like a boa constrictor around her waist from behind, the unmistakable metallic hardness of the revolver in his jacket pocket pressed against her back. The bastard brought his freaking gun! *I guess he doesn't go anywhere without it.*

"You can't force her, Ralo!" Kim heard the voice and all her strength left her. She collapsed like dead weight in Ralo's arms as the voice continued. "You can't make her if she doesn't want to. She has the right to choose."

No! God, No! He's going to kill that stupid girl! Kim glimpsed her would-be protector, standing unarmed and defiant, as Ralo whipped her around to face the challenge coming from behind him. Kim closed her eyes, hoping she might disappear.

"This is none of ju beesness, little girl!" He narrowed his eyes. "Bad things happen to people, they stick their noses in me beesness."

Kim's body stiffened as she struggled once more to free herself from Ralo's grasp.

"No, Lali!" Kim frantically struggled once more. "Don't. He'll kill you!"

Kim twisted suddenly, with a surprising strength she did not know she had and broke the body lock Ralo had around her waist. Ralo clamped onto her arms, as she turned to face him. "Just leave Lali alone. She didn't do anything wrong!"

Ralo faced Kim, his eyes terrible, his tone like the growl of a pit bull defending his turf. He squeezed her arms. "She sticks'er nose in me beesness, Kim. Ju know what happen when someone do that to me!"

Kim cowered as he gripped her arms, glowering over her. *I have to save this stupid girl!* Ralo would kill her, for sure. He might pull that gun out and kill her right here!

"Okay, okay. I'll do it, Ralo." Kim freed herself from his grasp in a sudden, desperate scramble, then smoothed her rumpled denim jacket. "Just leave her alone."

Kim stiffened her body as she resolved to ascend the steps of the clinic. *I will save that little fool! I can't let Ralo kill her.* As she took a step toward the clinic, Lali stepped in front of her, pleading, "No, Kim! Don't do this thing! God will protect you!"

Kim closed her eyes and calmed herself. She solidified her resolve. She placed her hands on Lali's shoulders and met her eyes. "No, Lali. He won't. But maybe, if I do this, He will protect you." She glanced at Ralo. "Maybe, if I do this."

Kim closed her misty eyes tightly and a tear wandered down her cheek when she opened them again. She turned and walked with Ralo to the steps of the clinic with Lali following. Kim sensed her presence behind her like an unwanted puppy hoping for attention from a new prospective master. She ascended the crookedly settled stairs with Ralo, to the landing before the door, confident that she had made the correct choice. Ralo opened the door and allowed Kim to enter first. *He's opening the door for me?* The bastard never did that before! After allowing Kim in, Ralo cut Lali off and entered the clinic, closing the door behind him and preventing Lali from entering. Kim sighed, as she turned and watched Lali open the door with a jerk, and step into the clinic waiting room. Kim turned to face the interior of the waiting room.

The receptionist, an attractive woman in her mid-thirties with short dark hair and green eyes that seemed to dart anxiously from person to person over her reading glasses, greeted them. On seeing Lali, her eyes narrowed as she tightened her lips into a skeptical smirk.

"May I help you?" She sat up straight and stiff, a cold sharpness in her tone. Ralo's body moved in front of Kim, his arm shoving her back. He answered for her. Kim's long stifled anger began to build, and she squinted at him.

"Jes, me girlfriend, she needs an abortion," he said, grabbing Kim's arm and yanking her forward. Kim shook her arm free.

"No, Kim, don't." Lali's hand fell gently upon Kim's shoulder. Kim glanced at it and closed her eyes for a moment. Kim's hands balled tightly into fists.

The receptionist glared at Lali. "And you? Are you looking for services?"

Lali stepped forward. "No, this man is trying to force this woman to have an abortion!" Lali sounded as if she were reporting a crime to a police officer.

I have to go through with this, or he'll kill her. Kim took a deep breath.

The receptionist's eyes narrowed at Lali, glancing occasionally at Ralo. She tightened her lips and shook her head.

"Well, if you are not here for services." She let out an exaggerated sigh. "I will have to ask you to leave."

Lali's pleading eyes once more found Kim.

Kim glanced at Ralo's smirk and she shut her eyes. She could not bear to see his gloating.

"But..." Lali stammered.

The receptionist cut her off. "Uh-uh, if you will not leave, I will have to call the police." She tilted her head and picked up the phone receiver, her finger dangerously close to the nine button.

"Just go, Lali," Kim said. "There's nothing you can do to help now. Having the police involved isn't going to help."

Lali slumped her shoulders and turned to leave the clinic.

At least I was able to save her. Kim watched the door open.

"Bye-bye, little girl." Ralo snidely wiggled his fingers at Lali as she left. Kim bit her cheek inside her mouth. *Let him gloat. She's out of trouble. At least for now...*

The receptionist pursed her lips and her head slowly turned from side to side. Then, ignoring Ralo, she turned to Kim.

"Okay, Miss. Is there something we can do for you?"

Kim glared at Ralo as he stepped in front of her, pushed her back, and answered for her, again. "Jes, she needs an abortion!"

The receptionist cocked her head and squinted at Ralo. She sounded like she was chastising a dog who had inappropriately jumped on the furniture against his training. "I was talking with the young lady."

Kim gasped, her eyes widening as Ralo glowered at the receptionist and stuck his hand in his jacket pocket. This one had better be careful, too. Or Ralo would shoot her right here. He was probably flipping the safety off right now...

The receptionist tilted her head toward Kim, and spoke softly, with gentle eyes. "Is there something we can do for you?"

Kim remembered Lali, and the women at the unwed mothers' home, how they had treated her with respect and compassion. *Maybe this woman can help me?* If Ralo didn't kill her, first. Kim started to cry. "I'm pregnant," she managed to say between sobs.

Ralo's arm pushed her back again, as he stepped forward in front of her. "Jes, and we want it taken care of."

Kim glared at Ralo, like a dog that had been beaten one too many times.

"Sir, the only one who can make a decision here is this young lady. I will ask you to step back and keep quiet, or I will call the police, and have you removed!" The receptionist's response seemed cold and aflame, like a judge delighting in sentencing some heinous felon who no one had thought would ever face justice.

You go, girl! Kim allowed herself a smile, then remembered the gun in Ralo's pocket. *God, I hope he doesn't just shoot her right here!*

Ralo glowered at the receptionist. "Look, beetch!" Kim carefully watched the hand in his jacket pocket. Surely, he had his finger on the trigger.

"We come here to get this taken care of, now let's get the doctor and get this taken care of!"

The receptionist scowled at Ralo. Then picking up the phone, flipping her hair, she raised the receiver to her ear. "Okay, that's it. We'll see what the police have to say." The receptionist began to dial.

"Okay, Okay!" Ralo waved his hands. "Ju no need to call the cops!"

Kim's eyes widened in amazement. She had never seen Ralo back down like that. *Never!*

The receptionist turned toward Kim once more.

"Well, okay, Miss, why don't we have the doctor examine you? Then you can discuss your options with him?"

Ralo's eyes narrowed, his hand still in his pocket. Kim instinctively stepped back as his body pushed its way in front of her once again. "Options? We no wanna discuss no options! We want this taken care of!"

"Sir, the young lady has options that she will need to discuss with the doctor. I suggest you take a seat, or I will have to ask you to leave!"

Ralo fixed his enraged stare on the receptionist. Kim watched his hand in his jacket pocket. Would he pull his gun and shoot her, right here, right now? Kim liked this crazy woman, but she was likely to get herself killed. Ralo's features relaxed as he reluctantly stepped to the couch in the waiting room and sat down, removing his hand from his jacket pocket and clenching his fists. The receptionist waited until he was seated, then handed Kim a clipboard with the patient information forms.

"Please just complete these forms with your information." The receptionist spoke softly, probably afraid Ralo would come bolting over. "The doctor will see you in a few minutes."

Kim remained at the receptionist's desk and completed the forms. Just the basic information: name, address, medical insurance, medical history, and the HIPAA privacy forms. Kim quickly filled out the forms and handed the clipboard back the receptionist, who glanced at the forms, then over at

Ralo still clenching his fists. The receptionist took a deep breath, shaking her head.

"No worries." She stole a quick glance at Ralo, then back to Kim. "The doctor provides an initial evaluation for no charge for people without insurance. If you decide you would like services, we will arrange for payment at that time."

Kim nodded, feeling like a frightened cat uncertain of how to get down from the unsteady limb on which she found herself. Did she spy compassion in the eye of this receptionist, as if the woman might reach out and take her hand and reassure her that it would be all right? Perhaps, but only for a moment, and then it was gone, and she returned to her cool, officious manner. She led Kim into the examining room, a cold, antiseptic, metallic place, a controlled environment where nothing unwanted could survive. The scent of alcohol and chemicals meant to control life and to permit it only where it was wanted, creating an environment where God and His creation were only welcome if they could be controlled and confined, sent a shiver through Kim's soul, somehow permeating deeper than just her physical body. The examining table with stirrups extended, resembled some kind of medieval torture device awaiting the accused for a terrible inquisition. The place seemed to demand a justification for anything that dared live. *Who is worthy to live?* it seemed to ask.

What am I doing here? I can't do this! I just can't! But Ralo! Ralo will kill me! Kim hugged herself, closed her eyes, and hoped to be somewhere else when she reopened them. The receptionist pulled the paper down over the examining table and ripped off the excess, placing it in the trash. Kim opened her eyes. *Oh, God! I'm still here!*

"Dr. Singer will be in to examine you shortly." The receptionist avoided any eye contact.

Kim seated herself on the examining table and shivered in the cold sterility of the place. Dr. Singer came in to examine her. He was a man in his mid-fifties, in a white lab coat, with a graying beard and bifocal glasses, not an unattractive man, but certainly not an attractive man, either. There was something a little off about this guy. Another shiver caught Kim unprepared, despite of the relief that another living being had joined her in the otherwise lifeless room.

Dr. Singer studied the paperwork that the receptionist had handed him and glanced up through the upper lenses of his bifocal glasses.

"So, Ms. Whiting, what brings you in today?" His pleasant voice sounded as if he was asking her how the weather was.

Kim rolled her eyes. What a phony! *What do you think brought me here, today?*

"I'm pregnant," Kim said, gripping the sides of the examining table. "My boyfriend wants me to have an abortion."

Kim noted a hint of surprise in the doctor's reaction. Why should he be surprised?

He cocked his head before answering. "But what about you? Do *you* want to have an abortion?"

"No, but he will kill me if I don't." Her anger building, tears began to cloud her eyes. Her fingernails dug into the palms of her hands.

The doctor tilted his head and raised an eyebrow.

Kim crossed her arms and legs. What was with this guy? Was he stupid or something? He was a doctor, he couldn't be stupid, could he?

"Was that your boyfriend in the waiting room?"

"Yes, Ralo." Kim shuddered.

"He looks like a pretty tough guy! What does he do for a living?"

What's he do for a living? This guy was a freakin' idiot! *What do you think he does for a living? He sells drugs and kills people!*

"Why don't you ask him?" Kim squinted at the doctor. *Yes, you and Ralo have a nice little chat about what he does for a living.*

Dr. Singer shrugged and placed the chart down on his lap.

"May I ask why you would like to keep this baby?" He sounded as if he were really interested, as if it were a legitimate question, like a dentist asking whether you flossed every day.

Kim was confused. The doctor's tone confused her. It was as though he thought she was crazy or something. Why would you like to keep this baby? Something about his question just did not make sense.

"Because it's my baby, and it would be wrong to kill it?" A strange sensation seized Kim, like she was guessing at an obvious answer in a nightmare where the obvious made no sense to anyone but her.

"But it's your boyfriend's baby as well, and he doesn't want it." Dr. Singer raised his eyebrows.

Kim's eyes widened, and she was unable to hide the anger and fear in her voice. "He's a killer. He doesn't care!"

"Do you think he would make a good father?"

Kim shook her head and blinked like she had just been slapped in the face. "Of course not!"

"Then why do you want to have his baby?" A false sincerity rang in Dr. Singer's tone, like a bad actor reading from a script.

This guy was the biggest idiot in the world! Kim hugged herself tightly, keeping her legs crossed, and wishing she could tighten herself into a ball. She could not imagine a stupider question.

"I don't want to have his baby! I'm pregnant, but I don't want to have an abortion. If I have an abortion, I'll be a killer like him!"

The doctor seemed unfazed. A deepening loneliness gripped her. If the threat of murder bothered Dr. Singer, he did not let it show. He didn't care! Who was there who would help her? No one. He glanced down at her chart, and then turned his attention to her, changing the subject.

"Do you drink alcohol, Kim?"

Kim pursed her lips and lowered her head. She did not want to answer any more of these foolish questions. *Would Ralo make a good father?* What an idiot! Her mind raced with confusion, anger, and fear.

"Sometimes," Kim kept her head down. She wished she could slide under the door and slither out of that God-awful place. Dr. Singer wrote something on the chart and looked up again.

"And do you use recreational drugs?" His eyes peeped through the upper lenses of his bifocals as if he were looking through her bedroom window and trying to see her naked.

Kim hesitated. Her boyfriend was the biggest drug dealer in town, and he would kill her if she ratted him out. Dr. Singer appeared to realize the legal implications of his question.

"Kim, anything you say is completely confidential. I would lose my license to practice medicine if I told anyone." Kim focused on the floor.

"Sometimes." She looked up, frantically. "But not since I knew I was pregnant! I swear! I stopped as soon as I knew it might hurt the baby!"

"But before you knew, you were using?" Dr. Singer wrote again on her chart.

Kim lowered her eyes, defeated. "Yes."

"Did you know that those drugs could affect the baby?" Dr. Singer lowered the chart to his lap.

Now, he was just pissing her off. "Yes, that's why I stopped!"

"But they may have already had an effect." Dr. Singer leaned forward, looking directly into her eyes like he was peering into her soul, and could see every sin she had ever committed, the clipboard on his lap ready to record it all.

Kim turned away and started to weep. "Doctor, what was I supposed to do? I didn't know."

Dr. Singer was ready with a tissue and handed it to her. She took a few deep breaths, calming herself. She hated that she had broken down. She hated all these infuriating questions. She hated this doctor. And, she hated herself, and her weakness. She wanted nothing more than to escape this dreadful place, and this prying creep. *Maybe I can tell him I'll go to that place Lali showed me? Maybe then he'll let me leave.*

"Are you prepared to care for a baby?" The doctor raised his pen to record another response. "A baby that may be sick because of the drugs?"

"I was thinking of going to the unwed mothers' home, the one that girl, Lali, showed me. The one who prays out front. They take care of girls like me and their babies." Kim's eyes widened with hope, seeking validation from the doctor.

Dr. Singer raised an eyebrow as if her answer surprised him. "Well, that is an option," he admitted. "But what would your boyfriend, what was his name?"

"Ralo." Kim cringed.

"Yeah, Ralo. What would he do if you went there and had the baby? Sounds like he really doesn't want you to have this baby and sounds like he's the kind of guy who doesn't take no for an answer."

Anger and resentment began to flare in Kim and her whole body tensed. She imagined herself a caged and abused animal tormented in this artificial, sterile environment, but even more terrified of what lay outside the cage.

"He'd probably kill me and the baby, and maybe everybody at the unwed mothers' home." Her voice grew louder, her face flushed.

"Wow." Dr. Singer nearly dropped his pen. "And you still want to have his baby?"

"It would be wrong to kill it..." Kim's voice trailed off. *How can I kill my child? How can I do it? I'm not a killer.*

"Wouldn't it be wrong to have this baby under these circumstances?" Dr. Singer sounded confused. "Do you really want to have Ralo's baby? Especially if he doesn't want you to? And put all those people in jeopardy?"

Kim was flummoxed. She did not want to put people in jeopardy. That was why she was here in the first place, to save Lali. Ralo surely would have killed that innocent fool. And now this idiot doctor kept asking these ridiculous questions! Why didn't he just do it? *Why is he making me decide?* If it was the thing to do, just do it! *Stop making me decide!*

"I don't know, Doctor," Kim said. "I just don't want to be a killer."

Dr. Singer smiled, like a serpent in an ancient garden long ago.

"Oh, don't think of it as killing. You're just not having a baby you're not ready to have and the father doesn't want. Wouldn't it be better not to have this one? Then you could get your life together, stop using drugs, get away from this guy, what's his name?

"Ralo."

"Yeah, right, Ralo. You can get away from him, find a nice guy, and when you are ready, have a nice, healthy baby that everybody wants and you're ready to care for?"

Kim lowered her head and let out a long sigh. "I suppose."

Kim imagined the serpent maintained his sly smile as she stared at the floor, not daring to raise her eyes to him, wishing he would just do it without making her decide. *If he would just do it, then he would be the killer, not me!*

"We could make this whole problem go away in just a few minutes. It's a very simple and safe procedure. I do it all the time for girls in your situation."

"I guess so." Kim stared at the floor, resigned and beaten.

"Okay, just sign these forms, and we can get started." Dr. Singer closed the deal.

Kim signed the forms, then sniffed and wiped another tear from her eye.

"I really don't want to." Kim raised her chin in hope, as if the doctor could absolve her sins.

The serpent smirked. "I know. We often must do things we don't want to do. But it really is for the best."

10

Mrs. Greene

ALICE GREENE, OR MRS. GREENE as she preferred to be called, peeked around some papers she had been pretending to read and spied the presumed impregnator pacing restlessly in the waiting room of Dr. Singer's Family Planning Clinic. The scar on his face slithered like a snake as he clenched his jaw and glared her way with his hand in his jacket pocket. She despised these men who bullied women into abortions. Not that she, herself, would ever have an abortion, nor need to be bullied into one. She did everything she could to make sure that would never happen. Everything short of abstinence from sex, which was just unreasonable. Mrs. Greene clutched the desk as she eyed the pacing impregnator. Her mind drifted from the terrifying ordeal of abortion to the more terrifying prospect of childbirth, to the completely horrifying idea of being made pregnant by this particular specimen of human maleness. How had that woman let this thug get her pregnant and why would she hesitate to rid herself of the creepy little thing inside of her?

Exhibit A of why abortion had to be kept safe and legal, the impregnator clenched his fists and glowered at her. No woman should be forced to carry the child of a Neanderthal like this guy! Just another reminder of why she had taken the job as office manager and receptionist at the clinic. Reproductive freedom, control of your own body, the right to say, "no, uh, sorry, I'm not going through this." But it was not exactly freedom when some spermist intimidated the woman into having an abortion. It was the woman who would have to have the little creature worming around inside her for nine months, so it was the woman's right to choose, and the sperm provider who had done the damage should just butt out. Why would any woman go through it, anyway, no matter who the impregnator was?

Mrs. Greene emerged from the terrors of her greatest fears and noticed the whiteness of her knuckles clutching the desk. She forced her mind to retreat to the web of rationality she had built around the issue. All those polite reasons why the right to choose was so important. She focused on one of her favorites, that some people just should not have children. She recalled sizing up this woman and her impregnator when they first came in. The girl was obviously on drugs. She looked like she hadn't eaten in days. And that guy with her? If this kid were born, it didn't have a chance. But they could not force her either way. Legally, the woman had a right to choose, and Mrs. Greene, if she were anything, she was a stickler for the rules, especially *that* rule. The woman would have to decide. She was sure Dr. Singer would talk some sense into her. Mrs. Greene loosened her grip on the desk and worked out the tension in her fingers. *This isn't about you, Alice. There's no creepy-crawler squirming around inside of you, so just calm down and stick to the procedure.*

The impregnator stopped pacing and eyed her. He seemed to be tightening his grip on whatever was in his pocket. He must have something in that pocket? Stick to the procedures. Things could get dangerous. She had warned the doctor that they needed more security, that many abortion clinics protect their employees with bulletproof glass barriers and bulletproof vests, and at minimum a security guard checking people in at the door. As business manager, however, she understood that they could not afford to pay someone to sit idly at the door all day, and bulletproof glass would clash with the generally carefree and safe mindset of the populace and put people off, though that mindset had begun to change. There were always trade-offs with security measures. If you are doing something mainstream and normal, you should not need to where a bulletproof vest and hide behind protective barriers. She had thought the threat would likely come from some nut-job trying to *stop* an abortion, not some impregnator demanding one. But she had easily gotten rid of the girl with the rosary beads and never felt in the least threatened by her. This guy, on the other hand, made her skin crawl with fear. And, whatever he had in his pocket, it was likely more dangerous than a string of beads and a cross.

"What the hell is going on?" The impregnator glared at her.

Mrs. Greene lowered the papers she hid behind to the desk. She sat up straight and assumed her businesslike posture, steadily maintaining eye contact with him over her reading glasses.

"Your girlfriend is consulting with the doctor." Her practiced, flat tone underscored the procedural authority as intended. Her tone became more pointed, as she changed her glance to look at the chairs in the waiting room. "It is her choice. I suggest you calm down and take a seat."

Just another day at the clinic. Another man commanding that his mess be cleaned up. The way he kept jumping in front of her, demanding an abortion? Mrs. Greene shuddered. Why had this woman even hesitated to abort the offspring of this brute? But only the woman could make the decision, though the men always wanted to decide for them. And when they showed up here, they had decided that they wanted an abortion. The doctor was very good at helping young girls to make the right decision, though, which just about always was to have an abortion. And in this case, that would make everybody happy. The doctor would get his pay. This jerk would not have to worry about a kid. And the woman? She would have to go through some pain, but soon she would be rid of this psycho's child. And, Mrs.

Greene would never have to see them again. Win, win, win, win! *Just follow the procedure, and let the doctor do his thing.* Everything would be fine.

Mrs. Greene glanced sideways at the impregnator, who crinkled his nose, now sitting on the couch, his knee bouncing up and down. The dude looked like a volcano about to erupt. He fumbled around again with something in his jacket pocket, staring at her.

"But why does it take so long?" His voice seethed with frustration and anger.

"This is not an easy choice for a woman." She repressed a smirk. Mrs. Greene grasped the irony of her position. Keep abortion safe and legal so women can abort critters co-created by men like this, the same men who were the ones demanding abortions, as if it were *their* right? And, under that kind of coercion, did the woman really have a choice? Men were the big winners in legalized abortion, but that wasn't how it was supposed to be. Her advocacy of abortion rights was based on the idea that women would be empowered if they could have the choice not to have an unwanted child, not so that men could bully women and avoid responsibility for the child. The de facto reality of legalized abortion many times negated any notion of sexual equality by making the woman into some kind of sex machine requiring the occasional maintenance of a trip to the abortion clinic. *That's not exactly what we feminists had in mind.* But certainly, the right decision for this poor girl was to rid herself of the child of this miscreant. Mrs. Greene glanced toward the examining room door, then back at the impregnator. *Just give Dr. Singer some time.* Look at this creep! It should be an easy decision for her. She rolled her eyes. "The doctor can be very persuasive, though, so I don't think you need to worry."

The impregnator snorted and glared at her. "This beesness better be taken care of!"

Mrs. Greene squinted at him over her reading glasses. If Dr. Singer failed to convince this girl, there would be trouble.

The door to the waiting room from the examining room slowly opened. The impregnator jumped up from his chair. Mrs. Greene glanced over at the door, and gasped, as her reading glasses fell from the end of her nose and dangled at her breasts from the chain around her neck. Girls often looked a bit ragged after the procedure and this girl looked a bit sickly going in, but something about this patient startled Mrs. Greene. *Jiminy Crickets, she looks almost like a reanimated corpse!* Kim shuffled silently into the waiting room barely lifting her feet from the floor, her normally pale skin ghastly gray, her face drawn, and seemingly drained of life. Her blank expression almost made her unrecognizable, something not quite human, as if something more than an unborn child had been removed from her body. The spark of life, what some people might call a soul, seemed to be gone.

"Is it over? Has it been taken care of?" the impregnator asked excitedly.

The ghastly gray figure nodded silently. Her expression appeared sadder now and more pathetic, but no less pale and drained.

Mrs. Greene turned her focus back to procedures, anything to avoid thinking about what remained of this poor creature that they had successfully liberated from pregnancy, and her gleeful impregnator. She had trouble thinking of either of them as human, something she did not understand. The doc had done the procedure before arranging payment. Mrs. Greene shook her head. Hopefully, he had gotten her signature on the authorization form. She squinted toward the procedure room, miffed that her boss had violated the process. She would have to try to get payment from this psycho after the fact.

"That will be three hundred fifty dollars." Mrs. Greene had recovered from her initial shock and wanted nothing more than to conclude the business and never to see these people again.

The impregnator took a roll of bills out of his pocket and peeled off four hundreds. He tossed them at her. "Keep the change. And, thank the doctor for me."

"We thank you for your business." Mrs. Greene accepted the cash. "This envelope has the post-procedure instructions."

The impregnator's eyes narrowed as he stared at the forlorn shadow of a woman that had been their patient. "Ju say the beesness was taken care of? What else ju need to do?"

The thing cowered, the little blood left in its face drained, leaving it impossibly pale for something still alive, but no words came from it. Mrs. Greene gasped. She reminded herself that the *thing* was a woman, their patient, a person they had helped.

"The instructions include prescriptions for antibiotics and managing pain and guidance in watching for signs of complications. There isn't anything else to do to avoid pregnancy, except abstain from sex." Mrs. Greene tried her best to remain businesslike, but an unmistakable bitterness pervaded her tone. She hoped the delight she took in telling this monster to avoid copulating remained more hidden.

"Well, that's no' likely. What else is she good for?" The impregnator smirked in a way that shriveled his face, distorting his scar and making him appear demon-like in the dim light of the abortion clinic waiting room.

The impregnator and the un-pregnated stepped toward the door. What remained of the patient staggered a bit, still appearing to be in a daze. Mrs. Greene instinctively jumped up, as if she could reach her and steady her, but she was too far away to actually help. The patient they had freed from the ravages of pregnancy struggled to turn the doorknob and open the door, while her impregnator impatiently waited behind her, tapping his foot, his hand still in his jacket pocket. Mrs. Greene watched from the reception desk, covering her mouth to conceal her dropped jaw. This asshole wasn't going to help her with the door?

"Ay, Dios mío, Kim! Just open the door! Ju no pregnant no more, so ju no have to act so needy!"

Mrs. Greene's eyes widened in horror as she watched the impregnator push the wretched un-pregnated creature aside and throw open the door.

She gasped as he dragged her through the door. She had hoped for a sense of closure as the door closed behind them. She would never have to see them again, but the thing did not seem to be over. She glanced at the four one hundred dollar bills the impregnator had tossed at her, and desperately searched her mind for some process that would make things go in a predictable way. Was there a procedure that might help her unsee, or at least forget, the callous cruelty of this particular patient visit? This exercise of a woman's right that she valued so highly? A woman's right to choose, a woman's right to choose. The words rattled around her mind. That was why she was here.

WHEN THE WOOD IS DRY

An Edgy Catholic Thriller

II
Crucifixion

JOSEPH CILLO, JR.

II
Crucifixion

For one is approved if, mindful of God, he endures pain while suffering unjustly...For to this you have been called, because Christ also suffered for you, leaving you an example, that you should follow in his steps.

1 Peter 19, 21

Warning!

When the Wood Is Dry: Crucifixion contains scenes of extreme violence and the brutal suffering of an innocent. The author intends the strongest warning be given to any reader who may be sensitive to such terrible things to venture no further and check out the synopsis for *Part II: Crucifixion* given in the appendix, which such readers may find disturbing enough, without being placed so intimately in the scenes of such horrible violence. In particular, **Chapter 14: Lali Spins**, is only meant for those with the highest tolerance for violence and should be avoided by all others.

For those who decide to venture onward, kindly remember that you were warned.

11

Are You Teaching Me About God?

LALI SAT ON THE STEPS of Dr. Singer's Family Planning Clinic, banished with a threat to be cited for criminal trespass. She still could be arrested for just sitting on the steps of the clinic and praying, but she did not care. Kim may have just placed her mortal soul in peril to protect her, as far as Lali was concerned. Theologians might argue that Kim's culpability may be mitigated by the degree of coercion, but that was only of little comfort. Lali's own welfare had been used to justify a terrible sin. A child had been sacrificed to save her, on the sterile altar of modern medicine, safe and legal. The stakes were much higher than technical violations of the trespass laws or whatever they were called. Thou shalt not pray too close to an abortion clinic or some equivalent legal gibberish! Were they really so afraid of rosary beads and prayer? Lali continued her prayer, the rosary beads hanging from her fingers, the cross dangling near the ground. The door opened, and she scrambled to her feet. Ralo and...was that Kim? *My God, what did they do to her?* She looked too pale to be alive.

"Go home, little girl." Ralo snidely brushed her away with a wave of his free hand, as he dragged Kim with the other. "The beesness is taken care of."

Kim, as if suddenly recharged with a hidden surge of electricity, became animated as Ralo spoke, her pale skin still gray like an apparition in an old black and white horror film. She pulled free of Ralo and glared at him. "Leave her alone, Ralo! She didn't do anything!"

Ralo turned to Kim, staring her down. She slunk back and shuddered like a dog about to be whipped. "Since when do I take orders from you?" Ralo grabbed her arm and dragged her toward the car. Kim struggled to get away from Ralo, but he overpowered her. Lali followed them to the curb, helplessly staring as Kim was manhandled and stuffed into the car.

"I will pray for you, Kim." The rosary beads dangled from Lali's fingers as she raised her hand toward Kim. "And for you, Ralo, and for your baby."

Kim started to cry as Ralo closed the car door behind her, muffling her sobs. Ralo turned to face Lali, his eyes filled with a deep, intense rage and hatred, smoldering below his usually cool and decisive manner.

"You should save your prayers for yourself, little girl. You be needing them if you don't stay out of my beesness," he spat with cool venom that made Lali shudder as he leaned forward over her, like a snake sizing up its prey. He turned and walked around the car and opened the door. Kim placed her hands on the window beside her head, looking like a forlorn puppy in an animal shelter begging to be adopted. Kim mouthed the words, "I'm so sorry," as if she had wronged Lali deeply, as if Lali's disapprobation might hurt her more than Ralo's deliberate abuse. Lali raised her hand, the tears running down her cheeks. The car drove off until it made the left turn at the corner and was gone.

Lali stood unsteadily under the weight of the emotional scene, recalling the spin in her dream, her deliberate disorientation. Only now a confusion was thrust upon her with no intention of her own. A godless world was spinning with no control, no point, no direction, no moral sense or meaning.

A child had been needlessly slaughtered to keep her from harm. She had stood where she felt compelled to stand, to protect that which was sacred, only to have the precious soul snuffed out in her stead. Was it all a cruel joke? She thought of Jesus in her dream, what He had said, *Sometimes we must suffer if we are to save souls.* Was this what He was talking about? But no souls had been saved, had they? Only a little innocent unborn soul, never to come into the world, lost and not saved? Or perhaps the child's soul was not lost. But the doctor, that receptionist, Kim, Ralo, what of their souls? It just didn't seem to make any sense. It all seemed like pointless pain, suffering with no purpose. And she had been willing to offer herself, but she was spared, while the child and Kim suffered in her place. And what of her prayers? If there were a God, why did He act like He was not there?

Lali took her cell phone out and noticed she had a little charge left. She paused for a moment, thinking about how she had failed. Was there more she could have done? How had anything she had done helped matters? A car drove by. The leaves swirled randomly, spinning and turning, the engine sputtering as it shifted its gears like a sick child coughing in the night. The light still shone from the clinic. She prayed for the children who had been lost there and imagined she heard them crying, but she could not make them stop. She pictured Kim's baby. Had it been a little boy? Or a little girl? Would she have had the same blond curls, the sad gray eyes of her mother? That little body torn up and thrown away like pages of a script for a movie that would never be made. The imagined cries of the lost children died away and the beating of her own heart thumped in her chest. She closed her eyes and let the tears run down her face. Opening her eyes again, she pushed the button on her phone to call her father.

"Hi, Papa." She closed her eyes, again, as she spoke into the phone. "I'm at the abortion clinic. Would you please come pick me up?"

"You're still at the clinic?" The worry in his voice made her shudder. "Is everything okay?"

Lali took a deep breath. *Just say your rosary and get out of there. That girl Kim is trouble.* His words echoed in her mind. But how could she let her walk into that place and then just leave?

"Well, something pretty terrible happened." Lali stared at her feet, as a chill ran through her. "But I'm okay. I'll tell you about it when you get here."

☩

I knew that place was trouble! Robert held the phone to his ear as he sat in his parked patrol car. Something pretty terrible happened? *I really wish she would just stay away from there!*

"Okay. I'm on my way. Just sit tight." He could only imagine what kind of mess she'd gotten herself into. Robert pushed the button to end the call and returned the phone to his pocket. As he approached the clinic, he caught sight of her sitting on the steps, with her rosary beads in her hand, and he realized he had forgotten her new look with the shaven head. He could not help but recall his poor, sick wife, hairless from the chemotherapy treatments. Those same beads that now draped his daughter's fingers, his wife's spiritual weapon, wielded in a battle doomed to failure. A useless token against cruel and chaotic forces that churned and turned and crushed the innocent and the guilty with the same mindless fury. But what innocent faith! What a beautiful thing! Made more beautiful in its failure, the failure it viewed as an ultimate victory, the hope of eternal life, brightly shining, even as grim death descended. This hope cried out for protection even as it trusted to the end. Life, here and now, persevering in hope when no hope could be found, defying the very clutches of death even as it succumbed to its cold, lifeless grasp. *To protect and serve*, it demanded of him.

Robert pulled his squad car to the curb in front of the clinic. Lali got up and slowly made her way to the waiting bubble of security as if counting the steps, her shoulders slumped, and her head bowed. She opened the passenger door and entered the car, sliding herself carefully onto the seat. She seemed so sullen and sad, so defeated, as if she had barely survived a losing battle. How fragile and sickly she looked. How beaten. Lali fastened her seatbelt and leaned against the door. Taking in a deep breath, her body seemed to relax as if she were finally safe, even in defeat.

"So, you didn't make it to the unwed mothers' home tonight?" He imagined the question would be the best way to find out what had happened.

"No." Lali placed her rosary beads into her purse. "I felt I was needed more here."

Lali glanced up at him, then toward the passenger window. Robert had hoped for a bigger opening. He had hoped he would not have to ask but he needed more information than she was offering.

"What happened?" He took his eyes from the road longer than he should have, trying to make eye contact. She was peering out the window as if there were nothing there at all. As if she did not want to look where there might be something to see. The darkening shade of fine stubble on her formerly smooth-shaven head, her body slumped against the passenger side door, Robert looked back to the road, unable to get her to face him.

Lali took a deep breath. A quick glance told him that her body was visibly heaving as the air filled and left her lungs, then she finally turned toward him, her eyes down, not yet able to meet his eyes. Give her time, just give her time. Robert refocused on the road, making quick glances toward her, then slowing the car and making a right-hand turn.

Robert heard her take a deep breath, her swallow that followed, surprisingly audible in the protective silence of the police car.

"Remember I told you about that girl, Kim, and her boyfriend Ralo?" She raised her eyes to meet his, pleading for understanding. Robert made eye contact with her.

"Yes," Robert said flatly, as if not wanting to interfere with a perpetrator's confession, then he turned his attention back to the road.

"Well, Ralo forced Kim to get an abortion, even though she didn't want one." Lali's voice cracked, then she turned toward the window again.

"How can that be? The doctor would not have done it if she didn't consent."

"She was coerced!" Lali turned her body toward him, undisguised indignation in her tone. "You know how these things happen!"

Robert sighed, took a quick glimpse at Lali, then faced forward.

"She did it, so he wouldn't hurt *me!*"

Her sobs became too distracting to continue driving, so he pulled his car to the side of the road. He removed his safety belt and unbuckled hers as well. He took her in his arms. Lali sobbed, gasping occasionally for another breath.

"Oh, Lali." Robert embraced his quaking girl, "I'm so sorry."

"Papa, it was horrible!" She lifted her chin, the tears running down her cheeks and dripping off. "It was the devil at work, pure evil."

"Yes, Lali, I know."

"She did it to protect *me!* I'm responsible!" Lali wailed and shuddered.

"No, Lali. That's not true." Robert wiped her tears with his rough hands. "Kim made a choice. If you hadn't been there, if she had never met you, she would have made the same choice. She may not have even hesitated."

Lali's eyes were wet with tears and filled with uncertainty. "Maybe, but now things are worse. Ralo may just kill her. I really tried to do the right thing, but I made matters worse!" Lali wept uncontrollably, burying her head in his chest.

"Oh, Lali." The tears filled in his own eyes and he blinked them away. He lifted his daughter's chin, forcing her to look at him. "Of course, you did the right thing. Sometimes when we do the right thing, it makes matters worse. We have to trust in God, that He will protect us when we do the right thing."

Lali's eyes widened and she tilted her head. "Papa! Are you teaching me about God?" The wonder and astonishment in her voice cut into his soul like a dagger to the heart. "I haven't heard you talk like this since Mama…"

Robert pulled his daughter close, ending her sentence, the thought drifting incomplete into the night air, in the safety of the protective bubble of his squad car. Robert started to weep. "I know, baby, I know," his voice cracked through his tears. "I'm so proud of you, and your faith. You're just like your mother. I've been lost. I'm still lost. You're all I have now."

12

Doctor Singer

D R. EMMANUEL SINGER CLEANED HIS TOOLS and disposed of the waste from Kim's procedure. The tiny arms and legs, the torso, the no longer beating heart within the chest still connected to the tiny head, and the blood. He had gotten the whole unwanted thing out of her and threw it away in the medical waste bin. Another drug-addled child of a drug-addled couple prevented from entering their drug-addled world. He had recognized Ralo, of course, as the newest, toughest drug dealer in town. They shared a lot of the same customers. Only Dr. Singer didn't have as much competition. Dr. Singer was the only abortion provider for many miles surrounding Santa Inés. He called it *Family Planning*, but, of course, a more apt title would be *Family Prevention*. He recalled the difficulties and travails of his previous practice. How much easier and safer it was to just dispense the birth control pills and perform abortions. He was still a baby doctor, but live births, well they were dangerous. He had been sued out of that end of the business. He made enough on the abortions, so live births weren't worth the bother. People did not usually sue when the baby dies after an abortion. He recalled the case where an obstetrician was sued for *wrongful life* when he delivered a child with birth defects that could have been identified before the child was born. At least Dr. Singer didn't have to worry about that.

It pays the bills, and I don't get sued. Dr. Singer let out a sigh as he disinfected his tools. Out here, in Santa Inéz, where things were quiet and the people tolerant, he didn't worry much about people checking his history or questioning the morality of his practice. They only had that one little moralist praying in front of the clinic. She might make trouble someday, if she started coming with friends, but there were laws protecting abortion clinics, so he would easily be able to deal with them, if it came to that. Not worth the bother, for just one person praying out there without even a sign or audible word of protest. Mrs. Greene had suggested more security, but it hardly seemed necessary. In many places, abortion clinics were under physical threat of violence, but that was why he had come here, where things were quiet. Quiet, that was the great virtue of this location. And quiet was good for business. The good people of Santa Inés could be assured. If ever there was a need for an abortion, he would be here, and he would keep the quiet. Dr. Singer picked up the curette from among his tools. And he would be ready to provide the needed services.

But, to be honest, he was not just a doctor with a curette at the ready. He dropped the curette into the sterilization unit with his other tools. He helped women make the right choice to not have a child. That was the more important part of his job. The women who came here knew that they should not have a child. They needed someone to help them see things clearly. He helped them make the right choice. Society needed people like him to help women rationally discern the most practical course of action. There was no shame in a woman making a mistake, and an easy solution to wipe away the consequences. Doctor Singer rolled his eyes. Imagine if all these women that came in here had their babies? Those kids wouldn't have a chance! So, he convinced them to do the right thing. A queasiness churned in his belly for a moment and he regretted the grilled cheese sandwich he had eaten at lunch.

Doctor Singer sighed. It wasn't like he forced them. It wasn't even a hard choice most times. He engaged the sterilization unit, and the chime rang signaling the beginning of its cycle, to be followed by the hissing white noise of the steam. Young women, suffering the scorn of their neighbors for having children without fathers, the burdens of caring for a child while trying to finish school, the loss of months of productivity when having a child, and even if an adoptive family could be found to provide the child a decent home, the anguish of giving up your child, your own flesh and blood. Not to mention the medical risks of having a child. Dr. Singer shuddered as he recalled the two patients he had lost. Sometimes the expectant mother died. And the doctor got sued. It was just all downside. Once you laid out the options, the choice became easy. Just get rid of it. Make the whole problem go away. Dr. Singer picked up Kim's chart and scanned the doodles he had made while he interviewed her. He had not noted anything that would answer the question that was bothering him, though. *So why was it so hard this time?*

He sighed again as he recalled his aspirations in medical school to help women bring babies into the world, and how just a couple unfortunate mistakes had landed him in the baby prevention business instead. Two women in a month! He remembered the two would-be mothers, so hopeful to be bringing home their newborns, and instead carried out themselves, and laid to rest. What bad luck! But the twinge of regret only lasted a moment before his thoughts returned to his difficulties in persuading this woman to have an abortion when it was such an easy choice! The girl was on drugs, for goodness sake, and her boyfriend, a drug-dealer, likely a murderer too from the look of him. Wasn't that what she kept saying? "He's a killer?" If ever there were a case for abortion, this was it! So why was it so difficult? He needed to talk to someone. *I wonder what Mrs. Greene thinks.* He washed his hands and something more than just a queasiness in his stomach seized him now, a twinge of conscience needled him as he recalled the ancient handwashing condemning the innocent man who claimed to be God. But that was a Christian thing? He dried his hands on a towel. *Why should I think of that? I'm not a Christian, am I?*

A spot of blood clung stubbornly to the back of his hand as he rubbed them dry, though he knew he had been careful with his surgical gloves. Examining it more closely, it was only the birthmark on the back of his hand where it had always been. He stepped into the reception area, hoping that Mrs. Greene might be able to help make sense of the peculiar events of the day. "That girl out there is trouble."

Mrs. Greene lifted her head and seemed to welcome the break in the awkward silence after the rough scene that afternoon.

Dr. Singer pushed his bifocal glasses up on his nose. "I used to think, what could it hurt? She's just praying. But here you have a drug-addicted pregnant woman with her drug-dealing boyfriend, and she's putting ideas into the girl's head that she can have the baby and stay in that unwed mothers' home and live happily ever after, even though she says that her boyfriend will kill her if she does. And, from the looks of him, I wouldn't be surprised if he did."

"Well, I'm not sure what we can do about it." Mrs. Greene shrugged. She seemed distant and distracted, like she'd been deep in thought. "It's legally the woman's choice, and there is no law against considering other choices. And I don't think we can stop people from praying."

"But, goodness, do you know what I had to do to get that girl's consent?" He leaned on the receptionist's desk. "It should have been such an easy choice! It was like she wanted me to just do it without having to consent. She kept saying, 'it would be wrong to kill it,' and 'I don't want to be a killer.' Even after she signed the consent, she said that she really did not want to do it, like she wanted it dead, but she didn't want to agree to kill it."

Mrs. Greene lowered her head. "We're not really *killing* though, are we, Doctor?" She raised her chin, her intense eyes pleaded like she wanted to be lied to. "I mean, we're just preventing life, not actually taking it, aren't we?"

Dr. Singer rolled his eyes. He knew well the awful truth of his trade. Of course, they were taking life! It was even a violation of the Hippocratic Oath. Even the ancient Greek knew, and forswore the practice in his oath to Apollo, well before any Christian moralists were around. Sure, he swore his oath to some phony god, but even if there were a real God, why should He have any say in it? It was the woman's choice. He made a conscious effort to calm himself, taking a deep breath. *But she said she really did not want to do it, and you did it anyway.* The unwelcome argument popped into his head like an old jingle for a long since forgotten product that was no longer available. The jingle, lasting and unforgettable, lying dormant for a time, now sang in his mind, unwelcome and unbidden, set off like a hidden, buried mine from a long-lost battle in a war unjustly concluded, though its terms long ago settled, with no one left with courage or desire to once again raise the banner and take up arms in its lost cause of justice. So, he had made the choice for her? Wasn't that what she wanted him to do? And the unwelcome voice haunted him, throwing his own words back at him. *Why should God have any say in it? It's the woman's choice. If God has no say, why should you?*

Dr. Singer took a deep breath to regain his composure and smiled uneasily at Mrs. Greene, who awaited his answer in the awkward silence of his reverie, an expression of concern bordering on dread washed over her face. "Of course, we're not taking life." He repeated the lie he long ago stopped telling himself. The lie he no longer needed to hear as he had become more comfortable with the dirty truth. The lie he told anyone who doubted the morality of his practice. "We're just helping women decide not to have children they are not ready to care for. That's how I got her to agree to it. I just had to try a little harder to explain it this time."

Mrs. Greene's shoulders relaxed, but her eyes flitted with uncertainty. She blinked a few times, as if something were in her eyes. "I was surprised to see she shaved her head." Mrs. Greene changed the subject. "She doesn't seem like the type to do something like that."

"Who shaved her head? The prayer girl?" Dr. Singer raised his eyebrows.

"Oh, yeah, I got rid of her quickly so maybe you didn't see."

"*She* came in here?" Dr. Singer regretted the degree of surprise in his voice.

"Yes, ranting about how the impregnator was trying to force the girl to have an abortion like somehow, we should stop it from happening."

"Really?" Dr. Singer mused, then rubbed his chin. "Well, if she's doing radical things like shaving her head, maybe she will be coming here for services soon."

A sinister smile crossed Dr. Singer's lips at the hope of such a victory for his cause and so soon after the doubts had come. Sooner or later, they came to him to erase their mistakes. The more devout, the more shame. The more shame, the more they wanted to hide the shame and just make it go away. *And that's what I do. I erase their shame.*

Mrs. Greene made a face like she had just bit into some bad fruit. "I wouldn't bet on that." Her lips pressed together for another awkward pause. "Well, anyway, I don't think we can do anything about that girl praying, as long as she doesn't stop anyone from coming in and stays far enough away."

"Yeah, there's probably nothing we can do." Dr. Singer allowed his shoulders to slump as he sighed. "But it's trouble. I mean, my God, where would this country be if all these people who clearly are not ready for the responsibilities of parenthood are allowed to keep having babies?"

13

The Trials Ahead

LALI SAT SILENTLY, HER EYES UNFOCUSED, her body slumped in the seat, held in place by the seat belt as the police car wove its way along the curving mountain roads toward home. A silence, a dread, a kind of pall enveloped the bubble of protection, keeping out the terror, but it was only a temporary shelter. The lengthening shadows had crept so close, wrapping their wispy fingers around her heart, filling her with dread, though no harm had yet come.

Lali had no more words to say and figured her father had nothing more to say as he silently drove the familiar route toward home. Having already said more than enough, only the sound of the car, the occasional blinker, the shifting gears of the engine interrupted the silence that neither of them wished to break. For Lali, the spinning had stopped as the solidity of the police car and the protection of her father had buoyed her like a life preserver thrown to a drowning man. Something to hold onto. Something firm, solid, unmoving. If the world spun without purpose, what was this that stopped the spinning? Was it love that proved that there must be a God? Could anything be pointless when there was love to hold onto, to steady the spinning, to give life its meaning?

Her father pulled the car into the driveway, the headlights illuminating the familiar home and breaking the dark envelope of the night and revealing their next, even more solid, bubble of protection. The car came to a stop, the engine ending its calm purring, the silence becoming more profound. But there were no words left to say. Or maybe just a few but not yet. Only the sound of the car doors opening and closing, the light footsteps changing their tone from the pavement, to the stones of the walk, to the wood of the steps, then onto the porch, each with its muted sad little song. The creaking of the storm door, then the main door and onto the carpet, the soft footsteps again. And then the faint, soothing scent of many burnt breakfasts lingering and reassuring her of the safety of home. Turning to her father, Lali gazed into his strong, sad eyes and paused. He averted his eyes as if begging her not to break the silence.

"I love you, Papa."

Her father released a long sigh and nodded as if speaking would break a secret code that no man dare break.

Lali cleared her throat and ascended the steps to her room. She tossed her clothes onto the chair next to the bed and sunk down onto her bed. The spinning thoughts of the trying day returned. Had she done the right thing? Had she made matters worse? Was she paving the proverbial way to hell with her good intentions? Was this what He meant when He said, *sometimes we must suffer to save souls?* Had any souls been saved? Or was there no point to the suffering? Was it all just a world of mindless cruelty? Surely not. Ralo's cruelty was not mindless. Pulling the pajama top over her head, she caught sight of the statuette of the Sacred Heart of Jesus. There He was, pointing to his most merciful heart. Surely, He would be with her just as He had said in her dream. *Oh, that dream!* How it had haunted her for years. The joy of meeting Jesus. The dread of His message of suffering. The loss of her mother. *Sometimes we must suffer if we are to save souls.* What did it mean? Perhaps she could bear it if souls were saved? Kim had killed her baby to protect her. What souls had been saved? An unexpected sense of relief filled her as she studied the little statue. She picked up the statue and kissed it. Placing it back on the dresser, she knelt before it and prayed.

Oh, Lord, please be with me tonight and in the trials ahead. Help me to do right and to stand with you and, if there is suffering, let it be for the salvation of souls. And be with me, just as you said. Thank you for being with me today in all the terrible things, for keeping me safe. Help Kim and the soul of her unborn child. And Ralo and Rodrigo, please come into their lives and turn them from their evil paths. You have the power to do all things and to turn all things to good. Thank you for Papa and for his strength and support. Help him to regain his faith. And, please, please, give me courage in the trials to come, that I may not faint from whatever suffering may be necessary to save souls. And please be with me as you said, when my time comes.

Lali crawled into bed and, with one last pensive glimpse of the statue, she turned off the light, her rosary beads draped on her fingers. *I'm just too tired to kneel and pray the rosary tonight, Lord. Forgive me.* Lali began her rosary. She drifted quickly into sleep by the prayer of the third bead.

The desert dust chokes her throat as the hot breeze lifts the grit, swirling it into the air. The sounds and clamor of the crowd beckon her onward to see what is there and what has roused such passion. A great commotion then in front of her, she makes her way through the crowd. The people gather stones, stones for throwing, weighty enough to do damage, light enough to throw with the needed velocity to inflict the intended punishment for sin. Among them, Kim and Ralo, and Rodrigo, all dressed in robes cinched at the waist with cords, appropriate for the time and place, but a time and place where they should not be. And there, the woman caught in adultery, the very act someone says, as the people ready their stones for throwing. And then she sees Him again. There He is crouching down and writing on the ground. The man from her recurring dream. The One who showed her His palm. The One they call Messiah. Jesus. The One she knows to be God. Writing in the dust of the ground, the wind catching and lifting the fine, powdered soil in swirls, his letters remain in an unfamiliar language on the transitory tablet of earth. He looks up at the crowd. "Let he who is without sin cast the first stone."

Ralo swaggers forward, his face lined with contempt and ridicule. He laughs at Jesus, a cruel, mocking laugh that echoes in Lali's mind.

"Since when do I take orders from you?" Ralo picks up a stone and throws it at the woman. Lali feels the rock hit her shoulder, finding she is now the condemned woman. She raises her arms to protect herself. Others of the crowd start throwing stones, as well. Lali covers her face and head with her arms as the incoming stones batter her from all directions.

Kim steps in front of Lali to shield her from the stones. "No! She didn't do anything wrong!"

Lali, blood flowing from her own head wounded by the stones, lifts her chin and sees Jesus, now tied to a pillar being scourged by Ralo and Rodrigo dressed as Romans, the lashes swooping and slapping and tearing his flesh mercilessly.

"Let he who is without sin cast the first stone?" Ralo scoffs. "Look what happens to he who is without sin!"

Lali woke up gasping. The rosary beads slipped from her hand, making their soft rattle as they hit the floor. She fell to her knees at the side of the bed and looked at the little statue of the Sacred Heart of Jesus.

"Oh, Jesus!" Her trembling voice broke the silence of her darkened room. "Please let me know what this is about! Be with me in this time of trial!"

"Lali? Are you okay?" her father called from the kitchen below. "You'll have to hurry, honey, if you want to have breakfast."

Lali quickly dressed, then descended the stairs to the sweet and burnt smell of another unsuccessful attempt at a hot breakfast. However, the burnt scent was different than usual. Her father stood over the frying pan, once more with his apron on, the one she had given him for Father's Day last year. "Rarely Well Done, But Always with Love" written across the front. She had it printed especially for him. Lali giggled, as her father stood over his latest breakfast failure sticking to the pan in an unseemly clump. He scraped it onto a plate and handed it to her.

"I thought I'd try pancakes this time," He stared at the ugly mess on the plate and shrugged. "I guess these are not much better than the eggs and bacon, though."

She sighed as she noticed burned spots and other places that appeared half-cooked. She smiled and pushed the plate away. "Thanks for trying, Papa, but I think I'll just get a bowl of cereal."

"Yeah, you'd think I would give up by now." Papa scraped the plate into the trash.

Lali sat in the passenger seat facing her father as he drove her to church for daily Mass. He was biting his lip. He must be worried about her. She had been acting erratically, first shaving her head, and then, having that dramatic scene last night. She was becoming a real piece of work. Her father glanced at her as the car wound its way almost automatically along the familiar route. Lali smiled uneasily at him. Finally, he broke the silence.

"Are you okay, Lali?" He signaled for a left turn.

"Yeah, sure. Just a little mixed up."

"I could take you home if you'd like a day off. You had a pretty tough day yesterday." Anxiety rose in his voice. It wasn't like him to suggest a day off. He usually pushed her to keep going. Was he testing her?

"Oh, no." Lali allowed herself a chuckle. "I'm all right."

Papa pulled up to the church and stopped the car at the curb. They sat for a moment in front of the church in awkward silence.

"I'll be going to the clinic to pray again, today." Lali broke the silence. "Then to the unwed mothers' home. I'll call you for a ride."

He rolled his eyes. "You know, most people might want to avoid a place like that after they had such a hard time?"

Lali leaned her head to one side. "Didn't you always tell me to stick with things? You know, get right back up and get back in the game?"

"Geez, Lali, this isn't a game! This is really serious business! We suspect Ralo of a good number of crimes. I'm really not supposed to talk about it though."

"Kim had her abortion. Ralo has no reason to come back. If you really don't want me to go, I won't go. I would never do anything if you told me not to."

She watched her father as he thought about it. He rarely made a request for her not to do something. But she resolved that she would do as he wished if he told her not to go.

"No." He let out a sigh in resignation. "You're right. I'm always teaching you the value of perseverance, and now I'm just worried. It's just getting harder to protect you." Papa tightened his lips for a moment. "But if you're not feeling well, just come right home. It's okay to take some time off now and then."

Lali kissed her father on the cheek. He was worried and did not want her to go to that place. She loved him more because he offered her the choice and rarely made demands. He would worry, but she had to go there, again. "Thanks, Papa. I'll be all right," she said, feeling loved and protected. "I love you, you know."

Papa sighed, closed his eyes and nodded.

She slid out through the car door and trotted to the church.

Lali entered the chapel at St. Sebastian's Church and knelt in a pew, focusing on the crucifix. Her head swam with the anticipation of suffering.

She recalled the scourging from her dream and Ralo's scoffing voice, "Look what happens to He who is without sin." Her mind reeled trying to make sense of the nightmare. The proceedings of the Holy Mass and her personal prayers and petitions did little to lesson her sense of foreboding. But, at the same time, the conviction lay on her soul to step forward and face whatever may lie ahead. She exited the chapel after Mass and walked past Father Fernandez without greeting him. Father Fernandez called after her.

"Lali? Lali? Are you all right?"

Lali managed an awkward smile as she turned around toward Father Fernandez. "Oh, yes, Father, I'm okay."

"You seem troubled. Is there anything you'd like to talk about?"

"Oh, no, Father. I'll be late for school." Lali shrugged her shoulder under her backpack in the direction of the school. "Maybe we can talk later sometime? I think maybe a confession. I've had some bad dreams lately."

"Anytime, my girl. You let me know. I'm always here for you."

"Thank you, Father. I'll be okay." Lali took a step but turned back suddenly. "Oh, uh, Father? Would you pray for me? I had a tough day yesterday. Just a prayer for strength, I think."

"Oh, yes, sure. I'll pray for the intercession of St. Michael and his angels! May they grant you strength."

Lali shifted the backpack on her shoulders. "Oh, thank you, Father. That's just what I need."

Lali followed her usual route to school. Any blessing from the angels and St. Michael did not last long as her steps became heavier and heavier. *They say an angel strengthened Jesus in the Garden.* Lali stopped walking for a moment. Why that angel? An angel had greeted Mary at the Annunciation, as well. She resumed her trek toward school without the usual spring in her step, her mind preoccupied with anxieties about the trials ahead and what they might be. The public-school girls once again snickered as she passed. Lali grimaced for a moment as if physically pained, then blankly moved on.

The girls seemed so carefree and unburdened, in contrast to the heaviness that weighed on her. She envied the superficial, teenaged concerns she imagined occupied their lives. She had seen a great evil and there was no unseeing it. What a luxury to be so concerned with such trivial things. *And what do I get? Suffering for the sake of souls. And do I have to bear their snickering, as well?* A pang of self-pity ached her soul as she ruminated on what might be her mission: longing for some ordinary existence that was now somehow out of her reach. Coming upon the school, she allowed her mind the luxury of wallowing in her sense of victimhood by keeping her head down, imagining a cup that could not be taken away, a moment of pleading in an ancient garden, a wish to avoid something that could not be avoided.

Lali walked past Principal Martinez, her head down. A burden weighed upon her in a way she had never experienced. The conviction came upon her soul that she should accept the cup, without complaint. What cup? She struggled to let her moodiness go. *Not my will but thine be done.* Jesus' answer to the cup that would not be taken away. Did she have the strength?

Principal Martinez interrupted her thoughts as she plodded silently past him. "Good-morning, Lali!"

"Oh, good morning, Mr. Martinez." Her eyes glanced at him, then away, not quite rolling.

"Is something wrong?" His mustache frowned at her, mocking her weakness. The heaviness remained on her soul. A stifling tightness gripped her spirit, like the coils of a serpent. She could not shake it off.

"Oh, yes, there are a great many things wrong, Principal Martinez." Lali's voice rang with exaggerated melodrama. "Our only hope is prayer."

A worry passed over Principal Martinez's face like a shadow. He seemed about to say something but turned suddenly as a dispute between a couple of boys erupted so he sighed and ran to intervene, leaving Lali to trudge into the school. She really didn't want to talk to him anyway.

✝✝✝

Daniel watched Lali lumbering toward her locker. She kept her head down, then slowly dialed the combination. Daniel met her there, smiling, his baseball cap covering his hairless head. "Hey, Lali!"

Lali glanced at him glumly, and the smile melted away from his face, a sudden flush of embarrassment took hold of him as though he had laughed at a funeral. Something was really eating her!

"Hi, Danny." Lali kept her head down as she peered into her locker.

"What's wrong?" Daniel changed his demeanor to fit the new circumstances that he did not fully understand.

Lali closed her locker and turned toward him. Daniel sensed a seriousness, a graveness he had never seen in her.

"Have you ever seen the devil, Danny? Do you know how he works?" Lali asked, as if she were interrogating him for a crime. She seemed to be right in his face, though she was at an appropriate distance for conversation in the clamorous hallway. Daniel took a step back. He shook his head, feeling like he could not speak, even if there were something he could think of to say.

"Yesterday, I saw the devil." Her voice held a terrifying intensity that seemed like madness. "I know how he works, now. He makes us think we can save others if we sacrifice our own souls. That's his trick. But we can't save others through sin. We only lose ourselves. We all must pay the price for doing the right thing, no matter the consequences. If you ever find yourself in that lion's den, Daniel my friend, don't fear the lions, fear yourself."

Lali plodded off to Mr. Trudeau's class. Danny took his hat off and scratched his head.

✝✝✝

Lali took her seat in history class. Mr. Trudeau appeared particularly ridiculous, his comb-over resting on his head like strands of overcooked black spaghetti.

"As you recall," Mr. Trudeau began. Did he ever start a class with any other words? "We were discussing the end of World War II and the trials at Nuremberg, where those deemed to be war criminals were tried by the victors. Let's take a quick look at a video of one of the German Officers."

Mr. Trudeau pointed the remote control at the monitor and started the video.

"I was just following orders," the German officer said. "If I did not follow orders, I would have been executed and my family disgraced and persecuted."

As the video clip ended, Mr. Trudeau glanced about the room. He met her eyes then quickly turned his head away. His comb-over dropped a bit over his eye and he brushed it back. "Place yourself now, in the position of the German Officer. What would you have done?"

Lali raised her hand, imagining the other students were yawning and rolling their eyes, or daydreaming about some boy, or girl, or some petty slight or insult, or whatever other thing might trouble a teen-aged mind, distracting them from schoolwork, or things more important than schoolwork. Was she the only one who cared about important things? *Did Mr. Trudeau just roll his eyes when he saw my hand?*

"Yes, Lali?"

"I would have died."

Mr. Trudeau's head snapped back as if he had been hit with a sudden gust of wind. He quickly regained his composure and checked to see if the wind had disturbed his comb-over. "You would have died? What do you mean by that?"

Lali squinted at him. He was her teacher, and yet he did not understand? "I mean, I would have died. If I were faced with a choice between sin and death, I would die. And my family would die. And everyone I know would die before I would sin to save them. And if God let that happen, it would be His will."

Mr. Trudeau appeared trapped like a rat in a maze looking for a piece of cheese, but there was no cheese to be found. As he scanned the classroom for some cheese, or at least a student who might break the tension, his comb-over fell over his eye, and he brushed it back to the top of his head. A sinister delight grew within her as she watched Mr. Comb-over and the distress she had caused him. He had no idea what to say. *Will he argue with me?* Lali sat, gripping the edges of her desk, her body tensed as though she were awaiting the headsman's ax. But inwardly enthralled by a sense of exhilaration, her heart raced. The awkward silence she had caused seemed to captivate the hushed students who waited to see what would happen next. She spied a hand going up in the corner of her eye, and she turned to face her accuser. Tommy Slater? It figured Tommy would bail him out. Lali glanced back at Mr. Trudeau, whose features relaxed as he recognized that Tommy Slater had raised his hand. *He's found his cheese.*

"Yes, Tommy." Mr. Trudeau was unable to disguise the relief in his voice.

Tommy addressed his comment to Lali. Mr. Trudeau raised his hand to his chin, his forehead lined with worry, eyes flitting back and forth from Tommy to Lali. Perhaps there would be no cheese after all.

"So even if a small sin would avoid a myriad of horrors." Tommy raised his smug little eyebrows. "You would not sin? Say, a white lie to avoid the detection of Anne Frank? You wouldn't lie?"

Lali glanced at Tommy as he spoke, then answered, glaring at Mr. Trudeau with the determination of a saint professing faith in Christ as she was fed to the lions. Or perhaps Saint Eulalia, anticipating the knives that would pierce her body as she made her spinning descent, rolling in that barrel down, down that Barcelonan street. "I would not lie." She tightened her grip on the edges of her desk. "I would stay silent and I would die. And in death, I would be free of such temptation."

✝✝✝

Daniel worried about his friend. She really had acted strangely that morning, and it had bugged him all day. And now, a wild rumor had spread that a girl had threatened to kill herself in Mr. Trudeau's history class. Lali was in that class. She was so moody this morning. Would she have threatened to kill herself? That was unlikely. But something was really eating her. He rubbed his upper arm. *Let's see how she is at lunch.*

Lali had already gotten her food and was sitting at a table by herself, looking glum and disturbed, when Daniel found her in the cafeteria. She usually waited for him and they got their food together.

"Hi, Lali." Daniel greeted his friend with an uneasy smile. "Are you okay?"

"Yeah, sure." Lali kept her head lowered and played with her food.

"People are worried about you," he stammered, unsure of what to say.

Lali cocked her head. She seemed amused and confused that people would be worried. "Why is that?" She chuckled but an underlying intensity burned in her eyes.

"Well, first, you shaved your head. That's a pretty radical thing to do." Daniel was determined to confront his friend over her strange behavior. "And now, you're all self-righteous and moody. I heard that someone in your class threatened to commit suicide? Was that you?"

Lali laughed, shaking her head. "I said I would die. I said I would not sin to save my life or someone else's. I never said I would kill myself. That would be a sin. That's like the opposite of what I said!" She forced an uncomfortable smile that came off like a grimace. "I'm sorry if I seem moody." She laid her fork down and met his eyes. "I had a bad time at the abortion clinic yesterday."

"What happened?" Danny tilted his head, softening his tone with compassion.

Lali took a deep breath and slumped her shoulders. She stared at the table.

"A girl had an abortion because she thought her boyfriend would hurt me if she didn't. She murdered her baby because she thought it would protect *me*." Lali kept her head down, as if she were counting the wood grains in the table.

Danny had not expected something so frightening and terrible, so beyond the high school experience, so worldly, so grown-up, so *evil*. As he looked at his friend, a kind of awe filled his spirit.

"Whoa!" he gasped, "that's pretty intense. I guess that explains it!"

"Yeah, it's freaking me out," Lali's eyes pleaded for help. But what help could he offer?

Danny paused, considering how to respond. He was out of his depth. He had been so focused on his own illness and troubles, he never even imagined other people could have troubles like this. He just had bad luck, having to fight cancer and dealing with the side-effects. She was up against something, well, it was not just random bad luck. It was intentional and violent. Standing up for what was right, and threatened with violence? A girl had an abortion to protect her? How could he help her? What could he say? There was a depth to the conflict he could see, but well-intentioned as he was, he just could not relate to or understand it well enough to suggest anything. *You can always pray;* the thought came to him.

"I'll pray for you, Lali." Danny hoped that prayers could help and was not sure what else might. Then he added, as the inspiration came to him, "And for the girl. And her boyfriend."

Lali grabbed his hand, pleading, "And the baby, Danny! Don't forget the baby!"

A tear welled in Danny's eye. "Yeah." His voice cracked as he gazed, into her plaintive eyes. "And the baby. Of course, for the baby."

"You're a good friend, Danny." Lali offered a sad, reassuring smile that Danny imagined covered a gaping emotional wound like a band-aid on a limb destined for amputation. "I really appreciate having you as a friend."

"Oh, Lali! You're the only friend I have." Daniel held back tears.

Lali smiled, that same sad, reassuring smile, and reached up and shuffled the hat on his head. Pausing a moment, she added, "I'm going back to the clinic to pray today. I could use some company."

Daniel lowered his head. "I'm sorry. I asked my parents, but they said, 'no way!'"

"I understand." Lali nodded, her lips pressing together.

"You take care of yourself, Lali." Danny made eye contact with her and hoped she could see the worry in his eyes.

Lali reached under her blouse and pulled a medal out. The Miraculous Medal, Danny recognized it. She moved it back and forth on its chain.

"She's always looking out for me." Lali's smile and voice appeared more confident now.

14

Lali Spins

LALI WALKED TOWARD THE ENTRANCE to the abortion clinic and stopped on the sidewalk in front of the building. She took out her rosary beads and prayed for a peaceful day, especially after yesterday. But she was unable to shake the sense of foreboding that seemed to wrap her like a cloak. Her dream troubled her again. *That dream!* Had she suffered to save souls? No, not really. Kim had suffered to spare her. Rodrigo had suffered her rejection. Daniel had suffered from his illness. All she had seemed to suffer was from guilt. Hadn't she been doing what was right in everything? But she had only caused other people to suffer. She had even offended Daniel, in shaving her head and thinking it was a sacrifice. How could she have been so wrong? All around her was suffering. And people like her father and Kim were willing to suffer to help her, but had she suffered? And yet the thought kept running in her head, *sometimes we must suffer if we are to save souls.* What did it mean? As each bead slipped through her fingers to the next one, Hail Mary after Hail Mary, her thoughts focused more on her own confusion than on the sorrowful mysteries that were her meditation. The Agony in The Garden, the anticipation of suffering, bead after bead, but it was only her own lack of suffering that occupied her mind. *Sometimes we must suffer if we are to save souls. What does it mean?* She glanced at the crucifix dangling from her rosary beads and thought of Jesus in the Garden of Gethsemane. *If it is possible, let this cup pass, but not my will but thine be done.* The gospel verse rang in her ears. *What cup, Lord?*

The rumbling rattle of the tan Chrysler sedan broke Lali's meditation as it pulled to the curb in front of the abortion clinic. Lali glanced up from her beads and drew in a breath as she recognized the car with its darker shades of brown in places where dirt and mud from some unpaved surface seemed to have become part of it. Ralo flung the driver's side door open and scrambled out, rushing frantically around the front of the car toward her.

"Ju needs to help me!" He extended his arms as he spoke with his palms up, pleading, almost begging. "Kim's freaking out!"

"What? Is she okay?" It must be bad if Ralo was asking for help.

"She flipping out!" Ralo said, his tone on the verge of a shout. "She may be suicidal. Says I force her to kill her baby!"

Lali paused a moment, sizing up Ralo.

"Well, Ralo, she's right about that, you know." Lali remained calm, her tone almost smug.

"Jes, sure, sure. Is me fault," Ralo admitted, "but ju have to help her. Calm her down."

"Where is she?"

"She at our place. Come on! I drive you!" Ralo hurried around the car to get back in, assuming Lali would follow.

Without thinking, Lali stepped to the front passenger door and opened it, letting herself in. She grabbed the seatbelt but as she buckled herself in, she heard Ralo chuckle. Lali looked at him suspiciously.

"Is something funny, Ralo?" Lali kept her hand on the seatbelt buckle, ready to unlatch it and make a dash from the car.

"No, no," Ralo assured her. "Is just we never use the seat belts."

"My father's a cop, Ralo," Lali said, shaking her head and adjusting the seatbelt across her shoulder. "He's seen a lot of bad accidents, so he always insisted."

Ralo started the car and pulled onto the street. An awkward silence permeated the interior of the car like an unwanted smell. Lali sat uncomfortably in the front passenger seat, her hand still on the seatbelt buckle, watching the road carefully as Ralo passed the house where he had been sharpening the machete, when she had walked Kim home.

"Isn't that your house?" Lali looked back over her shoulder as Ralo drove on.

"Oh, jeah, I took Kim to the cabin to rest." Ralo glanced over at her.

Lali eyed him suspiciously for a moment, then rolled her eyes, grabbing the cell phone from her purse.

"What ju doing with that?"

Lali narrowed her eyes and scowled at him. "I'm calling my father to make sure he knows where I am." Her cell phone appeared to be off, so she pushed the on button. A sudden sense of dread ran through her as she realized in all the excitement last night, she had forgotten to charge her phone and it was now completely dead. "Oh, shoot! I forgot to charge my phone again! There's a pay phone at the corner here. Could you stop? It will only take a second." She kept her tone as casual as she could manage.

"Ju can call him from the cabin, there's a phone there, at the cabin." Ralo did not look up at her but kept his eyes on the road.

"Well, I'd rather not wait. Do you have a cell phone I can borrow?"

"Uh, no, I never use those things. Is just a short way to the cabin. We be there soon. Ju can call from there."

Ralo continued driving in awkward silence for several miles, well beyond the borders of the town and up a mountain road, down the long driveway to a secluded shack out in the woods. The sun descended toward the horizon, peeking over a mountain ridge. The thick foliage obscured much of the light. Eerie, long shadows here and there where the light managed to pass through made ominous shapes on the forest floor as Ralo pulled up to the shack.

Ralo seemed less frantic and more confident as he opened the driver side door to the muted sounds of the early autumn forest and the dampness of the place where sunlight rarely directly penetrated. Lali entered the strange darkness, interrupted here and there where the light penetrated the trees, the shadows clawing at the light. She focused her attention on the wellbeing of her friend and braved the damp gloominess of the place. Had Kim taken her own life? Were they too late?

"Kim?" she called as she climbed the front steps to the door. "Are you okay? It's Lali!"

Ralo fumbled with his key in the lock then opened the door, which made a muffled squeaking noise as the forest absorbed the sound.

Ralo stepped aside to allow Lali to enter first as if he had discovered better manners now having need of assistance. As she entered the small, rustic cabin, deep in the darkness of the forest, an abrupt shove from behind her thrust her forward, landing her roughly on the couch in the main room.

"Just who do ju think ju are?" Ralo shouted angrily, "Telling Kim she could have that baby? What beesness is it of jours?"

Lali, confused, lifted her chin to watch Ralo, her eyes wide, as she raised herself off the sofa. "Where's Kim?"

"That beetch is no' here!" Ralo yelled. "Is just ju and me, miles from nowhere"

"Can I call my father now?" Lali asked.

Ralo responded incredulously. "No! No, ju can no' call ju father, the cop!" Ralo rolled his eyes. "Ju still don't get it, do ju?"

The stupidity of her question, the danger of her situation seeped slowly into her mind like spilt milk into a soaked sponge.

Ralo picked up a baseball bat and swung it. "Now, take off ju clothes!"

Lali's eyes widened and she stiffened in defiance. "I will not!" Her mind tried to wrap itself around a demand that seemed to come from nowhere.

"I say, take off ju clothes!" Ralo showed Lali the baseball bat. "Or I bash ju head in!"

Ralo took a few practice swings, and she cowered back, raising her arms in defense.

The danger of her position hardened into reality. Alone. Isolated. With this maniac. No one even knew she was here. *I have to get out of here!* But how? Lali glanced at the door. She would never make it. Even if she got out the door, could she make it to the road? There was no way. Lali took a deep breath and closed her eyes. *I would die.* In horror, she remembered her words from Mr. Trudeau's class.

"Ralo, don't do this. Please! It is a terrible sin. You'll go to hell!"

Ralo laughed at her. "Ju think I wanna go to heaven? All that singing and goody-goodies? Hell is the place for me, if there is such a place!"

Lali's mouth fell open, horrified. Who would want to go to hell? "It's a place of torment, Ralo! Eternal torment!"

Ralo snorted. "Then, I might as well get some pleasure now!" He dropped the baseball bat and pushed her down on the couch.

Lali reached inside her blouse, grabbed the Miraculous Medal she wore around her neck, curled up in a ball, and started to pray. "Hail Mary, Full of Grace…"

Ralo pried the Miraculous Medal from her fingers and ripped it from her neck, breaking the chain.

"No!"

"So, what do we have here?" Ralo tilted his head and studied the medal with the image of the Blessed Virgin on it, her hands extended, palms up. Ralo scoffed. "So, ju think She will save you, *mi cabronita Católica?*"

Lali fell on her knees, with her head down and prayed. "Please, Lord Jesus! Protect me!"

"Ju really belief this crap, don't ju?" Ralo shook his head, almost a look of pity in his cruel eyes. He spoke softly, as if to a child. "No, me little *cabronita*, there is no one there to hear ju. Just ju and me, miles from nowhere. No one to hear. No one to help. No one to protect."

Ralo tossed the Miraculous Medal across the room. It clanged lightly and spun on the floor, making its little call for help before dying away in the night. Ralo grabbed her wrists and pushed himself on top of Lali, managing to trap one of her arms behind her and holding her down with the full weight of his body. She struggled but could not free herself from his grasp. Overpowered, she closed her eyes and desperately prayed. *Lord Jesus, help me!* But the answer to her prayer offered no assistance and little solace. *Sometimes we must suffer.* The horrifying words echoed in her mind as her eyes opened wide, glimpsing the image of the Blessed Mother, her Mother, lying silently in the corner of the room, unable or unwilling to protect her. Her mind grasped for something solid, as the world spun, her body pinned, her throat raw from screams unheard in the suffocating damp of the forest, her innocence undefended, her spirit broken. *Mommy's with Jesus now.* She watched her mother die, death the only solid thing left to grab. Her mind abandoned her body and drifted elsewhere.

Afterward, Lali sat sullen and withdrawn on the couch, her mind not fully back from wherever it had gone. Her arms and legs crossed over her body, her back arched forward. Had this really happened? *Was I really just raped? Why didn't God protect me?* Where was the Blessed Mother? Where was Jesus?

And, horribly, she recalled her dream again. *Sometimes we must suffer if we are to save souls. I will be with you when your time comes.* But where was he? *Had He been with me and done nothing?* And what souls had been saved?

And a voice came to her. *Remember the cross? Who was there to protect me?*

Across the room, the glint of her Miraculous Medal softly glimmered in the dim cabin light. She imagined the Virgin was crying, as She had cried at the foot of the cross. Her own tears began to flow, and she started to weep.

And she imagined that it was her beaten and broken body that the Virgin Mother held, as she wept, Our Lady of Sorrows. And she thought of Saint Eulalia, her namesake, rolled in a barrel, the knives thrust through, cutting her endlessly as she tumbled down the street in her spinning descent. Her breasts cut off, crucified, decapitated. Who was there to protect her?

Lali sniffed and wiped her eyes, captivated by a vision of Jesus on the cross, *Father, forgive them. They don't know what they are doing.*

Was this what he meant when he said, "I will be with you when your time comes?" She sat on the couch, her arms crossed, her hands holding her plaid skirt against her legs, her eyes fixed on the glint of the miraculous medal on the floor, across the room. *Is it just a reflection of the metal or is it a tear drop?*

I was there the whole time at the cross, she heard her Mother say as she stared at the medal away on the floor. Lali bowed her head and squeezed her eyes shut, the voice of her rapist on the telephone barely registering, her body tensing, limbs tightly crossed. Events in the real world came faintly back into her consciousness.

"Rodrigo? Jes, come up to the shack." She heard Ralo speaking into the phone. "I have some beesness for ju…But is especial, this time…Sure. I think ju like it. Think of it as a present from me to ju. Just get here!"

Lali heard the oddly faint sound of the receiver roughly slammed down like a distant echo, the bell of the old-style rotary phone sending out its faint chime. She glimpsed Ralo, a blurred figure in her peripheral vision as she stared blankly ahead.

"Ju believe that clown was tryin' to make excuses no' to come?" Ralo shook his head and rolled his eyes.

Lali kept staring blankly ahead, his words almost unintelligible to her. *Is it a tear drop?*

"I'm talking to ju, beetch!" Ralo raised his voice. He picked up the bat again, "So ju no like to talk after sex? I like that." Ralo sniggered.

Lali continued staring at the medal on the floor, glimmering in the dull light of the cabin. *A tear drop, I think it is a tear!* Oh, how could it be a tear? Lali heard the rustling crackles as a car pulled up to the cabin, then the purr of the engine stop, and the car door opening. *I was there, at the cross.*

A knock on the door, and Ralo stepped away to answer it. "Hey, Rodrigo! Got something especial for ju!"

"Hey, Ralo." Lali heard the anxiety in Rodrigo's voice. "I thought we agreed? No more shack duty for me?"

At the sound of Rodrigo's voice, Lali came out of her daze. Had she missed a chance to escape while she sat there meditating in shock? With Ralo's back toward her as he stood at the door, she scanned the room. Was there another way out? Was there a back door? Lali quietly got to her feet and crept into the small kitchen at the back of the cabin, but found the back door barricaded. She would never be able to move the couch and table away from the door. The window!

"Oh, but this time is especial." Ralo's exuberance at showing off his prize made Lali gag as she unlocked the window over the sink and slowly slid it open. She climbed onto the sink, pulling the top part of her body through the window, the clanking of her knees and feet against the sink unavoidably ringing out into the cabin.

"Who is it, Ralo?" Rodrigo's suspicious voice reached her ears. She more urgently pulled herself through the window. Her breath left her body with the shock of landing with a thud on the cool ground. She gasped in the brisk autumn air. "Who do you have in there?"

"Oh, I think she's a friend of jours. Or she used to be?" The voices grew fainter as she clambered to her feet.

"She? Ralo? She? What have you done?" The alarm in Rodrigo's voice reverberated in her ears.

"Jes, she! I told ju, is especial this time."

Breathing the chilly air, the scent of freedom exhilarated her as she scrambled ahead, trying to get her bearings. Though the moon was full, much of its light was obscured by the large trees in the forest. She scrambled forward, every broken stick, every rustling leaf echoed in her ears as if screaming: *Here she is!* Finding a large bush, she pulled herself well beneath it, fully obscured from the view of any passerby. Pain, she bore it with only the lightest of gasps, as the thorns gouged her flesh, scraping her face and her recently shaved head. She curled herself into a ball, and breathed heavily, trying to calm herself so she could think. *How can I get out of here?* She figured she would have to make her way around the house to the driveway and then to the road. *Can I make it without being seen?*

"Holy chee, the beetch got out!" Ralo's voice rang out with menacing alarm.

"Who, Ralo, who got out?"

"That beetch Lali, ju know, ju little lovebird!" Ralo's voice was frantic.

"Lali! The cop's daughter? You brought the cop's daughter here?" She heard Rodrigo, incredulity sounding in his voice. Was he only concerned because he might get caught? Was she just "the cop's daughter" to him now? Lali squeezed her eyes shut. *Lord, please help me to escape them! Be my protection. Be my savior!*

"Sure, Rodrigo. She stuck her nose in me beesness." Ralo's voice was icy calm. "And, ju know what happen to people who stick their nose in me beesness."

The muffled scraping and crashing of the barricades being pulled away, deadened by the dense forest, rose above the sound of her breathing, like a reality penetrating the depths of sleep. She barely made their forms in the dark through the brush, as Ralo and Rodrigo scrambled out the back door. She hugged herself, lying on the cold ground.

"Ju go that way! I look over here." Ralo's shadowy form pointed as his voice commanded. The dull thudding crackles of one set of footsteps quickly receded. Another more deliberately, carefully approached.

Lali breathed deeply, trying to control her shivering in the cool night. She took a deep breath and held it. But only so long, and she had to breathe again. The presence was close now. She heard the dampened crunching of the small twigs and leaves under the approaching footsteps. And then the quiet as they stopped. Gripped with fear, she gasped for another breath. A couple more steps came even closer.

"Lali? Is that you?" She heard the whisper, relieved to a degree to hear Rodrigo's voice, but still careful to keep herself hidden.

Lali held her breath and did not answer. She trembled on the cold ground and held herself still, doing all she could to control her sobs.

Rodrigo whispered again. "Look, I'm not going to hurt you. Just stay here."

I have to tell him. He has to know. Lali took a deep breath. "He raped me, Rodrigo," she whispered. Lali closed her eyes tightly and shivered in the awkward pause.

"Just stay quiet. If he finds you, he'll kill you. I won't be able to protect you."

"Don't sin to protect me!" she whispered in hushed urgency.

"Shut up!" Rodrigo snapped back in a hushed tone. "I don't want to hear about sin right now."

✝✝✝

Rodrigo put as much distance between Lali and himself as he could, walking quickly in the dark night toward Ralo, who had given up his search of the front of the house and was doubling back. He had to keep Ralo away from that bush! Lali was breathing like a horse after a race. He'd hear her, for sure. Ralo's visage loomed in the darkness. "I can't see anything in this dark. Do you have a flashlight?" *Try anything to gain some time, distract him.*

"I think I hear whispering." Ralo sounded suspicious. "Did ju find her?"

"Just whispering to myself about what bad luck." Rodrigo scuffed his feet, kicking up fallen pine needles among the forest ferns. "You know I do that sometimes."

"Jes, but it esounded different this time." Skepticism rang in Ralo's voice. "More like a conversation. Ju would no' be playing some kind of hero-Romeo, would'ju?"

"Come on, Ralo! Why would I care about that bitch? She dumped me, you know!"

"Ju went up this way, did ju no'?" Ralo looked toward the bush where Lali was hiding. The blood drained from Rodrigo's face. His characteristic coolness slipped away. Would Ralo notice in the shadowy moonlight? Ralo followed his trail like a bloodhound, making his way toward the bush where Lali was hiding.

"Yes, Ralo, I already looked up there! Maybe she's gone deeper into the forest."

The shadowy specter in the moonlight skeptically tilted its head, an imagined sinister smile on Ralo's faceless form. *He doesn't believe me. No way he believes me! I'm going to get us both killed.*

"Jes, I'm sure it was right about here." The dark form nodded its head. "So, this is the bush ju was talking to about such bad luck!"

"Ralo, I wasn't talking to the bush. I was talking to myself!"

"Oh, jes. So ju say. Why do ju no' go look deeper in the woods, and I look under this bush?"

He knows I'm lying! What can I say? Rodrigo stood frozen and silent, paralyzed with fear.

"No? Don't wanna look deeper in the woods? Well, that is *interesante!*" The shadow chuckled knowingly. Rodrigo took a deep breath.

The form cupped his chin mockingly. "Now if I was a little beetch, where would I hide? Maybe in the bush? Oh, but look at those prickers! I hate prickers!" The shadowy form drew a handgun that caught just a glint of moonlight in the dark, damp of the forest. "Well, no sense in getting estuck by those things. We just make sure there nobody in there."

The gun raised and pointed at the bush.

"No, Ralo!" Rodrigo shouted, reaching out and pulling the gun down.

"So, she is in there!"

"Lali! Come out!" Trapped like a rat. *Like the rat I am! Now, I'll be shot like a rat.* Like Juanito, the rat. Only worse. *He'll make me watch him shoot Lali first.* Lali slithered out of the bush, hanging her head.

"So, ju would betray me for this piece o'chee!" Ralo angrily waved his gun, motioning toward Lali. "I should shoot ju both right now!"

"No, Ralo! Wait! It's not like that!" The despair ringing in his own voice made Rodrigo cringe.

Ralo chuckled, shaking his head in disbelief. "Well, Rodrigo, tell me? What is it like? I like a good estory."

"Ralo, I know you." Rodrigo struggled to regain his cool, logical manner. "I know what you're planning, and it won't work. Lali's father is a cop! They won't stop looking for her, like the others. People care about her, and they will figure it out, not like those other pieces of shit."

"So, ju was thinking of what's best for me, when ju was hiding this beetch!" Ralo tittered, his rolling eyes barely visible in the darkness.

He's clever in his own way, you need to be more clever if you are going to get out of this! Don't underestimate him! "She can't just disappear, Ralo. No one will buy it. They'll keep looking, and they'll find this place. And they'll find the others."

Ralo paused and looked around, glancing toward the shallow graves, where the ground was mounded up, and the grass had not yet regrown as if recalling the body buried in each one. Rodrigo imagined a self-satisfied expression washing over his face, invisible in the darkness. He looked like he was measuring the ground for two more. Or was he buying it?

"Oh, jes, that make some esense, Rodrigo." A certain slyness in his tone, the dark form motioned with the handgun toward the cabin. "Let's go back to the shack and think this through."

Rodrigo and Lali marched to the shack, Ralo following them with his gun drawn, the small sticks and ferns crackling under their feet as they walked. They entered the cabin through the back door, the barricade remnants strewn all over.

"Okay, now, Rodrigo, *mi amigo*." Ralo pointed the gun at him. "Let's hear the rest of ju estory."

"We have to make it look like an accident, or a suicide." Rodrigo avoided Lali's eyes. In his peripheral vision, he glimpsed her covering her mouth. He had to be strong if he was going to save her. Ralo had to believe it, and so did she! "The body must be found, or they will keep looking until they find it."

"Sure, me friend, the body must be found," Ralo said calmly, then his eyes narrowed as he shouted, "But that no esplain why ju was hiding this beetch!"

"Calm down, Ralo." Rodrigo raised and lowered his hands, as if he were throwing a blanket over a fire he wanted to put out. "I thought I could handle it a little more subtly."

"So, *Señor* Romeo, ju want me believe that ju was going to kill her subtly, with no involving me?" Ralo raised his eyebrow in his smug smirk. "Do ju take me for a *cabrón?* Why would ju do that? She no has nothing on ju!"

Ralo waived his revolver around enough that it might just go off accidentally. Rodrigo once again tried to put out the fire with his imaginary blanket, this time more urgently.

"Calm down, Ralo!"

"Ju know I no like it when people tell me calm down!" Ralo's angry voice crescendoed to a shout. "Especially when rats like ju tell me calm down!"

That was what got Juanito killed! Got to avoid that! Get him to calm down and listen. Win his trust, somehow. *Can I save her? Not sure. But if I can get him to listen, maybe I can get out of this!* Ralo was an experienced killer. Rodrigo had witnessed it. And Rodrigo was just as much a rat as Juanito. Had to be something really clever. Something that helped him. Could he get them both out? He didn't see how. A plan began to form in Rodrigo's genius level mind. A long shot, but it might be the only shot! *But first, I have to survive this altercation.*

"We can still make this work." Rodrigo confidently glanced at Ralo, and avoided eye contact with Lali, who stood arms folded and shivering. *What must she think of me? Discussing with Ralo how to get rid of her?* The last thing he wanted to do is get rid of her.

"And why would ju wanna do that'?" Ralo smirked in disbelief. "She no has nothing on ju? How could I trust ju? Jou'd turn me in to her cop father as soon as ju could!"

"No, no, Ralo, never!"

"But, oh, what about this? *Señor* Romeo?" A sinister smile caused his scar to curl on his cheek, like a cobra preparing to strike. "What if she has something on ju, as well? Jes, what if ju in this with me? All the way?"

"I don't know what you mean?" The sweat built on Rodrigo's brow. *Uh-oh, the psychopath has an idea!*

"Rape her." Ralo calmly waved the gun in Lali's direction.

"What?" Rodrigo blinked a couple of times. His mouth fell open.

"I say, rape her!" Ralo raised his voice.

Rodrigo looked helplessly at Lali for a moment, then back at Ralo. *God, how can I rape her?* "But, Ralo…"

Ralo glared. "I say, rape her! If ju with me, ju rape her, and we kill her together. If ju with her, ju die with her, just like Romeo and Juliet."

How did an uneducated drug-dealing thug with a ninth-grade education know the story of Romeo and Juliet? Rodrigo tried not to roll his eyes at the thought.

Ralo appeared to notice Rodrigo's puzzled look.

"Oh, Mister Smart Guy, ju no think Ralo knows about this Romeo an' Juliet? They make me read that crap the one year I went to high eschool." Ralo nodded his head and smiled.

Rodrigo could think of nothing to say.

"Jes, I know this rat Romeo betray his family for a woman and got his friend killed! Jes, I know this little meddler Juliet, sticking her nose in family beesness!"

"Ralo, I'm no rat, I'm not like Romeo." No time to ponder the psychopathic interpretation of the great bard's play, just reason on his level. *For God's sake, he's going to make me rape her!*

"We see, Rodrigo-Romeo." Ralo grinned, then turned almost whimsical. "Ju know the best thing about that estupid play? The thing I like most?"

Rodrigo assumed it was a rhetorical question and waited for Ralo to finish, but the time became awkwardly long.

"Uh…no…Ralo…uh…what did you like best?" *He's playing with us like a cat with a mouse!*

"They all die in the end! Romeo, Juliet, Romeo's friend, Juliet's brother, Romeo's mother! Everybody, toes-up dead! Now that's my kind of ending!"

Ralo pointed his handgun at Rodrigo. "So now is time for Romeo…" Then, pointing the gun at Lali. "…rape Juliet!"

Ralo scratched his head with the revolver, then pointed it back at Rodrigo, shrugging, "Or maybe we just keep it they die together? I'm okay either way. So what ju say, Romeo?"

Rodrigo looked at Lali, who had watched the argument silently, her mouth agape. The shock appeared to wane, replaced by the slow realization of horror. Her face scrunched, as she closed her eyes tightly. Rodrigo watched her eyes open again. How could he do this to her? *But if I don't, we're both dead!* He had to win Ralo's confidence, and this was the test. *If I can't rape her, we're both dead!*

"No! Rodrigo, no!" Lali seemed to suddenly regain her senses and came out of her shocked state. "You'll go to hell! Don't sin to protect me!"

Ralo turned to her derisively. "Will ju shut up, already! Ju dead either way! And Rodrigo is already going to hell, if there is such a place!"

Rodrigo nodded in acquiescence. "Okay, Ralo," he said, solemnly. "I'm with you. All the way. I'll rape her."

Lali's eyes widened in horror. "Rodrigo! No!" Her mouth gaped open. She blinked incredulously as if she were trying to awake from a nightmare.

Maybe she would live to hate him for this? He didn't see another way. *He'll kill us both if I don't. I may not be able to stop him from killing her, but there is a chance.*

Rodrigo passed close to Lali, avoiding her eyes, his focus lowered to where the wall met the baseboard. "Will you let me do this thing?" he whispered.

"No! It would be a sin!" Lali's eyes widened.

Ralo laughed. "It no counts if she let ju, Rodrigo! Now rape her. Ju know ju' wanna for a long time. Here she is! Take her! Or ju no' man enough?"

Rodrigo grabbed Lali and threw her against the couch.

Lali screamed. "No! No! Jesus, No!"

Ralo laughed. "Romeo, Romeo, wherefore art thou, Romeo," Ralo chided with glee.

Romeo the rat.

"I'm sorry," Rodrigo whispered to Lali, pinning her to the couch, his body forcing her down as she squirmed to free herself. "It's our only chance. It's the only way I can protect you."

"Rodrigo?" Ralo said, "Ju no whisper words of love when ju raping a woman!"

Good, the bastard couldn't hear me.

Ralo chuckled.

"No, no!" Lali wailed. "It's a sin! It's a sin!"

"Look what happen to them no wanna sin!" Ralo laughed.

When it was over, Rodrigo got up off of Lali. Ralo shook his hand.

"Go, get jouself clean up," Ralo said. "ju know, from the blood and all."

Rodrigo nodded and lowered his head. He quietly slunk to the bathroom, and left Lali sitting on the couch, staring at the floor.

✝✝✝

Lali searched for the Miraculous Medal on the floor, her vision unstable and blurred with tears, spinning as in her dream, staggering, grasping for something stable. Where was She? Her eyes scanned and blinked desperately until finally catching the recognizable glint in the blurry whirl the world had become. Was it a tear drop? Had Our Lady watched it all and done nothing? Was she really there?

"Get up!" The command came from far off as in a dream.

Lali kept staring at the medal on the floor.

"I say, get up!" A shout, then a hand grabbed her by the wrist and dragged her up off the couch.

Lali kept her head down, leaning her body to look past the man with the baseball bat at the medal on the floor. Where had she been? Was she there the whole time? The female voice came, *the whole time I watched at the cross.*

"Walk to the door." Hands roughly turned her body and shoved her toward the door.

Jesus, on the cross once more, looked heavenward. *"My God, my God, why have you forsaken me?"*

A flutter of air as the bat swung, almost silently in the dim light of the cabin, and a crack as the barrel found the back-left side of her skull. And Lali, spinning, just a half turn this time, a flash of light brighter now than the blue sky of her dream. *"I will be with you when your time comes."* She crumpled to the floor in a thud.

15

Did She Jump or Fall?

RODRIGO HEARD THE CRACK OF THE BAT and the unmistakable, sickening thud of a body hitting the floor. That sound from when Ralo shot Juanito. No gunshots this time. No ringing in the ears. Just a crack and then that sound, the sound of death, of brutal murder. *My God, what has he done? What have I done?*

Rodrigo caught the briefest glimpse of himself in the mirror, as if he were seeing himself, or what he had become, for the first time, and he did not like what he saw. He frantically shut off the faucet and rushed back into the living room.

"Ralo! What have you done?" His tone more anguish than alarm, his hands cupped his cheeks, his mouth dropped open. Then catching himself, he said more calmly, "You can't kill her here!"

"She is going with the rest of them." Ralo spoke with determination. He had made up his mind. "Can no have her walking around with this on me!"

"They'll find her, Ralo." Rodrigo calmed his tone to sound more reasonable. "And all the others. Because they won't stop looking!"

"Jes, jes, so ju keep saying."

I have to convince him. "I know a place, Ralo." Rodrigo could not disguise the plaintiveness in his voice and feared it was not convincing. "We can make it look like she did herself."

Ralo leaned on the baseball bat and narrowed his eyes.

Rodrigo pressed his case. "Look at her! She's been all freaked out lately. Shaving her head and all. People will believe it! We'll make it look like she jumped! I know a place. She goes there all the time. If she were going to do it herself, it's where she'd do it. They'll assume she hit her head on the way down."

"So, *Señor* Romeo, ju make it look like Juliet off herself, is that it?" Ralo snapped the baseball bat into his hand. "I no trust ju, Rodrigo, no' with this one."

"It's the only way. I raped her, too. I'm going down if we get caught."

"If we get caught, ju be dead before ju get to prison." Ralo coldly examined the baseball bat, as if looking for a crack. "Just remember that!"

"Yes, I get that!" Rodrigo nodded. "But we have to make it look like an accident or suicide. She can't just disappear. That cop father of hers will not stop looking. He'll find her. And he'll find this place and all the others if we bury her here."

Lali groaned on the floor.

"So, the beetch is still alive!" He took his stance and readied the bat to swing.

"No, Ralo!" Rodrigo stepped in front of him. "It's good she's still alive! The fall will really kill her! There'll be no evidence that the body was moved after death."

Ralo put the bat down at his side and appeared to be thinking for a moment.

"Ju know, Rodrigo, Ju a pretty smart guy. But ju be a pretty dead guy, if this no work out!"

Rodrigo smiled. "I'll be waiting in hell for you."

Ralo laughed. "Ju, and the rest of them, *mi hermano.*"

Rodrigo bent down to pick up Lali, then paused.

"Just a minute, Ralo. We need to clean her up."

Ralo leaned forward and scowled. "What ju talking about, now? Clean her up?"

"We want people to think she jumped, not that she was raped. When they find the body, we need her to be clean. If she looks like she had sex, her father will come after me, for sure. I'll be tops on his list." Her father wouldn't wait for a trial if he found her like this, even if she were alive! Ralo wasn't going to wait for a trial, either. *Not much chance, but I have to try…*

Ralo's eyes narrowed. "Well, *Señor* Romeo, maybe that's a good reason they find ju both?"

Rodrigo thought quickly. "If they find us both, they may start looking for someone who killed us both. That will lead them to you. Better for you that they come looking for me."

Ralo raised his eyebrows. "Once again, me little friend, thinking about what's good for me!"

He wasn't buying it! *If I can get her out of here alive, she'll have a chance…*

"Ralo, it's better for me too, if you don't kill me."

"Jes, everybody win!" Ralo chuckled. "Ju one esmart guy, Rodrigo. But just one bullet away from being one dead guy, remember that'."

Okay, for now, he's going for it. Now for the dirty work. *If this doesn't convince that cold-hearted bastard that I'm with him, nothing will…*

Rodrigo went to the bathroom and got a washcloth. The water from the washcloth dripped as he returned, the drops falling silently on the floor beside him as he knelt and examined Lali. Seeing a trickle of blood on the side of Lali's head where a thorn had torn her skin, he wiped it away. Then he wiped down her body and, closing his eyes, he found himself praying, *Lord, help me to get her out of this!*

"Should we clean the couch?" Ralo nodded toward the couch, stained with Lali's virgin blood.

"If they find the couch, they find this place and everything around here." Rodrigo motioned with his hands. "They are, for sure, going to find her so that's most important. But it may not be a bad idea to just burn that old thing."

Ralo chuckled. "Ju are always thinking, Rodrigo, I give ju that'."

Having cleaned Lali, Rodrigo asked, "Where are her panties?"

"Oh, I pull them off. There they are."

Ralo picked up Lali's panties and tossed them to Rodrigo. Lali groaned slightly as he moved her legs, slipping her panties over them. Her innocent body made its plea for protection. *Lord, please help me to get her out of here safely. We may need a miracle, but we're not dead yet.*

In the car, Rodrigo glanced over at Ralo, as he drove. Lali lay in the large trunk of the Chrysler. They traveled up to the coastal trail entrance and parked by the curb. *If I had a gun, I could shoot him right now.* Rodrigo pinched his lips, regretting the aversion to violence that had led him to eschew arming himself. He was just going to have to be clever. *Anyway, if I shot him, I'd be the one going to jail.*

Rodrigo opened the car door and got out. The fresh smell of the ocean breeze and the faint sound of the surf crashing on the rocks far below the cliffs reminded him of his walks with Lali. Rodrigo opened the car trunk. Its familiar squeaking disrupted his memory of the soft sounds of the sea in the distance. He studied Lali for a moment. She looked peaceful in the dim light of the trunk, breathing slowly and heavily, the swollen and wounded back of her head not quite visible as her body lay curled on her side. Rodrigo resolved to do what must be done, what would likely get him killed, as the call of the innocent for protection drew him into mortal peril, or perhaps, immortal peril. *Lord, help me to get her through this.*

Rodrigo closed his eyes. Ralo's presence loomed up from behind and looked over his shoulder.

"Is she dead?"

"Shh!" Rodrigo hushed him, whispering. "We're not at the cabin! People walk here sometimes."

Ralo's eyes narrowed angrily as he hissed quietly through his teeth. "I no liking this plan, Rodrigo."

"It'll be fine. Just keep quiet," Rodrigo whispered.

Rodrigo hoisted Lali over his shoulder, carrying her along the familiar route to the cliffs. Did she fall, or did she jump? Rodrigo could not shake the memory from his mind. Ralo followed quietly, anxiously looking around, his hand in his pocket. The pocket where he always kept his gun.

Rodrigo carried Lali toward the edge of the cliff and placed her down on the ground as gently as he could manage, though not as gently as he had hoped, as her dead weight landed with a dull thud. He looked back at the footprints on the path leading to the cliff. They would have to do something about them. He turned back around, and there, Ralo had carried Lali to the fence before the cliff. Hoisting her up, Ralo prepared to toss her over.

"No! Ralo! Not yet!" Rodrigo hissed through his teeth.

Ralo scoffed. "Oh, come on, Romeo! Is time for Juliet to jump."

Rodrigo grabbed Ralo and pulled him back from the edge.

"Ralo! It has to look like she jumped!" Rodrigo motioned toward the trail where they had come from. "Look at the footprints!"

Ralo dropped Lali on the ground, taking no care to be gentle. She landed with a thud.

"Rodrigo, I losing me patience." Ralo tilted his head, petulantly. "Let's dump her and get going!"

"She's a cop's daughter!" Rodrigo whispered sharply. "Not some drug dealer that nobody cares about! They'll be looking for evidence that she did not jump."

"So what ju wanna do? Wake her up and tell her to jump?" In the pale moonlight, the scar on Ralo's face slithered with his sarcastic smirk.

Rodrigo shook his head, tightening his lips, holding his tongue. He took off Lali's shoes and carried them back to the point on the path where their footprints became distinct. He squeezed his feet into Lali's shoes and walked back. He carefully hopped the fence and leaned back against it at the edge of the cliff. Simulating a jump, so that the shoes dug into the ground and left deeper imprints, he lost his balance. His heart raced as he turned quickly and grabbed the fence, narrowly avoiding falling off the edge himself. Rodrigo stared out over the cliff, at the ledge below. *I pray she fell.* " Lali's words rang in Rodrigo's head.

"Be careful, Romeo, or maybe they find ju at the bottom in Juliet's shoes," Ralo chided.

Rodrigo hopped back over the fence, careful not to leave any more footprints. He took off Lali's shoes and put them back on her feet. "There! Now if they search for footprints, it will look like she walked to the edge and jumped. Once they see that, they won't look at the other footprints. People walk here all the time."

"Ju are a clever one, Rodrigo."

"We have to be careful. They will be looking for anything unusual. Go back to the car and make sure she didn't drop anything." Rodrigo nodded toward the path.

"Ju giving me orders, Rodrigo?" Ralo put his hand in his jacket pocket.

Careful, Careful. Remember who was boss. The guy with the gun called the shots. Come up with something more unpleasant to do! "Just being careful. Just want to check, again, want to make sure it doesn't look like she was raped. Do you want to do that, and I'll check the car?"

Ralo shook his head and headed back to the car. *I figured not, you son of a bitch!* Lali groaned. Was she waking up? Rodrigo leaned over her.

"I'm going to try to get you out of this," he whispered, "but I don't know if I can."

"Rodrigo? What?" Lali moaned, confused.

"Shh! Keep quiet. He's coming back."

Ralo came back down the path, carrying Lali's book bag and purse. Rodrigo glanced over the edge of the cliff.

"Sorry, Lali, this is going to hurt a bit…" he whispered.

Rodrigo picked up Lali and dropped her over the fence before Ralo got there. Her body rolled gently over the edge and was gone.

Rodrigo ran to meet Ralo and grabbed the book bag and purse from him, then trotted back, and tossed them over the edge. "Okay, let's get out of here before somebody comes along." Rodrigo put his arm out to stop Ralo and turn him around.

"No so fast, Romeo!" Ralo said suspiciously. "Why ju so jumpy all a sudden? I wanna see her broken, little body at the bottom of the cliff."

Rodrigo stepped in front of him.

"Shh! Ralo!" he whispered urgently. "Someone's coming."

In the darkness, the beam of a flashlight bounced toward them on the trail. Rodrigo and Ralo ran down the path back to the car. Quickly getting in, the two sped off.

Thank you, Lord. She's in your hands, now. Old man, just do your thing. Find that little girl on the ledge and get help this time, before it's too late…

16

Mr. Hennessey

HOW COULD SHE JUST BE GONE? Mr. Hennessey glanced ahead, retracing the route to where he had last seen his little girl, as the flashlight beam fluttered in front of him on the paved surface of Coastal Drive, the way to the trail, the cliff, the ledge. The trees, if only they could talk. Perhaps they had seen? Maybe they knew what happened? But on that ledge, even they likely would not have seen so small a thing, tucked away over the edge. Maybe the rocks knew. Or the waves. But who could coax the secret from them?

The *Lost Girl,* they called her. But how could she be lost? He had left her on the ledge and gone for help. Had she tried to climb back up and fell? He had told her to wait. He should have stayed with her. She was all by herself, when she…*No, I don't know that she died. She was just…gone!*

Mr. Hennessey lowered his head and closed his eyes for a moment. Now, these fools said she was a ghost and she haunted the trail. That Katherine Kelly and her Channel 23 news spreading that crazy story! They didn't even know if she…*Oh, who am I kidding? She's gone. She must be, she must be…* His mind would not let him complete the thought as he followed the road past Rosie's Dinette, the place he had run to for help. And, they had called for help. But it was too late. They said she jumped? Why would she jump? *Yes, yes, she was in pain, but we were with her, to comfort her, her mom, her sisters, and me. She was loved!* Maybe she just tried to get a better look, a different angle, and slipped? *Hold tight! I told her, just hold tight! I'll get help!* How could she just be gone?

Mr. Hennessey ran over the details of the loss of his girl in the well-worn tracks of his mind. He had enough money, so he did not need to keep busy with work and that gave him the time to search, to walk the cliffs, to question, to doubt, and to wonder. They all thought he was mad. Plodding around the cliffs three times every night, stopping at the spot where he had last seen his little Claire.

His wife and other two daughters, they worried about him, as well. Mr. Hennessey recalled his conversation with his wife earlier that day. His daughter Michele, the expert skier who had nearly qualified for the Olympics, was asking what they thought about naming her baby, his granddaughter, Claire. He didn't know what to think about it. Perhaps they were thinking a new little Claire would help him forget? Life had gone on for his other girls. Michele, the skier and Siobhan, the collegiate gymnast, both such great athletes, so healthy, had recovered from the loss of their little sister and worried for him. But, the reality of a possible new little Claire only drove him deeper into his memories of his lost girl, and her athletic sisters. *Remember how we all used to cheer them on?* How excited Claire was for them when they won an event? He still had some of her drawings of the sisters. Claire was always drawing something.

She never went anywhere without that pad and pencil. But she was always so frail, so sickly. *We always worried it was something serious.* But, that crooked little smile! She always seemed so happy. She just never said very much, though. Mr. Hennessey reached the entrance of the Coastal Trail for the third and final time for that night. *I guess we weren't all that surprised when the doctor's said it was cancer.*

He entered the trail and hiked along following the twists and turns toward the sea, listening as the sound of the surf got louder. The chemotherapy had only weakened her more, causing her hair to fall out, wasting her body away. But her spirits were always high, and her little, sideways smile always so bright, even when she was weak and in pain. But she was just a child! *Lord, even in her sickness, didn't she deserve more life?*

She used to love to walk here with him, look out over the ocean and draw that scene. Always looking for a different angle, or time of day, or season, even different weather. Remember that time in the rain?

"But how she loved to draw the sunset!" Mr. Hennessey said out loud. He recalled where he had stood, waiting for her to finish her drawing. How he used to marvel at how she could capture the glint of the sunlight on the water with just some graphite on paper. The waters that day were rougher than normal, slamming on the rocks with great fury, and sparkling into the air catching the setting sunlight like little crystal prisms. Would little Claire be able to capture such beauty and drama with just her pencil? She would need time to work undisturbed. He left her to her work, and wandered a bit on the path, thinking that even should he just be too close to her, it would distract her. *Give her room, give her time.* He waited, looking down the trail, breathing in the scent of the evergreen trees mixed with the ocean breeze from far below, and listening to the sounds of the late summer insects. His gaze wandered, looking around in the dappled, dimming light, as the sun had begun its descent. Glancing up into the heights of the great trees of the forest, he caught sight of an owl high in one of the trees.

"Look, Claire, an owl, way up high," he remembered saying, in a hushed tone. He turned to her, but she was gone. She had not made a sound, had not cried out in fear, she simply was not there, as if she had never been there.

"Claire!" he had called, frantically running to the edge of the cliff, the owl taking flight and fleeing.

"I'm here, Daddy." Her small voice, not a hint of panic, came from below on the ledge, her pad and pencil in hand, her arms and legs scraped from the fall, or the jump, onto the ledge.

"Claire!" His heart had raced with alarm. "Don't worry, honey, I'll go and get help. You just hold tight! I'll get someone to help!"

He had run to Rosie's Dinette, not far from the entrance to the trail and had gotten the police. When they returned, she was gone. Her pad, her pencil, whatever it was that she last drew on the paper, gone with her.

The roughness of the waters churning at high tide caused rip currents along the shore. Her frail little body was never found, presumably swept out to sea. Here it was! Here was the place! The place he had stood. He shined the flashlight up at the tree where the owl had been. He turned and took a deep breath and closed his eyes for a moment, as the beam from his flashlight caught the cross beams of the fence, the fence meant to prevent any future lost Claires. *Hold tight, Claire! Just hold tight!* In the moonlight, now, Mr. Hennessey made his way to the fence at the edge of the cliff, as he had so many times before, little noting the sound of the starting car from the alternate trail entrance where he planned to later emerge on his circular route, focusing instead on the sound of the surf so far below, an echo of long ago. The policemen he had called on the night long past had looked over the edge with him and found, nothing. Gone. Lost. He looked out over the waters, so calm tonight, unlike that day so long ago. He fell to his knees and prayed, aloud.

"Oh, Lord! Have mercy on my little girl! I know she did not kill herself. My poor, beautiful, sick, little girl!"

Mr. Hennessey heard a groan from the ledge below. Startled, he got up off his knees. He peered over the edge. There his little girl lay, dressed in her school uniform, the skin of her scalp visible in the moonlight. But she was bigger and healthier. She was all grown up? How could it be? Oh, how could it be? But there she was!

Mr. Hennessey stared at the sky and blinked a few times, then back down. He hopped over the fence, carefully holding on and shining the flashlight down at the girl on the ledge. *It's her! After all these years!* It did not matter how.

"Claire!" he called down to her. "Claire! Hold tight! Daddy will get help! Just hold tight!"

Mr. Hennessey snapped open the door of Rosie's Dinette with a frantic yank, the bells chiming louder than normal. Flushed and out of breath, he charged to the counter where Rosie O'Neal glanced up from her near constant wiping, her hair bound up in its usual net.

"Rosie, you have to help! Call the police! Please!" Mr. Hennessey blinked his eyes as they adjusted to the light.

"Now, Mr. Hennessey. Try to calm down. What's this about?"

"She's there! She's on the ledge! You have to help!" He gasped to catch his breath. He had to get help! They were going to think he was crazy, but he had to get help!

Rosie's eyes softened with patronizing compassion. "Now, Mr. Hennessey, that was many years ago. Don't you remember? Little Claire is gone."

"No, No! I saw her!" He leaned over the counter. "Just tonight! On the ledge! Please! Call the police!"

Rosie smiled calmly. "Okay, okay! I'll call the police." Rosie turned over a glass and filled it with water. "But can I get you something? A glass of water maybe?"

"No, no! Just call the police! Please!"

Rosie picked up the phone and called the police. *Oh, thank God! She's calling them!* Even if they thought he was crazy, they'd have to look for themselves.

"Yes, this is Rosie O'Neal from Rosie's Dinette," she said into the phone. "I have Mr. Hennessey here. He's quite upset. He says he just saw his daughter Claire on the ledge at the cliff…" Rosie nodded at Mr. Hennessey. "Yes, that's right, that Claire. I think you better send someone quick. And send an ambulance."

"Yes! Thank you! She may be hurt." He wiped his sweaty face with a paper napkin from the counter. An ambulance. Yes! Exactly what they needed!

Rosie reached over the counter and touched Mr. Hennessey's hand. "Yes, Mr. Hennessey." Her smile was almost as crooked as little Claire's had been. "We don't want to take any chances."

She was humoring him. She thought he was nuts, but he didn't care! He was getting help. Just like he said. *Just hold tight Claire! Daddy's getting help! This time, not too late! Just hold tight! After all these years!*

"Oh, thank you, thank you, Mrs. O'Neal!" Mr. Hennessy squeezed her hand, filled with gratitude, and hope. "I'll wait for them outside." Mr. Hennessey hurried out the door.

17

Officer Kincaid

OFFICER DENNIS KINCAID TOOK THE CALL from dispatch in his patrol car. He raised the radio microphone to his lips. "This is Three-One-Adam responding. We're talking about *the* Lost Girl? Claire Hennessey? And her *father* says he found her?"

"That's right, Three-One-Adam," the radio chimed back, "we're sending the ambulance, just try to keep him calm."

"Roger, on my way to Rosie's Dinette." Officer Kincaid returned the mic of his police radio back to its hook. They got doped-up teenagers reporting seeing the *Lost Girl* up there all the time but the *father?* He must have finally cracked. Officer Kincaid rolled his eyes. The *Father of All Cliffwalkers,* as Rosie called him. Poor old guy. It must be a tough losing a daughter. *I never had a daughter.* Something about the thought made Officer Kincaid feel queasy. *And, I was hoping for a quiet night.* He made his way along the winding mountain roads toward Cliffside Drive and Rosie's Dinette.

Officer Kincaid pulled his squad car into the parking lot of the dinette and breathed a deep sigh. Mr. Hennessey rushed out to greet him. Officer

Kincaid parked vertically, next to the front entrance steps, and held his hand up as Mr. Hennessey tapped on the window of the car before it came to a full stop. Officer Kincaid lowered the window.

Mr. Hennessey leaned on the car door and put his hand through the window.

"Officer, Officer!" he cried, leaning forward. "You have to help! She's on the ledge! After all these years!"

Oh boy, he really did believe he saw her. And it was not some teenage stoner this time reporting a ghost.

"Okay, okay, Mr. Hennessey." Officer Kincaid tried his best not to roll his eyes, "Just try to calm down. Please, just step away from the car, so I can get out."

A very agitated Mr. Hennessey stepped away from the car. Officer Kincaid stepped out of the car and heard the bells of the dinette door ring quietly. Rosie peeked out from behind the door, her head tilted, the vertical wrinkles between her eyebrows visible even from this distance. Her hand moved to her chin. Officer Kincaid took a deep breath and turned to face Mr. Hennessey.

"Okay, now, Mr. Hennessey. What's all this about?"

Mr. Hennessey frantically grabbed his arm. "I was walking on the cliffs like I always do, but this time when I looked over, there she was! I don't know how. But there she was! All grown up, too. Like she was somehow hiding all these years. I don't know how it can be?"

"Okay, Mr. Hennessey. That does sound a bit strange. But let's go see. It can't hurt to take a look."

Officer Kincaid winked at Rosie.

"Oh, thank you, thank you, Officer," Mr. Hennessey blubbered. "I know this must sound crazy!"

Officer Kincaid nodded to Mr. Hennessey, who nodded back, calmer now but still in anxious anticipation, like a pet dog in urgent need to be let out on recognizing his owner's movement to get the leash.

"Just let me check back in with dispatch." Officer Kincaid reached back into the squad car and grabbed the radio mic.

"Dispatch, this is Three-One-Adam. I am proceeding on foot to the scenic overlook with Mr. Hennessey. Please have the ambulance stand by at the entrance. Will continue communication with the walkie."

"That's a roger, Three-One-Adam," the radio chirped back.

Officer Kincaid hung the microphone back in its place. He would have less range with the walkie, and there was a radio dead zone along the trail, but communication from the scenic overlook should be adequate. Hopefully, walking to the scene would keep Mr. Hennessey calm, and give the ambulance time to arrive. Perhaps, demonstrating for him that there was no one on the ledge would snap him out of it? If he tried to make Mr. Hennessey wait, in his agitated state, they might have to subdue him to get him into the ambulance. And, nobody wanted that. *Let's see if we can diffuse the situation.* He turned to Mr. Hennessey. "Okay, Mr. Hennessey, let's go see what this is all about."

Officer Kincaid shined his flashlight ahead of them and allowed Mr. Hennessey to lead the way back to the trail. The night was eerily silent, the pale moonlight formed shadows from the trees. The flashlight beam wobbled as they walked along, with Mr. Hennessey tugging Officer Kincaid's elbow to hurry him along. They entered the trail and Officer Kincaid engaged his walkie-talkie radio and checked in with dispatch.

"Three-One-Adam to dispatch. Entering the Coastal Trail. Will be out of contact for approximately ten minutes."

"Roger Three-One-Adam."

Officer Kincaid reattached the radio to his belt. He glanced ahead at the dark trail and had second thoughts about the wisdom of his plan. He did not know how unstable Mr. Hennessey might be, and they would be alone, with no communications for a time, even though only a short time. He glanced at Mr. Hennessey, who had been pushing the pace almost to a jog, and now seemed to be trembling restlessly, glancing at his watch. He had hoped that dispatch would have volunteered an update on the ambulance, but he had thought better of asking, not wanting to possibly upset Mr. Hennessey.

They entered the trail and made their way through the dead zone emerging on the other side. Officer Kincaid lifted the flashlight and the beams revealed the fence in the distance. Mr. Hennessey started to jog toward it.

"This is it! This is it!" he stammered.

"Please, Mr. Hennessey! Don't run ahead in the dark! We don't want you to trip and fall."

"Oh, yes, of course, but we need to get there. We can't be too late! Not again!"

Officer Kincaid grabbed his radio. "Dispatch this is Three-One-Adam. Reestablishing communications."

"That's a roger, Three-One-Adam."

Officer Kincaid breathed a heavy sigh. At least, if there were any trouble with the old guy, he could easily call for help. The way he was running ahead, after making such a strange report, there was no telling what might happen. Now, just keep everything steady and predictable.

They walked together toward the fence guarding the scenic overlook. Mr. Hennessey ran the last few steps to the fence and looked over.

"There she is! There she is! My God, she's still there this time! My God, my Claire, oh my Claire!"

Worry seized Officer Kincaid. He had not thought carefully enough of the implications of coming out to this isolated location with Mr. Hennessey. The man was clearly hallucinating. *If he falls or gets hurt or, jumps, for God's sake, that's on me.* He hoped he could keep the old man calm until the EMT's arrived with the ambulance. Officer Kincaid took a deep breath as he studied the desperately hopeful old man. It would look really bad if he had to subdue him. He should have waited at Rosie's and let the ambulance guys take care of him there.

"Oh, hurry, hurry, please!" Mr. Hennessey pleaded. "We have to help her!"

"Okay, okay, Mr. Hennessey, but it won't do any good for us to get hurt trying to run in the dark." Officer Kincaid walked deliberately, the flashlight beam gently bobbing the way toward the old man, already at the fence.

"Oh, no, no. Here we are. She's over the edge. There's a ledge!" Mr. Hennessey began to lean forward over the fence.

"Mr. Hennessey! Please step back!" Officer Kincaid commanded sharply. "We don't want you falling over the edge as well, now do we?"

Mr. Hennessey stepped back from the fence. His mouth dropped open, his hands cradling his chin. Officer Kincaid carefully approached the fence and leaned over. He shined the flashlight down onto the ledge and there, unconscious, lying on the ledge, a girl in a Catholic school uniform, her head shaven, her body broken. The light of the flashlight reflected off her shaved head.

"Oh, my God! She really is there!" Officer Kincaid exclaimed.

Mr. Hennessey fell to his knees and wept.

"Oh, my God! Thank you! I'm not too late. Not this time!"

Officer Kincaid pulled the walkie-talkie radio off his utility belt and raised it to his mouth.

"Dispatch? This is Three-One-Adam. We need a rescue squad over at the Coastal Trail by the scenic ocean view look-out. There's a girl unconscious on a ledge."

"Three-One-Adam, can you repeat? Not sure we copied? Did you say there's a girl on the ledge?"

"Roger, Dispatch, there's a girl on the ledge. Please send the rescue squad."

Officer Kincaid met the rescue squad when they arrived carrying their portable lights that cast long, strange shadows in the dull moonlight.

"What's up, Denny? We got a report that the *Lost Girl* is on the ledge?" Pablo Martinez, one of the EMT's asked.

"Well, Pablo, not sure if it is *the* Lost Girl, but it looks like there is *a* girl on the ledge, and Mr. Hennessey thinks it is his daughter, the *Lost Girl.* We have to keep an eye on him. I'm not sure how stable he is."

"Okay, well, first things first. If there's someone down on that ledge, let's get to her and see if she's okay."

"You guys do your thing. I'll keep an eye on Mr. Hennessey. You may need room for him in the ambulance. Just keep that in mind."

Pablo nodded, and the rescue squad quickly went about their business setting up portable lights around the scene, to allow them to complete their work. Officer Kincaid stood next to Mr. Hennessey and watched the rescue operation while keeping an eye on the anxious old man. There was no way it was Claire. He had to watch the old guy to see how he might react when he found out. Hopefully, he would not need to do anything physical to restrain him.

The rescue workers deployed a backboard and secured it to a rope harness, then tied the end of the rope around one of the fence posts. They tied a second rope to another fence post and connected to the harness of one of the rescue workers. The rescue worker rappelled down to the ledge where the girl lay unconscious. Once he got to the ledge, he felt for a pulse.

"She's alive! She's got a pulse."

An audible sigh of relief spread through those waiting at the top of the cliff.

Mr. Hennessey gasped in relief. "Oh, Claire! I wasn't too late! Not this time!"

Officer Kincaid put his arm around the man to comfort him. Officer Kincaid saw no way that the girl on the cliff could be little Claire after all these years. And there was no way it was a ghost either. Could it be some other bald, Catholic School girl here on the same ledge?

"Lower the backboard. We have to get her out of here. She's hurt pretty bad. Looks like she landed pretty hard on an outcropping, so the impact was focused on her right side."

The rescue team carefully lowered the backboard down to their teammate on the ledge. He guided it to where the girl lay and where he would be able to get her onto it.

"Let's get a harness on her first," the rescue worker said.

The rescue team worked to attach the harness, securing her first in the narrow space, so that she would not fall while moving her to the back board. How the heck did another girl get on that ledge? This time with a fence in the way?

An EMT cupped his hand around his mouth like a megaphone. "Would you like me to come down and help?"

"It's pretty narrow down here, so there's not a lot of room," the man called back. "I think if I get a harness around her, you can lift her while I secure her head and neck and get the full board underneath her. She has a head injury for sure, not sure about her neck and back."

The EMT's managed to get the girl on the harness and lift her, and the worker on the ledge secured her to the backboard. They lifted the girl back up the side of the cliff.

"Easy, guys, easy!" The rescue worker called up from below, still strapped into his harness, as the backboard began to sway and turn. "We don't want her to spin."

The workers managed to lift the girl on the backboard to the edge of the cliff. Stepping over to the edge, they hoisted her to safety onto the short space between the fence and the edge. Officer Kincaid glanced at Mr. Hennessey, who watched anxiously, tightening his fists and biting his lip. Lifting the backboard over the fence, they got the girl securely to the ground. She lay there, silent and motionless, secured on the backboard, her baldness mostly obscured by the brace around her head, her face scratched and bruised from the fall.

Officer Kincaid stood between Mr. Hennessey and the girl who was rescued, thinking to hold him back to give the EMT's room to work. Gripped by pity for the old man, he let him go and stepped aside. Mr. Hennessey ran to see what he believed to be his long, lost daughter, somehow resurrected, after all these years. He studied the girl.

"No, no!" The old man, his fists relaxed, as his hands raised now to hold his face. "That's not Claire! No, that's…that's that girl! Oh, God, not her!"

"Mr. Hennessey, do you know who this girl is?" Officer Kincaid's eyes widened.

"Yes, yes! She's that girl, the one who told me I could think of her as a daughter. Years ago. I just couldn't. I told her to leave me alone. I always regretted that. She comes here with her boyfriend now. I see her here all the time. Oh, God, not that one!"

The old man was rambling, but he seemed to know the girl. Officer Kincaid needed to get more information from him, but the man would have to calm down and focus.

"Yes, Mr. Hennessey. Please look at me. Do you know this girl's name?" Officer Kincaid grabbed his upper arms and gave him a light shake. "It's really important."

"Yes, yes, her name?" Mr. Hennessey stammered, "It's something sing-songy? Something like Lala? No, that's not quite it?"

"Lali? Lali Russo? Is that it?" Officer Kincaid squeezed his arms, his eyes wide with surprise and anxiety. If this were Officer Russo's girl, there would be trouble. The kind of trouble no one in a small town like Santa Inéz wanted. The idea that it could be Robert's daughter raised the stakes of the investigation and piled on additional questions. How did she get here? Who shaved her head? The case was no longer just worries about rescuing some unknown girl on a ledge, but now the child of an impulsive police officer, who would likely not wait for the wheels of justice to slowly move forward. If Robert thought someone did this to her, that crazy bastard was liable to do anything! And, he wouldn't want to hear anything about procedures, or warrants or courts.

"Yes, yes! That's it! But what happened to her hair? God, I hope she's not sick! Oh, not that sweet, sweet girl!"

Officer Kincaid took a deep breath and put his radio to his mouth again and pressed the call button. "Dispatch?" He tried to hide the tension in his voice. "This is Three-One-Adam. We have a possible ID on the injured girl on the ledge. We believe it may be Lali Russo, Officer Russo's girl. You better give him a call."

The radio crackled as Robert's voice broke in. "I'm on my way, Denny. No need to call."

18

Officer Russo

OFFICER RUSSO SIGHED as he lowered the radio microphone and hung it on the hook. *Lali, what have you gotten yourself into this time?* Robert pulled into a driveway and turned his squad car around. No need to check that damned clinic now.

Robert had been searching for his daughter since she had not called for a ride. It had gotten late, and he had begun to worry as his shift was coming to an end. He had called her cell and left messages. He had texted. He had gotten no answers. He recalled Officer Kincaid's voice on the radio just before he began his search. "…we're talking about *the* Lost Girl? Claire Hennessey? And, her *father* says he found her?" Officer Kincaid was the perfect guy to handle that one. Calm the old guy down and get him help. Robert had his own lost girl to worry about. It hadn't occurred to him that it could be Lali. Robert signaled for a left turn, the tires squealed as he took it faster than he should have. *I should have known it was you, Lali. I should have taken that call but, I thought, I guess I hoped, I would find you at the unwed mother's home or the abortion clinic. Anywhere but there.*

Robert tensed, the anger within him building. Every stoner west of the Mississippi had been hiking the trail and spotting the ghost of a girl on that cliff since they ran that ridiculous story on Channel 23. The police had been investigating several reports every month. He figured it must have pushed Mr. Hennessey over the edge. Katherine Kelly! Robert engaged his siren so the car in front of him would let him pass. *Really knows how to spin a yarn? Wasn't that what Rosie said? Good for business? Amazing!* Robert rolled his eyes in disgust. *Irresponsible, I say!*

Robert ran over his actions in his mind. He had been back tracking where Lali was supposed to be and had stopped at St. Elizabeth's, but Mrs. Howard reported that Lali had not shown up. He had spent too long with Mrs. Howard. Thinking she would show up. Hoping…

The next place to check was that damn clinic. And then he heard in his mind Denny on the radio, again. "…we believe it may be Lali Russo, Officer Russo's girl…"

How had he not seen it? Wasting time, hoping! Robert gritted his teeth, his anger with himself began to redirect to the true villains. How did she end up on that ledge? A new mission formed in his mind as his anger grew, as his mind drew the only conclusions he knew to draw. *If that punk hurt her, he's dead.* He would not be going to juvenile court. Nor reform school nor juvenile detention. *He's going in the ground. I don't give a crap about his potential for rehabilitation!* His mind so filled with rage, vengeance pushed out all else, including concern for his daughter's well-being. *To protect and serve. I failed her. I failed to protect her.* Without her, who was there to protect and serve? His mission and his purpose now mortally wounded, blinding, avenging rage filled the ranks. His new orders, issued from no commanding officer, demanded decisive action and superseded love and care for the injured, even his own daughter. The red, the blood, his faceless comrade again, his hand in the goo, trying to clear an airway. He shuddered. *Kill them all! Kill them all!* The voice present again, more than a mere memory. Robert pulled the car to the side of the road. *Kill them all!* The sounds of battle, the cries of "Take cover!" The charging ahead. Turn, look, shoot!

"No!" he screamed, his voice filled the small cab of the squad car as he pounded his fist into his thigh. "I have to get it together! They will never understand! They will assume she's just a crazy high school kid! I must be there for her. I can't allow them to make assumptions in this investigation! I have to get it together!"

Robert adjusted the review mirror, so he could look at himself. A tear tracked down his cheek. He had failed to protect her. That seemed clear. Now it would be a matter of justice. "Remember your training, Officer Russo!" he said, aloud, his voice grating and hoarse.

He had to keep control. He was an officer of the law. There was a crime to investigate, and a victim who deserved justice. He had a job to do, to investigate, to pursue justice. She was a victim of a crime, not his daughter.

Officer Russo took a deep breath and shifted into drive, then pulled away from the curb. Making his way on the winding mountain roads, he came up to the entrance of the coastal trail. The Channel 23 news van was parked at the curb, and a redheaded woman with a microphone was stalking his squad car as he pulled to the curb ahead of the van. The woman waived to her cameraman to get a better shooting position, taking the high ground for her ambush as she jogged to keep up with the rolling car and moved to cross in front of it as it came to a stop.

"Well, *All hail the back-bar,* Katherine Kelly, the Spinner of Yarns!" Officer Russo muttered to himself. *Remember your training. We have nothing to say to the press. That's the Chief's job.*

Officer Russo exited the car quickly and turned to go around the back with the redheaded harpy close on his tail. By making his unanticipated move to go around the back of the car, he had blown the ambush shot and he had the car now for cover. But that would not be enough to stop the Spinner of Yarns.

"Officer, Officer." The reporter hurried behind him, holding the microphone like she was passing a baton in a relay race, as her cameraman quickly maneuvered to cut him off as he passed the back of the squad car. "We heard that the victim may be the daughter of a police officer? Lali Russo? Can you verify that?"

They must be monitoring the police frequency.

"No comment," Officer Russo muttered, without turning to face her, and preparing to stiff-arm the cameraman who scurried to take a position in front of him. "Please, sir! You are interfering with a police investigation. Please, get out of my way." Officer Russo held out his hand like a halfback fending off a defensive end on a sweep play. His hand covered the camera's lens coming dangerously close to making contact with it.

The cameraman gave way and re-centered his camera on the redhead, who flipped the hair from her eye as she chased behind him.

"Officer Russo? Is that your daughter that they found on the ledge?"

Officer Russo stopped in his tracks and closed his eyes. The rage built within him despite all his effort to suppress it. *All Hail the Fucking Back Bar! The Spinner of Fucking Yarns knows who I am!* He turned on her like a viper spitting venom but fortunately, the cameraman was still behind him, focusing the camera on the reporter.

"She's somebody's daughter, that's for sure." Officer Russo released an intense smoldering rage and condemnation that seemed to shake the earth like a volcano on the verge of erupting. "She's not a ghost. She's not some toy for your amusement. And she's not your ticket to fame and fortune. She's a person who needs help, and I'm going to help her if you will stop your childish antics and let me through. How did something like you ever ooze from the sludge and acquire the gift of life?"

The cameraman lowered his camera and stopped filming. Katherine Kelly's jaw dropped so that Officer Russo could have counted her perfectly aligned teeth if he had a mind to. She slowly flipped a strand of red hair from over her eye.

Officer Russo took a deep breath, calming himself in the awkward silence. Remember your training, Officer! Protect and serve, even when they were jerks. Be courteous.

"I'm very sorry, Miss. You in no way deserved that. I forgot myself in the heat of the moment. Please accept my apology. Please direct any press inquiries to Chief Greeley. I am not qualified to answer any of your questions."

The cameraman gave way as Officer Russo raced to the entrance of the Coastal Trail, past the police tape that cordoned off the crime scene. The Emergency Medical Services team were just about to lift Lali's gurney into the ambulance. Officer Russo stopped them and examined her. She was not his daughter now, but a crime victim. And he was Officer Russo now, not Robert Russo, Lali's father. *Examine the victim, Officer.* He ran down the details in his mind. A young girl found on a ledge, obvious head injury. Fall? Improbable. There was a fence that would need to be scaled. Suicide? Possible, but victim was known to have strong beliefs against it. Still, she had been acting erratically. By the book, looks like she jumped. *I know she didn't jump, but that's what they will think. I have to make sure they don't jump to conclusions.* Robert gritted his teeth, clenching his jaw. Remember your training, Officer! Protect and serve! *We failed to protect, now we must obtain justice for the victim!* Officer Russo returned to the possibilities. Staged scene to look like suicide? Probable. The victim had been mixing with some gang members. Possible suspects? Rodrigo Alvarez, member: *La Hermandad. If that punk did anything to her…*Procedure, get back to the investigative procedure. The next step was to get the status from the EMTs…

"What's the status, Pablo?" Officer Russo interrupted the paramedic examining the victim on the gurney.

"She has severe trauma to the back of the head." The paramedic, Pablo Martinez, motioned to the back of his own head. "She must have hit it when she…" Pablo paused for a moment. "Fell."

"Fell?" Officer Russo glared skeptically, sensing the tentativeness in the paramedic's voice as indicative that he may not believe it was a fall.

"Yes, or jumped." The paramedic avoided eye contact.

"Jumped?" Officer Russo's piercing eyes waited to meet Pablo's.

Pablo sighed. "Yes, Robert. It looks like she may have jumped. They are examining the scene."

Officer Russo squatted down, to get his eyes level with the victim's head and examined the wound, or at least what was not obscured by the brace on her head and neck.

"Yes, that must have been some impact. Looks like her skull may be fractured in the back on the left side. But it also looks like there are bruises on the front right side of her head. And you have her right leg splinted?"

"Yes, it looks like she has a skull fracture and her femur is broken," the paramedic explained. "We will x-ray her, of course."

"Odd, though," Officer Russo mused. "I would not expect if she jumped onto a ledge, she would do such damage to the back of her head on the left, and also to have these bruises on the front, mostly on the right? And her right leg broken, but also severe damage to the back left of her skull?"

"Yeah, she must have tumbled a bit, but landed on the back of her head?" The paramedic tried to make sense of the inconsistent evidence.

"Yes, that's possible." Officer Russo conceded the possibility for now. *Just gather the facts, for now, we have to get the victim to the hospital as fast as possible.* He straightened and nodded to the paramedics, who loaded the victim into the ambulance.

"Would you like to ride with her in the ambulance?" Pablo asked.

Officer Russo shook his head. He had to take charge, or at least, influence the investigation. He could not allow them to conclude the obvious. He had to make sure they considered all the evidence and did not jump to conclusions. "No, I'd like to take a look at the scene."

"Of course." The paramedic closed the rear doors of the ambulance enclosing Lali in the back almost, it seemed, like they were rolling a great boulder in front of a rock-cut tomb in some ancient place. *Why should I think of that, now?*

As the ambulance sped off with the siren blaring and lights flashing, Officer Russo clenched his jaw. "No way this was a suicide attempt," he said audibly, under his breath. "No way."

Officer Russo stomped up the path toward the scene of the investigation. Officer Kincaid surveyed the scene and was trying to recreate what had happened. He looked like he was doing some form of new exercise, bending his knees and pushing off, in a simulated jump, then looking at the footprints he left behind. Officer Kincaid sighed and slightly rolled his eyes as Officer Russo approached. *Officer Kincaid will think I'm interfering with his investigation, but there are things he needs to know about the victim.*

"Hello, Officer Kincaid." Officer Russo nodded somberly.

"Hi, Robert. Wish we could meet under better circumstances." Officer Kincaid glanced down at the footprints he had made in doing his strange exercise.

"We're cops. Our jobs are to deal with lousy circumstances. So, what's it look like?" Officer Russo took out a small notepad and pen.

"It looks like she jumped," Officer Kincaid pointed. "See the footprints leading to the edge, and then the deep ones at the edge? That's just how you would expect the heals to dig in if she jumped."

"She didn't jump." Officer Russo spoke as if it were a truth etched in stone and carved by the finger of God. There was no way she jumped. "The scene has been staged to make it appear that way."

Officer Kincaid raised an eyebrow and stroked his chin. "How can you be so sure?"

"She's a Catholic." Officer Russo fought to stifle a fatherly defensiveness building within him. Keep it to the facts. "And not just an ordinary Catholic. She goes to Mass every day. To commit suicide to her would condemn her soul to hell. She would never do that."

Officer Kincaid raised a skeptical eyebrow, a frown forming. "Listen, Robert, I know she's your daughter, but we have to follow the evidence."

Robert clenched his jaw to try to hold back his anger. "Officer Kincaid, the fact that the victim is Catholic and would regard suicide as a sure route to eternal damnation is evidence against a motive for suicide. You have to treat this as an attempted homicide."

Officer Kincaid's eyes widened. "There's no evidence to support that!"

"Officer Kincaid, a young girl is found unconscious on a ledge of a cliff with severe blunt-force trauma to the back of her head. That's evidence!" Officer Russo squinted at his fellow officer.

Officer Kincaid gave in with a sigh. "Okay, Robert, we cannot rule out an attempted homicide, but it sure looks like attempted suicide. Teenagers attempt suicide even when they're Catholic. It happens. And sometimes they even make a lame attempt that leaves them on a ledge where they will be found and not at the bottom of the cliff. Look, it's your daughter, man! You're too close to this one. You have to let us do the investigation. If there is foul play involved, it will eventually come out."

"I just want to make sure we don't jump to any conclusions. She was in with a bad crowd, Denny. She had just broken off a relationship with a known gang member, Rodrigo Alvarez. If that punk had anything to do with this, I'll..."

"You'll what, Robert?" Officer Kincaid cut him off. "You're an officer of the law. You must work within the law. Look, I know you're trying to keep your emotions out of it, but you can't. It's your daughter. You wouldn't be human if you could investigate this with a clear head."

Robert stormed off angrily, knowing that Officer Kincaid was right. But he would not be bound by the law, not when it came to his daughter.

19

Dead Pull Hitter

RODRIGO CLOSED HIS EYES, his mind reeling from the events of that night. He had gotten Lali onto the ledge, and given her a chance, but only a slim one. It was a nasty drop to the ledge, and Ralo had hit her hard. If that old dude found her, maybe she'd be okay.

Rodrigo entered the kitchen of his mother's two-bedroom duplex apartment and buried his head in the refrigerator, nosing around for something to eat, enjoying the feeling of the coolness on his face. *God, I hope she's all right.*

The doorbell rang. Rodrigo lifted his head from the refrigerator. Who would be visiting at this time of night? Rodrigo walked to the door, smoothing his hair, trying to look more presentable for the unexpected visitor. He peered out the peephole. Officer Russo? Have they found her already? Rodrigo's heart pounded. He took a deep breath to calm himself.

Rodrigo opened the door and stepped back as if surprised.

"Good evening, Rodrigo." Officer Russo looked as if he had swallowed a grenade and was trying not to burp. "May I come in? I think we need to talk."

Oh, they found her, for sure. But was she okay?

"Talk, Officer Russo?" Rodrigo played dumb. "I'm not sure what we need to talk about?"

"It's about Lali. May I come in?"

"Sure, sure." Rodrigo motioned for the policeman to come in. "Is Lali okay?"

Officer Russo stepped inside the door and slowly scanned the room.

"You asked if Lali is okay?" The policeman began his interrogation. "Is there any reason why she wouldn't be?"

Rodrigo cocked his head. *He's trying to trap me. It won't work.*

"It's late, Officer Russo, and you're a policeman here at my door, asking about Lali? Is she okay?"

The policeman's eyes narrowed in suspicion. "When was the last time you saw Lali, Rodrigo?"

Rodrigo hesitated. He had not expected this visit so soon and had not prepared a story. He would have to make it up as he went. And be careful not to spill the soup.

"Lali broke up with me." Rodrigo instinctively answered evasively. "That was two days ago."

"That's not what I asked, Rodrigo." Officer Russo squinted at him, then repeated his question. "When was the last time you saw Lali?"

"Two days ago." Rodrigo squared his shoulders and assumed an air confidence. "When she broke up with me."

"So, you did not see her tonight, then?" Officer Russo pried.

"No, of course not!" Rodrigo hoped he had not overacted his part. Keeping his cool was his strength, not feigning emotion. "She broke up with me! Okay? What's this all about?"

Officer Russo's eyes were like x-rays, staring into his soul. *Careful, he's a tough man, and he's not stupid.* He would examine every word, every move.

"Lali's in the hospital, Rodrigo." Officer Russo broke the news, abruptly.

"What? Oh, my God! What happened? Is she alright?" Rodrigo expressed surprise and concern, convincingly. Okay, show no relief. You didn't know. How could you?

Officer Russo hesitated. *His eyes, just let him look.*

"No, Rodrigo, she is not all right." Officer Russo leaned forward. "Somebody tried to bash her skull in."

"Oh, wow." Rodrigo stepped back and widened his eyes, as if surprised. "Who would want to do that?" *That bastard, Ralo. That's who!* But how did this cop know that? *Keep it cool, just keep it cool!* Fresh as lettuce!

Officer Russo smirked. *He thinks I'm lying. I can tell. Just stick with it, though. He can't prove anything...*

"Where were you tonight, Rodrigo?"

"I've been in all night. I haven't felt like doing much since Lali broke up with me."

Officer Russo eyed him up. *I think he's buying it. Just keep cool!*

"Is there anybody who can vouch for your whereabouts tonight?"

"Not really, I've just been hanging out here. My mother works at night."

"What about the neighbors in the apartment next door?" Officer Russo leaned forward. *He's looking for a tell. Just keep cool.*

"That apartment's been vacant for a couple weeks now. Mrs. Jimenez got evicted after her husband left her and she couldn't pay the rent." Rodrigo was relieved to be telling a verifiable truth. The police could check that one out! That was totally true.

The police officer nodded, cocked his head, then narrowed his eyes, skeptically. "So, you've been here all night?"

"Yes, that's right. I sure hope Lali is okay?"

"I do too, Rodrigo." Officer Russo's x-ray eyes seemed to be examining his soul, or trying to, and now they squinted at him again. Rodrigo sensed a depth of hatred, a smoldering lust for vengeance behind the policeman's terrible eyes, eyes that seemed to peer into his guilty soul. Something beyond a desire for justice, though justice would be bad enough, burned like embers waiting to be kindled to flame. There was a murderous intent more terrifying than even Ralo's more casual deadly calculations.

The calm veneer with which the father of the girl he had raped attempted to conceal his rage succeeded about as well as a wet blanket covering a volcano. "If I find out you had anything to do with this, you won't just have to answer to the law; you'll have to answer to me. Do you understand me, Rodrigo?"

Rodrigo blinked several times, then swallowed. "Of course, Officer Russo."

Officer Russo walked to the door. Rodrigo rolled his eyes behind the policeman's back and his body relaxed. Turning around, the policeman asked a final question.

"Oh, one more thing, Rodrigo. Did you ever play baseball?"

Rodrigo's body tensed once again. The police couldn't possibly know that Lali was struck by a baseball bat, could they? His mind raced through the possibilities. The bat was at the cabin. They could not have found it. The wound? They must suspect from the wound. Was there evidence, or was it just a guess? Rodrigo cleared his throat. "Why, yes. I played Little League. I made the all-star team."

"And did you bat left-handed or right-handed?" The policeman leaned forward, too close to him.

Rodrigo, stepped back and hesitated again, keeping his focus on the baseboard. Left-handed or right-handed? What was this about? Then he remembered, Ralo batted left-handed. His eyes opened wider for just an instant.

"Right-handed." He made steely eye contact with the policeman, testing that his answer might be a surprise. "A dead pull hitter. I always envied those lefties. Makes it so much easier to hit the curveball."

The policeman raised his eyebrows. He didn't expect that answer. He's looking for a lefty. How could he suspect that? *He's x-raying me with his eyes again! Just stay cool! Fresh as lettuce! He doesn't know anything.* Except the baseball bat? And, left-handed? Did he have something, or was he guessing?

"Only from a right-handed pitcher." Officer Russo smirked. "Well, I'm sure we will be asking you more questions, Rodrigo. You better hope nobody saw you out tonight."

"Of course not, Officer. I've been here all night." Was it finally over?

Officer Russo turned and walked out the front door the way he had come in. Rodrigo fell to his knees and began to weep.

Oh, God, thank you! Thank you! She's alive and they found her!

20

Smile and Show No Fear

OFFICER RUSSO MARCHED THROUGH THE DOORS of the County General Hospital Emergency Room, his hand never far from his holstered sidearm. His pace and the rigidness of his stride unnerved the staff and patients as they made way to let him pass. *Assess the victim's condition. Determine the source of her injuries, if possible.* Officer Russo's mind focused only on his duty, blocking out his emotional connection to the victim.

A large black man in a white lab coat with a stethoscope dangling at his chest smiled broadly as Officer Russo approached. He didn't appear the least bit intimidated and appeared to be a person in charge.

Officer Russo stepped forward to shake his hand. "Hi, I'm Officer Russo. I understand you were taking care of Eulalia Russo? She was brought in by ambulance?" He paused, the next words stuck in his throat. "We believe she may have been the victim of a crime."

"Hi, Dr. Okolo." The doctor answered with an African accent and took Officer Russo's hand with a confident shake. He glanced down at his clipboard, "Ah, yes, we had a Eulalia Russo come in by ambulance, and I examined her."

The doctor continued his grinning. Officer Russo cocked his head. There was something strange about this doctor. What was with all the smiles? It was like he was greeting people at a cocktail party.

"What is her condition, Doctor?" Officer Russo asked officiously, as if he were completing paperwork for a report.

"Oh," Dr. Okolo raised his eyebrows in surprise, as if it were an unexpected question. "She's just come out of emergency surgery. She was badly injured. We had to operate to stop her internal bleeding and relieve the pressure on her brain. We also were able to set her leg. She's in pretty rough shape, but her vitals look strong."

Victim had survived, for now and had obtained emergency care for her injuries: internal bleeding, head injury, broken leg. Prognosis unknown. "Do you think I could go see her?"

"She is in the recovery room, and we only allow visits from family. You may visit her when she is moved to a regular room." Dr. Okolo put on a big, inappropriate grin. "Oh, unless you obtain a court order."

Robert sighed, his hand brushing against his sidearm. He closed his eyes anticipating the pain of what he had to say. "She's my daughter, Doctor. I am family."

Dr. Okolo's eyes widened and his mouth fell open for a moment, then he grinned broadly again.

"Oh, why then, yes, sure. She's in the recovery room. It's this way." Dr. Okolo motioned toward the recovery room like he was inviting him in for tea. Dr. Okolo and Robert entered the recovery room, and there she was, lying motionless, the ventilator making its gasping then clicking sound as it breathed air into Lali's lungs for her.

"She'll be on the ventilator for a while," Dr. Okolo said more seriously now. "We believe she also has suffered a pulmonary contusion. As you can see, it looks like she landed pretty hard on her right leg, which is broken, and her side, which ruptured her liver. That's what required surgery. That was where the bleeding in her abdomen came from."

"Would you say that her injuries are consistent with a fall from about ten feet or so?"

Dr. Okolo thought for a moment. "Well, broken legs, fractured skulls, pulmonary contusions, these are common in falls. A ruptured liver is not very common, unless the body fell on something pointed, that might focus the impact. I thought that one was a little unusual."

"The EMT report says they found her lying on her right side, with a raised outcropping under her body."

"Yes, that would likely explain it." The doctor grinned again.

"I was interested in the wound to the back of her head?"

"Yes, that is most concerning." Dr. Okolo lost his grin and frowned, then glanced away. "Her skull is fractured, and there was some bleeding into the brain cavity. We were able to relieve the pressure and give her some medication to reduce the brain swelling. But if she survives, there is a chance of significant impairment."

Dr. Okolo lowered his head. Robert tightened his lips for a moment. At least he stopped smiling for now.

"Yes, Doctor," Officer Russo continued his inquiry. "I'm a little curious, though, how she might have come by such a wound?"

Dr. Okolo furrowed his brow. "Well, we were told she suffered a fall?"

"Oh, yes, no doubt, no doubt there was a fall." Officer Russo nodded. "But it looks like most of the other damage from the fall is on her right side. The bruises on her head here," Robert pointed to the bruises on the right side of her head, "her right broken leg, even the internal hemorrhaging, that's on the right side as well, isn't it?"

Dr. Okolo's eyes widened with interest. "Yes, now that you mention it, that does seem a little strange. The impact must have been hard on her right side to rupture her liver." He rubbed his chin curiously, then smiled broadly again. He turned more serious, as Officer Russo cocked his head. *Why would he grin like that?*

Officer Russo tightened his lips, then floated a theory. "Do you think it might be possible that she suffered that blow to the back of the head first, and then was thrown off the cliff, and that's when she got the wounds to the right side of her body? The wound to the back of the head almost looks like it might have been made with a club or a baseball bat."

Dr. Okolo paused for a moment, thinking. "In my country, Nigeria…uh… I have seen many wounds from clubs that are like this, that is true. But I'm not sure it would be much different if she had hit her head in a fall."

"But you think it is possible?"

"I guess it might be possible." Dr. Okolo's brow furrowed in thought, then he grinned broadly again. "We don't dwell too much on how they get injured here. We just patch them up and try to save them."

"Yes, Doctor, I understand that. We, as the police, though, have to give some thought to how it happened. I've seen these kinds of wounds before." Robert took a step back and simulated a left-handed baseball swing as he explained. "When you hit someone from behind with a baseball bat with a left-handed swing, with the left hand on top of the right hand like this, the wound will be on the back, left-hand side, just like this." Officer Russo demonstrated the swing on an imaginary head.

Dr. Okolo tilted his head. "Of course, she may have hit her head on the way down and got spun around. We know for sure she suffered a fall."

Dr. Okolo made eye contact with Robert, smiling broadly again. "I think you should consult a forensic pathologist."

"Yes, maybe that would be best. Thank you, Doctor." Officer Russo concluded his interview.

"Well, perhaps she will come out of it and be able to tell us what happened?" The doctor continued his inappropriate grinning. "We will have to wait and see. The longer she is unconscious, the more likely she will not come out of it. She may have considerable impairments, however, even if she does. Which means that she may not remember. It is really a miracle that she is still alive. If we had gotten her a few minutes later, she might not be."

Robert grinned back at the doctor. "Dr. Okolo, this one has angels watching over her. They will take her when the time comes, but not a minute before."

The doctor resumed his inappropriate cheeriness. "Well, Officer, why don't you leave your number and go home and try to get some rest? I'll have the nurses call you if there is any change in her condition."

"Thank you, Doctor." Officer Russo gave Dr. Okolo a business card with his contact information, then reached out his hand, and Dr. Okolo shook it firmly. Officer Russo turned and headed toward the door, then turned around to catch a glimpse of the doctor, shoulders more slumped now, shaking his head dubiously.

"Uh, doctor, uh, just one more question." Robert noted how the doctor squared his shoulders and smiled broadly again. It almost seemed a conditioned response. "It's kind of personal, so you don't have to answer if you don't want to."

"I have the right to remain silent in this country, I know."

Robert shook his head and chuckled. "We've been talking about a lot of grim things, and you seem to be smiling about them. I'm just curious. Is that common in your culture?"

"Well, Officer, you carry a weapon, do you not?"

Robert nodded, glancing down at his sidearm.

"Where I am from, we have many troubles and much violence. We find it best when talking to someone who is armed to smile and show no fear."

21

Meeting at the Cabin

RALO FLIPPED THE TELEVISION to channel 23 just in time to catch Katherine Kelly's update on the *Lost Girl* story in progress. Katherine flipped her red hair like she always did as she stood outside the emergency room of County General Hospital.

"...Not a ghost, this time, no, not at all, though we've often heard stories of how the ghost of the *Lost Girl* haunts the coastal trail beckoning hikers to join her on the ledge. This time, the girl is very real — and very much alive — at least for now. There were some, including Mr. Hennessey, the original lost girl's father, who thought it might be the long-lost Claire Hennessey, somehow come back and found on the same ledge from whence she disappeared long ago. But we can now confirm the girl's identity as Eulalia Russo, or Lali, as her friends call her. She was taken here to County General Hospital last night and was rushed into emergency surgery. No one knows for sure how she ended up on that ledge with her extensive injuries. The Emergency Room doctor here, Dr. Okolo, says it may be some time before she regains consciousness, if she ever does."

Ralo's eyes widened with interest as he watched the reporting. She was *supposed* to be a ghost. They found her, and she was *alive?* Ralo's fury grew as he continued watching. A large, black man in a white lab coat began talking with the reporter.

"Oh, here is the Emergency Room doctor now. Dr. Okolo, would you please talk with us for a few minutes?"

The doctor smiled broadly and looked directly into the camera. "Yes, well, the patient is entitled to privacy about her condition, but I may be able to say a few things."

"So, how is she? Do you think she will recover?"

"We list her status as stable but guarded. Her vital signs are strong for now. It is hard to say if she will recover. Right now, she is in a coma. She may not survive, or she may not come out of the coma. Those are the bad things that can happen. Or she may wake up and be fine. We don't know."

Ralo's jaw dropped. *Stable but guarded?* Dead! It didn't get any more stable than dead. She was supposed to be dead. *Wake up and be fine?*

"We heard that the police are investigating the case as a possible suicide attempt. Would you say that is consistent with her injuries?"

The doctor smiled like an idiot again, as Katherine Kelly flipped her hair, and glared at the doctor as if he had stepped on her foot.

"Well, we don't hypothesize about the cause so much in the emergency room. Her injuries are consistent with a fall. She has broken bones, including a fractured skull and internal hemorrhaging. If she had gotten here just a few minutes later, she may not have made it. She still may not. We must wait and see."

"Thank you, Doctor."

The doctor smiled another toothy grin and walked on.

Katherine Kelly continued. "So again, the police have officially released the name of the girl; it's Eulalia Russo, daughter of Robert Russo, a member of the Santa Inés police force. We have her picture from the St. Mary's High

School yearbook, though she apparently shaved her head since this photo was taken…"

Ralo snapped the power button to off as Lali's yearbook picture came on the screen. She was dressed in the same Catholic school uniform, with her beaming, innocent smile and her long dark hair pulled forward over her shoulders.

"Faucking' Mister Smart-guy!" Ralo shouted at the now blank television screen.

There should be no news. Not so soon. Or maybe just a report of a girl missing, not a body found. After all, they had just dumped her last night. A day or two, at least, so she was sure to be dead and rotting, that was what he expected. Maybe animals eating her? That was dead!

"The body must be found, Ralo?" He mimicked Rodrigo's admonition from the previous night. "That *cabrón,*"

Ralo ran the events of the previous night through his head. How was it that someone falling from that height onto the rocks, who had already been bashed in the skull with a baseball bat had only *attempted* suicide? *Attempted suicide?* It was supposed to *be* suicide, not *attempted* suicide! Ralo fumed as he recalled the events. She must not have gone all the way down?

Ralo began piecing it all together. "Faucking Rodrigo-Romeo drop her on a ledge! He would no' let me see! If that girl spills the soup, we efaucked!" That *cabrón,* Rodrigo-Romeo pulled a fast one! He tried to save Juliet? After he raped her? Mr. Smart-guy?

"Oh, that's no so esmart, Mister Smart-guy. No esmart, at all!" Ralo vented aloud.

Faucking Romeo pulled a fast one! Surely there was some business to take care of! Ralo shook his head grimly and picked up the phone, one of those old landline phones with the coiled wire leading to the handset. He called Rodrigo.

"Good morning, Rodrigo," Ralo greeted him with a false pleasantness. He paused to listen to Rodrigo's answer. "Jes, I just watched the news report...Jes, that's right, channel twenty-three, with the redheaded beetch...Jes, she esay some interesting things... Jes, look like our girl *try* commit suicide... No, that's no' what we plan! No' what we plan at all! We no plan that she try commit suicide, we plan that she *would* commit suicide. So why is the beetch still alive?"

Ralo's voice became more hoarse as it crescendoed steadily to a shout. He coiled the phone cord around his finger, smirking, as Rodrigo explained that she must have fallen onto the ledge and not all the way to the bottom of the cliff.

"I think we have to talk about this." Ralo rolled his eyes, maintaining the same false pleasantness in his voice. "Jes, I think a little chat at the cabin is in order."

A sinister and knowing smile tightened on his lips through the awkward pause as he awaited Rodrigo's answer.

†╬†

"Look Ralo, she's in a coma." Rodrigo's voice quavered, and he cringed at his lack of control as he spoke into the phone. "She can't hurt us..."

"Oh, no, she can no' hurt us." Ralo's voice cut him off and dripped with false sincerity from the handset speaker. "No, everything is all good, *mi hermano*. Nothing to worry about."

Ralo's voice became more demanding and ominous. "We can talk all about it, at the cabin."

"Sure, sure. I'll meet you at the cabin. We can talk there."

Rodrigo pushed the button and put the phone handset back on its base. He had not attempted to explain to his mother the advantages of a wired handset, though Ralo had urged him to. His mother was not someone who was overly concerned that her conversations might be monitored. He walked to his bedroom, to the dresser and opened a drawer. He reached into the drawer and took out his newly acquired pistol. He had not even considered trying to explain the advantages of having a handgun to his mother. He slid a loaded magazine into his handgun, and chambered a round. *I was hoping I would not need this so soon!*

Rodrigo pulled into the driveway of the cabin. He glanced at Ralo's car, the tan Chrysler, with its seemingly permanent coat of cabin driveway dirt clinging to it parked next to the house and shuddered. He gasped in a deep breath, trying to calm his racing heart. He reached into his jacket pocket. He ran his trembling fingers along the cool, hard metal of the gun. They stopped their shaking and his heart slowed. The safety, he flipped it off and kept his finger safely next to the trigger, but not on it. One more deep breath, a glance at himself in the vanity mirror, then he closed his eyes for a moment. It was time to face the unavoidable. Remember Juanito? Fear, that was what got him killed. If you turned and ran, you got shot in the back. *You have the gun, if it comes to that. If you're going down, go down shooting.* He opened his eyes, gritted his teeth, and pulled himself out of the car. The steps of the cabin creaked as he slowly ascended. He knocked, then opened the door.

Rodrigo entered the shack. Ralo was taking left-handed practice swings with his baseball bat.

"Still batting lefty, Ralo?" Rodrigo's finger traced along the trigger of his pistol, hidden in his jacket pocket.

"I too old to switch, now." Ralo took another swing. "Like I told you, me brother taught me to swing layfee when I was a kid. Say it would be easier to hit the curveball. But I could never hit for much power layfee."

Ralo took another swing. "Obviously, no enough power, or else that beetch would be dead!"

"She must have fallen onto a ledge, which would have been okay if that old fart hadn't found her. How was I supposed to know he would find her so soon? Christ, the doctor said in the news report that if they'd just gotten to her a few minutes later, she would be dead!"

"My friend, these things ju have to know." Ralo spoke like some murderous mentor, then he took another practice swing. "If ju going to kill somebody, they have to end up dead. That's just how it works."

"But she's in a coma, Ralo. That's just as good. She can't talk."

Ralo shook his head and leaned ominously on the baseball bat. "No, Rodrigo, is no' *just as good*. People come out of comas. And when they do, they talk. Dead people? They no talk. That's the difference."

Ralo picked up the bat again and swung it lightly, from side to side, eying Rodrigo. Ralo glanced toward his jacket pocket where Rodrigo's finger rested on the cool metal of the pistol alongside the trigger. *Does he know I'm armed?* Had he guessed? *Should I shoot him right now?*

Ralo tilted his head and narrowed one eye. "Back there, at the cliff. Ju no let me go and look, remember? Why no'? I wonder?"

"The old dude was coming! You saw his flashlight."

"Jes, they say he come there a lot." Ralo nodded and smirked. "Something, maybe, somebody should have known. Me? I know nothing about cliffs and walks, and old dudes and lost girls. Ju? I wonder. Ju say this was the place to take her."

"You think I wanted to save her? I raped her, for God's sake!"

"For God's sake, *mi amigo?* Maybe? For my sake? No' so sure?"

Psychology, Rodrigo! He respects courage, be courageous! But put your finger on the trigger in case it comes to that! "Ralo, if you think I crossed you to save that bitch, just go on and shoot me and bury me out back. I didn't know that dude would find her, and when I dumped her over the side, I thought she hit bottom."

Ralo paused a moment, sizing up Rodrigo. "I don't know, *mi amigo?* I no can decide. Kill you, no kill you? Here's what I do." Ralo took his revolver out of his pocket and removed three bullets.

"Now, is fifty-fifty. So, to kill or no to kill? Let's see." Ralo spun the cylinder then locked it in place. He pulled the hammer back casually cocking the revolver. Rodrigo focused intently on the revolver pointed without aim in his direction. The cylinder seemed to move in slow motion as it advanced and locked into place, aligning the next chamber with the firing pin of the revolver. Ralo coolly pointed the barrel at Rodrigo's head. Rodrigo fingered the trigger of the gun in his pocket for a moment as he stared into the barrel of Ralo's revolver. *Should I pull it? Is this it?*

Rodrigo lowered his head, and chuckled. Then, he lifted his head and smiled, as he looked Ralo directly in the eyes. He took his hands out of his pockets, leaving his loaded gun inside and spread his arms wide.

"Do it, Ralo! Go ahead! Pull the trigger!"

Ralo shrugged, pointed the gun carefully at Rodrigo's face and pulled the trigger.

Click.

Rodrigo took a deep breath and exhaled. Ralo laughed.

"Okay, *mi amigo*, ju get to go home today." Ralo's grin showed off all the prominent gaps in his teeth. "I so happy. I no want to see jour big brain esplatter against the wall. What a mess! Can ju imagine? But just remember, there is a nice place for ju out back if that beetch wake up and finger us."

"I know, Ralo, there's plenty of room back there; I'm not so big."

Ralo laughed. "No Mister Smart guy, ju no so big. But ju balls? They big, *mi hermano,* They really big. But I sure, we make them fit."

Rodrigo closed his eyes a moment and nodded. "I may have big balls, Ralo, but they're not so big that I think I can cross you. Who could walk with balls so big!"

Ralo chuckled. "Mister Smart guy always remember that, and I no have to point me gun at ju, again!"

Rodrigo put his hand back in his jacket pocket, putting his finger on the safety, but decided to leave it off. "I really think we're okay, Ralo. The news report said you fractured her skull, for Christ's sake. She probably won't remember, even if she does come out of it."

A sinister and self-satisfied smirk crossed Ralo's lips, creasing the skin around his eyes. The serpent-like scar on his cheek seemed prepared to strike. "Jes, even layfy, I bust that bitch's skull!" Ralo took another hard practice swing with the bat. Then, placing the bat before him, with both hands gripping the knob, he leaned forward on the bat. "But probably is no' enough, me friend," he said. "There is too much at stake. If that beetch wakes up and tells people what happen, I am efaucked. And if I am efaucked, ju dead!"

Rodrigo nodded. "If you don't kill me, her crazy cop father will. I'm dead either way if she wakes up and talks. I'll keep an eye on her. If it looks like she's coming to, I'll finish the job," Rodrigo volunteered, moving his finger onto the trigger of his pistol hidden in the pocket of his jacket. *I could probably kill him right now.* No way he was expecting it. Rodrigo bit his lip. *But you're not a killer,* the voice that was not quite his own rang in his head. He took his finger off the trigger.

Ralo gave him another gap-toothed grin. "Just remember, Rodrigo, there is no prison for ju if this goes wrong. Ju will most certainly be dead before ju can go to trial or make a deal."

"Yes, I know." Rodrigo nodded. "You don't have to remind me."

Ralo took another big swing with the bat.

"Oh, and Ralo," Rodrigo said coolly, as if giving a tip on how to improve his batting average, "if anyone asks, tell them you bat right-handed."

Ralo squinted and cocked his head to one side. "Why is that'?"

"Because Lali's father, the cop, he's asking about left-handed batters. I think he suspects something."

"Oh, and what else is Mister Daddy-cop asking about?" Ralo leaned forward on the bat again.

"Just asking what I was doing that night and whether I had seen Lali. I told him I was at home alone. But, come to think of it, you better ditch that old piece-of-shit car. If they search it, they will find evidence."

"How would they know to search it? Ju no tell them ju were with me, did ju?" Ralo pulled the bat back and laid it on his shoulder, as if he were in the on-deck circle. "They better no' come looking for me!"

"No. I told him I was alone, but if anyone retraces her steps, you know, puts you and her together at the clinic, in that car or whatever. She's a cop's daughter. They are going to investigate. And if they find that old piece of crap, they will find evidence of Lali in the trunk, hair, skin cells, blood, fibers from her clothes. You know, evidence."

"Ju better hope they no find anything, *mi amigo,*" Ralo chuckled. "Because ju no have so many friends, me friend. No one will come looking for ju if ju disappear."

Rodrigo gripped the gun in his pocket, his finger on the trigger and readied himself to pull it out, the cool metal of the gun having warmed in his hand. "Yes, Ralo, neither of us have many friends."

Ralo laughed. "Jes, I guess all we have is each other, *mi hermano.* But no count on any friendship if that girl comes to."

"Yes, you've made that clear." Rodrigo loosened his grip on the pistol. *He thinks I've got balls of steel! I wonder if he'll figure out that with that revolver, I could see the three loaded rounds in the cylinder? It's a lot easier to be brave when you know the gun isn't going to go off.* Then he changed the subject. "So, how's Kim doing, anyway?"

Ralo rolled his eyes, letting slip a sinister chuckle. "Well, she no' pregnant no more. She be fine now."

22

Aborting Ralo

KIM PACKED HER THINGS QUICKLY. Only one suitcase would hold most of her possessions. Where would she end up? It didn't matter. She couldn't think that far ahead. But she would get away. She would take Ralo's car. She would have the money and the drugs. She could sell the drugs. She could find a place. Far away. But first, she just had to do what needed to be done.

Closing the suitcase, Kim lugged it down the stairs and left it in the living room. She glanced at the mat and the gun cleaning kit on the kitchen table. She couldn't do anything about his gun. He always carried it with him. She had hidden the machete upstairs. She took a deep breath, then walked to the stove and stirred the chili. Ralo would be home soon. He always loved her chili. After he ate, she would leave. It would be that simple. She would just leave, and he would not stop her. Unless he shot her, first. That was always a possibility. At least he would not be able to chop her up with the machete or bash her head in with the baseball bat he had left at the cabin. What about Lali and the unwed mothers' home she had shown her? Could it really have been different? Could she have raised her child there? Ralo would not have let her. She gave the chili another stir. That doctor? She rolled her eyes. *Do you think Ralo would make a good father?* What a stupid question. She wasn't even sure if Ralo *was* the father. She added more cayenne pepper to the chili and stirred it some more. But what had the doctor said? Maybe she could get away from Ralo and find a nice guy? Maybe she could get her life together, have another one? But first, she had to get away.

Kim stirred the pot again, looking into the steam from the chili, like the mist of a dream. Or, perhaps, the fumes from a witch's cauldron. She heard Ralo's car pull into the driveway and peeked out the kitchen window. Why had he gotten a new car? *No matter, as long as I can get the keys...*

She walked back to the stove and stirred the chili.

✝✝✝

Ralo pulled into the driveway and got out of the green Ford sedan that he had just purchased, very clean, no road dirt, no DNA evidence, nothing that would tie him to the cabin or the cop's daughter. He came through the back door, entering directly into the kitchen where Kim stood at the stove, stirring something. Ralo inhaled the scent of the chili she liked to make for him. Maybe, all was well with Kim, after all.

"Ay, that smells great, baby." Ralo inhaled a big whiff of the chili. "Mmmm! Ju know, ju make the best chili, even if ju are a gringo."

Cheer her up. She'd been moody and distant since the abortion. Kim had always been easy to push around and compliant but this time, had he pushed her too far? Had he broken her? Would she heal in time? Not that it mattered much. He could easily just dump her, command her to leave and not come back. Oh, she might resist for a while, but it would not be hard to get rid of her if she was just going to sulk around and be useless. Or, worse, if she would start defying him and causing him trouble.

Kim served Ralo a bowl of chili without saying a word. Her hand trembled as she placed the bowl in front of him. He tilted his head and smiled. He liked keeping her on edge, but she had been especially skittish since the abortion. Maybe a little reassurance would help get her back to where they could get their relationship back to normal. It made no sense to whip a dog that was already cowering, and it just was no fun.

Ralo took a fork full of chili and raised it to his mouth and blew on it to cool it down. Her eyes followed the fork to his mouth, as if she were desperate to know if the chili pleased him. Her characteristic nervous smile creased her lips, the one she always wore when she was unsure whether she would gain his approval. Or was it a little different this time? A little more anxious, a little more nervous. Well, she had been through a lot, hopefully, she was not completely broken.

Ralo opened his mouth and in went the chili. A chew, a smile, he opened his mouth and breathed heavily to cool down the spice. He pounded his fist on the table as he swallowed. "Now, that's what I talking about!"

"I'm glad you like it." Kim's face relaxed into that relieved smile. The one she managed when she gained his approval. Or was it something other than relief? Was it almost sly?

"Baby, ju the best!" Ralo tried his best to build her up, reassure her. She'd been through a lot. He had had to physically drag her out of the car, toward the clinic, after all. "I really sorry we have this little disagreement." Ralo ate another large forkful of the chili.

"Little disagreement?" Kim cocked her head as if confused.

Another forkful of chili.

"Ju know, about the baby, and all." Some sauce from the chili trickled out of the corner of his mouth and he wiped it with a paper napkin. He mumbled his words with his mouth full. "Is just no' a great time, Kim. I just no' ready to be a father."

More chili.

"Maybe when things get a little more settled." He had begun to sweat from the spice and wiped his brow with the paper napkin.

Another bite.

"Ralo, this wasn't some little disagreement." Her sly smile gone, a smoldering anger took its place.

Maybe, he would need to beat her back down, soon? If the dog should get its growl back, he would not have to keep trying to be nice.

"You forced me to have an abortion!"

Another big forkful of chili.

"Jes, but ju know it was the right thing." His mouth full of chili, he muffled his words. "What kind a father would I make?" Ralo breathed out, heavily, "Ay! This is some hot chili!" Ralo winced in pain, his abdomen suddenly cramping. "Maybe is a little too espicy, this time, Kim." He gasped for a breath.

Ralo cringed in more pain. He doubled over.

"Ralo, you made me kill my baby, our baby. I can never forgive you for that."

Her voice was calm. No fear. No anxiety. She sounded like a different person. Like a judge passing a sentence in a secure courtroom. He had seen the smoldering anger in her eyes, but there was none of it in her voice. She was totally in control. How unlike Kim? How unacceptable!

"Kim!" Ralo forced himself to stand and stepped toward her. She stepped back, the fear back in her eyes. "Ju better no have…"

Ralo's legs fell out from under him and he crashed to the floor. Poison. He seethed with anger, but he could not stand, the cramping pain in his abdomen was too much. He wriggled on the floor, trying to get up, but realized he hadn't the strength. He was totally in her power now. He had made her a killer. She would calmly wait for him to die, like a venomous spider who had delivered her bite. All she needed to do was stand clear and watch from a safe distance. It was a woman's way to murder. He never imagined her capable of it, though. Not Kim.

He tried to get up, once more, to strike back, but crumpled back to the floor. She seemed to drift from side to side, as his vision became unsteady. He thought of all the men he had killed. Bullets and baseball bats. Bloody messes. Why had he never thought to use poison?

"And so now, I'm aborting you, Ralo." Her words were cold and calm, like a doctor's tool in a sterile procedure room. "Just like your mother tried to do all those years ago."

Ralo wretched and pulled his knees to his chest. Mixed in with his pain, he found a little pride. He had made her a killer. And, not just that little nothing in her womb. Not some hapless cabrón. She was killing a killer. A dangerous man. A man she dared not raise a hand to.

"And that poor little girl tried to help me, and you threatened her!"

Now, some anger rang in her voice. No longer a cool sentencing. Now, he could hear the killer in her. He could see the fire he had started.

"I only agreed to have the abortion to save her from you."

Ralo chuckled but the pain cut him off and he gasped for a breath. He looked up at her swirling image, with vindictiveness, blinking to try to focus better. "Well, it no work," he stammered, gasping for another breath, between waves of pain.

"What didn't work?" Kim's voice echoed cold apathy, once more.

"Ju no esave that girl." Ralo gasped for another breath. Perhaps his last? "I rape and kill...that little beetch... for meddling... in me beesness." Writhing in pain on the floor, unable to protect himself, he braced as best he could, as Kim stepped toward him and kicked him in the face. He spit out one of his front teeth. The gap would be more prominent now. No doubt, he had made her a killer. A kick to the face? That was personal. She had killed him, a dangerous man. That took courage. Another wave of pain and cramping from his abdomen made him forget the pain in his mouth and teeth.

He found a strange respect for her. Not much more time. But he at least had taken some of her delight. Spoiled her motive. She had saved no one. Protected no one. She had murdered and only served herself. That made it darker. Less satisfying. Colder. No solace that she had saved an innocent by her sin. *She's a killer, like me.*

"So, I was too late to save little Lali? Well, at least I'm ridding the world of you!"

She stepped over him to the living room. Her steps then back to the kitchen. He heard the keys jangle. But he was not dead yet? Had he taken from her so much delight that she would not wait for the moment to see him die? Ralo chuckled and writhed in pain, another searing wave brought on by his laugh. Perhaps it would be his last laugh? *Maybe, she no' so good a killer after all.*

†Ħ†

Kim grabbed her packed bag from the living room. She picked up the car keys off the kitchen table had left them and jangled them, finding the ignition key. On the way to where Ralo the door, she calmly stepped over Ralo's crumpled body, doubled over on the floor, still writhing in pain. Just a matter of time, and he would be dead. No need to wait for it. Strange? She had imagined enjoying watching him take his last breath, his soul leaving his body bound for hell, if there was such a place. But she sickened at the sight of him. And Lali. That poor girl. Had he really raped and killed her? Probably. A bad taste formed in her mouth, like rancid flesh. But at least she was rid of him, at last.

Kim opened the door, lifted her head and saw the sunlight as if for the first time. She hesitated and closed her eyes. The free, fresh air filled her lungs. The great burden lifted from her shoulders. What awaited her? She did not know. But she was free of him. Free, at last.

Did she hear the shot or feel the pain first? She crumpled to the floor, her legs now useless, as the bullet had severed her spinal cord and now lodged in her liver causing the hemorrhage that would ultimately kill her. She flopped for several minutes on the floor bleeding. Her last thought was incomplete, *what if I had…?*

No skilled physician with a curette at the ready to be found to do the job, Ralo died with his revolver in his hand, the poisoned chili still burning on his tongue. The abortive procedure judged ultimately to be a success, though the abortionist had not survived.

23

Officer Kincaid Investigates

OFFICER KINCAID STOOD BEFORE THE STAIRS and read the sign's faded letters, *Dr. Singer's Family Planning Clinic*. He lowered his head and stared at the steps that had settled unevenly. Just a touch of his hand to the cool, metallic railing, and it all came back to him, that awful day many years ago. A deep breath, then the pain in his long-ago injured knee reminded him how, if he had not been injured, he might never have had to come to a place like this. What might have happened to that child and her mother? She would be seventeen now! The mother had told him it would have been a girl, thinking that would make it easier for him. *I would not have forced her to! I would have supported her!* She wanted to do this. And then a voice, not quite his own. *But you paid for it.* The former linebacker sighed, a tear forming in his eye. She had told him that he would never be able to support her and the baby with his injury. He wouldn't be able to walk for months, never mind work to support a family. She told him just three hundred bucks and it would all be over. She wasn't old enough to be a mother. She wanted it taken care of. *I took her to that awful place. I paid the three hundred bucks.* Seventeen. She'd be seventeen.

Officer Kincaid wiped the tear from his eye. He had told Robert he would follow the evidence, and the evidence led here. The last place Lali said she was going before they found her on that ledge was the last place in Santa Inés that he ever wanted to be. *Jesus, Robert! Why'd you let your girl come here?*

Officer Kincaid straightened his shoulders, marched deliberately up the steps and opened the door to the clinic. He stepped into the waiting room in his policeman's uniform, the shining badge, the gun holstered on his hip and his broad-shouldered imposing presence, aching, though, from his freshly awakened emotional turmoil. The receptionist looked up over her paperwork and sat up straight. Her reading glasses fell off her nose and dangled on their chain. Officer Kincaid, his teeth gritted, approached the receptionist's window.

"May I help you?" The receptionist cleared her throat.

"I'm Officer Kincaid of the Santa Inés police department. We're investigating an incident with a girl named Lali Russo. She often comes here and prays in front of the clinic."

"Oh, uh, yes," The receptionist stammered. "Uh, I read about her in the paper. Is she going to be okay?"

"Well, we don't really know yet…uh…Miss…uh?"

"Greene. Mrs. Greene, that is."

"Yes, Mrs. Greene." Officer Kincaid wrote the name down on a pad. "She was hurt pretty bad and is in a coma as of now."

"That's really too bad." Mrs. Greene looked away and closed her eyes for moment.

"Did you know her, Mrs. Greene?" Officer Kincaid readied his pen to record her response.

"Well, not really." Mrs. Greene shrugged, and blinked her eyes. "I used to see her outside praying, though, if that's what you mean."

"Uh, huh." Officer Kincaid raised his eyes from writing on his pad. "And did you ever talk with her?"

"Well, just that one time when she came in. But it wasn't much of a conversation. I asked if she was here for services and, if she wasn't, I told her she had to leave. But that was the day before yesterday. I don't think she was here yesterday, or at least I didn't see her."

"Oh, so she came in here once? And did she request any services?"

"Well, no," Mrs. Greene said with a chuckle. "I don't think that girl would ever need anything that we offer here." She scrunched her face, as if she had said something she had not meant to say.

"Interesting." Officer Kincaid wrote down his observations on the pad. "So, why did she come in then?"

Mrs. Greene quickly glanced right and left, as if trying to make sure there was no one else to hear. She spoke softly. "Uh…she…uh…was suggesting that a man was trying to force his girlfriend to have an abortion."

Officer Kincaid raised his eyebrows. He had not gotten this part of the story from Robert, only that Lali's boyfriend was in that gang, *La Hermandad*. Evidently, there had been some kind of altercation at the abortion clinic. "And was that true?"

"Oh, well, you know, uh, some men, you know, are more convinced that abortion is the right decision than their partner is."

With his chin lowered, Officer Kincaid raised his eyes from writing on his pad. "So, would you say that this gentleman was not very happy with Lali?"

"Yes." Mrs. Greene's head bobbed emphatically. "I would say most definitely he was not very happy with Lali, or anyone else who might interfere with him getting what he wanted. But I wouldn't call him a gentleman."

Officer Kincaid nodded. Mrs. Greene's expression became quizzical, as if an idea had just occurred to her.

"Huh!" Mrs. Greene tilted her head, her short hair long enough that a strand flopped close to her eye. She brushed it back. "Do you think this guy did something to that girl? The newspaper said it was a suicide attempt."

"We have to investigate all the possibilities. So, we're trying to retrace Lali's steps to see how she came to be on that ledge."

"Well, that guy was quite capable of hurting someone, but I figured it was more likely to be his girlfriend."

"Okay, Mrs. Greene, do you know who this guy is? I think we need to talk with him."

"Why, no." Mrs. Greene glanced down at a file on her desk. "He paid in cash. But we have the girl's name, if that will help, and her address and phone number, but I can't share her information without a warrant. There are privacy laws, you know."

A man in a white lab coat popped his head into the waiting room.

"Uh, Officer, so good to see you!" The man extended his hand to Officer Kincaid. "Dr. Emmanuel Singer."

Officer Kincaid hesitated before extending his hand to the doctor. "Officer Dennis Kincaid, Santa Inés Police. Mrs. Greene here just advised me that I would need a warrant to obtain some information about one of your patients. We're investigating the Lali Russo case."

"Oh, yes, what a tragedy!" Dr. Singer raised his eyebrows, then leaned on the receptionist's desk. "Well, Alice, I think in this case we can make an exception. We want to be as helpful as possible to our friends on the police force."

"Uh, there's a law about…"

"Uh-uh, Mrs. Greene. I think we can make an exception in this case. I think these are special circumstances."

Mrs. Greene glared at Dr. Singer. "Well, okay, Doctor." She handed him the file with a sharp flip of her wrist. "Here's the patient's file, if you would like to share anything, just I think you should know…"

"Uh-uh, Mrs. Greene, thank you for the file," Dr. Singer cut her off. "Now, let me see. Oh, yes, here's the name, Kim Whiting, yes, and the address, 321 East Maple Street. Is there anything else, Officer Kincaid?"

"Why, thank you, Dr. Singer. You've been very helpful." Officer Kincaid wrote the name and address on his small notepad and hurried out the way he came, thankful that he wouldn't have to come back with a warrant.

†††

Mrs. Greene glared at Dr. Singer after the policeman had left. "You know that's a HIPAA violation to give that information out! You know better than that!"

"Yes, I am well aware. But we don't want the police subpoenaing that file. It would be worse for us than a HIPAA violation that will likely go unreported." Dr. Singer's face was fraught with anxiety.

"Why is that?" Mrs. Greene eyed the doctor suspiciously. What was he so worried about? She crinkled her face in a most unflattering way.

"There's media all over this story, so we don't want it to get out."

"What are you talking about? We didn't do anything wrong. I make sure we follow all the rules. You know that!"

"Take a closer look at the file, Mrs. Greene. In particular, the authorization form."

Dr. Singer handed the file to Mrs. Greene.

"Don't see it, yet? Look at the signature." Dr. Singer rolled his eyes.

Mrs. Greene gasped.

"Yes, she signed it *Ralo Rodriguez*." Dr. Singer took a deep breath. "Wasn't that the boyfriend's name?"

"Well, you did say she kept telling you she really didn't want to."

"Let's just hope the police don't start digging into her file. It won't look good for us to have the boyfriend's signature on the consent form, even if the girl wrote it. We'll deal with HIPAA if anyone reports us, but it isn't likely."

✟

Officer Kincaid glanced at his notepad with Kim's address, 321 East Maple Street. He started his squad car. The radio crackled.

"Three-One-Adam, proceed to 321 East Maple Street. We have a report of a shot being fired."

Officer Kincaid's eyes widened as he checked the address he had written down. "Damn." Then he spoke into the radio. "Three-One-Adam, responding, I'm on it!"

Officer Kincaid arrived on the scene at Kim and Ralo's place and found a female he presumed to be Kim dead in a puddle of blood in the doorway, a suitcase filled with money, drugs, clothes and a few personal items still in her hand. And a man he presumed to be Ralo dead on the floor, traces of foam and regurgitated food around his mouth, a revolver still in his hand.

There was little mystery about what had happened. Not much detective work to be done to piece it together. The scene certainly validated a lot of suspicions of possible foul play in the Lali Russo case, but all they really had were suspicions. Later, a forensic search of the premises found no physical evidence that Lali had ever been there. No fingerprints, no DNA, no physical evidence whatsoever. There were no computers nor cellphones with electronic records that might give a clue. There was an old landline telephone and checking the phone records, calls made to Rodrigo Alvarez the day before but nothing more. The pot of chili on the stove as well as the half-eaten bowl on the table tested positive for six different poisons and a lethal dose of heroin. Apparently, Kim was taking no chances. They did a thorough search of Ralo's car, the green Ford sedan parked in the driveway but found no forensic evidence, the car having been fully detailed before Ralo had bought it. There were some records at the Department of Motor Vehicles suggesting that Ralo owned a tan Chrysler sedan, but it was never found. Whatever else Officer Kincaid had hoped he would learn about the events leading to Lali's discovery on that ledge died in that small house, lost forever, an unintended victim of the remorseless effects of poison and hot lead.

24

The Annunciation

SIX WEEKS HAD PASSED since the *incident,* as Rodrigo referred to it in his mind. Since Ralo had died, his worries were less. Though prison still loomed as a possibility, at least he did not expect to die before having the pleasure of going there. Of course, the police had interrogated him about Ralo and Kim, but he had kept his cool and not given them anything incriminating. Sure, he had told them that he knew Ralo and Kim, but all he had to say was that Kim was pregnant and Ralo was not happy about it. The police filled in the blanks that Kim was likely resentful and had poisoned Ralo. And Ralo, realizing that he had been poisoned, shot Kim before she could make an escape. Rodrigo was safe. There was nothing to tie him to Kim or Ralo's deaths and nothing that tied him to what happened to Lali. What happened to Lali? *What I did to Lali.* Technically, he had managed to save Lali's life, but lying there like a corpse was not much of a life. Was there another way? Maybe he could have stood up to Ralo? But then he would likely have gotten them both killed.

Rodrigo ran the thing over in his mind. Was there a better solution? He had not thought of one. Maybe if he had gotten that gun sooner? But he wasn't a killer. *I don't think I could have done it.* Now, the cabin was the key. That's where all the evidence was. If they ever found that cabin, he was done. Rodrigo shook his head. A shudder ran through his body. Even if Ralo burned that couch, evidence was all over that cabin.

There was nothing other than the evidence in the cabin connecting Rodrigo with any of it, even though no one could vouch for his whereabouts on the night of the incident. Sure, there were some phone records of Ralo calling Rodrigo at his home. The police asked about what they talked about. "Oh, nothing real important. I don't even really remember," Rodrigo had said. Rodrigo was smart enough to know that, as long as he didn't give anything up, there was no way the police could know anything about his connection to Ralo. Sure, they had found drugs at Ralo's place, mostly in Kim's suitcase, but Rodrigo had flushed his stash down the toilet and since Rodrigo kept the books, the financial records were easily disposed of. Rodrigo had made it out. He had escaped all the snares and traps. He had left the drug trade for good. They really could not connect him with any of that. The police assumed Ralo may have had something to do with Lali's emergence on the ledge, but there was no physical evidence to support the conclusion, and Ralo was dead so there was no one else to look for. Lali's father might suspect him of being involved somehow, but he couldn't prove anything. People would think he was just a father made mad by grief for his daughter, if Officer Russo accused him. Rodrigo could just deny it all.

Rodrigo kept a watchful eye on Lali, visiting most every day, hoping to be there if she woke but no longer having anyone to whom he needed to report the news, no one to force him to finish the job. Lali was the only loose end. If she woke up, she could implicate him, and even though Ralo had forced him to rape her, he figured there were lots of things they could charge him with if she awoke and was able to tell the police what happened. What happened? *What I did! I raped her. I raped her because that cabrón would have killed me if I didn't.* Worse, he would have killed her. *I raped her to save her.* And Lali's voice rang in his head. *Don't sin to protect me!* Rodrigo shook his head. *It was the only way!*

But he desperately wanted her to awaken. So, he kept watch, hoping to catch her if she woke up to see if she could clear him of culpability, though he was willing to go to prison as long as she was okay. *What will my mother say? My God, that's worse than prison! She has such high hopes for me.* He watched as Lali lay on a hospital bed unconscious, no longer on a respirator but with a feeding tube and an IV in place. Lali stirred restlessly, hopefully a good sign. Was she dreaming? Hopefully, she was not dreaming of what he had done that night. Rodrigo breathed a deep sigh and left the hospital.

†††

Lali is in the cabin again. Her dread and fear palpable as she looks at the couch on which she was raped, still stained with her virgin blood. She gasps and turns and looks for it, on the floor, the Miraculous Medal, her Mother. And there she is, a girl even younger than herself, in a blue outer robe belted at the waist over a white gown, no icon of faith, no sacramental, but the Immaculate Conception, herself. A joy unknown to Lali fills her spirit. The girl's eyes widen as if she sees something, something special. A glow comes from behind Lali and lights on the girl's face, her shadow forming on the wall behind her. Lali turns to see what it is and becomes a little girl again, as the fire blazes to a brilliant white and the angel appears. Formless, yet with form, a spirit without a body, as we know bodies, his wings retract behind him as the brilliance subsides.

"Hail, Full of Grace!" The angel's voice like that of a choir singing sotto voce, full and yet quiet, fills little Lali's ears, or seems rather, to pass her ears and to materialize directly in her mind.

Lali turns to gaze on Mary, Full of Grace.

Mary appears troubled, her eyes askance, her mouth falls open.

"Do not be afraid, Mary." The angel's voice fills Lali's mind, as she mouths the words she knows by heart. "For you have found favor with God. Behold, you will conceive in your womb and bear a son, and you shall name him Jesus."

Little Lali turns to face the angel. The angel smiles, his eyes like flames, flickering, seeming to focus everywhere and nowhere at the same time. She feels a presence in her soul, a presence of love, as if she, herself, is filled with grace, truly known, and truly loved by God, the Creator of all things, filled to the point where she might burst, unable to breathe but wanting no breath nor anything else.

"Behold, I am the handmaid of the Lord," Lali feels herself saying, but knows that Mary is the one saying it. "May it be done to me according to your word."

†╫†

Robert parked his squad car at the hospital. Dr. Smith, one of the attending physicians on Lali's floor, had said that they should meet at Lali's room, that there was something they needed to discuss. Robert hoped for the best but did not know what to expect. His daughter had lain there in much the same condition for six weeks. *What could it be, that he could not just tell me on the phone?* Had her condition worsened? Was there some complication? She was in a coma. How much worse could it be? Robert hurried to the elevators and pushed the button, hoping it would be faster than walking the steps as he usually did. He tapped his foot as the numbers descended until the chime rang and the door opened. He checked his watch, not really caring what time it was but maybe knowing the time might get him there faster? It didn't have to make sense. When he arrived at her room, Lali lay on the bed as she had for six weeks. The monitor showed a normal heart rate and oxygenation level, the same IV and feeding tube still there and the cast on her leg. He sighed, and his shoulders relaxed, then his heart rate slackened. She seemed to be okay.

Robert stepped to the bedside and gently took hold of Lali's hand. He heard someone in the hallway and glanced toward the door. Dr. Smith and Nurse Richards, an attractive nurse he had met many times while visiting Lali, stood by the doorway. Dr. Smith flipped through some papers in a file folder, chatting with Nurse Richards, glancing now and again over his half-moon reading glasses at the pretty nurse, with hair more orange than red, who had always expressed care and concern for Lali. The doctor turned another page as if he were making sure of some unexpected result, carefully examining the page. He took a deep breath and entered the room. The doctor shuffled his feet to a stop, then glanced at Robert, then quickly away, back at his papers. He sighed and began speaking while staring at the papers on his clipboard.

"Mr. Russo, uh," Dr. Smith glanced up from his clipboard. "I'm not quite sure how to tell you this, but, uh…" The doctor again scanned the clipboard, then he faced Robert. "Lali's pregnant."

Robert gasped. "W…What?"

"I don't know how we could have missed this," the doctor stammered, "but she is most definitely pregnant."

The wheels of logic had already begun to turn in Robert's mind.

"Pregnant?" He squared his shoulders. "Well, that settles it. There must have been foul play. The only way my daughter is pregnant is if she was raped!"

Shocked and stunned, the doctor and nurse exchanged glances. Nurse Richards brushed her nurse's uniform, stood up straight and faced Robert. "Now, Officer Russo, that is a common reaction among parents when they find that their daughters are pregnant, but it is rarely true."

Robert paused. He closed his eyes for a moment, collecting himself. "Nurse, you do not know my daughter." Robert spoke in a calm deliberate tone. "I'm telling you, the only way she is pregnant is if she was raped, or the Holy Spirit is involved."

"Now, Officer Russo!" Nurse Richard's eyes bulged making her orange hair look more like part of a Halloween costume.

"Nurse Richards, are you Catholic?" Robert raised an eyebrow.

"Why, no." Nurse Richards' head slanted skeptically. "I'm a Presbyterian."

"Well, my daughter is a Catholic. She is as Catholic as they come."

Nurse Richards and Dr. Smith traded glances, again. Clearly, they didn't understand.

Robert continued. "She goes to Mass each morning before school, and after school, she prays the rosary in front of the abortion clinic, then she helps at the unwed mothers' home."

Nurse Richards and Dr. Smith both scowled and avoided eye contact. Clearly, they were not getting the point. Robert could feel his exasperation increasing. His voice grew louder. "If you asked her about sex, she would tell you that she will not have sex before she is married because she loves her husband too much, even though she doesn't know who he is yet."

Nurse Richards and Dr. Smith both stood with dropped jaws, blinking in disbelief, each leaning their heads as if somehow that would help them better understand his slant. Once they stopped blinking, each had an eye half shut. After an awkward pause, Dr. Smith said, "Yes, well, Officer Russo, if a girl with such convictions were to fall to temptation, and not live up to those standards, well, that might be a motive for suicide."

Robert clenched his fists. His voice crescendoed. "Suicide? You're not listening to me! My daughter was as pro-life as they come! There is no way she would even contemplate suicide!"

It was as if he were on some alien planet trying to communicate with creatures who had no basis to understand what he was saying, even if they understood the language perfectly. The nurse's freckles were like dots that defied connecting, as the furrows in her brow pushed them into entirely different planes. "Now, Officer Russo, surely you can see how such a girl might fall victim to despair if she did not live up to such high ideals?"

Robert shook his head in disbelief. Time to try a different tack. He attempted to regain his policeman's demeanor, squaring his shoulders, calming his voice but he was unable to disguise his agitation. "Nurse Richards, do you believe in hell? Eternal damnation?"

Nurse Richards paused.

Maybe the wheels were turning now.

"Well, not for believers," she explained haltingly. "We believe that if you accept Christ as your savior, your salvation is assured."

"But you know what hell is? You have some concept of what I mean when I say, 'eternal damnation'?"

The nurse nodded slowly.

"Well, my daughter believes in hell, eternal damnation. All that sulfurous hellfire and eternal torment. Worse than you can possibly imagine it. She believes it's as real as you or me, or this hospital room, or anything else on this planet. And not just for unbelievers, as you call them. But for those who die in mortal sin. And fornication and suicide would be mortal sins to Lali. If my daughter were guilty of fornication, she would have gone to Confession. She would be tormented that she could not receive Holy Communion until she went to Confession. She would be terrified that she might die before she went to Confession and was granted absolution. She would not have further damned herself by committing suicide."

Nurse Richards and Dr. Smith glanced at each other dubiously. Robert finally gave up, with a sigh, they just would never be able to understand. It was all just too foreign to them. "I can see it is senseless to argue with you.

All I can tell you is that there is no way that my daughter attempted suicide, and the only way she can possibly be pregnant is if she was raped."

Dr. Smith nodded, seeming to placate Robert for the moment. "Well, okay, let's all just agree that she is pregnant, no matter how it happened. That brings us to the next question." Dr. Smith paused a moment. "What to do about the pregnancy. We can end it, of course. We'll just need you to sign the authorization."

Robert's mouth fell open, shocked by the complete disconnect.

"End it?" It was Robert's turn to be incredulous. "Haven't you been listening to me? My daughter would never forgive me if I did anything to end her pregnancy!"

Dr. Smith let his clipboard fall to his side. He started to speak, but he was not quite able to. Nurse Richards' eyes were wide, and mouth gaping; Robert imagined he could see an unfilled cavity in one of Nurse Richards' molars.

"But we don't know…if she can survive…in her condition?" the doctor stammered.

Robert squared his shoulders resolutely.

"If I am to speak for my daughter, there is no way I can consent to an abortion." He folded his arms and stiffened his back.

The doctor and nurse would just never be able to connect the dots. Robert figured it was just not worth further effort to try to make them understand. All they needed to understand was his decision, not the reasoning.

Dr. Smith blinked a few times. "You said you believe she was raped? Would she really want the child if she had been raped?"

"Absolutely." Robert nodded his head, not expecting the doctor would understand. "She would say the child is innocent of any crime of the father. I don't think she would want an abortion even if she knew for sure that she would not survive, especially if she were confident the child would survive."

Dr. Smith and Nurse Richards again traded glances of disbelief.

Dr. Smith looked down at his clipboard, then back up. "Well, Officer Russo, we will do all we can to comply with your wishes, but if that girl's life is in jeopardy and you refuse to terminate this pregnancy, you may well be guilty of child abuse."

Robert waved his hand for emphasis as he spoke. "Doctor, my conscience is clear. I know what my daughter's wishes would be. And there is another child to be considered here."

The doctor faced the nurse, eyebrows raised, then turned back to Robert. "What other child? Do you mean the father?"

Robert threw his head back and laughed. Then he put his head in his hands and rubbed off his face as if he were washing it. He turned to the doctor. "No, of course, I don't mean the son-of-a-bitch who raped her! I'll likely wring that bastard's neck myself when I know for sure. The child in her womb! You have another patient in the equation, Doctor. Lali's baby!"

Dr. Smith and Nurse Richards left the room, both shaking their heads but not saying another word.

Robert walked to the bed and took his girl's hand and kissed it. "Well, my crazy, beautiful girl, this is a fine mess!" He raised her hand and held it against his cheek. "I have faith in you, and I think I know what happened, but I cannot do anything without proof. Once I know for sure what he did to you, I will set things right, regardless of the consequences."

WHEN THE WOOD IS DRY

An Edgy Catholic Thriller

III
Resurrection

JOSEPH CILLO, JR.

III

Resurrection

For if we have been united with him in a death like his, we shall certainly be united with him in a resurrection like his.

Romans 6:5

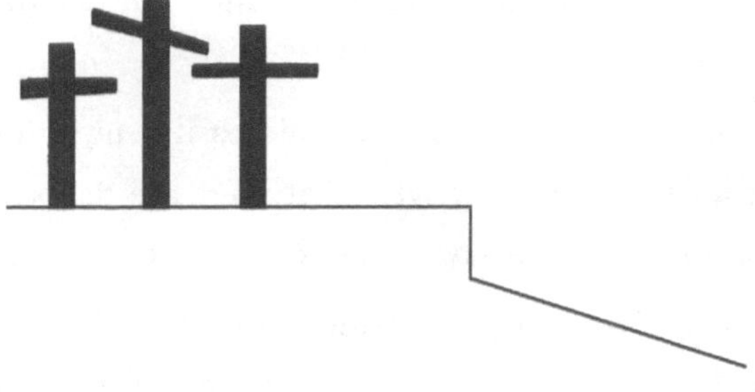

25

No Evidence

O FFICER KINCAID WAS WAITING for Robert at Rodrigo's house and tensed when Robert's squad car pulled up. A Nurse Richards had tipped off the police that there might be trouble with one of their officers, who was convinced his daughter had been raped and had threatened violence against the alleged perpetrator. Threatening a suspect in front of witnesses? Even a hot-head like Robert should know better than that. Officer Kincaid sighed and bowed his head a moment, like a football player in a huddle deciding on the next play. *Now we must protect our own, even when they don't want to be protected.*

Robert stepped out of his squad car and stormed toward the front steps. Officer Kincaid met him at the bottom of the steps, his large athletic frame effectively blocked the way as if he were playing offensive guard rather than his usual position of linebacker. "I can't let you go in, Robert." Officer Kincaid held his hand out, as if directing traffic to stop. "You have to let us handle this."

"Denny, you know what that piece of shit did to my daughter!"

"Yes, Robert, I know, but he says it was consensual. And your daughter is in no condition to dispute the point."

Robert made a move to get past, but Officer Kincaid easily cut him off and blocked his way. "Don't let him get away with that! Get the dates and times! Where and when? Don't let him just say it was consensual!"

"Come on, Robert!" Officer Kincaid put a hand on each of Robert's shoulders and pushed him back. "Do you really want that kind of detail out there when your daughter cannot even respond? He'll just choose a time when they were together and say it happened and you won't be able to refute him. He's not stupid! In fact, he's smart as hell. And he's keeping his cool and you're not. You threatened him in front of witnesses. To *wring his neck?* That's pretty personal, Robert. You're going to have to trust us. If you continue to interfere with our investigation, we will have to arrest you!"

"That piece of shit raped my daughter, beat her, and left her for dead!" Robert pounded his fist into his hand.

"We can't prove it, though. We can't." Officer Kincaid slowly shook his head. "We've got almost no evidence. Nothing that places him at the scene. We know they had sex because she's pregnant and he admitted as much. But we can't prove it was rape. We can't even prove your daughter was beaten and did not just fall off the cliff onto the ledge. We can't prove she didn't jump. And that other guy who you say threatened her…"

"Ralo," Robert sneered.

"Yeah, Ralo. Well, he and his girlfriend are both dead, so they ain't talking either. Forensics was all over their place looking for anything that might tie them to Lali. We called in a specialist from San Francisco. There was absolutely nothing. We know there was a dispute at the abortion clinic the day before she went missing. But we don't have anything suspicious on the day of the incident. There's just not much to go on. All we can do is look for more evidence. If we had a weapon, or a witness, something! But we don't have anything. All we have is a father's suspicions and his beautiful daughter in the hospital in a coma and pregnant, unable to tell us anything."

Officer Kincaid escorted Robert to his car, keeping his large frame between Robert and the Alvarez residence, as he guided his friend to the squad car and opened the door for him. Robert stepped inside, and Officer Kincaid closed the door behind him. Robert rolled down the window.

"I don't know if I can take this Denny." Robert's voice cracked, as he stared forward through the windshield.

"You have to let the process work, Robert." Officer Kincaid laid his hand on Robert's shoulder through the window. Robert turned toward him. "I know it's hard. We'll keep looking. Just go home. And try to stay out of trouble."

Officer Kincaid scuffed his feet as Robert drove off. "If only we had something…"

✝✝✝

"Well, *All Hail the Back-Bar!* What the hell is this?" Robert signaled to turn his squad car into his driveway. A crowd of reporters, complete with video cameras and lights, were camped out in his front yard and up onto the front porch of his house. Robert slowly pulled up his driveway as the media crowd parted to let him drive through. The news media must have gotten word of a seventeen-year-old girl who was pregnant and in a coma. Robert noticed major networks from out-of-state, so the story must have gone national. Robert stepped out of the car and ducked as a microphone with a large 23 nearly hit him in the face. An attractive redheaded woman, smartly dressed and sharp-eyed held the thing in her pretty little hand.

"Is it true that your daughter tried to kill herself because she discovered she was pregnant?"

Robert batted the microphone away from him and glared at her. *Katherine Kelly, Spinner of Yarns.* He remembered his apology to her and regretted it. It was the part of this job that he hated. Thou shalt be courteous to jerks, especially jerks with microphones or pens. He recalled her reports on the *Ghost of the Lost Girl* and the later report of the *Lost Girl Found* with disgust. She had not used the footage at the crime scene of his berating her, likely because her cameraman had not gotten a decent angle on him, and what she caught on audio made her look bad, especially with the video of her open-mouthed gaping. She had, though, deceptively created the story that people had sighted the ghost of the *Lost Girl* inspiring every dopehead in the west to share in that hallucination. And then she invented a scenario where more people than poor Mr. Hennessey had thought it was Claire Hennessey on that ledge. Storytelling, sensationalism, anything to get attention, that was Katherine Kelly's brand of journalism. And it made Robert's stomach churn. *The Lost Girls are men's daughters, you bitch, not just props for your storytelling.* Katherine flipped her hair from over her eye, then turned to blab something into the camera as he pushed past. The other reporters joined in, shoving microphones in his face and barking their questions at him as they walked beside him toward his house.

"Is it true that the doctors recommended an abortion for your daughter and you refused?"

"Isn't there an ethical question about using your daughter as an incubator for a baby?"

"Do you really think it's okay to bring a child into this world when its mother clearly cannot care for it."

Robert ignored all their questions and pushed on toward his home. When Robert got to the top of the steps on his porch, he found his path to the door blocked by more reporters. Robert's seething anger built upon itself, like water filling a bucket, a bucket about to overflow. Remember your training! Taking deep breaths, he managed to calm himself enough to interact with them.

"Please, please!" he cried to be heard over the din, his voice loud but controlled. "Please stay off my porch. This is my home! This is private property!"

The reporters continued to shove their way onto the porch. As he made his way to the front door, a reporter leaned down to peer in the window next to the door, blocking his way. Robert un-holstered his sidearm and extended the business-end toward the reporter, tapping him on the shoulder with the barrel. The crowd of reporters hushed and murmured; all the video cameras zoomed in on the scene. As the reporter turned toward him, Robert grinned as the barrel of the revolver fit itself over the reporter's nose. The reporter slowly stood up, raising his hands. Robert lifted the gun up with him, keeping it in contact with his nose.

"Now, please get off my porch!" Robert motioned with his service revolver toward the stairs of the porch, his voice assertive and directive but not angry.

The reporter tried to make his way around, but the crowd was too thick. Robert turned and faced the hushed and gawking crowd. "Please, give him room!" Robert waved with his gun. "All of you, please get off my porch. I will make a statement once you begin to respect my property."

The crowd of reporters gradually began to exit the front porch. Once they were all off the porch, Robert holstered his gun and addressed them. "I know you are all reporters, and sometimes reporters will do bold things to get a story. I get that. But please respect that this is my life and my property, and I am armed and able to protect what is my own. Please do not approach my home or disrupt my life. I will do my best to tell you what I know."

"Will you answer questions?" A reporter waited with a pen and pad in hand to record an answer.

Robert grimaced. The last thing he wanted was these bastards twisting his words. "I will not answer questions that are shouted out like a mob scene. I don't want to say things off-the-cuff that might be misconstrued. I will make a statement. If you have questions, please submit them in writing. Does that sound fair?"

"But people want an unfiltered reaction." Katherine Kelly thrust her microphone forward while smoothly flipping a lock of her red hair from over her eye.

Spinner of Yarns. Robert peered out over the hushed crowd awaiting his words. They looked like a pack of pathetic hungry dogs, waiting for scraps to be tossed to them. But if they were not fed, they'd become more dangerous. "People will have to make do with thoughtful and considered answers." Robert nodded, then repeated his question and added, "Does that sound fair?"

Even from the considerable distance, Robert could see the roll of Katherine Kelly's green eyes.

The rest of the reporters nodded. *They're afraid I might pull the gun again.*

"Now, let me give you the facts as they occurred. On October 9th at about 8:30 pm, my daughter was discovered on a ledge of a cliff at the scenic overlook on the Coastal Trail. She was badly injured with a fractured skull, internal bleeding from a ruptured liver and a broken leg. My daughter remains in a coma and cannot speak to what happened to her. Today, as most of you know, my daughter was also discovered to be pregnant. As I have discussed with my daughter's doctors, if I am to speak in this matter for my daughter – who cannot speak for herself – I cannot consent to terminate her pregnancy. My daughter is a staunch pro-life advocate and a devout Catholic who would never consent to an abortion. My daughter could not have known she was pregnant at the time of the incident, so any suggestion that she attempted suicide as a result of discovering a pregnancy is false. Also, owing to her strict Catholic beliefs, I do not believe an attempted suicide is a possible explanation for this incident. Nor do I believe that her pregnancy resulted from any consensual activity on my daughter's part, even though her ex-boyfriend asserts as much. My firm belief, which I do not have the evidence at present to prove, is that my daughter was brutally raped, beaten, and left to die."

The reporters gasped and murmured. They didn't see that coming. Likely, they were thinking of a religious nut who would not consent to an abortion for his daughter in a coma. The idea of a rape? Probably never crossed their minds. What would they think of him now? In their minds, he would be crazy for thinking his daughter was raped, and even crazier for denying a rape victim an abortion. They would never understand, but he was doing what his daughter would want. Glancing over the crowd, he noted several head scratches, and even more dropped jaws. *Give it a little time to soak in. It's all I can do.* After a pause, Robert continued. "Because of the extent of her injuries, the doctors focused on saving her life which, thank God, they did, but they did not look for evidence of rape. I cannot explain why the perpetrators of this heinous crime were unsuccessful in completely disposing of my daughter, and how she came to be resting on that ledge to be found there by Mr. Hennessey in the same place where he lost his daughter all those years ago. I believe that it is only by the grace of God that she survives, and it is only with the grace of God that I will be able to make decisions on her behalf."

Robert scanned the crowd. The hungry dogs looked well-fed but puzzled. "Thank you. That is all I have to say right now. I would appreciate it if you would submit any questions you may have in writing."

That should hold them for a while. Robert turned to go into his house.

One intrepid reporter hazarded a question despite his instructions. "But if you think your daughter was raped, why won't you let her have an abortion?"

Robert stopped in his tracks, his body tightened. *I'll bet it's that bitch from Channel 23, the Spinner of Yarns.* Robert's anger grew. The other reporters hushed to silence. Robert closed his eyes. *Just let it go!* He squeezed his eyes tighter and gritted his teeth. *My daughter was raped.* The rage and despair roiled and heated to a rolling boil. *Let my daughter have an abortion? Let My Daughter... LET MY DAUGHTER...*

Robert stood for a moment that seemed an eternity until he felt his hand on his sidearm. He glanced at his hand on the gun and closed his eyes. His heart pounded in the hushed silence. *The red, the blood, The Red, The Blood, THE RED, THE BLOOD!* His mind filled with rage. *KILL THEM ALL! TURN, LOOK, SHOOT!* In his mind, he gunned them down. *All hail the back-bar! If your God is so great…*

Robert took a deep breath. *Remember your training, Officer!* Robert willed his hand off his gun. Turning to face the reporters, tears filled his eyes as he began to speak. "Let my daughter have an abortion? Let my daughter… I wish that I could let my daughter do whatever she wanted to do. I am making this choice for her because I know she would have made this choice herself. I don't have the luxury of letting my daughter do anything!"

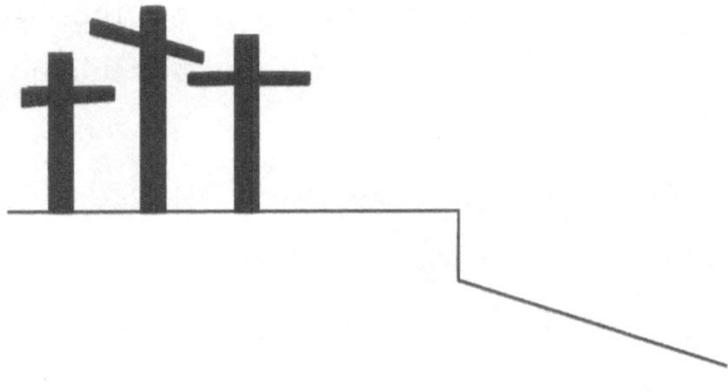

26

Dr. Singer Floats a Theory

"I knew that girl was trouble!" Dr. Singer slapped the newspaper down on Mrs. Greene's desk. "I told you something was up with her when she shaved her head. I've seen these kids before. They get all that talk about the virtue of chastity from the Church and then it's just a matter of time before they're pregnant and doing crazy stuff like shaving their heads and jumping off cliffs."

Mrs. Greene rolled her eyes and chuckled to herself as her employer ranted. *Well, I guess the old doc is on a roll.* Religious girls came to the clinic for services all the time. If the response to an unwanted pregnancy by the faithful was to shave their heads and jump off cliffs, the clinic would be less busy and there'd be more bald, dead girls on the rocks. Mrs. Greene decided to goad the old man along and see where it went. "So, you think it's a religious thing? It's just a matter of time before Catholic girls are pregnant, shaving their heads, and leaping to their deaths because of what the Church teaches them? I thought they taught that suicide is a sin?"

Dr. Singer laughed. "Sure, it's a sin! So is sex for them. So, the shame drives them from one sin to another. If there were no sin, there would be no shame and no suicide."

"And maybe no abortions? Don't you always say that religion is the best thing for our business? You know, the more shame, the more they come to us for services? If girls are killing themselves, that's not so good for business." Mrs. Greene smirked at him.

Dr. Singer paused. "Well, yes, it is good for business, as long as the shame leads them here. That's why we have to encourage them to come here. But this girl didn't come here. She took a leap."

"But if she did it the Church's way, I mean, if she remained chaste, she would not need to come here, and she would not have been tempted to jump, so I'm not sure you can blame the Church? Most girls don't listen to the Church. If they did, we would not be in business."

"Nobody listens to the Church! I mean, it's not natural."

"Well, if nobody listens to them, why would a girl jump off a cliff because of something they said that she chose not to listen to?"

Dr. Singer pinched his nose and closed his eyes. Mrs. Greene imagined puffs of smoke coming out of his ears, as the rusted and little used cogs of his brain struggled to turn, but in the end, the more well-oiled circuits took over. "It's because they shame them."

Mrs. Greene laughed. "I thought the Church recognized that they were all sinners, so why would there be so much shame? Look, Dr. Singer, I think you are a fine doctor providing a needed service, but you really don't understand women very well."

Mrs. Greene had thought a lot about why girls came there for services. Girls who got knocked-up and came to the clinic to fix things probably felt pretty stupid, especially if it happened when they were virgins. But girls these days knew the options. There just weren't many pregnant, Catholic girls with shaved heads jumping off cliffs. There had to be more to it than that.

"Of course, I don't understand women. I'm a man, after all."

Mrs. Greene rolled her eyes. "Look, Doctor, it's not that complicated. Women like to shop. And when they shop, they like to try things on. So, if you're buying something that you expect to keep for the rest of your life, you want to make sure it fits right. They just aren't going to listen much to a Church that says you have to buy the thing without trying it on. Especially not when there are ways to avoid any negative consequences for giving it a go first. Most girls are not trying to do it the Church's way and get caught off-guard. They just figure it's time to start doing what everybody else is doing and get on with the shopping, so they find someone not-too-horrible and they let it happen, kind of a starter-guy, like a starter-home. Not where you plan to end up but okay for now. And they figure out what they like and don't like for when they trade up. If they've figured out birth control first, they don't get pregnant. If they haven't, they come here. They just don't try real hard to live by the Church's rules and then slip up, shave their heads, and go take a header off a cliff. I just think that's really unlikely." Mrs. Greene paused thinking of her own starter-guy. That guy Barry, ugh! *Thank goodness, I figured out birth control first!* Would have been pretty awful to get knocked-up on the first try, but not so bad as to take a leap off a cliff. Mrs. Greene's mind wandered down darker paths, searching for one that might lead to a shear drop to the rocks. But what if a girl were forced? If she didn't just let it happen? A girl who had never done it before? Now that would be really awful!

"So, you don't think much of my theory? What do you think happened?" Dr. Singer crossed his arms and waited for an answer. Mrs. Greene detected a certain snideness in the doctor's tone. She glared at him over her reading glasses. "The father says he thinks she was raped. How do you know she wasn't?"

Dr. Singer stared blankly at her and blinked a couple of times. There was that expression. He thought she was stupid.

"Come on!" Dr. Singer unfolded his arms and opened them as if he were pleading. "You don't take him seriously, do you? How long have you been working here? Have we ever had a girl say she was violently raped?"

"I do take him seriously. About six years. And no, we haven't." Mrs. Greene covered all the answers succinctly, as she often did when she was sufficiently annoyed. "You saw that girl's impregnator, that Ralo. Remember, that girl ended up poisoning him and he shot her? That thug very well could have raped her. Maybe that's why she jumped."

The whites under Dr. Singer's rolling eyes, the slightly opened mouth, the blank unbelieving expression as he paused, he might as well just come out and call her an idiot. "Oh, come on! Why did she shave her head then?"

"Dr. Singer, how long have you been performing abortions?"

"About fifteen years."

"And in all the time you have been working with girls who were pregnant and did not want to be, how many of them shaved their heads?"

"Well, none."

"And how many tried to commit suicide?"

"Well, there was one I remember that killed herself." Dr. Singer rubbed his chin. "But now that I think about it, it was after we performed the abortion."

"Yes, I've seen some of the girls after we've provided them services." Mrs. Greene glanced away. "Some of them are not dealing with it well."

"Well, that's beside the point. This girl did not receive any services from us, and she ended up jumping."

"Only she didn't really jump." Mrs. Greene raised her eyebrows, then squinted. "She was found on a ledge. That's a pretty lame attempt at suicide. I mean, just a few feet from a sheer drop to the ocean, and she's unconscious on a ledge. You think she couldn't figure out how to miss the ledge?"

"Yeah, so how did the bald little troublemaker get there?"

"I'm just saying," Mrs. Greene concluded, "that none of this case really adds up. I don't know if anyone really knows what happened, except maybe that poor girl herself. And she's in a coma, so she's not talking."

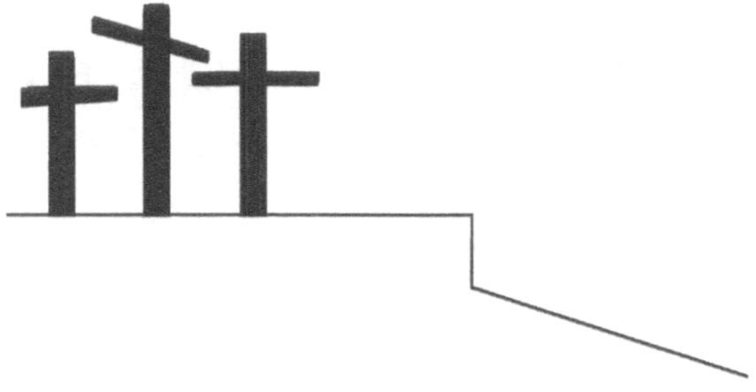

27

The Bob O'Malley Show

B OB O'MALLEY KNEW HOW TO GET RATINGS. Controversy and conflict, issues on which everybody would take a stand, and each side thought they had the moral high ground. When he heard there was a pregnant girl in a coma, he realized it should be the lead for the night, and he told the producers to shelve the story about the gorilla being shot to save the foolish kid who wandered into the cage at the zoo. "We'll do that one tomorrow." He closed the file and placed it on the desk. "Let's go with the pregnant girl in the coma with the crazy father who won't let her have an abortion. We get it all with that one. Religion, sex, abortion, the medical system, and wherever else the panel wants to take it. Everybody's going to want to take a position on this one, and every water cooler kibitzer is going to want to talk about it."

The panel would love this one. Allenby would have a field day! It's a softball for him. Bob O'Malley checked his makeup in his dressing room mirror. *The King of Ridicule.* Colm Allenby would bury the father mercilessly. Which way would Kimberly go? Not sure. Bob O'Malley straightened his tie. Former prosecutor, she's tough as nails on crime stuff, but the moral angle? Jill Kimberly would be hard to predict. But she'll look great, as always. Sharp and telegenic, that's always a ratings hit. What about Lesley? Bob O'Malley paused for a moment. Whitney Lesley, she's African American, liberal but Christian, civil rights activist, but pro-choice. She'll side with the father, defending his choice, his right to choose for his daughter. Bob O'Malley smoothed his hair. They would be tough on the father, though. Really tough. Not allowing his daughter in a coma to have an abortion? That was going to get people fired up! Bob O'Malley picked up the file again, reviewing the details of the case. This one was dynamite!

There was a knock on his dressing room door. Bob O'Malley put away the papers for the show prep and answered the door. Whitney Lesley greeted him. Shouldn't she be prepping for the show? She'd never tried to talk to him in his dressing room before. Looked like something was bothering her? Better hear her out. He let her in and closed the door behind her.

"Hi Bob." She glanced away. "Are you sure you want to go with this story about the pregnant girl?"

Whitney lowered the file folder with the notes for the show prep, resting it on her thigh. She frowned and avoided eye contact.

"It's a sure thing, Whitney." Bob cocked his head.

Whitney sighed. "The guy says his daughter was raped, and she was a virgin." She waved the file in her hand. "It's just too sad, even if it's not true. You know what Colm is going to do to this guy!"

The story was made for Allenby. He would tear the guy up. It would be great television. But they needed Whitney to balance him.

"Look, it is a sad story for the family, but the girl's in a coma. Whether she was raped or not, she's not going to be watching." Bob O'Malley desperately resisted rolling his eyes and tried to sound reasonable. "Sure, Allenby will be hard on the father, but that's what it's all about. If we don't hit hard, people don't watch. You can take the guy's side, if you want."

Whitney rolled her eyes. "I want to leave the guy alone."

Whitney had strong feelings on this one. She would be ready to fight, and that's just what the show needed.

"We can't leave him alone, Whitney. He's news, big news! Everybody is going to want to talk about this guy. If we don't do it, everybody else will."

Bob O'Malley ushered Whitney Lesley perfunctorily to the door. He had to keep her on board as a counterweight to the other panelists. They had to do this story. The fuse had been lit and it was ready to explode.

"Take his side, Whitney! Somebody has to. I was expecting you would. You're going to need to be on your A-game to counter Allenby, so go get ready!"

Whitney took a deep breath. Bob O'Malley noted the roll of her eyes. She really did not want to see this guy roasted. That meant she would be at her best, and she had better be. Allenby would not be holding back

"Is there anything more important to you than ratings, Bob?"

Bob O'Malley smirked. "I can't think of anything. I'll get back to you if I think of something."

Whitney Lesley shook her head and walked out the door. Bob O'Malley closed the door behind her. More important than ratings? *We're not a charity! Tonight, we are going to roast this guy!*

The theme music for the Bob O'Malley show sounded with all its exciting riffs, and the panelists had taken their places. Bob O'Malley scanned his panelists. They were all ready and prepped. Allenby looked like he was ready to jump out of his chair. Bob O'Malley smiled with delight. Kimberly appeared ready and confident, as always. He still wasn't sure which way she would go. But she really looked great in that blue dress! He glanced at Whitney Leslie, who stared down at the floor, her body tense, and her jaw clenched. Something was still eating Leslie. *Hope she doesn't choke!* If she blew this one, they would have to find someone else next time. The intro came to its sudden end, the music making its final cadence with a cymbal crash. "And now, here's Bob O'Malley!" Whitney Leslie closed her eyes and took a deep breath. Ready or not, the battle was on! Bob O'Malley smiled into the camera.

"Okay, for our first item, we have the case of Lali Russo." Bob O'Malley shuffled some papers he pretended he was reading. "A seventeen-year-old girl who was found on a cliff ledge a couple of months ago, an apparent suicide attempt. She's been in a coma ever since, and now it turns out that she's pregnant and the father has decided that she should carry the baby to term. So, what do we make of this?"

Okay, now, let them fight it out! Bob O'Malley leaned back in his chair and enjoyed the spectacle for which he had laid the ground. It was like overseeing a gladiatorial contest.

"Well, it is a pretty complex story," Jill Kimberly chimed in. "First of all, the father claims that the girl was raped and left for dead, and that since she was a pro-life advocate, she would not want to abort the baby."

Colm Allenby cut her off, "The father is being a father...."

Ooh! Kimberly lays out the case, and Allenby cuts her off and starts swinging! Bob O'Malley called the play-by-play in his mind.

"...No father wants to think about his little girl being sexually active. All the evidence points to the fact that this pro-life girl lost her virginity and tried to kill herself. Now she ends up in a coma and her father is forcing her to carry the baby. It's really a very sad story and really is close to child abuse, if you ask me!"

"All the evidence?" Whitney jumped in.

Okay, let's see what Leslie's got.

"There really isn't much evidence at all, except the word of the boy who, if the father is right and the boy raped her and left her for dead, we would expect *him* to lie. We really don't know what happened in this case."

Good, Good she's defending the guy. We need that balance.

"Oh, really?" Colm hit back. "It's really quite clear that here we have a girl who had all that religious talk about chastity beaten into her head so that when she loses her virginity, she tried to kill herself. She was obviously acting erratically when she shaved her head for no apparent reason. This really is an indictment of the Catholic Church and its teachings on life."

Ooh! Allenby's on a roll!

"And, if the father is right," Jill Kimberly added, "he's forcing his daughter to carry to term the child of her rapist! This is really sick stuff!"

Ouch! Kimberly's piling on! Whitney Leslie bit her lip and lowered her head. She was hopelessly outgunned. Bob O'Malley needed to get the conversation back to the facts and reframe the issue. He was Catholic, after all, and they were throwing his Church under the bus.

"Well, to be fair," Bob O'Malley said, "the father is saying that his daughter believed that even in the case of rape, the child is an innocent whose life should be preserved. That's in line with the teachings of the Catholic Church."

Colm would not let that just go by. "And just what is he going to do with this baby when it is born? Obviously, the mother can't care for it, and the child's father, if he's not a rapist, is at best an alleged drug dealer. If ever there was a case for legalized abortion, this is it."

Bob O'Malley's eyes widened as Colm Allenby spewed his venom, then he glanced over at Whitney Leslie, who glared at Colm Allenby. Whitney Leslie looked like she was ready to rip his face off. *Better be ready, if things get too bad...*

"Well, abortion is legal," she clarified, then laid into Allenby. "You seem to be cheesed-off not because there is no choice, but because you don't like the choice the father is making on behalf of his daughter? How do you know she wouldn't make the same choice? Isn't that the father's point? It's what the girl would want?"

Colm Allenby did not wait to respond. "Well, I just don't think that comatose women should be used as incubators for the children of rapists or drug dealers. The whole thing is just too sordid for words!"

Okay, okay, time to end this. Leslie held her own with logic and the facts, but Allenby overwhelmed her with emotion and false-characterizations. It was too much to ask for her to dig out of this one. Calling a comatose woman, who may have been raped a baby-incubator? That was just too much.

"Well, that will have to be the last word today," Bob O'Malley cut off the debate with a chuckle. "Hopefully, we'll have something a little less sordid to discuss next time. But we do wish the girl well, in this terrible situation. "Okay, so, coming up tomorrow." Bob O'Malley teased the next segment as the camera focused on him, then cut away to the video of a boy cowering before a gorilla in its cage. "To shoot, or not to shoot? That is the question for the zookeepers as this gorilla faces his day of judgment, and this boy's life hangs in the balance..."

✝✝✝

Robert watched the Bob O'Malley Show on his old vacuum tube style television set. He shut it off in disgust and fell to his knees, praying aloud in front of the Crucifix hanging on the living room wall. The arms of the God-man sacrificed for the sins of the world stretched open as if to receive the prodigal as he took his first step back toward faith. The bloody wounds in his hands and side seemed to drip as Robert beheld Jesus on the cross through his tears. "Oh, God, I am trying so hard to be true to your word and your will for the sake of my little Lali, even though I have lost my faith. But they are making me out to be a monster! If you are there, please help me!"

Robert gazed at the Crucifix and the broken and bleeding body of the son of God nailed to a cross. He recalled how the crowds had jeered and mocked Him, crowning Him with thorns, bowing to Him in mock adoration.

How wrong they were! "Lord, give me the strength to see this through." He humbly bowed his head and continued his prayer. "Please, Lord, if you are there, let Lali wake up and let justice be done. Let them all know from her own lips that I am doing just as she would have wished."

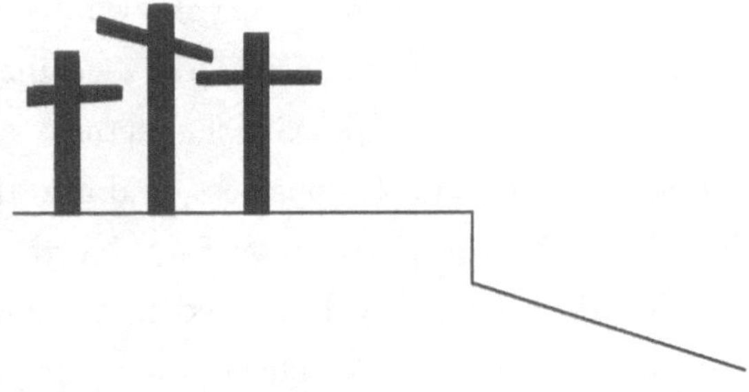

28

Katherine Kelly

KATHERINE KELLY WAS A GO-GETTER. An overachiever who had a nose for a story and knew how to play an angle. A news story was first and foremost a story and a story had a beginning, a middle, and an end. It was all about the entertainment, whether it was true or not, perhaps just a little nugget of truth was all you needed to build a good story.

Katherine Kelly placed the newspaper down on the seat in the news van as she waited for her cameraman to join her. Eulalia Russo, the coma-mama, she read the caption under the girl's picture. *I suppose they think that's really clever.* But the story lacked depth and was only surface mockery. Not really a story at all, just an opinionated perspective and a slanted list of facts. The angular perspective did not bother her. Nothing wrong with playing an angle. The lack of story-telling, that was the problem. Facts only mattered if they helped tell the story. Facts were like lemons to be squeezed. Bitter on their own but when sweetened with sugar, they made the lemonade of a good story.

She had the angle on this one, for sure. The story everyone wanted to hear. The one that validated what people already believed. Just feed them what they like to eat. She just needed to get it on tape. Get the pictures and make it all real. That was what got you ahead in this business, and into the bigger markets. She wouldn't be a beat reporter covering Northern California for the rest of her life. Almost nothing happened here worth reporting. She had resorted to making stuff up, like ghost stories, to get anybody to notice. Katherine rolled her eyes and flipped her hair, chuckling to herself. But they had noticed that one about the *Lost Girl*. What a great story! And then the *Lost Girl* was found. What a break that was. Played right with her little ghost story and was timed just perfectly to keep the story going. The perfect sequel. Bigger, more dramatic, even more real. And just as that one was settling down, bam, now she turned up pregnant in a coma! *Lost Girl 3: Pregnant in a Coma!* But maybe there was something real to work with this time? A real story to tell? About a girl pregnant and in a coma? The fall of the good girl? Or, rather, the jump? Found on the same ledge as the ghost girl? *I don't think I could make up something so good!* She just had to tell it. And telling a good story, that's how she would get out. That was the secret sauce that would get her into a big market. *Los Angeles? New York? Or how about DC, maybe?* But for now, skulking around Northern California for a story? *Ugh!* This coma-mama thing was her ticket! She could feel it in her bones.

Katherine had the Lali Russo story figured out and just how she would tell it. Get the interviews. The classmates would validate it. And, expert testimony from the abortion doctor, from the very clinic where the little fanatic was praying. Little coma-mama was just another troubled teen. This one, a bit of a religious nut. Praying at the abortion clinic? Who does that? But girls will be girls, and boys will be boys, and sooner or later, it comes down to fate, just like the old song said. Katherine had trouble laughing at her own joke, remembering how quickly fate had caught up with her as a sixteen-year-old girl. *That was long ago, Katherine. We don't need to go there.* She smoothed her skirt, talking herself back from the memory. But, for these church girls, birth control was out of the question because, well, they were not going to let it go that far. But eventually, they did. And maybe they got pregnant and maybe they didn't. And maybe they told their parents or went to confession or whatever, and maybe they didn't. But, likely, they did it again, and kept doing it, pretending they never had. Katherine closed her eyes. *No, there's no going back.* Something inside her ached but she held back the memory. But sometimes they felt so bad about it, like they couldn't tell anyone, like no one would ever understand, and that was when the good girl who everyone knew and loved, the one sitting in the front row at church, tried to kill herself.

Katherine had constructed the story in her mind and only needed to get the footage to validate it. She just needed to keep her own baggage out of it and get the work done. Of course, she had already started getting the job done with the father, the poor sap of a man who thought his virgin daughter had been raped. Good grief, what a fool! But what great television. There he was in his police uniform telling the world that the only way his daughter was pregnant was if she had been raped. Katherine picked up the paper again and stared at Officer Russo's picture, standing at attention, so rigid and proud. Katherine sighed. A proud man. But pride goeth before a fall, as they say. What had he called her? Ooze from the sludge or something like that? Katherine dropped the paper back onto the seat. *I guess it is a dirty business, but the world is dirty.* And this girl was part of that dirty world, no matter what fantasy world her father lived in. Katherine glanced at herself in the vanity mirror of the news van and flipped her hair. Something buried deep within her longed for the fantasy to be true. A place where men defended the honor of women and where women cherished the honor that was worth defending. A place where a statement like, *The only way my daughter is pregnant is if she was raped,* didn't sound like an absurdity. That Cinderella land was long gone, if it ever was real. *Our stories these days are only tragedies.* Katherine jerked her head back as though she were waking herself from a dream. Well, a good story often had a good fool, and good tragedy often had shattered illusions. Just get the story from the classmates. Sure, a lot of them would tell how nice a girl she was, how she just couldn't be doing it. But someone would let out the dirty truth. Katherine glanced at Lali's school picture in the paper on the seat, her long dark hair on her shoulders, her beaming, innocent smile. Pretty thing, but that nice girl act would never hold up. The girl was obviously troubled, suddenly shaving her head and all. Wasn't that how they shamed women in many cultures? The little fool was probably shaming herself, racked with guilt over her fall to the inevitable.

Paul Kruger, Katherine's cameraman, knocked on the driver side window of the van. She leaned over and unlocked the door.

"Sorry I'm late." Paul entered the van and took the driver's seat. "I don't think they get many visitors here in scenic Santa Inés, California. They couldn't find the key to my room. It's one of those old-style keys that you actually stick in and turn, you know, not a card key like in most places these days."

"No worries, Paul. I needed some time to strategize. I think we have a really hot one this time, so we need to get it right."

"Okay, Katherine, you're the boss. So where to?"

"We'll start with the abortion doctor. That will set the tone for the whole story."

"Alrighty, Dr. Singer's Family Planning Clinic, here we come."

Katherine scanned the scenery from the passenger seat of the news van as it made its way through the quaint town of Santa Inés, then ventured into the eastern end of the town where the decline in home values became evident as single-family homes became smaller and more rundown until they crossed the railroad tracks where single-family homes gave way to the row-house rental units just as they reached the clinic. The news van pulled to a stop at the curb in front of Dr. Singer's Family Planning Clinic. Paul removed his seatbelt and reached for the door.

"Why don't you wait in the van for now, Paul. Let me see if this guy will talk on camera. Pretty sure he will, though."

Katherine got out of the news van and ascended the obliquely-settled steps to Dr. Singer's Family Planning Clinic. As she entered, an unsettledness in her stomach assailed her as if a long-suppressed memory of an illness had come back, though not the illness itself. She swallowed hard and strolled up to the receptionist's desk.

"May I help you?" The receptionist's head tilted, an eyebrow raised. "I mean, are you okay?"

Was it that obvious? *Keep it together, Katherine!* That was a long time ago.

"Uh, yes." Katherine smoothed the wrinkles in her blazer. "Uh, I'm Katherine Kelly from Channel 23 News. We would like to get Dr. Singer's opinion on the Lali Russo case. Is he available for an interview?"

"Well, we don't comment on patients, ever." The receptionist's demeanor of concern transformed into officious curtness, almost annoyance.

"Oh, was Lali Russo a patient here?"

"Well, no." The receptionist paused and pursed her lips. "Let me check with Dr. Singer." The receptionist pushed her finger down on the intercom. "Dr. Singer?"

"Yes?" came the voice from the intercom.

"I have a Katherine Kelly here who would like you to comment for Channel 23 news on the Lali Russo case."

Dr. Singer popped his head into the waiting room then stepped fully in, wearing his white lab coat and his stethoscope around his neck. "Why sure, Mrs. Greene, I'd be happy to comment on the case for Ms. Kelly."

The receptionist rolled her eyes.

Katherine held her hand out. "Hi, Katherine Kelly, from Channel 23 News."

"Hi, Dr. Emanuel Singer."

"Okay, I have my cameraman in the van. It would be best if we can set up in your office. It will be more credible that way."

Katherine had Paul set up the equipment in Dr. Singer's office. Dr. Singer sat behind a large oak desk closing some open files. His diploma from medical school hung on the wall behind his head, and various medical texts rested on the bookshelf behind the desk. Dr. Singer's chair was higher than the chairs on the other side of the desk, allowing him to look down at patients as he counseled them. Katherine squirmed a little in the chair across from him. *Keep it together, Katherine! You're on a story. You're not here for that! Not this time.* Paul held the camera on his shoulder and would pan between them as necessary, since there was only one camera available.

"Hello, this is Katherine Kelly, reporting for Channel 23 news, we have today Dr. Emanuel Singer from the Dr. Singer Family Planning Clinic. We will be discussing the Lali Russo case, the young girl who is now pregnant and in a coma. So, Dr. Singer, first, do you know Lali Russo?"

"Why, no, not really. She used to pray in front of the clinic. She never came here for services, though I thought she might one day."

"Why do you say that?"

"Well, we get a lot of Catholic girls coming here when they get in trouble. They tend to be very ashamed when they get pregnant and usually want to quietly terminate the pregnancy. We are very discreet about it, of course."

"But Lali never came here?"

"No, well, the poor thing, she could not even have known she was pregnant when she tried to kill herself. I mean, she was probably just so ashamed to have lost her virginity."

"So, do you think that was the motive for her attempted suicide?"

"Well, it's just a supposition, but it makes some sense. Catholics teach that girls should remain virgins until they are married, so if they fail at that, they could be ashamed. A possible indication in this case is that she shaved her head. That's something that many cultures do to shame women."

"But Lali appears to have shaved her own head."

"Well, yes," Dr. Singer explained, with just the perfect nod of his head. "Lali was likely very devout and wanted to shame herself."

"So, Lali's father claims that the only way his daughter could be pregnant is if she were raped. What do you think of that possibility?"

"Oh, it's absurd." Dr. Singer was a natural, his look of disdain just perfect. "I mean, it's understandable for a father to believe something like that, but it's unlikely to be true. I understand that the boyfriend said they were having consensual sex. That's more likely the reason she is pregnant."

"So, you don't really think it's possible that the boyfriend could have raped her, beat her, and left her on that ledge?"

"Oh, it hardly seems likely. If he wanted to kill her, why wouldn't he have made sure she was dead? Look, I deal with pregnant girls all the time. It's just a shame these religious girls are kept away from places like this where we can help them to avoid getting pregnant or can help them out if they do get pregnant. I think we really could have helped Lali. This was totally avoidable."

"So, what do you think of the father's decision for her to carry the baby while in a coma?"

"I think it's monstrous! The girl is likely to be severely impaired if she ever comes out of that coma. She won't be able to care for that child, which would be hard enough to do if she were a healthy seventeen-year-old. The pregnancy should be terminated, without any question. It's only some kind of weird, religious fanaticism that would lead to any other decision."

"Thank you, Dr. Singer," Katherine said, then added, "This is Katherine Kelly, from Channel 23 News, reporting."

Okay, that was the hard part. Katherine took a deep breath and swallowed, trying to repress the queasiness in her stomach. *Now, let's get some of her classmates from school.*

Katherine walked from the parking lot with her cameraman toward the entrance of St. Mary's High School. She smiled, *Blessed Mary, Ever-Virgin.* Wasn't that what the Catholics believed, after all? Perpetual virginity? Right up until the time they jumped off a cliff. Katherine chuckled to herself and turned to her cameraman, Paul Kruger.

"Okay, Paul." She dusted a windblown leaf from her jacket, all business now. "Let's get the principal first."

Principal Martinez was greeting students as usual as they came into the school. The reports of Lali's pregnancy had spread throughout the school population. There seemed to be a somberness as the students quietly entered the school, as if the place were in mourning or maybe just in a state of shock over the unexpected news. Katherine approached the principal with the camera rolling. *Let's catch his reaction even if he refuses to talk.*

"Hello, Principal Martinez." She approached him, holding the microphone forward. "I'm Katherine Kelly of Channel 23 News. Would you be willing to answer a few questions about the Lali Russo case?"

Principal Martinez shooed a couple of students into the school and then turned to greet Katherine. "Good morning."

Katherine noticed how he stared directly into the camera with a surprised smile sneaking past his down-turned mustache. The startled gape into the lens would look awful on television. A bad start.

"You say you would like to talk about Lali?" His great mustache added weight to his serious demeanor, giving him the impression more of an undertaker than a high school principal.

"Yes, Principal Martinez." Katherine brushed some windblown hair from her eye. She hoped Paul had the camera on her for that perfect little gesture.

"Well, you know, we're all a bit shocked by this turn of events. We've been praying for her recovery."

"So, what was Lali like?"

"That girl was the best we had. She was the real deal." The principal peered directly into the camera as if he were being stalked by a tiger.

Didn't they teach these teachers camera presence? Maybe they could find a way to edit it out, or it would just look ridiculous.

Principal Martinez anxiously glanced back at Katherine. "But I don't think we need to talk about her in the past tense?"

Katherine ignored his question and moved the interview onward, where *she* wanted it to go. "So why do you think she tried to kill herself?" Katherine was confident that her practiced look of concern and sincerity would look just perfect on the recording. She was hitting her marks perfectly.

Principal Martinez chuckled, his mustache bouncing a bit, though still turned decidedly downward, then he became more serious. He stared directly into the camera once more. Katherine scowled. Did she have to stop the interview and tell this idiot to stop looking into the camera? Katherine glanced at the camera and noticed Paul smiling and shrugging his shoulders.

"I don't think she did," Principal Martinez said flatly. "I mean, I don't know how she came to be on that ledge, but I don't believe she tried to kill herself."

The principal's response puzzled her. He didn't think she tried to kill herself? *Keep it together, Katherine, the camera's rolling.* He was just another fool who got it all wrong. *And don't you start looking into the camera!* It was like it was contagious.

"Why do you say that?" She suppressed her smirk and kept her tone polite.

Principal Martinez grinned, his mustache obscuring his facial expression making him appear as grim as an Old Testament prophet calling the people to repent, despite his smile. "Well, she just wasn't wired that way. She always put others before herself. People like that don't end their own lives." Principal Martinez checked his watch. "I'm sorry. I really must get to work now." He stared into the camera lens a final time. He glanced back at it as he turned away, as if expecting a viper might strike at his heel before he could escape.

Principal Martinez headed into the school. Katherine lowered the microphone, her head listed to one side, and her mouth fell open as she glanced at the camera. The principal's perspective caught her off-guard. He was so confident that she had not attempted suicide. The girl was supposed to be some disturbed teenager, not a real-deal, whatever that meant?

Paul, the cameraman, took his eye away from the camera viewfinder and called to Katherine. "Hey, boss! You know better than to gape into the camera like that!"

Katherine rolled her eyes. "Sorry Paul, I think I caught it from that principal. I mean, I'm trying to interview him, and all I keep thinking is that he's staring like a dope into the camera. We'll have to see if we can clean it up in editing."

An uncommon queasiness in her gut, she closed her eyes and for a moment she was a teenager again, back at the clinic signing the consent forms. *Come on, girl! This isn't about you! But you know what it's like, that a girl might just jump, if…Stop it! It's not about you! You know there's a big story here! Just get the footage! Get to it now!* Katherine blinked a few times. She perked up when a teenaged boy sauntered toward the school with his shirt untucked and his confident gait. This kid was trying to look rebellious. Maybe he would give her the dirty truth?

"Hi, Katherine Kelly from the Channel 23 news. We're interviewing people about the Lali Russo case. Would you like to comment?" She pushed the microphone in his face.

"Sure," the boy said, with a wink.

"What's your name?"

"Jake Turner. Maybe you should write that down, so you'll remember?" Jake raised his eyebrows, and half-smiled.

The queasiness in her stomach worsened. "So, what do you think of Lali Russo?"

Jake rolled his eyes. "None of the things they are saying about her make any sense."

Katherine cocked her head, trying to hear better. Interesting. But at least he wasn't staring into the camera.

"What do you mean?"

"Like, that she was having sex and all. No way that girl was putting out! She was God-Squad all the way!"

"So, you think she was raped?" Katherine was unable to hide a certain snideness in her tone. This place was just filled with fools!

"Listen, lady," he said, as if she had poked him in a particularly sore place, "it's more likely that she conceived by the Holy Spirit than that punk Rodrigo got her!"

Katherine physically stepped back. Her head bobbed at the unexpected answer.

"Really?" She regained her composure. "So, you don't think much of Rodrigo?"

"He's a drug dealer. How much should I think of him?" Jake scoffed as he walked toward the school.

Katherine overheard him say to his friend who had stopped and watched his interview, "What an idiot! Too bad because she was kind of hot."

The Holy Spirit? Conceived by the Holy Spirit? *And I'm the idiot?* It wasn't the Holy Spirit! It was a guy like that! *One like that got me! Just sixteen, and I let him…* Katherine found herself looking directly into the camera again. Paul chuckled, and Katherine glared at him.

Another boy hurried toward the school. He was well dressed. The kid looked like a good student, one who might have a more intelligent perspective. *My God, I forgot how much I hated high school.*

"So, what do you think about the Lali Russo story?" Flustered, she forgot to even request an interview or ask his name.

The young and studious boy chuckled. "I think you guys got it all wrong."

Katherine furrowed her brow. Had she gotten it all wrong? Or, were all the people here just nuts? Was the doctor the only sane person in this town? "What do you mean?" She was caught off-guard by this young man's smooth confidence.

"Well, you're talking about a girl who said she would die before committing a sin, even a small sin to save someone's life. She said this the day of the incident. There's no way that girl tried to kill herself because she would consider it a sin. And there's no way she was sleeping with Rodrigo."

Katherine cocked her head again. No point trying to make sense of it now. Just get the footage. "So, what do you think happened?"

"I think someone raped her and tried to kill her but couldn't go through with it and left it in God's hands. Probably Rodrigo. It can't be easy killing someone like Lali."

Katherine squinted her eyes in puzzlement. It was supposed to be a suicide, but now it's someone who would be hard to kill? She was just a high-school girl? Why would she be so hard to kill?

"What do you mean by that?" More true confusion echoed in her voice than was appropriate for a professional television reporter to express. *Keep it together, Katherine!* Keep it all business!

"Well, she's not afraid to die." The well-dressed boy glanced briefly at the camera, as if he were unsure if this were a secret he should share with the world. He shrugged, meeting her eyes once more. "And she wouldn't fight back, but she would stand her ground. I mean, that's what she said, what she rehearsed. I argued with her about it, so I know. She said that if someone tried to force her to sin, she would die, and if God let it happen, it would be

His will. She wasn't afraid to die. It would be like killing a saint. If there is any good left in you at all, you would have a hard time killing a saint."

A saint? Really?

"So, you don't see any way that she lost her virginity and fell into despair?" Katherine finally laid out her theory of the case.

"You know, that might make sense for some girls but not for Lali. She worked with troubled women. She knew what that was all about. And there's another thing."

"What's that?"

"If Lali had tried to kill herself, she would have succeeded." The boy confidently nodded for emphasis. "She didn't do things halfway."

The boy smiled and walked on into the school. Katherine lowered her microphone. Maybe they did have it all wrong! Maybe it wasn't like what happened to *her?* Maybe, the Holy Spirit…Oh, that's crazy… Paul laughed, which brought her out of it. Katherine realized she had been staring stupidly into the camera again.

"Don't worry, we can edit that out."

Katherine regained her composure and glared at him. A pretty girl walked up. Katherine eyed her up. Check this girl out! She looked like she should be on a runway, not in a Catholic School. Maybe the pretty, catty girls would give her some dirt? She was becoming desperate.

"Hi. Katherine Kelly, Channel 23 news. We're interviewing students about the Lali Russo case. Would you like to comment?"

"Well, sure!" The girl tittered.

"For the record, what is your name?"

"Suzie Parks." The girl flashed a smile, and Katherine stepped back and blinked a few times. Then, she cleared her head and continued.

"So, what do you think of Lali Russo?"

Suzie smiled her pretty-girl smile that seemed to light up the otherwise ordinary morning, her full lips parting just enough to reveal each tooth perfectly aligned, sparkling white. She fluffed her long, curly blond hair. Katherine noticed the camera wobble. Her sparkling blue eyes seemed to have caught Paul off-guard.

"Well, I don't know," she said.

"Do you know her?" Katherine asked hopefully.

"A little." Suzie giggled.

"Do you think she tried to kill herself?" Katherine asked bluntly.

"Well, you know, she was a little crazy." Suzie raised her eyebrows, and her eyes sparkled the more. "I mean, she used to have this gorgeous hair, but she shaved it all off! I mean, who does that?"

Suzie tittered and walked on.

My God, what a bubble-head! All she saw was that the girl shaved off her pretty hair? Was there anything usable in that footage? Especially up against the kid saying Lali was a saint? Not likely. Too bad, she would look really great on television. Katherine lowered the microphone as her mind wandered. She noticed Paul, grinning with the camera on his shoulder as she realized she was again gaping directly into the lens. *Ugh, I did it again!*

Dismayed and confused, a sense of failure swept through her spirit. She did not see how she could piece together that perfect interview from the doctor with the contrary interviews from the people from the school. Would she be able to make the story she wanted to tell hold together? Katherine raised her chin, slowly. A slight, sickly, bald boy walked confidently toward her, a glint of the morning sunlight gleamed off his uncovered hairless head. Katherine's eyes were drawn down to meet the intense, angry eyes, set in his gaunt face.

"That girl doesn't know what she's talking about." The pale boy glared at her, speaking before she had a chance to raise the microphone.

"Oh?" Katherine regained her reporter's stance, microphone ready to capture each word. "Then what do you think of Lali Russo?"

The boy ignored Katherine's question. "Lali shaved her head because kids were making fun of me. My hair fell out from chemotherapy."

Katherine's eyes widened for an instant, then she regained her composure. This might be something, not what she thought, but something. "So, Lali shaved her head in sympathy?" Something less than hardboiled and businesslike rang in her tone, something more human than reporter.

"Yes." The boy squinted at her. His eyes seemed to search and judge her soul, tearing through the jaded exterior she had been failing so miserably to maintain and finding the frightened sixteen-year-old girl, pregnant and waiting in the cold, sterile procedure room for the doctor to remove the unwanted and unexpected child from her body. *I let it happen. My God, why did I let it happen? I wanted it to happen, and then, the doctor, the... Oh, God, why? Why did I let it happen?*

The boy's words became more and more choked as he continued. "She was the kindest person in the world and brave. She was the only friend I had. I should have gone with her that day, but I was scared. I really miss her."

The boy began to weep. Distressed, Katherine waved to the cameraman to stop filming. She put her arm around the boy and accompanied him into the school. She returned to the cameraman, picking through the shattered pieces of the fantasy she had created in her mind, piecing the cold reality of the story back together like jagged fragments of black ice in the coldest dark, separating out her own experience that had so colored her jaded viewpoint. *I thought it was like me. But I wanted it to happen. I was so young. But I wanted it. She shaved her head in sympathy... Not shame... Not despair... She's not afraid to die... She's like a saint...She's not like me...She didn't let it happen... She... She was... Like a saint....*

As she approached the cameraman, she stood up straight. She wiped a tear from her cheek as smoothly and confidently as she had pushed the windblown hair from over her eye. *All business now, Katherine. Now, we get the real story.* The story no one wanted to hear. The one no one wanted to believe...

"This isn't what I expected, Paul." She opened the door to the news van with a decisive jerk on the handle. "Either this kid is the Virgin Mary, or she was raped. We can't run the story the way we planned."

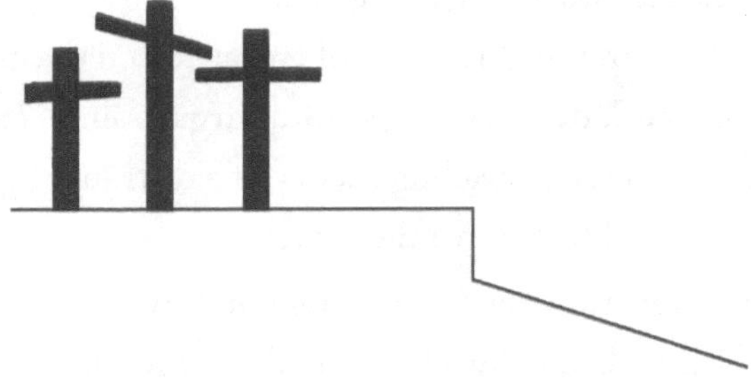

29

Setting the Record Straight

KATHERINE KELLY BIT HER LIP as the news van made its way to the Russo home. She would do whatever it took to get the story and the pictures, but it would not be easy, especially since the man with the gun had referred to her as something oozing from the sludge, and he had made it clear that there would only be written answers to written questions. The guy must be even more on edge now given the latest news coverage. They needed pictures, though. They couldn't just read answers to written questions on television. That just wouldn't work. She glanced at Paul in the driver's seat. There was a big story here, that no one else had gotten. She could feel it in her bones. A story of a father's vindication against a jaded press and an equally jaded society, so ready to believe the worst. Katherine glanced out the window at the lengthening shadows cast by the tall trees along the mountain road. Or maybe not ready to believe the worst? So ready to believe what was easiest to believe. The lies she had been so ready to feed them. Katherine sighed. Not much was worse than the truth if it's true that this virgin girl who her peers at school thought was like a saint had been brutally raped and left for dead on the edge of a cliff. Katherine smoothed her skirt, and checked herself in the vanity mirror, as the news van entered the driveway of the single-family home, a short walk from the Coastal Trail entrance and the cliff where Lali had been found on the ledge. The rape of a virgin saint? *That would be most definitely worse than the prevailing theory of a distraught girl attempting suicide, so no one wanted to believe the worst.*

She had Paul park the news van at the end of the long driveway to avoid arousing any suspicions. The Russo house awaited her like some old castle with a moat, archers standing at the ready in the turrets, except that it was just an ordinary farmhouse with the now infamous front porch, from which the man with the gun had chased them. Every news outlet had gotten a good shot of that one. She raised her eyes up toward the Russo house with trepidation. Her knees buckled as she stepped out of the van onto ground that seemed so unfamiliar to her. *Play it straight, Katherine.* No spinning this time. There would be no video of her knocking at the door nor of Officer Russo answering surprised by the camera. They could likely get some nice shots of the officer brandishing his sidearm if they did it that way. Katherine chuckled to herself. But that was not what they were after. Not this time. Katherine walked toward the house, carrying her laptop computer in its black leather bag. This time it was about setting the record straight. No reporter heroics. Just letting a man defend his daughter and her honor from all the cynical conclusions of a corrupt world. *The conclusions I was so ready to draw.* This time, it was about defending the innocent.

Katherine stopped in front of the steps to the porch and took a deep breath. Gain his confidence, first. But it would not be easy. Surely, he'd seen the news, and had seen himself depicted as just a father blinded by love, defending the honor of his daughter when no one thought there was really any honor to defend. Katherine bowed her head. She had been just as guilty as everyone else. But she had always used innuendo rather than coming right out and saying it. She just asked the question and let the viewers decide the obvious, that the man was a fool. *How clever, Katherine!* She sighed and squeezed her eyes shut as she recalled the copy she had written and read for her report. "Was he right? Had some fiend raped and beaten his daughter, leaving her for dead on the ledge of a cliff? Or is he just a father, blinded by love, clinging to hope that his daughter had not done this to herself?" Oh, how very clever! Report what he said and lay the groundwork to show he was a fool all along. Hint at what everyone wanted to believe, without coming right out and accusing the man of being a sap. Katherine pursed her lips as she ascended the steps to the Russo home, recalling his armed threat when reporters last crowded onto his porch. Taking a deep breath, she knocked on the front door. The door opened, and the off-duty policeman grimaced as if the pain of some old, hidden wound had unexpectedly flared up.

"Hi, Officer Russo?" Katherine cleared her throat.

"Yes?" Officer Russo held the door ajar and looked ready to slam it shut.

"I'm Katherine Kelly from Channel 23 News." She reached her right hand toward him but seeing his right hand remaining on the door, she let her hand fall back to her side.

"I'm sorry, Ms. Kelly, I don't do interviews. Please submit any questions you have in writing." Officer Russo began closing the door.

"No, Mr. Russo, please you don't understand." She put her hand forward to stop the door from closing. "I don't have any questions to submit. I want to show you what the people who know your daughter best are saying about her."

Katherine motioned toward her laptop case as she spoke. He looked curious. He hesitated a moment. "If I let you in, anything that I may say is off the record, right? I don't want to hear any of it on the news or read about it in the paper, okay?"

"Strictly off the record. I'm here as a fellow human tonight, not a reporter. You really need to see this."

Robert slowly opened the door. He eyed her like a dog guarding a bone. *Tread lightly, Katherine! Gain his confidence!* Katherine entered the living room and took a deep breath. She noted the crucifix on the wall, but there was little else to suggest the religious fanaticism ascribed to this man in the press accounts. A picture hung on the wall of a woman with kindly, dark eyes, eyes that called her with a kind of gentle persuasion, demanding nothing, yet inviting her to a better way. That must be his wife. How sad. She died of cancer many years ago, they had said on the news. *How is it that we forget so easily that we are messing with people's lives!* A newspaper lay on the coffee table with a picture of Lali on the front page. That article made him out to be a religious nut. That was why she was here. *I have to set the record straight.*

"The more people I interview who know your daughter, the fewer people I find who believe she tried to kill herself. I don't believe the true story has gotten out, and I'd like to try to correct that. Let me show you what I have."

Katherine set up her laptop on the kitchen table, started the video player, showing the interviews with the kids and the teachers, all of them saying they doubted the prevailing story.

"You see, you're not the only one defending your daughter's honor or your choice on her behalf."

Mr. Russo sighed. The video of the boy with cancer nearly brought him to tears.

"This is very heartening, but it still doesn't give me the proof I need."

"No, we can't prove anything." Katherine lowered her eyes a moment. She raised her head, again. "But we can try to change perception. Would you be willing to be interviewed?"

Katherine held her breath as he paused for a moment.

"I know how you reporters work." He cocked his head and thrust forward his jaw. "You'll say anything to get an interview, and then once the cameras are rolling, it's gotcha time. I'll only do an interview if I know the questions beforehand, and if there is any deviation from those questions, I'll stop the interview. I won't let you make me look like a fool."

Katherine took a deep breath. How many times had she thought this man a fool? He was absolutely right to be suspicious. But it would look like a hostage tape if he knew the questions beforehand and he prepared his answers. Katherine placed her hand on his, "Yes, I understand your concern. But it will not look natural if you know the questions beforehand."

"I know." Officer Russo drew his hand back and wiped it on his shirt. "But I'm not sure I'll answer correctly off-the-cuff. And people will twist what I say. You've seen that creep Allenby on the O'Malley Show?"

Katherine paused. She had stuck that microphone right in his face in their last encounter and made sure they had gotten a good shot of him holding his gun on the reporters. They had ambushed him! Staked out his house and waited to pounce. No wonder he was apprehensive. *Be human, Katherine.* She had to set things right. Forget that crap about objective journalism. It's never objective anyway. They told stories that they wanted to tell. This time, they needed to get the truth out. Give this guy what he needs to feel safe without it sounding staged.

"Okay, how about this? You let me ask the questions freely, and if you don't think you got it right, we'll let you change it. This won't be about confrontational journalism; this will be about you getting your side of the story out. Giving you equal time, as they say. This will be about me giving you the chance to set the record straight."

Robert stared at her, his head tilted and his eyes squinting. "Nothing goes on the air unless I approve?"

"Nothing."

"And if I want to change my answer, you ask it again?"

"We do whatever it takes, so you are comfortable."

Robert paused. "No gotchas?"

"No gotchas. If you don't approve, we won't use it. If my cameraman tries to run off with the tape, you can shoot him."

Robert laughed and threw his head back. "You know I had the safety on when I pulled my gun that day? I was never going to shoot anybody. It's just you people are so annoying."

"Yes, I know. Sometimes we forget we are people, and that we are reporting on people. Our cameras are in some ways more dangerous than your gun."

Robert reached out his right hand. "Okay then."

Katherine shook his hand and grinned. "Let me get my cameraman; he's in the car. Just don't shoot him unless he tries to run off with the tape." She chuckled.

An excitement built in Katherine's soul as she stepped toward the Russo home with Paul Kruger. Life had led her here, to this point, to do this thing, what she was created to do. Reporting the truth, a big story, not making things up to get noticed, but being part of something she always was meant to be part of.

"Paul, this one's going to be big and all we have to do is play it straight. Nothing sneaky this time. Just make the guy look good. He's the victim in all this."

"Sure, Katherine, this is one of those rare times when we get to feel good about our jobs." Paul winked. "I've really liked this guy ever since he suggested you must have oozed out of the sludge."

"Oh, shut up!" Katherine smacked him playfully on the arm.

"And I really loved him when he put his gun to that guy's nose. I zoomed right in on that one!"

Katherine laughed. "We really have behaved like something oozing from the sludge but today we get to set things right. You know I told him he could shoot you if you tried to keep anything he didn't approve of?"

"Anything to get the interview." Paul rolled his eyes with a laugh.

"Well, here we go." Katherine took a deep breath and knocked on the door.

Officer Russo opened the door, an apprehensive smile creasing his lips.

"Hello, Officer Russo, this is my cameraman, Paul Kruger. We'll need a little time to set up and get the lighting right, then we can begin. I'm really looking forward to helping you get your side of the story out."

Mr. Russo nodded as he let them in. "I'm a little nervous, but I'm looking forward to clearing things up."

Katherine stepped into the Russo home and studied the room. Katherine maintained her best business-like manner despite the excitement of the big moment bubbling over within her. "Okay, Officer Russo, we need to be positioned so Paul can pan between us and zoom out to have us both in the shot. I think we can manage well in the living room, but we will need to bring in some additional lighting."

They would have to do the best they could with just one camera. Paul Kruger set up the portable lights.

"What do you think, Paul?" Katherine said. "It would be best if we sit at a right angle, then you will have plenty of space to move in and out and change the shot angles?"

"Sure, Katherine," Paul's confident voice responded. "I think the warm lighting in here will work well, and if I position them this way, we can add a little drama to the shots. I think we can make it look really great."

Katherine glanced at Robert as he sat on the big recliner in the living room. "Officer Russo? I think it would be best if you sit on the divan, and I'll pull this chair over cattycorner. I don't think that big chair will work well."

Robert smirked as he made his way to the sofa.

"Paul, would you please arrange the lights for us over here instead?" Katherine pointed towards the other end of the coffee table. "I think we can hang the mic above out of the shot, so we can talk more naturally."

"Sure, Katherine, I think that will actually work much better."

"Okay, Officer Russo, I think we're all set." Katherine said, straightened herself on the small chair they had brought in from the kitchen, placed it next to the divan, with the coffee table in the living room filling in the corner. "Are you ready to give this a go?"

Officer Russo nodded. A bead of sweat dripped down his cheek. Katherine leaned over and wiped it with a tissue.

"Try to relax, Robert. I know this is likely to be painful in many ways but we both need to be strong, for Lali's sake. Let's get the truth out. I'm going to try to make it as easy as possible." She nodded reassuringly.

Katherine took her position, standing behind her chair. "Okay, Paul, let's start with the camera on me."

"This is Katherine Kelly from Channel 23 News reporting. We have an exclusive interview today with Officer Robert Russo, father of Lali Russo, the seventeen-year-old girl in a coma who is pregnant. Many people have said a lot of things about this case and made assumptions about Lali, her father, and Lali's beliefs. We would like to give Officer Russo a chance to set the record straight on some very difficult decisions he had to make on behalf of his daughter. "

Katherine smoothly glided around to the front of the chair and extended her hand to Officer Russo. "So, first, I'd like to thank Officer Russo for allowing us into his home."

He stood and shook her hand. "You're welcome. I'm looking forward to this opportunity to clear some things up."

Katherine nodded, then they seated themselves. "Officer Russo, so there's been a lot of talk and theorizing about what happened to your daughter. But, most of the theories have been based on assumptions that there may be reason to question. So, let's try to step through the facts. First, I'd like to ask you about the relationship between your daughter and Rodrigo Alvarez, the boy who says he is the father of Lali's unborn child."

"Yes, well, I was very concerned about that relationship because I had learned that Rodrigo had become involved with some pretty dangerous people. He had joined a gang that was selling drugs in the neighborhood. Lali – God bless her – thought that she could be a good influence on him." Robert kept his eyes on Katherine.

"So, you urged her to break it off?"

"Yes, I did." Robert nodded. "And, typical of Lali, she did not just listen to me blindly but evaluated the situation for herself. She ran into some of the people associated with that gang and discovered the truth. Then she confronted Rodrigo about being in the gang and selling drugs, and finally gave him an ultimatum: to either quit the gang or she would end the relationship."

"Now, this relationship, as far as you know, was not sexual?"

"Oh, no." Robert shook his head. "My daughter believed that sex before marriage was a betrayal of your future spouse. She was very serious about that. I know that people will say I'm just being a father, and that I just don't want to think that my little girl was sexually active, and I cannot know for sure, but I'm as sure as anyone can be. It would be totally against everything she stood for and Lali was pretty immovable when she took a stand."

"Well, I've also interviewed Lali's friends and classmates at school and could not find anyone who believed the relationship was sexual either." Katherine gave a single nod of her head.

Robert paused a minute, then answered, "It can be difficult when you take your Catholic faith seriously, because so few people can relate to it. Lali goes to Catholic school, where the kids understand the faith better, even if they don't always agree with it or live up to it. They know who the kids are who really believe, though."

"So, you believe that Rodrigo Alvarez raped your daughter?" Katherine addressed the question directly.

Robert shifted his position on the sofa. "Well, Rodrigo claims he had sex with my daughter and my daughter is pregnant. I believe that the only way he could have had sex with her would be if he forced her. And I know my daughter was beaten and left for dead on that ledge."

Katherine caught the camera in her peripheral vision zooming in on her. She paused and raised an eyebrow.

"So, you believe your daughter was beaten?" She leaned forward. "That she was not just injured in a fall?"

"Yes, that's right." Robert nodded confidently. "As a police officer, when I look at the evidence, I cannot reconstruct a way for her skull to fracture on the left side, while all the other injuries are on the right side of her body, including a ruptured liver, which requires a significant, focused impact. She must have landed hard on her right side on some kind of protrusion to cause that injury. But she would also need to land with focused energy on her left side to have fractured her skull. Some speculate that she might have tumbled in the fall, but the ledge is fairly narrow. If she had tumbled much, she likely would have fallen to the bottom. It seems more plausible that the head injury occurred before the fall."

Katherine followed up, her voice intense. "So, you believe she was struck on the back-left side of her head, and then tossed over onto the ledge where she fell on the right side of her body?"

"Yes, that is correct. I believe that explanation best fits the evidence. To fracture her skull like that would require a good deal of concentrated force, and if the force from the fall were concentrated on her skull on the left side, how did she get all the other injuries, including a ruptured liver, on the right side of her body?"

"But why wouldn't the person trying to kill her just toss her over where she would not fall on the ledge?" Katherine tilted her head and raised her eyebrows.

Robert shifted his position in the chair and cocked his head and said with some exasperation, "I don't know. Perhaps they wanted to be sure the body would be found, and they wanted it to look like a suicide? If the body fell all the way down, it could be swept out to sea and never found, so people would spend a lot of time and effort looking for a missing girl, a girl like Lali, who no one would expect would go missing. If it looks like a suicide, you don't spend a lot of time looking for a killer or a missing person. Maybe that was their plan? Or maybe it wasn't a plan at all, and they just didn't see the ledge? People walk the cliffs, even at night, so they may have had to hurry. There are more reasons for her to be on the ledge because someone put her there than if she tried to commit suicide. If she wanted to kill herself, she easily could have jumped where there was no ledge. Especially Lali, who was very familiar with the terrain there. It makes more sense that someone staged it to look like a suicide."

Katherine nodded and paused. She studied her notes for a second, then glanced up. "Okay. Now I'd like to talk to you about your choice for your daughter to carry the baby to term while she is in a coma."

Robert sighed. "Yes, well, it is a difficult thing for many people to accept, but Lali believes that the best thing to do, even in the case of rape, is to have the baby. She has worked with victims of sexual abuse and rape and talked with them, and the ones that have the babies are best able to make sense of the tragedy and are happier with their lives. They see something good coming out of a horrible situation."

"But your daughter is in a coma?" Katherine half closed an eye. "She may never be able to come out of it and have to make sense of anything?"

"All the more reason why she would want to preserve a life, if her own life is of less value because of injury." Robert's voice rose, and his open hand gesture underscored the point. "But I am still hopeful that she will come out of it, and she will validate all the decisions I have made on her behalf. I am confident that I am making decisions for her that she would make herself."

"So, what would you say to those who suggest that you are using your daughter as a baby incubator?" Katherine leaned forward.

Robert chuckled. "They just don't know what they are talking about." He instinctively turned to face the camera, his face reflecting an earnestness and seriousness as if speaking an eternal truth lost in the modern age of psychology and science. "Once the baby is born, my daughter will be a mother. She may be disabled, and she may not be able to care for her child because of her disability, but she will be no less a mother who sacrificed for her child." Robert moved his gaze back to Katherine. "I just don't understand people who would think of a mother as a baby incubator. I think it is a pretty twisted way to think."

Katherine sensed the drama of the moment. *Now that's how you face the camera and make a point.* She narrowed her eyes and leaned forward. "Even if it is a child produced by rape?"

Robert sighed. Then gazed directly into the camera again. Paul maneuvered closer for the shot as Robert spoke. "However this child was conceived." He lowered his head, biting his lip. An underlying anger seemed to grip him before he composed himself and finally looked up at the camera. "It will be Lali's child and she would want her child to have life and to be loved, regardless of whether she can care for the child herself. That's who my daughter is, and I could not be more proud of her."

Paul stepped back and re-angled the camera to capture them both in the shot. Katherine paused, to let the point sink in, looking sympathetically at Robert. "Okay, Officer Russo." She nodded. "I'm glad we had this opportunity to let you tell your side of the story." Katherine smiled, pressing her lips together.

"Thank you for giving me the opportunity." Robert stood and shook Katherine's hand.

Robert and Katherine Kelly sat together in Robert's living room, watching the interview when it aired that evening on the Channel 23 News program. Once the interview concluded, Robert shut off the television set. "Well, at least I was able to get my side out, not that many people will listen."

"Yes, and we didn't have to edit or retake anything," Katherine said.

Robert chuckled. "And I didn't have to shoot your cameraman!"

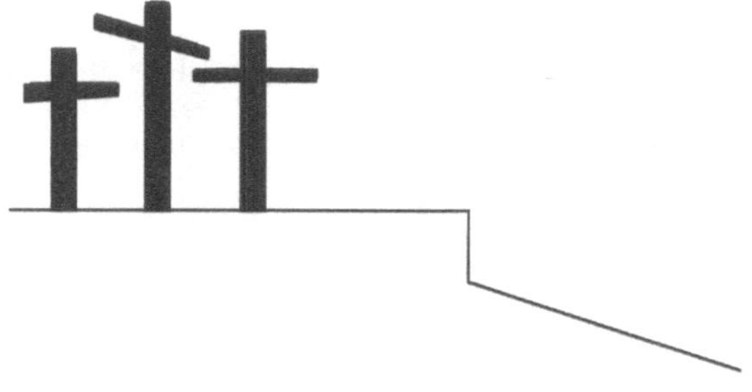

30

Suzie Parks

LIKE MOTHER LIKE DAUGHTER. Suzie glanced at the picture of the two of them together, looking particularly stunning, looking more like sisters. Why did Daddy want nothing to do with them, after all these years? Was he still afraid of the law? *I guess I wouldn't be here, if he hadn't broken the law.* Suzie sighed. But that was long ago? They couldn't still come after him for that? *But his wife probably wouldn't like it, if he visited us.*

Suzie had often looked for her father's name in the movie credits as they scrolled, sometimes even in the beginning of the movie as producer or executive producer, but mostly at the end, as production assistant or some other behind-the-scenes role in the film-making business. *Executive producer, Gavin McCreedy, or Produced by Gavin McCreedy, Hollywood bigshot, my dad.* The oldest Hollywood cliché. He knocked up Mom when she was only sixteen. *Thank God.* She laughed. *I owe my life to a criminal who got away with it!* They really should find a different word for that. Mom just started having sex with older men when she was young. It wasn't anything forced or violent. *Maybe I should have started having sex with someone older?*

Suzie pulled the hairbrush through her thick blonde hair. Why did Mom work so much? Daddy sent them enough money to live on. Mom never talked about *the arrangement*. Suzie chuckled at how her mom always scrunched her face when Suzie referred to Mr. McCreedy as Daddy. She glanced in her mirror and tried to mimic her mother's appearance. Suzie giggled. *I guess she doesn't like Daddy very much.* Suzie applied her lipstick, smiling at herself in the mirror. Mom sold a lot of houses, though. She made enough money that they didn't really need Daddy's money. All those fancy homes, with their ocean views and mountain views. Those Hollywood people looking for quiet vacation homes were always happy to work with Mom. After all, she was one of them.

Suzie put down the lipstick and studied herself in the mirror. She pulled her thick, curly hair back exposing her full forehead. Like Lali and her shaved head. She giggled letting her thick hair flop back. Then a pang of regret gripped her. It's terrible what happened to Lali! Now she's pregnant and in a coma! The wheels and gears of her mind turned slowly into even darker, more secret places, where old hurts waited to surface. *I was pregnant once. But I killed it.*

The tears spilled from her sparkling eyes transforming her reflection into a sloppy watercolor portrait. She left the mirror and sat down on the bed, sobbing quietly. *Why did I let him do it to me?* That Teddy Logan! *I didn't even know what he was doing.* Just thirteen years old. And Mom taking me to that doctor, that Dr. Singer! The old wound gnawed at her. Nobody knew, except her mother and the doctor. They all looked at her, they desired her, but nobody saw her, certainly not that part of her, the part that ached. Not even Mom. *She thinks it's the best thing I ever did.* They all saw her hair, her make-up, her sparkling eyes, but they didn't see her, or what she had done. The dark secret that she and her mother never talked about. Her sexual encounter with a seventeen-year-old ne'er-do-well with no law to call it illegal. Just a couple of kids who got into trouble. Nothing to see here. Just go to Dr. Singer and get it taken care of.

Why did people think that was okay? If he were a year older, he would have been in big trouble. The same kind of trouble Daddy was in. Only, he didn't have any money, so there would be no arrangement. *But what about my baby?* He'd be almost ready to start pre-school. Mom didn't even ask me about what to do. She just took me to that Doctor. Teddy Logan, whatever happened to him? He's probably in jail now. He was always in trouble back then. And she had just let it happen. *Why didn't I stop him? I just didn't know.*

Suzie's anger with herself ended her sobbing. She walked to the mirror and shook her head. *Oh, now look at my makeup!* She grabbed a tissue and started wiping around her eyes, then stopped again, noticing her Catholic school uniform. That was why Mom sent her there. *I mean, I like it there, but the boys still…well, I guess they all do.* She wasn't thirteen anymore and she had the pills, so it was okay. Dr. Singer and his pills!

"Now, Suzie," Dr. Singer had said, "just make sure you take the pills in order every day, and no matter how many boys you are with, you won't need to worry about having this done again and you won't have a baby."

"But what if I want a baby?" She had asked innocently.

"You don't want to have a baby until you're much older," her mother had said.

"Suzie," Dr. Singer had said, "if you stop taking the pills and you have intercourse with a boy, you might have a baby. So just take the pills, and everything will be okay."

"But what if I don't have intercourse with a boy?"

"Just take the pills, Suzie!" Mom had snapped. "Stop bothering the doctor with all these questions!"

I'll bet nobody ever made Lali take those pills! She just never did it. And it wasn't like she wasn't pretty, but the boys left her alone. It was like there was something about her that made them behave. *Oh, what am I thinking? She's pregnant now and in a coma.*

Suzie put down the tissue and stared at herself in the mirror. A horrifying reality surfaced and confronted her. Lali was pregnant and in a coma and her father was letting her have her baby. Even though he thought she had been forcibly raped. *And, my mother, my mother made me kill mine.*

Suzie sat back down on her bed, hanging her head and weeping. It was no use trying to fix her makeup.

Suzie goes to see Lali in the hospital. She wanders through the corridors and sees a young mother, who looks as if she is her own age, holding a three-year-old child, just about the age her own child would be. The boy glances up at her and smiles and it is as if she is looking in a mirror at her own blue eyes, his with the same hidden light and sparkle. She smiles back at the boy and notices all the women have children, some holding their infants, some holding hands with toddlers, little girls with their pigtails, little boys running and stomping, generally making a nuisance of themselves. A warmth encompasses her, seeing all these happy children with their parents, some with fathers, some with mothers, all happy and content. She wanders past the hospital nursery and marvels at all the newborns, mostly sleeping quietly, a few crying. Suzie smiles playfully at one baby, who is awake and not crying and the little girl smiles back, seeming to wave her little hand at her. Suzie waves back. Another young woman comes up beside her and asks, "So which one is yours?"

Suzie's eyes widen at the question. She shakes her head and flees back to the corridor, the children everywhere, but a dread knowledge seizes her that none of them are hers. She gasps as she wanders on and finds Lali's room. She expects to find Lali unconscious in her hospital bed, but the bed is empty. The fear leaves her as she marvels that Lali must be all right. She must have come out of the coma. Suzie steps into the room and sees Lali sitting on a chair next to the bed, making faces at her cooing, giggling baby, dipping her back and then up again. Lali looks up and sees Suzie. "Hi Suzie." Lali raises her baby to her shoulder. Then, she tilts her head and half closes an eye. "Where's your baby?"

Suzie woke with a start from her dream, her sweat drenching the sheets. A deep panic and dread gripped her soul. She clutched the sheets with her terrified, if carefully manicured, fingers.

"Where's my baby?" she cried. "Where's my baby?"

After that dream, Suzie resolved to stop seeing boys altogether and stopped taking her birth control pills. If Lali could do it, she could do it! If she didn't have sex with boys, she didn't need the pills. Even Dr. Singer would have to admit that.

But while her plan was sound in theory, she had difficulty in executing it. When boys dared, her natural reaction was still to passively let things happen, starting with Teddy Logan, but continuing with other boys. She wanted to please them, to make them happy, for them to like her, but often, they avoided her afterward, once they had gotten what they wanted. What did they really think of her? They didn't even take the time to get to know her. Dr. Singer had said that as long as she took the pills, it didn't matter and the boys all wanted to, so she did. *But now I'll just tell them I don't do it anymore.*

The boys, however, just didn't seem to get it. It was like they didn't believe her. They got all hurt and offended, or they just kept trying. It was like they didn't think she was allowed to stop doing it. Like there was something wrong with her.

And she found her own desire was stronger than she thought, as was her desire for their approval, or rather, her dread of their disapproval. Suzie began to realize that she was fighting against an inclination she was not fully in control of. And having taken her infertility for granted for so long, she did not fully appreciate the consequence of failure. Why was it so hard for her to just say, "No?" And, why didn't they just leave her alone when she said, "No?" Why did she even want to do it, if she didn't want to have a baby right now? *But I do want to, I just know I don't want to. My God, that just doesn't make any sense?*

"Come on, Suzie, just a kiss?" Jake Turner turned toward her, as he closed the math book. He leaned closer, as they sat at the small desk in her bedroom. The light from the hallway shone through her half-closed bedroom door.

"No, Jake, I don't do that anymore." Suzie pointed back to the math book on the desk in her room while Jake glanced toward her bed. "Besides, you're supposed to be helping me with my algebra."

Jake smiled slyly. "Here, let me help you with your alge-BRA!" His hand slipped around her back, going for the clasp to her bra. Suzie stood up and slipped away and stood by the door. She laughed. "No, Jake, math! You know, numbers."

Jake became sullen. "Yes, I know. You don't like me anymore. I don't need algebra to figure that out!"

Suzie rolled her eyes and sighed. "It's not that I don't like you anymore, Jake. I just don't want to do *that* anymore."

"What do you mean you don't want to do that anymore? Are you seeing someone else?"

"No, I don't want to see anyone for a while."

"For how long? It's been like months!"

"Well, I don't know."

"Well, I don't think I like the sound of that! You used to like kissing me."

"I do, I still do." The dread of his disapproval gnawed at her. "It's just that…"

Jake rose and moved in closer, putting his arms around her, smoothly kicking the door shut. He brushed the long blond, curly hair away from her face, and gazed into her sparkling, blue eyes.

"So, if you like it?"

Suzie sighed. And her experiment in chastity ended.

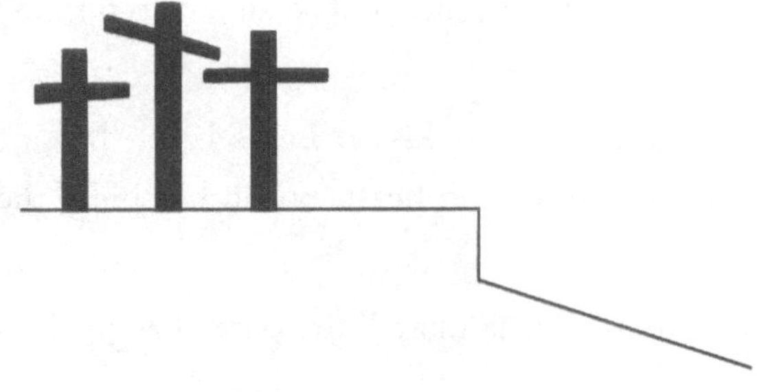

31

Coming To

ROBERT WAITED BY LALI'S BEDSIDE in County General Hospital while Nurse Richards attended to Lali, adjusting the IV line, cleaning the feeding tube, checking her vital signs. Lali let out a groan and stirred. Robert glanced hopefully at her and then the nurse.

"After six months, it's unlikely she'll come out of it."

Any sign of movement was a sign of hope for Robert. He took Lali's hand and raised it to his cheek.

"I think the baby's kicking her." The nurse adjusted something on the monitor. "That's why she's groaning. It would be nice if he kicked hard enough to wake her up."

Robert returned a smile at the nurse and turned his eyes to Rodrigo. The punk came here every day. Robert gritted his teeth and tried to suppress his rage. *Just keep watching him. Maybe he'll slip up. Say something stupid. Let me know for sure..."*

"Such a beautiful girl." Nurse Richards ran her hand along her regrown hair, speaking softly, almost to herself. Lali's hair had grown back considerably, framing her delicate features, her expression serene. "She seems strong, considering."

"Six months and still no change." Robert kissed Lali's hand, her arm limp and lifeless yet warm and soft. He placed her hand on her belly then pulled the bed covers over her.

"Well, at least it looks like the baby is okay." Rodrigo shrugged and smiled.

Robert gritted his teeth and glared at Rodrigo. *If only I knew for sure!*

Rodrigo took a deep breath, lowered his head then glanced at Lali. Her features had darkened, it seemed. A pained anxiety erupted on her face, as she rolled her head a little to the left.

Robert looked hopefully at the nurse.

"She's been moving like that for a while." The nurse shaking her head. "It's a hopeful sign, but I wouldn't be too hopeful unless we see it increase."

Robert's eyes returned to Rodrigo, who sat in a chair on the opposite side of the bed. If only he could be certain. He wouldn't do anything until he had more to go on. If the punk would just say something. Not just some stupid crack about how the baby was okay. Something incriminating. *Just give me a reason!*

Rodrigo stood up. "Uh, well, I'm going to stop down at the cafeteria for lunch."

Robert narrowed his eyes at Rodrigo. One day, he was going to slip, one day… "Yes, I think it would be good for me to spend a little time alone with my daughter." Robert continued to glare at Rodrigo. Rodrigo walked out of the room, his shoulders slightly hunched, looking like a dog who had lost a fight. If he had a tail, it would be between his legs.

"You know, you're being pretty hard on him," Nurse Richards said. "He's been visiting here almost every day."

"He raped my daughter and left her for dead." Robert seethed with a rage that no smooth talk from a nurse could assuage. "I don't think he can win me over by visiting her in the hospital."

"You don't know that, though."

"Oh, I know it, I just can't prove it. If only she would come out of it and let us know what happened!"

"It's been over six months," Nurse Richards said. "It would truly be a miracle if she came out of it now."

Robert gazed at his beautiful little girl, sleeping calmly on the hospital bed, so small and lonely. A sadness seemed to have taken hold of her as if she were dreaming of an old friend's funeral. Or was it his own hopelessness that made her look that way?

"Lali always believed in miracles." He remembered when he had believed in miracles. But those days were long gone.

✝✝✝

Lali looks up at the grieving woman who holds her small five-year-old hand gently in Hers as She walks along following His steps, grieving, yet beautiful beneath Her strangely familiar Semitic garb. Her long, dark hair juts out from beneath the cowl covering Her head, Her sad dark eyes heavy with tears. The coarse material from Her robe gently scrapes Lali's hand as they slowly walk. Lali knows Her to be her Mother, but not the mother who bore her, the Mother who protected her all those years when her birth mother was unable to, the Mother whose visage was on the medal Lali wore on a chain around her neck, the Mother who had wept, lying on the floor when she was brutally raped. The Mother who had failed to protect her in her time of greatest need.

She was there. She saw it all. And did nothing. Lali remembers questioning how that could be, as she saw the glint of the medal on the floor of the cabin.

Had She really abandoned me? Or had She been there all along? But She didn't do anything. And here She is again now, holding her hand as they both walk, watching an even greater crime unfold, the Son of God, Her Son, carry His awful burden, the burden of all our sins, through the streets of Jerusalem. *And what can we do?* Nothing.

Little Lali sobs, as she walks with this mother onward, bearing the jeers of the crowd, staying as close to Jesus as they can. And now, a group of women awaits Jesus coming with the cross. They are weeping, weeping for the beaten and bloody form of a man, so marred as to be almost unrecognizable, the one they had hoped would be their redeemer. Holding their little ones close, hoping to protect them from the horror before them, they weep.

"Daughters of Jerusalem. Do not weep for me; weep instead for yourselves." Jesus looks directly at Lali, His blue eyes pierce her heart like a sword. "And for your children. For if these things are done when the wood is green, what will happen when it is dry?"

A tear falls from Lali's eye, making little impact on the dry dust of the road. *I thought only of myself. I asked, "Where is He? Why doesn't He protect me?" He isn't asking for help. He's thinking of me!*

"My poor, poor, Jesus!" Lali's small voice cracks with grief.

The Blessed Mother holding Lali's hand, gazes at her with a sad, consoling smile. A tear falls from Her chin into the dust. Her Mother, She lays aside Her own grief for a brief moment to give comfort to Lali, Her child. They continue their walk with Jesus, up the hill. The dry dust kicked up from the road mixes with their tears and forms tracks down their faces. They watch as Jesus staggers and falls.

"My poor, poor Jesus." Lali's only comfort the warm, gentle hand of the Mother beside her. She squeezes her hand affectionately. Three times, He falls. Then He gets up and walks on, carrying the wood on which He will be crucified. And with each fall, Lali says, "My poor, poor Jesus."

At the top of the hill, they watch as the executioners strip Jesus of His garments. His scourged and battered flesh clings to the fabric, as they roughly tear the clothes from His body, opening the wounds once again.

"My poor, poor Jesus," Lali whispers. Another tear falls, swallowed in the sea of dust on the road. They watch the soldiers drive the nails into His hands and then His feet, piercing His flesh. The merciless sound of the hammer rings out over the groans of the God-man bearing the burden of sin, laying down His life willingly for the love of mankind.

"My poor, poor Jesus." Lali turns her head away, as the final blows of the hammer nail her Savior to the cross, unable to watch, lest He might look at her again and see her weakness. *How I despaired in my suffering but how much worse was His, yet He accepted it willingly.* Who is there to stop this? No one.

The soldiers strain and grunt as they raise the cross, the wooden thud of it falling into place as vivid as the sound of her body as it hit the floor, the sign atop the cross, "Jesus of Nazareth, King of the Jews," in mocking tribute.

"My God, my God," Jesus gasps for another breath. "Why have you forsaken me?"

He felt abandoned. Like me! Oh, my Jesus! My poor, poor Jesus!

Lali sobs uncontrollably now, her little body heaving as she weeps. The hand she feels on her shoulder, her Mother's hand, His Mother's hand, warm and tender, love in the sadness, hope in despair. A gentle hand raises her chin and she sees her Mother through her tears.

"Do not cry, Lali." Her sad, comforting smile like an embrace. "You know this must be."

"My poor, poor Jesus." Lali chokes out the words between sobs.

"He was with you through it all, just as you are here with Him now through it all. And, I... I was with each of you the whole time at the cross."

Lali looks up through the blur of her tears at Her Mother, smiling sadly through Her own tears. "Jesus' suffering is not in vain. You know this. Nor is your suffering. Your faith will be rewarded."

Lali feels the Blessed Mother's arms wrap around her like a warm blanket. "My poor, poor Jesus," Lali whispers in her ear.

As dusk approaches, Lali opens her eyes and glimpses the soldiers coming, dragging His lifeless body, the red of His blood a swirl in her tears. They place His beaten, bloody body across her Mother's lap, His Mother's lap. The Blessed Mother lifts her gaze toward the heavens in grief as if She is offering Her son to the Father in heaven as a sacrifice. And, for a moment, Lali sees her own broken and battered body, lain across this Mother's lap. Then, a dizzying swirl and she is back in the cabin where it all happened and sees her full-grown self, sitting despondently on the couch scanning the floor, searching desperately for her Miraculous Medal and spying the glint, pondering, could it be a tear? Little Lali finds it glimmering now on the floor with more light than could possibly be reflected in the dimly-lit cabin. She rushes toward it, leaving her older self to her searching grief, and bends to pick it up as it lies still tarnished, yet sparkling, in a pool of tears.

"It was a tear!" she gasps aloud. "She *was* with me the whole time!" Lali snatches up the medal and holds it to her heart as the world spins and swirls again, and in the swirl, she sees Them, standing together, hand in hand. The Mother of God and Her Child weeping, swirling, spinning.

Then she is at her earthly mother's bedside where her mother lies frail and dying. "Take my medal, my little Lali." Her frail voice is no louder than a whisper. "Always remember, you have a Mother in heaven who loves you and who will be with you always, even if I'm not able to."

And then, the same soft, gentle, consoling smile, as her mother puts aside the grief of her own pain and imminent passing to comfort her child. Lali places the tarnished medal around her little neck, the medal she never dared to polish, lest something of her mother be scrubbed away and lost. She holds her mother's lifeless hand in her own small hands and traces a circle around her palm. Lifting her head to her grieving father, she says, "Mommy's with Jesus now."

Another dizzying swirl and she is again with His Mother, her Mother, the Lord of Lords lying bloody across Her lap. She gazes heavenward, a glimmering about Her, the same impossible reflection of light as from the medal in the cabin. Lali, transfixed by the awesome, solemn beauty of her Mother's grief and humble submission, holds the medal to her heart, the broken chain restored. She lets it go to dangle on her chest, shielding her eyes against the shimmering light surrounding the blessed scene. As the light fades, the sword pierces her heart again as Lali shares for a moment the full measure of this Mother's sorrows and her soul staggers with the certainty.

He was with me through it all, as I am with Him now, and She, She was with each of us, at the cross of our suffering.

Lali dares to approach her Mother, His mother, and the body of the Son of God. She takes Jesus' bloody, wounded hand in her little hands. Overwhelmed with grief and wonder, she traces her finger around the wound.

"My poor, poor Jesus," she whispers.

In her hospital bed, hidden beneath the bed covers the index finger of her right hand, traced a circle on her left palm.

✝✝✝

Robert glanced out the window while Nurse Richards replaced a bag on the IV stand and connected it to the line in Lali's arm. He imagined he heard his daughter, not more than a whisper. A prayer, though, surely it was a prayer. Then a scrambling sound from behind him and he turned from the window to see Nurse Richards drop the IV bag and rush to Lali's bedside, her eyes wide.

"Are you talking, Lali? Are you waking up?" The nurse placed her hands on her shoulders and looked into her half-closed eyes.

Robert rushed to the bedside. Nurse Richards pushed the button for nursing assistance. Another nurse promptly popped her head into the room.

"My poor, poor Jesus." Lali's hoarse voice was barely audible.

"Go get Dr. Smith! I think she's waking up!"

"She's waking up?" Robert gripped the rail to the bed. "My God, she always did believe in miracles!"

"My poor, poor Jesus." Lali moaned.

"Stay calm, Lali!" Nurse Richards reached for her hand beneath the covers and took it in her own. "You're going to be fine! And so is your baby!"

"Baby?" Lali mumbled in groggy confusion.

"Oh, that's right." Nurse Richards raised Lali's hand to her cheek. "You don't even know you're pregnant!"

"Pregnant?" Lali groaned.

Robert could say nothing. Tears of joy streamed down his face. He blinked his eyes, uncertain if it might be a dream. Awe and wonder filled his soul.

The other nurse hurried back with Dr. Smith, whose face was bright with joy.

"It's a miracle, Doctor!" Robert's heart raced. "She's coming out of it."

Lali began to cry.

"Are you crying Lali?" Nurse Richards asked. "Why are you crying? You're going to be all right!"

Robert waited in anticipation for the next words, the validation of the miracle he had hoped for. All his fears forgotten, hope overflowed his heart. Gone was the feeling of failure for allowing her to be harmed. Gone the feeling of impotence in not finding the culprits who had harmed her. Gone were all his fears that his safe haven had been lost, and that the monsters had invaded and won. All was made new and restored. But the wispy fingers of the long shadows that had lain hidden and dormant in the depth of coma and controversy reappeared and choked the life and joy from the wondrous and unexpected realization of all his hope, as if the sufferings of the cross were made known only at the moment of the Resurrection. The cruel reality descended upon him like dirt falling onto a coffin. The words, he had expected might come, but no one wanted to hear.

"I was a virgin." Lali sobbed. "And I was raped."

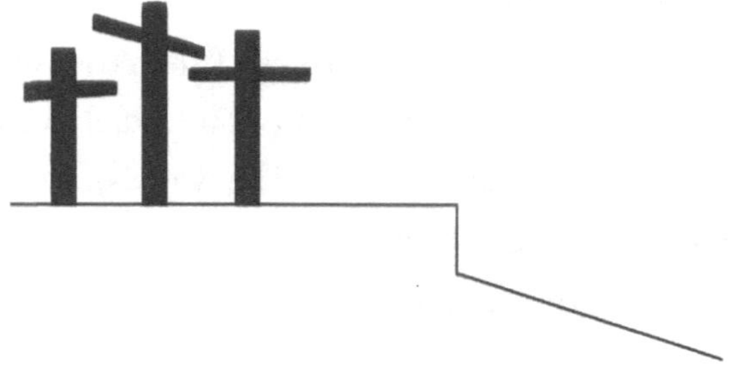

32

Vengeance

THE WORDS TOOK A MOMENT TO REGISTER. The great moment of joy descended into the abyss as quickly as a tear falling to the ground, lost in the drizzle of rain as he stood at his wife's grave. The anger welled up within him, filling him with rage. But that time, it had been God who was responsible and God at whom his anger was directed. What could be done when God was the culprit? This time, however, this time there was a man, or rather a boy, who had done this. This time, there was someone to pay. This time, there was something to do, something that *must* be done.

Robert furrowed his brow with determination. While the other mouths dropped open and hands raised to cover them as the shock of the moment set in, Robert clenched his jaw. He grasped for the service revolver at his side. Yes, it was there. He clicked open the strap that held his sidearm in the holster as he turned around. Exiting the door, his hand ready to draw the gun at any moment, and with deliberate speed and grim determination, he hurried down the hospital corridor. His heart raced, his breath heavy and audible, the din and commotion of the hospital made way for him. He marched past the doctors and nurses with their clipboards and reading glasses. The sound of his own breath, then the creaking of the stairwell door and then his footsteps down the stairs clacking on the hard-tiled floor, the sounds crackled like fire in his enraged mind. Down, down, round and round, he descended the flights of stairs to the main floor. Pulling the door open, he emerged into the hallway like an angel of death spreading his wings on his mission of vengeance. His hand grazed the hilt of his gun. The muttered, unintelligible sounds of the conversations of visitors unable to command his attention, he heard only the sound of his own breathing and his footsteps. Onward, onward, toward the cafeteria, where his prey awaited. Had he not told the fool? Had he not warned him of the consequences? Now it had to be done.

A twinge of guilt pricked Robert's conscience, interrupting the safety of his rage, as the reality of his failure assailed him. He had failed to protect his daughter. He had not stopped her from going to that awful place, confronting those awful people. He had let his innocent be raped. And now? All he could do was deliver justice. *But is it justice?* The voice within him asked. Wasn't he part of a system designed to deliver justice? Was it not his job to deliver the accused to that system of justice as an officer of the law? *But I'm a father first! To protect and serve.* He heard the voice again, louder, *but how does this protect or serve?* The law — no, the law could not be trusted. He'd go to juvenile detention. He'd be out when he's eighteen. What was that, a couple months? An honors student, so much potential. He could hear the bullshit already. And that was if they even believed her! Remember that smug bastard, Allenby? They'd say anything to keep him from justice. *But not from my justice!* What father could trust the law? *I'm a father first! If I love, I must protect.* The voice, not quite his own, interrupted again, *but are you protecting? She's in no danger now. What can you win with a gun?* the voice asked. *But I warned him. I warned him not to harm her! And he raped her! He raped her! He raped my crazy, beautiful girl! Now, I have to...* The voice protested, now a screaming siren, a deafening alarm, *NO, YOU DON'T. YOU DON'T HAVE TO!*

Robert entered the cafeteria. Rodrigo stood in line, various items on the tray he held, the last meal he would never enjoy. The chicken breast sandwich, the french-fries, the soup, chicken with rice, the bottle of water. Robert's eyes widened with rage. No longer Officer Russo, but now Mr. Russo, the father of the victim, face to face with the perpetrator, her rapist, his conscience screaming, "NO!" but ignored, the angel of death unsheathed its sword of justice and spread its wings. Its shadow fell on Rodrigo, her rapist. Mr. Robert Russo, father of Eulalia Russo, the murderer drew his revolver.

✝✝✝

Rodrigo saw the gun. His heart filled with terror. The tray with his intended lunch dropped to the floor. The last words he heard, shouted by the father of the girl he had raped. The girl whose life he had saved. The girl he still loved.

"You did it! You raped her, you bastard!"

✝✝✝

BANG! BANG! BANG! BANG! BANG! BANG! click, click, click, click.

Robert emptied his service revolver into Rodrigo. He collapsed on the floor, the blood pouring from his body into large pools on the hard tiles. Robert fell to his knees on the floor, weeping, the screams of terror, the sounds of flight, the fire alarm someone had pulled, like distant echoes of a dream long forgotten, lost in the mist of his passing rage, the fog of a battle finally ended. The red, the blood, the blood, oozing toward him on the floor. He placed the gun on the floor and slid it away. He looked up at the cashier, a young woman, not much older than Lali, whose mouth gaped open and whose eyes, wide with horror, stared through him into his soul, the soul of a murderer.

"Call the police." Robert allowed his bottom to settle back onto his calves as he knelt, his body curling forward, his arms on the floor.

"It is finished."

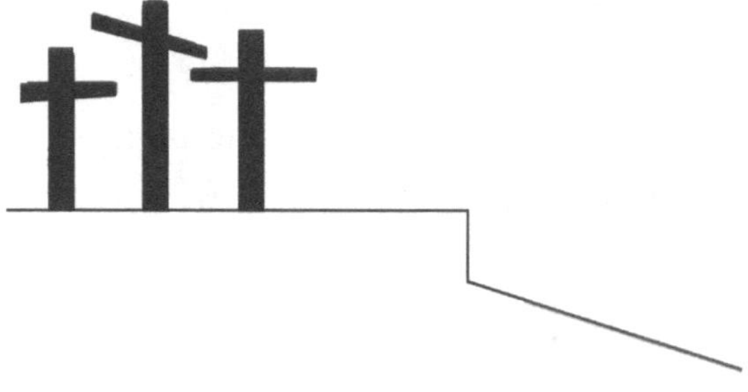

33

Lali's Statement

OFFICER KINCAID ENTERED COUNTY GENERAL Hospital with Chief Greeley, who wanted to get Lali's statement as soon as possible before anyone had a chance to influence her. They had already placed Robert under arrest for murder and taken him into custody. The hospital's active shooter protocol had been in place for a short time, then cleared, as Robert gave himself up willingly. The path now into the future would follow the well-worn trail with few surprises, not many doubted. For now, they had to collect the evidence, take the eyewitness statements, and write the report. Sure, there would be mitigating circumstances in the sentencing, but few doubted that the rather long legal process would yield a conviction. But there were lots of questions for Lali. How she had ended up on that ledge, the biggest one.

They made their way to Lali's room. Chief Greeley wanted to be there for the interrogation. The chief would need to handle the questions from the press, and he expected a lot of media attention. He wanted Officer Kincaid to be there, since he had completed the investigation on the Ralo Rodrigues and Kim Whiting case, and they knew that Lali had been in some altercation with them the day before being found on the ledge. He also thought it wise to have an officer who was a member of a minority, and he hadn't yet hired a Latino. He expected that there would be racial concerns raised by the media, who were already buzzing around the hospital looking for new sensational angles to drive their ratings.

They entered Lali's hospital room. A doctor had just finished examining Lali and removed the stethoscope from her swollen belly. He glanced at them, his eyes above his reading glasses seemed worried with cares other than the physical health of his patient.

"Hi, Lali." Officer Kincaid struggled within himself to find the correct tone. "We would like to get a statement from you, if you are up to it."

The doctor spoke up. "Officers, do we have to do this right now? The girl is pregnant and just came out of a coma after six months. She is still pretty weak, and we don't want to upset her in her condition."

"We just have a couple of questions," Officer Kincaid insisted. The Santa Inés police force didn't get many big media cases, and they couldn't afford a screwup. They wanted to get her statement before any other information tainted her account.

"Where's my father?" Lali seemed to be dazed and unaware of the events in the cafeteria.

"Your father is under arrest for the murder of Rodrigo Alvarez." Officer Kincaid spoke with as little emotion as he could manage.

Lali began to cry. "No, no! Not Rodrigo! Papa, what have you done?" Her words were not much louder than a whisper, but with a poignancy that made them more audible than if they had been shouted.

"Lali, you said you were raped." Chief Greeley's tone rang with confusion. "Was Rodrigo the one who raped you?"

"Yes, he was one of them. But he forced him."

One of them? He forced him? Officer Kincaid exchanged glances with Chief Greeley, who seemed to be trying to form words into a sentence but could not manage it.

Officer Kincaid broke the awkward silence. "Forced him? Who forced him?"

"Ralo." Horror and disdain crinkled Lali's face as though she had just tasted something rancid. "Ralo raped me, then threatened to kill Rodrigo if he didn't. Rodrigo tried to save me. He dropped me on the ledge." Lali's voice faded to a whisper as she looked away into the corner of the room.

"But Rodrigo did rape you?" Chief Greeley rubbed his neck.

"Yes, yes," Lali's eyes darkened, her speech crescendoing as she continued. "He damned himself to save me. And now, Papa too. Ralo, Ralo was evil!" Lali shuddered, squeezing her eyes shut and shaking her head, her entire body tightening in fear and horror.

"Ralo is dead, Lali. He can't hurt you anymore." Officer Kincaid hoped the news would calm her down.

"Dead?" Lali looked confused.

"Yes, looks like he was poisoned by his girlfriend." Officer Kincaid listed the fact in his flat policeman's deadpan.

Lali paused a moment. Her head tilted, and her body began to sway. Her fingers began to tighten on the bedsheets, as though she feared the bed might slide out from under her as her eyes widened with the realization. "Kim? No, not Kim too?"

The policemen traded glances, confused.

"What do you mean, Lali?" Chief Greeley leaned forward on the edge of the bed.

Lali sighed and shook her head, then closed her eyes tightly. Then she looked into the corner of the room, avoiding their eyes, and explained calmly. "Kim agreed to have an abortion because she thought it would save me from Ralo." Lali continued to shake her head, her expression as if she was having trouble holding down her food. Her voice gained volume as she spoke. "But all it did was lose her soul! She damned herself for me! And now, another murder on her soul! To protect me! All this sin to protect me."

Lali's voice had just about reached the level of a shout. She began sobbing violently.

The doctor stepped forward and took Lali's hand. "Officers, we really need to stop this now."

"Yes, yes, of course." Officer Kincaid nodded and glanced toward Chief Greeley.

Officer Kincaid walked toward the door with Chief Greeley, leaving the doctor to console Lali.

"There, there, Lali," Officer Kincaid heard the doctor say as they were leaving the room. "You must try to stay calm. Think of your little baby."

Officer Kincaid trudged down the hall with Chief Greeley, not knowing what exactly to make of Lali's statement. More than one rapist? A man forced to rape a girl? That poor girl, the victim of such horrible crime, grieving for the souls of those who had tried to protect her, but not really for their lives? Damning themselves? Sin, what was all this talk about sin?

Chief Greeley broke the silence. "Do you think we will be held to account for the sins we commit to protect the innocent?"

"My God, I hope not!"

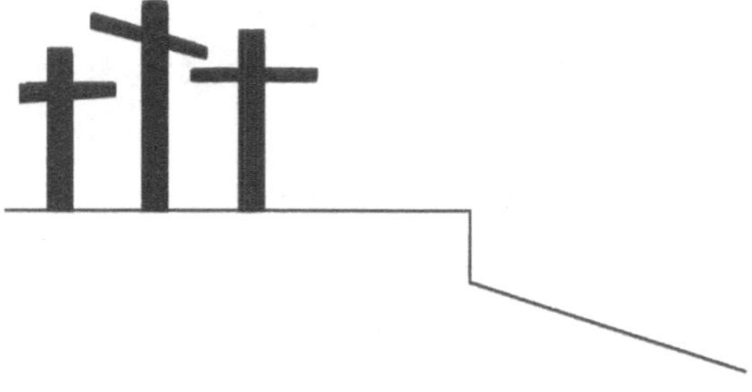

34

Suzie Parks Is Late

THERE COULD BE NO DOUBT ABOUT IT. Suzie was late. How had she let this happen again? Suzie closed her eyes, feeling the weight of dread upon her soul. It was that darn dream! *Where's your baby? Where's your baby?* She just couldn't take it! It was that Lali, lying there in that hospital, raped, having her baby. *And me, I killed mine!* And those dreams, those awful dreams! *Where's your baby? Where's your baby?* She had to do something to be better, but now it was worse! She was knocked-up again. Why had she stopped taking those pills! And it was just that one time with Jake! How could it happen? Why didn't she stop him? She could have just said no. He wouldn't have forced her. *I mean I did say no, but then... Just one slip!* Where's your baby? Where's your baby? *My baby?* Another one! Another one will be thrown in the garbage! Then it will be "where are your *babies!"* *Oh God, no! Please God, no!*

Suzie Parks' ruminations turned into prayer. What her mother would say, what her mother would do, she had little doubt. They would go to Dr. Singer and have it taken care of. *But I can't do it. I can't kill another one! I just can't!* But how could she tell her mother?

Suzie opened the home pregnancy test package. She held her breath and prayed, crossed her fingers and hoped. She peed on the stick. Maybe she wasn't! Maybe she was late for some other reason, not *that* reason? *Maybe? Oh God, please!* And then she waited. And waited. And then she looked. She fell to her knees and wept.

"Suzie? Are you okay, honey?" her mother called up from downstairs.

Suzie caught her breath. *Oh, God, please help me!*

"I'm okay, Mom." She glanced up at the bathroom ceiling. "I'm just… I'm just late is all."

"Late, honey? Late for what?"

Suzie tried to compose herself as she knelt on the bathroom floor. *Oh Jesus, please help me.* "Uh, I'm late, you know, late." Suzie closed her eyes and clenched her fists. She heard the hurried footfalls of her mother as she raced up the steps. She was just outside the door now. *Oh, God, please help me!*

"Uh, oh, you mean you're…" her mother's voice stammered through the door, "*late.*"

Suzie sobbed, her body heaved as she gasped for another breath.

"Oh, honey, you're on the pill," her mother said hopefully. "You can't be pregnant."

Suzie cried louder as her lungs filled in an uncontrolled gasp. *Oh, Holy Mary, help me!* "I stopped…" The air pushed forcefully out of her lungs, then wildly filled them, again. "I stopped taking them."

Suzie heard her mother's audible gasp through the door. Her mother would kill her for stopping! She would never understand! Suzie didn't fully understand, herself. *Why did I stop taking them?*

"Honey, it's okay." Her mother tried to calm her. "We'll go see Dr. Singer, and if you are… uh… if you are, we'll get it taken care of."

Suzie gasped in horror. She knew it was coming, but it was like knowing the shots were coming from a firing squad. That knowledge did not stop their deadly effect. "I can't Mom, I just can't!" Suzie wailed. "I can't do that again!"

There was silence outside the door.

"Baby-doll," her mother finally ended the agony of silence. "Open the door. We need to talk. It's okay."

Suzie wiped her face and opened the door.

Her mother smiled at her, a tentative, nervous smile.

Suzie lowered herself to the floor, then glanced down at the piece of plastic she held in her finely manicured fingers, knowing her mother would follow her eyes.

"I guess you are pretty sure."

Suzie nodded. "I'm so sorry, Mom."

Mom grabbed the box of tissues from the top of the sink and sat down on the floor of the bathroom putting her arm around her. She pulled out one of the tissues and wiped her tears, her eye makeup having run down her face in black trails against her pale skin.

"Baby-doll, if we don't get this taken care of, you're going to have a baby."

"I know." Suzie kept her head down.

"You're too young, honey. You're just too young to have a baby."

Suzie lifted her chin, her heart full of hope, and met her mother's gaze.

"That girl, Lali, she was unconscious, and her father, even though she was raped, he wouldn't let them…you know. And even now, I mean, she was raped and she's still having hers."

Her mother took a deep breath and her eyes narrowed. "So, is that what this is all about? You think you should have a baby because she's having one?"

"No, no, Mama!" Suzie shouted, "I just wanted to be good again. I wanted to be like Lali, you know, like she never does it. And the boys, the boys don't…well, I mean, she was raped!"

Her mother's eyes widened.

"Baby-doll?" Mom's voice filled with concern and anxiety. "Did a boy force you? I mean, were you? Uh?"

"Oh, no, Mama, no!" Suzie widened her eyes. "No, he didn't force me. It's not like that! He just made me want to, and I didn't stop him. That's how it happened. It was just once, just once since I stopped taking the pills. I thought I was being good!" Suzie started crying again. Her mother's arms wrapped around her.

"There, there, Baby-doll. We'll get through this."

Suzie regained her composure after a few moments. *Maybe she'll let me? Maybe, she'll let me keep my baby?* Through the blur of her tears, she snuck a glance sidelong at her mother. "So, can I keep it?"

"Oh, honey." Mom shook her head. "You're just too young. It's a big responsibility and a sacrifice. You won't be able to do a lot of things you may have wanted to do. And what will the boys think of you if you have a baby?"

"What do they think of me now, Mom?" Suzie heard her voice strain with the anger welling up within her as if it were from someone else. *They think I'm a whore.* Susie closed her eyes for a moment. Her mind drifted toward hope. "Maybe if they think of me as a mother, they won't... they won't make me want to, anymore."

Her mother shook her head and sighed. "Oh, Suzie, that will only stop the nice guys, the guys you might really want to be with. The others won't care. It will be hard for you. I just don't want you to make the same mistake I did." Mom gasped, closing her eyes.

The mechanism of Suzie's mind clicked forward like a gear in an ancient torture device. Her eyes widened in shock with the realization. Her mouth fell open. She stared at her mother.

"So, you wish you had... you wish you had... Dr. Singer?" Suzie was unable to put the whole thought together into words, her mouth open with horror at the idea.

Mom closed her eyes. then pulled her close in her arms.

"Oh, Baby-doll, no!" Mom held her for a moment that seemed like an eternity, then pulled back, placing a hand on each of her shoulders, and peered directly into her eyes. "No, I didn't mean it like that! It's just hard to raise a child when you're young and single, is all. But it wasn't a mistake. Never, I don't wish I'd... no, no, it's not like that!"

✝✝✝

Almeda Parks closed her eyes as she recalled sitting on the floor with Suzie, her pregnant weeping daughter. And the horror of the thought, the words that had slipped from her lips, her daughter's sparkling eyes wet with tears, careened about her mind colliding with all her lost dreams of stardom and her sense of the injustice of her coerced motherhood. The ugliness of the idea that had long occupied her mind remained the sole survivor of the psychological maelstrom. *I should have gotten this thing taken care of, but my parents would not let me.*

Almeda looked at the phone receiver she held in her hand, then down at the ad for Dr. Singer's Family Planning Clinic and the number. For years she had resented that her parents had forced her to have her child and made the arrangement with Gavin McCreedy that sent her north to Santa Inéz. The jerk didn't want her hanging around LA where his wife might find out, and demanded she relocate as part of the deal.

She had been too young to have a kid. Her life had been spoiled caring for her child, when she could have been pursuing an acting or modeling career. And, while the ugliness still permeated her idle ruminations, it just wasn't true. Sometime, long ago, the idea had become a dirty lie, repeated only in her own mind, and never aloud. And only now, when her daughter needed her most, the words had irrevocably slipped past her lips.

How could I let myself think that? How could I tell her she was a mistake? If it had been my choice she would have never been born? The irony that an illegal act had produced her child and the prevention of her exercising her legal right had ensured her birth struck her as never before. One law demanded she not be conceived, the other allowed for her not to be born. The law had conspired in every way against Suzie's existence. Her beautiful girl never should have been. Yet, there she was. She put the phone down. *I can't make her do it.* It would be like asking her to abort herself. Almeda took a deep breath and glanced back at the phone. But she's just too young! She picked the phone back up as her eyes widen with a realization. *I'm too young! I'm too young to be a grandmother! Oh, we have to get this taken care of!* Almeda dialed the first three numbers, then stopped and disengaged the phone. *I can't make her do this! Not after I said that!* She dropped the phone on the table again. But, Almeda could not be like her parents, and force her to have the child. She had to let Suzie choose. Know all the options and make an informed choice. Maybe she would choose to get it taken care of? *I can't be a grandmother! I'm only thirty-three years old!*

Almeda picked up the phone and dialed the number for Dr. Singer's Family Planning Clinic. She closed her eyes and took a deep breath as she pressed the last number. *My daughter is pregnant and needs to discuss the options. All* the options. She rehearsed the conversation in her mind. Then Suzie could make an informed decision. As the phone began to ring, Almeda took another deep breath. She could be there for support, but it must be Suzie's choice.

"Dr. Singer's Family Planning. Mrs. Greene speaking. How may I help you?" The voice was not very pleasant but businesslike.

"Hi… uh… this is Almeda Parks." Almeda took another deep breath. "Uh… my daughter is a patient of Dr. Singer's, and she's… uh… at least we think… uh… she's pregnant."

"Would you like an appointment to terminate the pregnancy?"

"Uh, no, no!" Almeda pulled the phone away from her head and looked at the handset in dismay. She returned it to her ear. "Uh… we need to discuss all the options, so she can make a choice."

There was an awkward silence.

"Uh, okay." The voice from the phone sounded tentative and unsure. "But we really only offer one option here for girls that are pregnant."

Almeda closed her eyes and took a deep breath.

"Uh… look, my daughter Suzie, uh… we're pretty sure she is pregnant, but I can't just bring her there for… uh…services… uh… if you know what I mean. We need to discuss all the options, you know. Like having the child, or giving it up for adoption, or… uh… you know, the other thing."

"Ms. Parks," the voice continued after another awkward pause. "We don't really provide other options other than contraception and pregnancy termination here."

What kind of family planning was that? If you considered abortion or contraception the only choice? What if you actually were planning to *have* a family? A level of irritation that she did not really understand welled within her at the answer. Her anger and frustration grew as she replied. "But you call yourself a Family Planning Clinic? And the only options you can provide are family prevention? That's a pretty dirty business."

There was another awkward pause. Finally, the voice answered. "Well, Ms. Parks, I understand this is a trying and emotional time. Why don't we schedule you for an appointment for…uh… Suzie, to just have a consultation with Dr. Singer? We have an opening today at three. He can confirm that she is actually pregnant and make his recommendation. Then you and Suzie can decide what is best." The voice from the phone then hesitated. "You may also want to talk to some people… uh…on the other side, like…uh…maybe the folks at that…uh…place for unwed mothers, oh, what is it called? Oh, yeah, St. Elizabeth's Home. They probably can talk about other options."

Almeda breathed a deep sigh. Suzie would have to decide after considering the options. Almeda was not ready to be a grandmother and her daughter certainly was not ready to be a mother. But she could not force the choice on her daughter. *How could I say she was a mistake right to her face?* "Uh…okay, we'll take the three o'clock. Uh, I'm sorry. It's just really difficult this time. I…uh…just can't ask my daughter to have an abortion again. Not after she found out…"

Almeda let the thought drift off and wished she had not added it. Why was she confiding in the abortion clinic clerk? The whole thing must really have her rattled.

"Oh, so Suzie terminated a pregnancy before?" The voice stammered on, with some surprise evident in the tone. "Dr. Singer usually puts the girls on the pill after they have a procedure. Let me check her chart."

Almeda closed her eyes and held the phone to her ears, not wanting to say anything else, but the doctor would need to know the rest, that Suzie had stopped taking her prescription for oral contraceptives.

"Uh, it says here that Suzie has been taking oral contraceptives." The voice responded with the expected confusion. "So, what happened that makes you think she's pregnant?"

"She stopped taking them."

"Why on earth would she do that if she was still having sex?" The voice rang out with unexpected alarm.

Almeda drew another deep breath.

"Because she wanted to be good again, like that girl in the coma."

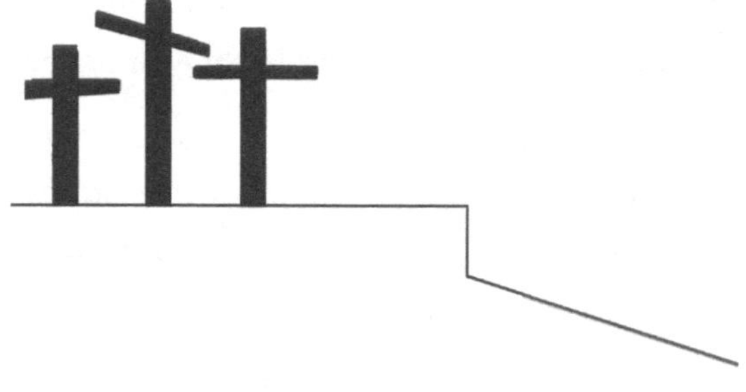

35

Mrs. Greene Finds Her Conscience

As Mrs. Greene hung up the phone, the words rang in her ears, the idea of it filling her mind and convicting her soul. She wanted to be good again? *I want to be good again.* But what did that have to do with stopping your birth control? How could that kid be so stupid? And she'd been through it before? Hoky Finoky! *I want to have the option for an abortion, but I never want to go through one, certainly not twice!* Maybe that was why she had mentioned St. Elizabeth's home? *That's not like me? Not like me at all!* Mrs. Greene's mind raced on as she checked the schedule for the day again, but there were no appointments coming up to distract her. She slammed the appointment book back down on the desk hoping maybe the sound would distract her, or maybe the doctor would hear and poke his head in. Anything, so she did not have to listen to herself. *What's up with me today?* Was it that Kim, what's-her-name? Poisoning her impregnator? Or, maybe it was the girl in a coma having a baby? It was like everything, all of a sudden, had become an extreme situation. Nothing was going as expected.

A churning in her stomach, the same churning that seized her whenever she contemplated being pregnant herself, raised a bilious taste into her mouth. Pregnancy? No danger of that! No siree, Bob or Billy or Buddy! Or Ray? Mrs. Greene sighed. Ray. No chance with Ray, not anymore. Poor Ray! They had planned very well not to have a child. But that's all they did here. They didn't really plan families here, did they? It was like that woman said! They only planned not to have families. It *was* a dirty business. Mrs. Greene swallowed hard, her hand passing over her belly. But what was this sickening feeling? What is this idea that she wanted to be good again? Why did she feel so queasy?

Mrs. Greene stood up and got herself a glass of water, unable to shake the unsettledness in her stomach. She returned to her desk and put her head in her hands. *What is wrong with me?* Her eyes focused on the clock. Another hour-and-a-half before they'd be here to discuss the options. Options? What options? She was pregnant. The only option they offered was an abortion.

Mrs. Greene watched as the minute hand clicked forward. Only an hour and twenty-nine minutes now. Why did she stop taking those pills?

Mrs. Greene was relieved to see Almeda and Suzie enter the clinic seven minutes early for their appointment. She became concerned when she studied Suzie, her arms folded defiantly, looking like an animal being dragged on a leash to a place she did not wish to go. This looked like trouble. Better stick to the procedure.

"May I help you?" Mrs. Greene's eyes darted above her reading glasses between the woman and her daughter.

"Yes, I'm Almeda Parks. I have an appointment scheduled for my daughter for this afternoon."

Mrs. Greene smiled, trying to catch Suzie's eye, but Suzie appeared to be intent on not making eye contact. Mrs. Greene swallowed hard and glanced down at the schedule.

"Yes, I have the appointment here for Susan Parks. Would you please take a seat and the doctor will be right with you?" She glanced again at Suzie, who stood with her arms crossed, eyebrows knit, staring down at the corner of the room. Would Dr. Singer be able to convince this one? She looked like a tough nut. The girl and her mother seated themselves in the waiting room.

Dr. Singer poked his head into the waiting room. "Susan Parks? Step right this way."

Suzie did not respond but sat with her arms crossed.

The mother turned to her. "Suzie, please! We have to have the doctor check. You don't have to do anything else, but we have to get his opinion first. I'll go with you."

The mother turned to Dr. Singer. "It's okay, right, if I go with her?"

"Sure, lots of girls want somebody to be with them."

Suzie let out a huff, stood up, and stomped to the examining room with her mother following.

Mrs. Greene glanced at the clock again and noticed the minute hand had just clicked forward. Did a sudden desire to be good have the side effect of slowing time to a crawl? She waited, watching the second hand on her watch to make sure there were not more than sixty seconds before the minute hand on the desk clock clicked forward again.

✝✝✝

Almeda accompanied Suzie and followed Dr. Singer into the examining room. She noticed Suzie shiver and hold herself more tightly with her folded arms. A sense of cold sterility chilled her as she noticed the metal instruments laid out on a cart next to the examining table. Her daughter stared intensely ahead, tight-lipped, a smoldering anger burned behind the sparkle of her eyes. The doctor ripped off the paper the last patient had sat on, making available fresh paper and motioned to Suzie to sit down on the examining table. Suzie complied, keeping her arms folded, and avoiding eye contact with anyone. Almeda took a deep breath. This would not be easy. But they had to consider this option. She was just too young.

Dr. Singer sat on a stool and rolled toward her looking at her chart. "Okay, Suzie, so, it says here that we had you on an oral contraceptive. Is that correct?"

Suzie avoided eye contact and did not answer.

"Yes, Doctor, that's correct but she stopped taking them a while ago." Almeda answered for her.

Dr. Singer raised his eyebrows and nodded to Almeda. Then he looked back at Suzie, who was staring off at the corner of the room.

"And when exactly did you stop, Suzie?" The doctor glanced at Suzie through the upper lenses of his bifocals.

Suzie finally made eye contact with the doctor, the embers of anger kindling to a small flame. "When Lali turned up pregnant in the hospital and her father refused to force her to have an abortion!"

Dr. Singer rolled backward on his stool. "I see, so you felt if Lali was having a baby, you should have one too?"

Suzie's building anger seemed to flame out from her crystal blue eyes. Almeda winced. She had never seen Suzie like this. Maybe it was a mistake to come here, after all?

"No, doctor. I did not want to have a baby. I wanted to be good like Lali."

Dr. Singer tilted his head and pursed his lips. "Good like Lali? I'm not sure I understand."

Suzie rolled her eyes. "I didn't want to have sex anymore! If I don't do it, I don't need those stupid pills!"

Dr. Singer nodded. "Ah, but then you did do it?"

"Yes."

"And when was that?"

"Just the one time, a couple months ago."

"And so now you think you're pregnant?"

"Yes."

"I see. So, when did you have your last period?"

"About five weeks ago, but it was a little different. I thought it was because I just came off the pill."

Dr. Singer closed his eyes and sighed. "Okay, so, let's take a look. Just lie back and open your blouse so I can move the probe on your belly."

Suzie appeared reluctant to unfold her arms but slowly complied, lifting her blouse and exposing her belly. Dr. Singer rolled over the ultrasound machine.

"This is going to feel a little cold and there will be a little pressure, but it won't hurt at all." The doctor applied the jelly to the probe.

The doctor rolled the probe over Suzie's belly and nodded his head as the unmistakable form of the fetus came into view. Almeda watched Suzie intently. Her eyes widened and began to tear as she watched the monitor. Almeda glanced at the monitor. The little head seemed to nod, and the eyes to blink. The little arms and legs to wave and kick and plead. She glanced back at Suzie, then back to the monitor. She covered her mouth.

"So, that's what it looked like?" Suzie's face filled with horror, her eyes clouded with tears.

Dr. Singer cocked his head, then shrugged slightly. "Yes, that's what it looks like. I'm sorry. I probably should have positioned the monitor where you could not see it if it is upsetting you."

"No, that's what it looked like last time? When you killed it!"

"Suzie!" Almeda was shocked by the ugly assertion and embarrassed for the doctor.

Dr. Singer shut off the machine. "Miss Parks, you are most definitely pregnant. If you no longer want to be pregnant, you don't have to be."

Suzie paused, staring at the doctor, the dark track of a tear running down her left cheek carrying her mascara as it dripped off to the floor. "So, you're asking me if I want you to kill my baby?"

Almeda covered her mouth and glanced at Dr. Singer, who seemed to take it in stride.

"No, Suzie, I'm asking if you want to have a baby. If you don't, you don't have to."

"Where's my baby, Doctor?" Suzie's blue eyes seemed to rip through the doctor like a laser. Almeda watched the tear from Suzie's right eye track down her cheek, her eyes tearing but filled with rage, glaring like blue fire in the snow.

Dr. Singer's head leaned to one side as he fidgeted on his stool, pushing it back a bit, as if attempting to avoid the flaming glare of Suzie's eyes. "Well, Suzie, you don't have a baby. You have a fetus in your uterus."

"No, Doctor, not the baby I'm carrying now. The one you killed four years ago? I need to know where it is."

Dr. Singer's mouth fell open. Almeda watched the drama unfold, covering her mouth with her hand. She never thought about what they did with it afterward. The image of the little person on the sonogram came to life in her mind. Waving her little hands. The crystal blue eyes of the daughter she had been forced to have lit a fire in the depth of her soul. Almeda had had a child like that in her womb and had wanted it gone. Where had she wanted Suzie to go? What *did* they do with it afterward?

The doctor still seemed a little shaken by Suzie's question. "Uh, Suzie, I did not kill your baby. I stopped you from having a baby."

"Yeah, Doctor, you did. But you didn't stop me from having the dreams, the dreams where everybody is asking me, 'Where's your baby? Where's your baby?' So, the only person who knows the answer to that question is you, Doctor, and maybe if you tell me, I won't have these dreams anymore."

Almeda Parks sat with her hand over her mouth, horrified, tears slowly filling and overflowing the reservoirs of her eyes and trickling down her cheeks. Suzie had never mentioned any bad dreams. Had she forced her child to do something that had hurt her psychologically? *I thought you just stopped being pregnant and moved on with your life?* Any remaining doubt that Almeda's parents had made the right decision for her in not allowing her to terminate her pregnancy was gone. *God forgive me for letting them do this to Suzie!*

There was an awkward pause while Dr. Singer considered what to say. "Suzie, you never had a baby. The products of conception of your pregnancy were discarded with the other medical waste."

Almeda gasped in horror. *Medical waste? Suzie?*

Suzie started to cry. "Products of conception? Products of conception? That's what you call my baby? My baby? Where's my baby? Where's My Baby? WHERE'S MY BABY?" Suzie's shout progressed to a bloodcurdling scream. Until at last, she broke down completely and whimpered plaintively, "Where's my baby, Doctor? Where's my baby? Where's my baby?"

Almeda threw her arms around her daughter. "Oh, Baby-doll! What did I let them do to you? My poor baby!"

Almeda glared at Dr. Singer. "You keep away from my daughter, you monster." Venom dripped with each word. Almeda turned to her daughter. "I'm so sorry, Baby-doll! Let's get out of here! You never have to come back here again!"

✝✝✝

As the woman and her daughter stormed through the waiting room and out the door, Mrs. Greene gripped her chair with both hands as if the fury of the storm might rip her out of her seat. She had heard Suzie's terrifying screams of "Where's my baby," something that seemed so unreal to her, like something out of a horror movie.

Dr. Singer was not far behind. He needed someone to talk to. "Holy crap! I've never seen anything like it! She wanted me to tell her where her aborted fetus was? Holy crap!"

Mrs. Greene tried to think of something to say. *Where's my baby?* The words kept ringing in her ears.

"Holy crap!" was all she could manage.

As Mrs. Greene drove home that day, she continued to feel queasy. She tried not to think about the crazy girl who stopped taking her birth control pills and her terrifying screams. Her husband, Mr. Brown, or Ray, as he liked to be called, she focused on him. He should be home when she got there. She chuckled to herself about how she liked to be known as Mrs. Greene, so everybody would know she was married but did not accept her husband's last name. "After all, who would change from Greene to Brown?" she would quip. She had always been so clever. And, poor Ray had always put up with it. Feminism just made everything so complicated.

Mrs. Greene swallowed hard as she turned left, not able to shake the uneasy feeling. Why did Ray put up with her anyway? The things she had made that man do. *If he had asked me to do anything like that, it would have been, adiós muchacho!* Not that she could have ever found anyone better. Oh, the doofuses she had sent packing! Those were experiences, never what she would call a relationship. *No, siree Bob, Jacob, or Justin! Or any of the other ones! Barry! Oh, what a nightmare!* Thank goodness or badness or whatever, she had never gotten knocked up! Thank the doctors for those pills!

The idea of pregnancy made her physically gag as she turned right at the stop sign. *Ugh!* Those women talking about their episiotomies! Her mind had begun to descend to her greatest fear. The little alien growing inside of you, bigger and bigger, until he bursts out, ripping you apart! And the little bastard could kill you! Oh, the doctors slice you to make it more controlled, but, Uh! No! No! NO!

Mrs. Greene slammed on the brakes, almost rear-ending the van in front of her stopped at the light. "Holy crap!" she said, out loud.

But despite the real danger narrowly avoided, her mind returned to her greater fear. Why would anyone do such a thing? No siree! Such interlopers were to be ushered to the door! Thank you, very much! Oh, no! No motherhood for Alice Greene. Out of the question!

Mrs. Greene considered herself to be an intelligent woman, despite her fears and anxieties which were numerous and well beyond merely the fear of childbirth. She developed mechanisms to make the world safer and less chaotic. Process, following the rules, doing what was expected, with no surprises. Make everything happen the way it was supposed to happen, and everything is easier to deal with. But something was happening to her now that was unexpected, and she had no procedure for it. For some reason, she wanted to be good? Whatever that was? And it was making her sick.

Mrs. Greene chose her opinions carefully, most of which were not too far from the conventional wisdom and stuck with them. She was an avid feminist, for example, and an advocate of the pro-choice position. The last thing any woman should be required to do is allow some alien life that has taken up residence inside her to grow and threaten her life. She slowed the car and stopped at the light, glancing over at the young mother holding hands with her five-year-old. *But maybe it's not an alien. Maybe it's a person.* A voice she barely recognized as her own butted in. It really bugged her when Dr. Singer talked about that girl not wanting to kill it and she signed that impregnator's name, Ralo or whatever! What a psycho that guy was! That woman had not chosen to have an abortion! She allowed Dr. Singer to kill her baby because that psycho would have killed her. And he did kill her! That's not a choice!

The light changed, and she started rolling forward again, leaving the mother and child by the side of the road. *Kill her baby? Jiminy Crickets! Did I even think that? Holy crap, we can't be killing babies?*

Mrs. Greene swallowed hard again, making the last turn for home. Well, that girl, the one who was in a coma in the hospital and her father would not let them do an abortion? She sure thought it was a baby! If ever someone should have had an abortion, a girl in a coma who was raped? But even after she woke up, she wouldn't have done it? But if it's a person? And now this girl screaming like she was in a graveyard on Halloween and the corpses were rising or something? *Where's my baby? Where's my baby?* Why in the name of Gracie Allen would she stop taking her pills? She wanted to be good? *I want to be good! Holy crap! I'm the oddball here.* She always knew that. Normal women had children. They had their episiotomies! *Ugh!* But people like her, they could not be forced. *We have the pills! We have, well, what I made Ray do! We can stop it before it starts!*

Mrs. Greene did not see the flashing lights in her rear-view mirror until after she heard the siren. She pulled to the curb, gasping for a breath.

She recognized Officer Kincaid, as he tapped on the window, and Mrs. Greene sheepishly lowered it.

"Good day, Officer. I hope I didn't do anything too bad?"

"License and registration, please." Procedures! He was sticking to procedures! *Why do I still feel sick?*

Mrs. Greene reached into the glove compartment and retrieved the papers, handing them to the police officer, who glanced at them. Then he raised his eyes over the papers.

"You were going forty-seven miles per hour in a thirty-five mile an hour zone." The policeman gazed at her with a level of concern that surprised her. "Are you, okay, uh, Miss?"

"Uh, Mrs., uh…Mrs. Greene."

"Well, Mrs. Greene, you…uh…*look* a little green. Are you okay?"

"Oh, well, yes, I…uh…I'm not feeling well. I just have a short way to go to get home." This couldn't be procedure! What on earth was coming?

"Well, you know, you look a bit like my wife did when we had our first kid."

Shock and horror flashed through her like lightning. Her eyelids pinned open. "Oh, no! Officer, it can't be that! We are doubly careful. Almost foolproof. It's not that!"

Officer Kincaid chuckled. "I meant no offense. Just keep the speed down through here. There are lots of kids in this neighborhood. We don't want any kids getting killed if they wind up in a place they're not supposed to be, like the street, you know."

Mrs. Greene gasped. Why in God's name would he use such confused phrasing! *God's name? I don't believe in God? What's wrong with me?*

"Thank you, Officer, I'll be more careful. Just not feeling well today."

"Okay, Mrs. Greene. I hope you feel better." The policeman handed back her documents.

Mrs. Greene managed an awkward smile as she put the papers back into the glove box. Mrs. Greene took a deep breath and looked at herself in the review mirror. *We don't want any kids getting killed?* Wasn't that what he said? She closed her eyes a moment, then put her car in gear and drove slowly the few blocks to home, watching carefully for children who might be in a place where they were not supposed to be…but there weren't any.

✝✝✝

Mr. Brown, the husband of Mrs. Greene, sensed something was wrong when Mrs. Greene returned home that day.

"Why don't we have any kids?" Mrs. Greene asked, in that accusatory tone that warned Mr. Brown of danger as sure as the rattle of a snake.

"Uh," Mr. Brown stumbled for words. "Uh, maybe because you made me get a vasectomy and you are on the pill just in case that fails. And…uh…the only reason you didn't get your tubes tied was because you are so afraid of surgery?"

Mrs. Greene glared at him. Oh boy, she didn't like that answer…

"No, those are just the tactics for not having children. Why did we try so hard not to have children?"

Mr. Brown knew better than to try to answer that one. So, he redirected. "Uh, why do you think we don't have any children?"

Mrs. Greene smirked. "Because I am a fool and a coward. I made up a bunch of ridiculous reasons like there are too many people in the world already, or having kids would cramp our style, or it's like having an alien living in you, but it's really just that I'm scared out of my wits about it."

Mr. Brown knew better than to agree with her. "You know I love you."

Mrs. Greene laughed. "I gave you the perfect opportunity to just agree that I'm a fool and a coward, and all you have to say is that you love me?"

"Uh, yeah, well, I'm no fool and…uh…perhaps a bit of a coward."

Mrs. Green laughed again. She approached him and put her arms around him. As she pulled back, an odd sight caught him by surprise, something he had rarely witnessed. A tear rolled down Mrs. Greene's face, and he remembered she was Alice, after all, his wife.

Alice sniffled and wiped the tear from her eye. "No, you're not. You're not a fool or a coward. But you must really love me to put up with me. I'm so sorry. I had a tough day. I don't think I can work there anymore. I finally figured it out. We've been killing babies. I just can't do it anymore."

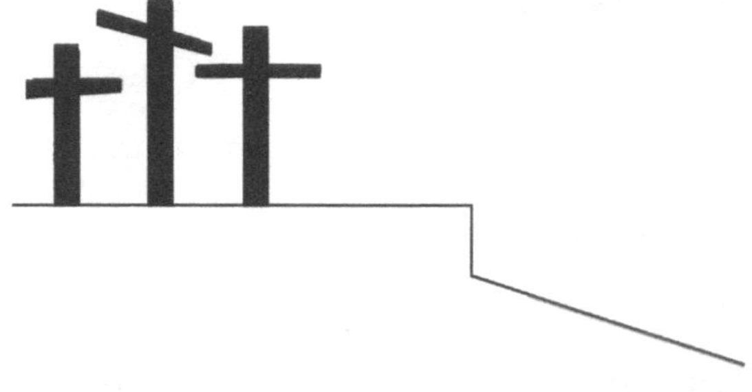

36

Going Home

A COUPLE OF DAYS HAD PASSED SINCE LALI'S unexpected waking from her coma, the revelations of her trials, and the act of vengeance still staining and scarring the hospital cafeteria. She had undergone a battery of tests, and of particular concern, the neurological tests for residual damage from her fractured skull. Dr. Smith entered Lali's hospital room to review the results. Dr. Smith looked over the papers on his clipboard. "Well, my dear girl, it looks like, besides a little weakness from being off your feet so long, you are in near perfect health."

Lali rubbed her swollen belly. "Well, that's good news. And my baby?"

"Oh, yes, your baby too. It really is quite a miracle." The doctor's eyes peered at her over his glasses.

"Thank you, Doctor. Thank you for all the care you gave me, even when things looked really bad."

Dr. Smith smiled sheepishly. "Your father knows you very well. He knew you would want to keep your baby."

Lali stared wistfully across the room at nothing in particular. "Yes, Doctor, he made the right decision for me. But he made the wrong decision for him."

Dr. Smith paused a moment, then smiled. "Well, my girl, I think it's time we send you home!"

"Really?"

Dr. Smith rested his hand on the bed as he leaned forward toward Lali. "Yes, I completed the discharge order this morning, my little miracle girl! You're free to go!"

✝✝✝

Jake Turner had not thought much about Suzie since he had helped her with her math homework. He had moved on to more challenging targets. After all, he was young and could afford to play the field. And Suzie, while she was really pretty, was just too easy. And she never stuck with one guy very long anyway. Not that he was interested in sticking with one girl, no matter how pretty. But the field had turned cold for Jake as he moved down his list of possible dates.

"Well, Jill, if you're not available, you're not available," Jake Turner said into the phone, feigning apathy, but feeling the sting of rejection from a girl he considered beneath him. "It's not like I don't have other options."

Jake aggressively pushed the button ending the call. Jill was the fourth girl he had tried. *Jeez, I thought she would be easy.* And that's when Jake remembered the girl with the sparkling blue eyes and the curly blond hair, who often needed help with her math because, well, she was just not that bright.

I wonder what Suzie's been up to? Jake looked at his cell phone. She was always good for a laugh. Maybe he could help her with her alge-*BRA* again.

Jake chuckled at the clever euphemism he had created. Helping her with her alge-BRA, that was too easy. Jake pushed the button and the phone dialed up Suzie.

"Hi Suzie." Jake smirked in the anonymity of the phone.

"Oh, hello, Jake. I think we need to talk."

"Hey, I'd love to, that's why I'm calling. We haven't talked in a while."

"Yes, Jake, can you meet me tonight at the coffee house, maybe around seven?"

"Sure! Looking forward to it." All too easy! He could always depend on good old Suzie.

Jake waited at counter of the Grindhouse Coffee Place, the popular Santa Inés teen hangout. The place hummed with activity. A folk singer strummed his guitar singing mostly those sappy songs of heartbreak that chicks liked so much. It would be just perfect. He noticed Jill, the girl who had turned him down, at a table with that little nerd, Tommy Slater. Really? *She turned me down for that nothing?* He caught Jill's eye and winked. She glanced away and took Tommy's hand. Jake chuckled to himself. *Wait till she sees me with Suzie.* This should be fun! Good-old Suzie. Algebra? Alge-*BRA!* Too easy!

Suzie stepped into the coffee house. He waved her over to where he sat at the counter. Suzie had her curly, blond hair pulled back in a ponytail and wore a pretty blue print dress with a light white sweater over her shoulders, unbuttoned in the front.

"Hi Suzie." Jake sized her up. "You look…uh…you look good."

She was really dressed down, tonight. Or not really down, like a little girl. She wasn't even wearing makeup? Was she trying not to look good? Jake grinned betraying not the least apprehension.

"Hi Jake." Suzie's smile seemed pensive, almost sad. Unusual for Suzie. "Do you think we can go somewhere more private?"

"Oh, yeah, sure, Suzie." Jake raised his eyebrows. "We can go somewhere more private. I have my car outside?"

Maybe she was into it, after all? Not sure what's up with the little girl act, though.

Suzie grimaced, almost like she was in pain. Probably not into it, after all...

"How about that table over in the corner? I have something I need to talk to you about."

The other patrons sipped their coffee. Their voices an indistinct hum as he walked with her over to the table in the corner. The folk singer sang, "You never really cared for me..." Why would he have to sing that stupid song?

Jake held her chair for her as she sat, and noticed her eyes rolling. The singer finished his song, "I never really cared for you." Jake rolled his eyes. How about something I little more romantic? The singer announced he was going on a break. *Thank God.* Jake took his seat, he made eye contact with Jill again, and smirked. Jill quickly glanced away. Yeah, he was under her skin. Just a matter of time.

"So, what would you like to talk about?" Jake put on an easy smile. *Just let her talk, make sure she thinks you really care about what she's saying.*

Suzie took a deep breath. "I'm pregnant."

Jake cocked his head and scrunched his nose. Did she just say she's *pregnant?*

"Uh, I'm sorry. I'm not sure I heard..."

"I'm pregnant, Jake."

Jake squirmed in his chair. He opened his mouth, but nothing came out.

"It's yours, Jake. You were the only one I was with for months."

"Uh...but, uh...you told me you were on the pill?"

"I stopped taking them. I wasn't going to do it anymore but then you insisted, remember?"

"Uh, but I thought, I thought you were…"

"Yes, I know you did. I'm not blaming you. I should not have let you. I slipped."

"Oh, Suzie, you should have told me."

"I told you I didn't want to, but you insisted."

"But you didn't tell me you stopped taking the pill! I could have used protection."

Suzie rolled her eyes then the blue crystals stabbed him, like shimmering icicles. "That's all you have to say to me? You could have used protection?"

"Well, I could have, if I had known." Jake leaned forward and lowered his voice. "Now you'll have to, uh…"

"Now I'll have to what?" Suzie's tone grew louder.

Jake glanced side to side, not wishing anyone to overhear. "You know, get it taken care of." He lowered his volume, so his voice nearly got lost in the low rumble of noise in the crowded coffee house. "I'll go with you, you know, and pay for it."

Suzie closed her eyes and took a deep breath. She whispered through her teeth. "Jake, I'm not going to kill this baby. This baby is going to be born. You are going to be a father."

Jake's eyes widened. "I'm too young to be a father!" He kept his voice to an intense hushed tone, slightly louder than a whisper.

Suzie rolled her eyes then squeezed them shut like she did not want to see his face. "Jake, if you are old enough to have sexual intercourse, you are old enough to be a father. That's just how it works."

Jake folded his arms and leaned back. "What the fuck do you want from me? You're pregnant? Like, what do you want me to do about it? I'm going to be a father? What the fuck?" He paused, then leaned forward. "I suppose you want me to marry you."

Suzie shook her head and sighed, "Of course I don't want you to marry me!"

"Then why are you even telling me? Just go get it taken care of."

"You're the father, Jake, you would want me to just kill your child without even telling you?"

"Yes, of course, why would I even want to know? Just get rid of it." Jake rolled his eyes and crossed his arms. "Are you trying to trap me? One little hook-up, and now you want me to be father to your kid! What the fuck!"

Suzie closed her eyes. The blue sparkles of light snuffed under determined lids, then opened reflecting the low light of the coffee shop like ice in winter moonlight; the pooling of held-back tears magnified their power. Jake was paralyzed by the strength of her gaze.

"Okay, I'll handle it on my own." Suzie tightened her lips and set her jaw, her voice low and intense. "But I'm having this baby. What you're telling me is that you want nothing to do with your child and that's fine. But it will still be your child. I'm not having an abortion!"

Suzie's voice had gotten loud enough to carry beyond their table in the corner of the coffee house and some of the people at the adjacent tables could probably hear her. The word *abortion* seemed to echo throughout the place. Holy crap! Why didn't she just use a megaphone!

"Shh!" Jake widened his eyes and glanced side to side. "Do you want everybody to know?"

"Yes, Jake, I do. I want everyone to know that I am not having an abortion. That I am not going to kill my baby. I have the right to choose and I'm having my child, your child."

Jake's hands covered his ears without having willed them there, as if his subconscious mind did not want to hear anything she had to say and somehow reasoned that if he did not hear it, no one else would. But it was out there now. Jake put his head in his hands. "It's just not fair."

Suzie's shoulders slumped, and she tilted her head. "Look, Jake, I'm not going to make a big deal about this. It's your child but it's not like I'm going to tell everybody. I'm going to have this baby. I'm considering adoption or something, but I want to know where the baby will be. That's very important to me. I have to make sure I do what is best for this child. You're the father and obviously, you don't care, and you never really cared much for me. I mean, I get it. It wasn't supposed to happen, but it did. Now I have to make sure the baby is okay."

Jake lifted his chin to gaze at Suzie. She had never looked more beautiful but then, she had never really been a person to him before. She was now a beautiful person not just a beautiful girl, so vulnerable, and so determined to do what was right for her child. *My child.* He gasped with fear. *But she's not afraid!* Her blue eyes twinkled as a small, sad smile cracked her lips. "Suzie…" He glanced away, then down at the table. "I'm really sorry. I never should have done it with you that day. You said you didn't want to, and I never even asked you why. I just wanted to change your mind because I wanted to. I'm sorry. I just didn't know. I didn't know you… uh… you had changed."

The warmth and softness of her hand unexpectedly on his, Jake looked up into her sparkling blue eyes, so determined, yet filling with tears. She rolled her eyes, and a tear spilled out and tracked its translucent course down her cheek. "Jake Turner, that is the nicest thing you could have said to me."

Suzie wiped the tear from her eye, then got up from the table and walked away from him and out of the door to the coffee house.

✝✝✝

Lali had not thought much about what it meant to go home until Dr. Smith had discharged her from the hospital and she realized that the place she had called home would no longer be her home. Her father, her provider, her protector, had taken up residence elsewhere, and she had no way to maintain herself in the home he had once provided for her. Her father had gone to a new home, one that she could not share with him.

Lifting her head, Lali stared at the entrance to the county jail where her father would be staying while awaiting his trial. Not a place anyone could call home. Though no one doubted her father had shot and killed Rodrigo, the lawyers could not come to terms on a plea agreement. Her father's lawyer figured there was a pretty good chance of catching a sympathetic juror, considering his war record, history of PTSD, and the fact that he had shot a boy who had raped his daughter. Just one such juror could hang the jury and delay a conviction. That was the leverage the lawyer used to try to get a reduced charge and sentence. But the prosecutor depended heavily on Hispanic votes for his election. A light sentence without a trial would likely be controversial and might alienate his voters, so the lawyers just could not agree. Was her dad an off-duty cop who had gunned down a promising, Hispanic honors student, or a war hero who executed an evil villain who had raped his daughter? A jury would have to decide. If the jury did hang, a plea bargain might be possible with considerably better terms. But few doubted that her father would eventually be found guilty and sentenced.

Lali took a deep breath. Visiting Papa in jail? She had trouble reconciling the idea with a lifetime of experiences with her father. She had not seen her father since he had murdered Rodrigo and only in a groggy haze in the hospital before that. He had been taken directly into custody after the shooting. She remembered him vaguely being there when she had found out that she was pregnant. He had seemed so happy, but then he was gone.

Lali entered the jail. She approached the guard at the reception desk and sighed. "Hi, I would like to visit Robert Russo."

"Name, please."

"Eulalia Russo."

"Relationship to the inmate."

"Daughter."

The guard spoke into the microphone. He glanced at Lali. "We have a Eulalia Russo here, to visit Robert Russo at Station 3."

"Thanks." Lali crossed her arms over her swollen belly, feeling a chill.

The guard tightened his lips together and nodded to Lali. The case had been highly publicized, so everyone was aware of who Lali was and it was a potential press event that she was visiting her father. Fewer people might recognize her full name, and she certainly did not want to gain the attention of any reporters who might be wandering around.

Lali went to Station 3 and met her father across a small table with a plexiglass screen separating them. The once proud police officer, her protector, her father, reduced to this sad figure who sat hunched over the table in his civilian clothes, a flannel shirt and jeans. They would not force him to wear a prison jumpsuit until he was convicted. He did not have to be there. He could have made bail and awaited his trial at home. It seemed as though he wanted to punish himself.

"Hello, Papa." Lali raised her hand and pushed against the plexiglass. Her dad seemed so small, like he'd been deflated. He raised his hand opposite to hers, as if touching through the barrier.

"You look wonderful, Lali!" He glanced at her belly. "I guess it won't be long now."

"No, not too much longer." Lali rubbed her belly.

"You know I was only trying to protect you." Her father stared intensely into her eyes. Lali shivered as a coldness she had never seen in him caught her by surprise. Then, his frustration seemed to build. "How could I know that Rodrigo was not the real culprit? I can't believe I killed the wrong man!"

She shook her head, her lips pressed doubtfully together, remaining calm and serene but sad.

"Oh, Papa." She closed her eyes a moment. "You weren't protecting me." She regained eye contact through the translucent barrier. "Rodrigo wasn't a threat to me, not anymore. You killed him out of vengeance, not for protection. Did you find peace? Did you feel relief?"

Her dad avoided eye contact and clenched his fists. "How could I? I killed the wrong man!"

"Oh, Papa! You had no call to kill anyone! Do you really think it would have done any good to kill Ralo? It would not have changed what he did to me."

"At least I would have killed the right man!" Papa pounded his balled fist into the palm of his other hand. *Lord, have mercy. Help him to see clearly.*

"I know you think you were helping me, but you weren't, not really. And look at you now! You will be going to prison. How will you be able to help me then?"

Papa hung his head low and squeezed his eyes shut. *Lord, help him.* He raised his head and gazed at her sadly, the coldness of his eyes receded, and she recognized the old gentleness and love were still there. "I miss you, Lali."

"I miss you too, Papa. I'll pray for you. Please, Papa, see a priest. Go to confession. It's the only thing that will give you peace."

He clenched his fists and turned away and did not respond. *Lord, have mercy. He's holding onto his anger. Help him to let go.*

Lali waited until he finally returned her gaze. She kissed her hand and pressed it to the plexiglass. Robert did the same.

Lali recalled the sad smile of the Blessed Mother with her at the cross. "You know I love you more than anyone in the world."

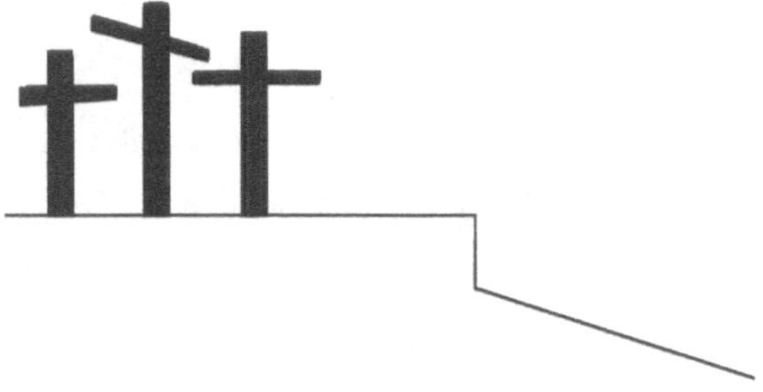

37

New Homes

LALI STOOD WITH HER POSSESSIONS IN A SUITCASE looking at St. Elizabeth's Home For Unwed Mothers. She chuckled to herself and shook her head. *My new home.*

Mrs. Howard greeted her, with a wide grin and animated shake of her head. "Well, Lali, never in a million years would I have expected that you might take up residence here!"

"Thank you, Mrs. Howard." Lali smiled in return. "With my father going to prison, there is really nowhere left for me to go."

"Well, we surely will take good care of you."

Mrs. Howard showed Lali to her room, a small bedroom with a twin bed, a dresser, and a desk, not unlike a room in a college dorm, except for the crib in the corner. An unframed poster taped to the wall next to the bed proclaimed the scripture reading from the Letter to the Philippians meant to reassure, a remnant from a past resident: "I can do all things through Christ who strengthens me." *Not something I will want to take down.* Lali lowered her head. She had hoped that Kim would have taken this room and had her baby here. A shadow seemed to cross Lali's mind as her thoughts turned to Ralo, and what he may have done if Kim had tried to come here. Ralo could be the father of the child in her own womb. She cringed. But Ralo could not hurt them anymore. Lali sighed, thinking of how Kim had sacrificed her soul. Perhaps she could be forgiven for the abortion under such coercion, but murdering Ralo? Of course, God is a God of mercy and compassion. Who can tell the depths of His mercy?

Mrs. Howard broke the silence. "You know, Lali, you really have quite a story to tell. And just seventeen years old!"

Lali wistfully rubbed her belly. "Yes, but first I have to make sure this baby is all right. That's my only priority right now."

✝✝✝

Mrs. Greene and Mr. Brown had an idea, *an inspiration*, Mrs. Greene called it. Her conscience had convicted her of a hard reality, but the circumstances of her conviction pushed her to explore possibilities she had long left unconsidered, having been so racked with fear over the process and possibility of pregnancy. Perhaps there was another way? Perhaps the events that led to her conviction of conscience had provided a way to help someone in a special way. Something she could do to be good in a way few others might be willing to? Maybe she could help the person who had helped her to see an ugly truth that had, in a way, set her free? At least, had set her free of her work at the abortion clinic?

Mrs. Greene stared with trepidation at the door knocker at Suzie Parks' house, then at her husband, Mr. Brown. She took a deep breath and reached out. Then glanced back at her husband.

"You do it." She tilted her head playfully.

Mr. Brown chuckled. "You know, we don't need to do this, if you don't want to."

"No, no. I want to. It's just, like…like…jumping into a pool. The water might be cold. And, well, you know you're going to get all wet."

"So, you want me to throw you into the pool?"

Mrs. Greene laughed. "I would never forgive you if you threw me into the pool. You know that!"

"Yes, I'm no fool. So, if you want to jump in, you're going to have to jump."

Mrs. Greene closed her eyes and took a deep breath. She grabbed the knocker and rapped three times.

Suzie opened the door; the smile left her face when she realized who it was.

"Uh…hi…uh…Suzie, right?" Mrs. Greene stammered.

"Yes, uh, I'm not sure I know your name? Uh, you work at the clinic, right?"

"*Worked* at the clinic." Mrs. Greene tilted her head and squinted a bit, as if the sun were in her eyes. "Past tense. I can't work there anymore. That's kind of what I'd like to talk to you about."

"Oh, really? Why would you want to talk to me?" Suzie raised her eyebrows and exposed the blueness of her eyes with a surprising innocence.

"Well, I think you helped me realize something…uh…important. Do you think we can come in?"

"Oh, yeah, sure." Suzie stepped aside and let them in. "I guess this is your husband?"

"Oh, yes, Suzie, I'm Raymond Brown, and this is my wife, Alice. You may know her as Mrs. Greene."

Suzie shook her head. "I'm sorry. I'm just not getting it. Raymond Brown, wife Alice, Mrs. Greene?"

"Oh, let me explain." Mrs. Greene rolled her eyes. "It's not Ray's fault. It's all me. I'm a feminist, at least I think I am. Anyway, I want everybody to know I'm married but I thought it would be…uh…I don't know, too traditional to take my husband's name, so I kept my maiden name and go by the name Mrs. Greene. But there is no Mr. Greene; there is only Mr. Brown."

Suzie laughed. "I guess that's why I'm not a feminist. It's just too complicated. I guess I like green better than brown, though…oh, uh…sorry Mr. Brown."

"Just call me Ray." Ray grinned.

"Anyway, we—Mr. Brown and I—wanted to talk to you about something, Suzie. I heard what you asked Dr. Singer. 'Where's my baby?' and it really…uh…got to me. I was, like…uh…fooling myself for a long time, thinking, like, we were preventing babies from being born, but I started to see that it was…uh…like we were…uh…well, you know, it was already a baby."

Suzie lowered her gaze.

"Oh, gosh, Suzie, I'm so sorry. I don't want to upset you."

Suzie lifted her head, sighed and pursed her mouth in a smile laying her hand on her belly.

"Oh, it's okay. It's just I've been haunted…"

"I know, I know. Let's not talk about it." Mrs. Greene laid her hand on Suzie's shoulder.

"Thanks," Suzie said.

Mrs. Greene nearly swooned when Suzie raised her sparkling blue eyes to meet hers. "Suzie, you just have the most beautiful eyes!"

Suzie laughed. "Yes, I know, I can't help it. I try not to."

Mrs. Greene laughed. "Oh, you know, I really like you."

Suzie laughed. "Well, Mrs. Greene, my mom will be home soon. Is there something I can help you with?"

Okay, Alice. It's now or never. Out with it. "Well, yes, uh, Suzie, there may be, or maybe we can help you?" Mrs. Greene said, trying to compose herself. "Uh…Mr. Brown and I, well, we can't really have children, so we were wondering if you had thought about adoption for your baby?"

Suzie's face brightened. "Yes." She rubbed her belly. "Uh…I've thought a lot about it. But I don't think I can. I need to know where this baby is and that he's being taken care of properly. If I let my baby be adopted, it's like I lose all contact. I just don't want to have any more of those dreams. You know, 'where's your baby?'"

Mrs. Greene nodded. "I was thinking you might say something like that. But if Mr. Brown and I adopt him, we'll let you see him as much as you want, and you will always know where he is. He'll be right here with us. You can come and see him anytime. Just, it would be better not to tell him for a while that you're his mother until he's older, so that he won't be too confused."

Suzie cocked her head in thought. "You mean, I could just be like a friend of the family or something? And visit and know that he's okay and well-provided for?"

"Yes, that's right," Mr. Brown said, "you can come and check out our place. I make a good living and can provide for him. We want to help you do what is best for your baby and for you. I mean, I know you could provide a good home for him but you're young, and it will be a sacrifice. Well, it will be a sacrifice either way, but we wanted to offer you another option."

"It's good to have options. Can I think about it a while?"

Mrs. Greene laughed. "Please! Sure, think about it. My policy is, don't make any decisions until you think about it. We want you to know that we are here to help you, no matter what you decide."

✝✝✝

Lali stared at the building that had been her home for some months, though she had been barely aware of it. But now she was drawn back to that place where she had lain unconscious, her hair slowly growing back, as the new life grew within her womb, while others debated and opined over what should be the fate of her child. *Our homes here are never so permanent as we think. But in the end, I guess we find our final new home.* Lali would be back here at the hospital soon as a patient to have her baby, hopefully for just a brief visit. She had not realized that she would return so soon to visit someone.

Her friend Daniel was back in the hospital. He had been there a week or so before she had found out, having been admitted the day after she had gotten out. She pushed open the door of the hospital that had been her home for several months and a heaviness weighed in her soul, an added burden well beyond that of the baby she carried in her womb. His prognosis was not good. A sense of foreboding and doom riffled through her as she passed by the cafeteria, the place where her father had gunned down the boy who had loved her and who had raped her, an incongruity of emotions matching the incongruity of the events. And now she went to visit another boy she loved who was dying. She made her way to Daniel's room, her belly swollen with a new, hopeful life as she journeyed to bid farewell to another once hopeful life.

When she arrived at his room, Lali recognized Jake Turner and his friend Ted Strickland visiting at Danny's bedside. The boys who had stolen his hat and had tormented him when she first met him now consoled their former victim as he lay stricken. She waited at the door while they talked with him. Danny looked so frail and small beneath the covers of the bed, his thin skeletal arms lying outside the covers, the IV line attached to his left arm, his face gaunt and pale.

"So, Ted, here, started up a *Bald Beneath Our Hair Club* at school. He's raised a couple thousand dollars for the Cancer Society." Jake proudly motioned toward Ted.

"We felt we needed to do something in your honor, Danny." Ted took Danny's frail hand in his own. "We really didn't know what we were doing when we teased you and all. We're really sorry about that."

"You don't need to apologize again." Danny coughed, his voice soft and weak. "It's been really nice of you guys to visit these last few days."

Lali lingered in the doorway listening to murmurs of the conversation. Ted Strickland? Set up a club to raise money for the Cancer Society? Lali pressed her lips together. He was never one to take the initiative, always following Jake around. Maybe it was a kind of penance? For having teased Danny with Jake?

"We have to get you well again, Danny, so you can join the club!" Jake patted Danny's shoulder. "We'll even let you wear your hat."

Danny laughed. "I'm not sure I'll need one anymore, now that we're all bald beneath our hair."

Jake chuckled, then turned and saw Lali in the doorway. He recognized her with a nod, then turned back to Danny. "You have another visitor, Danny. Ted and I are going to get going and leave you with her, okay?"

Danny tried to smile, but in his weakness, it came off as a grimace. "Okay, Jake. Thanks so much for coming. You guys have really been great."

Jake and Ted waved to Lali as they left, not revealing to Danny who the new visitor was.

Lali stepped to the bedside and took Danny's hand and raised it to her cheek. "Hi, Danny!"

"Lali!" Danny coughed. "Lollipop!"

The two friends laughed together. Lali gazed at Danny, her mouth forming a smile, she imagined the same sad smile the Blessed Mother had given to her in her dream. Danny winced and avoided eye contact. "I'm so...I'm so," Danny gasped for a breath, "sorry, for not coming with you."

Lali choked back the tears. "Oh, Danny, it was wrong for me to ask you to come. You were so weak."

Danny blinked a couple times, then refocused on her. "I'm weaker now."

Lali squeezed his hand. "Be brave, my little Daniel. The lions have nothing on you."

Danny smiled weakly and took another breath. "So glad you are okay. And the baby, don't forget the baby."

Lali put Daniel's hand on her belly, and felt the baby move within her. "Yes, I'm okay, and the baby too."

"I prayed for Kim and her baby, you know, you said." Danny's breathing became more labored.

A tear rolled down Lali's cheek. She could not say anything else. She raised Danny's hand to her lips and kissed it. Then she took Danny's hand in hers and traced a little circle on his palm.

Does it hurt?

Not anymore.

She remembered the answer from her dream.

Daniel died that night, leaving for his eternal home with his family by his bedside. His mother later told Lali his last words which she thought were meant for Lali and her child. But Lali knew better.

"And for the baby, don't forget the baby…"

✝✝✝

The rosary beads swing gently as Lali prays in front of the abortion clinic, her belly swollen with child. She glances up as the tan Chrysler sedan pulls to a stop at the curb in front of her. Her heart races as Ralo exits and thumps around the front of the car, his baseball bat firmly in hand. Her feet merge into the sidewalk as he glowers over her.

"Did ju get the beesness taken care of, little girl?" Ralo glares at her, cocking the bat for a swing.

Lali turns to run, but her feet sink into the sidewalk. Over her shoulder, she glances as the bat swings. The world spins, and in the clinic examining room, she sees Kim, frail and gray, stagger forward. Beyond Kim, the doctor, the curette in his hand drips blood, his face, her father's face.

"I can't believe I killed the wrong baby!" Her father's voice calls, as if from beyond. "It's a common procedure. I do it all the time for girls like you."

"It's my baby!" Lali screams in terror. "It's my baby! You can't kill my baby!"

Lali turns to run, but Ralo grabs her and throws her onto the examining table, pinning her arms down.

"Just who the fauck ju think ju are, keeping that baby?"

Her legs in the stirrups, she cannot move. The doctor, with the bloody curette, draws closer. She turns her head back and forth, struggling to free herself. Her blood flows onto the examining table. Spinning, spinning, spinning...

"No, not my baby! You can't kill my baby!" she screamed, feeling the dampness on the bed, more than sweat. "It's my baby! It's my baby."

"Lali, Lali! You're okay! It's just a dream. They can't hurt you no more."

Someone had hold of her hand. She recognized the voice. Mrs. Howard. St. Elizabeth's Home. Her room. The poster on the wall. The crib in the corner. The spinning stopped. The warm wetness on the bed, like fresh blood from her body. The terrible realization took hold of her.

"The baby! I lost the baby!"

Mrs. Howard cradled her face in her hands. "Lali, you did not lose no baby! Listen to me. It's time. Your water broke, is all. We have to get you to the hospital.

Mrs. Howard drove Lali to the hospital, where she was quickly admitted to the delivery room. Despite the terrifying nightmares which would continue, she had reached the end of her term and had arrived safely at the hospital.

Lali's labor progressed without complication. She found her mind drifting, wondering about the tragic events that had taken her to this point. The father, whichever he was, had been murdered, the grandfather would be going to jail. And the mother had been raped. Family planning? How far from something planned was the origin of this child! Was a child somehow of more value if planned? Would a loveless origin make a child less lovable? And yet she would do everything she could to raise this child, to love this child, despite the suffering she had endured. The suffering was certainly hers and she expected there may be more. Things would not always be easy. And she recalled the passage from the Gospel of John: *When a woman is in travail, she has sorrow, because her hour has come; but when she is delivered of the child, she no longer remembers the anguish, for joy that a child is born into the world.*

And she pondered her travails. Did it matter that they were worse than most?

Sometimes we must suffer...

I will be with you when your time comes...

"Okay, Lali, just one more push!" Dr. Smith said. "Okay, here she comes!"

Squeezing her eyes shut and scrunching up her face, Lali grunted one last time. Dr. Smith raised the crying baby and snipped the umbilical cord. The nurse washed the infant and handed her to Lali.

"A beautiful, healthy baby girl!" The doctor beamed.

Lali, sweating and exhausted, held her child to her breast.

"I'll name her Carmela after my mother." Lali stared off into the empty space of the delivery room, focusing on nothing in particular.

"Would you like us to do a paternity test?" Dr. Smith asked, directly.

Lali shook her head. "What would be the point? I'm the only one left to love this child either way."

"You are one special girl, Lali Russo."

Lali brought her child from the hospital to her new home at St. Elizabeth's Home for Unwed Mothers and placed her baby in a crib in the nursery. A new home for a new life. *Thank God for this place.* Sandra and Molly smiled at her baby.

"That is one beautiful little baby girl!" Sandra adjusted the covers over the child in the crib.

Molly took Lali's hand and squeezed it. "Just like her mother."

"Thank you so much for your help." Lali turned and hugged them both. "I don't know what I would do without you!"

Lali watched her baby sleeping. She hoped Rodrigo was the father, but she really did not want to know. One thing was certain. This little girl was *her* little girl, no matter who the father was. She remembered what Jesus had said. "Sometimes, we must suffer if we are to save souls." She thought about the souls, of Kim, Rodrigo, and Ralo, now in God's hands. She would not be their judge and prayed to God for mercy. She thought about her father, as well. There was still hope for him. Then she gazed again at her baby sleeping in the crib, who gurgled and turned her head. Surely, here was one soul that had benefited from her suffering, even if no one else had. This little child would never have been born without that suffering. And this little child was innocent. No matter what the father had done. Of course, all mothers suffered in bringing children into the world. Wasn't even the most uncomplicated pregnancy a great sacrifice, a sacrifice yielding the greatest of blessings? Sure, the circumstances of how her child was conceived were horrendous. But this great blessing had come forth from that terrible crime.

Was this what He meant when he said, "Sometimes we must suffer if we are to save souls?" Or was there more?

"So, have you thought about coming with us to the March for Life in Washington?" Sandra asked. "Molly and I are going to tell our stories, but your story is so much more interesting."

Lali cocked her head in thought. "My story is more tragic, you mean."

"Yes, but what a story! People have to hear it," Molly said.

"I think people have heard enough on the news and in the papers," Lali laughed.

"No, Lali, that's not your story, that's their story, what they want to believe."

Lali paused. *Sometimes we must suffer if we are to save souls.* She heard the voice again in her head. "Yes," she nodded with conviction. "I think it is time. I have to let people know the ending."

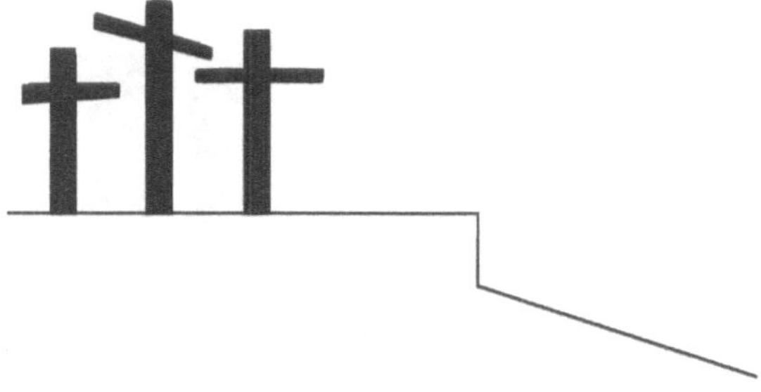

38

The Media Eats Crow

KATHERINE KELLY HAD TRIED TO LAND a follow-up interview with Officer Russo after the shooting incident at the hospital but on the advice of counsel, Robert had declined. There was however, a more important interview to pursue: Lali, the center of a vortex of rape, murder, and vengeance, the mother of her rapist's child, the enigma referred to in the media as the *Coma Girl*, or sometimes, *Coma-Mama*, or *Coma-Mom*. As much as they were trying to be clever, most reporters were too frightened to even attempt an interview with the actual person; the girl who did not want her pregnancy terminated even though she was in a coma and carrying the child of her rapist. The whole thing was just too foreign and incomprehensible. How would they criticize her to her face, this girl they had called a *baby incubator*, now that she clearly was a person and a mother? And, what would they say of her child?

A few of the more intrepid or brazen reporters had approached Lali and had been rebuffed. Katherine had bided her time, just a call here and there to check in, never requesting an interview. Just making sure the girl was all right, waiting for the time when she might be ready to face the media, and tell her story. Enough time having passed, she picked up the phone and called again to check in with Lali.

"Hi, Lali? Katherine Kelly. I just wanted to check and see how you are doing."

"Oh, hi, Katherine," Lali spoke into the phone. "I wanted to thank you again for the baby clothes."

"I thought that outfit was just too cute, and it just wouldn't look so special on any other baby than that beauty of yours. She's just adorable."

Lali laughed. "Yes, she's a cutie. And some people thought she shouldn't be born."

Katherine closed her eyes, knowing she had been one of those foolish people. "She's the cutest baby I've ever seen."

There was a pause on the line, and Katherine kept her fingers crossed as she waited for Lali to speak.

"You know, Katherine, I know you did that interview with my father, and I wanted to thank you for giving him a chance to tell his side of the story."

"It was the right thing to do, Lali."

"Well, I've been thinking. It's about time I tell my side of the story…"

Katherine smiled, pumping her fist.

The Channel 23 News crew set up in the living room of St. Elizabeth's Home for Unwed Mothers. Paul Kruger arranged the lights and this time had another cameraman to manage, ensuring more diverse and better angles of coverage that would be edited together. All the major media were aware of the big feature interview and would be covering it nationally, but it would be Katherine Kelly's production.

Katherine stood with Lali in the living room where the cameras were set to capture Lali in her place on the sofa. Katherine would sit in a chair across from her, separated by the glass coffee table. The camera lights yielded a surreal brightness to the place, almost a heavenly aura, that would only appear on screen as naturally well-lit figures in conversation, the intended effect of the artificial lighting.

"Okay, Lali." Katherine directed her attention to the camera. "We will have a camera here that will be capturing you, and this other one will be on me. Just focus on me, like we're having a nice little chat. It's best if you just forget the cameras are there."

Lali nodded, a slight apprehension seemed buried in her pensive smile.

"Oh, and we have some video clips that we will be showing, which we would like you to respond to, just some things that some of your friends have said about your situation. You can watch them on this monitor right here." Katherine pointed. "The cameramen know what to do, so it will look very natural when you look at the images on the screen. Just try not to let them distract you. If you start staring at the camera, it won't look right."

Lali nodded again. "Okay, Katherine. I trust you. I just feel a little strange."

"You're going to be great!" Katherine placed her hands on Lali's shoulders. "You're going to look really great on TV! Just relax. I'll make sure we get you at your best. Let's get your story out there."

Katherine turned to Paul. "Are we ready? Just let the cameras run on each of us. We'll edit it together later."

"You got it, Boss."

"Okay, guys. Let's start rolling." Katherine stood behind her chair as the camera focused on her.

"This is Katherine Kelly of Channel 23 News. We are onsite here at the St. Elizabeth's Home for Unwed Mothers in Santa Inés, California. We have tonight an exclusive interview with Lali Russo, the girl who was found to be pregnant while in a coma. As has been widely reported, her father allegedly gunned down the boy who allegedly raped her and left her on a ledge just off the Coastal Trail. Since much has been said in the media about the case, and a lot of people have had strong opinions either way, we wanted to bring you the perspective of the girl who actually lived through it all.”

Katherine strolled smoothly around to the front of her chair and seated herself as she continued. “So now let me introduce to you, Lali Russo. Good evening, Lali.”

“Good evening.” Lali nodded.

Katherine allowed Lali to review all her experiences leading up to her being found on the ledge. How Ralo had coerced Kim into having an abortion and then had used concern about Kim’s wellbeing as a ruse to take her to the secluded cabin in the woods. How he had raped her, and she had nearly escaped. How Ralo, to have Rodrigo prove his loyalty, had forced him at gunpoint to rape her. How she must have been hit from behind, as there was a flash, and she lost consciousness. Lali did not remember much after being hit in the back of the head until she awoke in the hospital, except that Rodrigo had said he would try to help her. And, as she understood it, she was found on the ledge where Claire Hennessey had been lost, and she was aware that Rodrigo knew that Mr. Hennessey always walked the trail, and always searched for his daughter there.

“Rodrigo was very clever,” Lali said. “He knew that if he could make Ralo believe I had fallen off the cliff, I would be relatively safe on the ledge, and that Mr. Hennessey would find me there. I believe he was trying to save my life.”

Katherine sat and nodded, guiding her through the story as necessary to make sure everyone understood what had happened. Then she started asking questions about Lali’s opinion of the issues surrounding the case. “So, Lali, when I first started investigating this case, I interviewed a lot of people at St. Mary’s High School, Principal Martinez, some of your teachers, and classmates. Let me show you some samples of what they had to say.”

Katherine showed Lali the clips of the interviews she had captured. Lali smiled, seeing how people viewed her as virtuous and highly doubted that she would have tried to kill herself. Katherine got to the clip of Tommy Slater:

"Well, you're talking about a girl who said she would die before committing a sin, even a small sin to save someone's life. She said this the day of the incident. There's no way that girl tried to kill herself because she would consider it a sin. And there's no way she was sleeping with Rodrigo."

"So, what do you think happened?"

"I think someone raped her and tried to kill her but couldn't go through with it and left it in God's hands. Probably Rodrigo. It can't be easy killing someone like Lali."

"What do you mean by that?"

"Well, she's not afraid to die. And she wouldn't fight back, but she would stand her ground. I mean, that's what she said, what she rehearsed. I argued with her about it, so I know. She said that if someone tried to force her to sin, she would die, and if God let it happen, it would be His will. She wasn't afraid to die. It would be like killing a saint. If there is any good left in you at all, you would have a hard time killing a saint."

Lali laughed, and Katherine stopped the clip.

"So why did that make you laugh, Lali?"

"Well, I never thought of myself as a saint. Tommy is a smart kid and he guessed nearly right, but I think he is exaggerating about the saint stuff. There is something we are all asked to do at the end of Mass. *Go in peace, glorifying the Lord by your life.* I'm always asking myself, *Am I doing it?* Maybe I'm doing better than I thought. But it's just what all Catholics are called to do. I would not call myself a saint. But I did say that about sin. I don't think it makes me a saint, though."

Katherine nodded again. "I'd like to show you one last clip, this one of your friend Daniel."

Lali watched as Daniel's image came up on the monitor. She closed her eyes a moment.

"Lali shaved her head because kids were making fun of me. My hair fell out from chemotherapy."

"So Lali shaved her head in sympathy?"

"Yes. She was the kindest person in the world and brave. She was the only friend I had. I should have gone with her that day, but I was scared. I really miss her."

The cameraman repositioned himself to zoom in on Lali, as she pursed her lips and began to tear up.

"So, that clip really gets to you? It gets to me too." Katherine handed Lali a tissue.

Lali straightened and wiped her tears. "Well, as you probably know, Danny didn't make it. He passed away a week or so after I got out of the hospital. It was unfair of me to ask Danny to come." Lali raised the tissue to her eye, again. "He was very sick and really could not be expected to. I was just scared. I was very shaken by my confrontation the previous day with Ralo. I felt like I might face a very difficult trial and did not want to be alone. But some things you must face alone. They can't be avoided, and there's no one who can come with you."

Katherine paused before continuing. "So, Lali, I'd like to ask you just a couple more questions about what happened to you and what you think of what your father has done. Now, you were raped by two men. Your father suspected that you must have been raped when they found that you were pregnant, and he decided for you that you would not want an abortion. Did he make the right decision for you?"

"Absolutely!" Lali's face lit up. "My baby didn't do anything wrong. She is totally innocent of what these men did to me."

"But doesn't it bother you that the child resulted from you being raped?"

"It bothers me that I was raped. That was a terrible sin. But the child is a child, my child, no matter what sins her father committed. She's the one surely good thing that came out of the horrible things that happened."

"But aren't you reminded of the rape when you look at the child?"

"Let me get my baby and show you." Katherine and the cameraman followed her as she went to the crib and picked up her baby girl in her pink pajamas and showed the baby to Katherine, the cameraman stepping closer, focusing in on the sleepy child. "When I look at this child, I am reminded of the goodness of God, that he can make such beauty come from such a terrible thing."

"But what if you had never come out of it? Then this baby would not have a mother to care for her?"

Lali laughed. "Take another look. This baby would be just as beautiful, even if I was not here to care for her. How would ending this precious little life have helped anything?"

Katherine nodded. "How could anyone argue with that? Now, I wanted to ask you about your father. Your father stood by you and made the right decision for you, but he also allegedly shot and killed Rodrigo Alvarez, one of the men who raped you, even though he was coerced into doing so. How do you feel about that?"

Lali took a deep breath, shifting her baby to her shoulder. "My father will need to answer to God for what he has done. God will be his judge. He thought he was protecting me but at that point, he really wasn't. And, even if he was, it would not excuse his sin. Please pray for my father. Pray for mercy on his soul. Pray that he will repent for what he has done. Pray that he will regain his faith."

Katherine paused. "Well, Lali, we certainly have enjoyed spending time with you this evening and giving you a chance to address some of the things people have been saying. You really are a very special person, and I'm sure I'm joining all our viewers in expressing how sorry I am that you had to go through this terrible ordeal. I'm certain all the people watching this wish you and your daughter well."

"Thank you, Katherine." Lali held up her baby girl to the camera.

The crew packed up their things and life returned to normal at St. Elizabeth's Home. Katherine received a thank-you note from Lali:

> Katherine -
>
> Thanks so much! Something I said to Daniel once: "If you stand tall and unafraid, sometimes you can have an impact."
>
> Thought you would like that!
>
> Lali

Katherine sent Lali a bib for her baby with custom printing: *Stand Tall and Unafraid!*

A sense of accomplishment and validation, a feeling that she had done something she was always meant to do, filled Katherine with a special kind of joy. The major media picked up her interview with Lali and it dominated the debates on the panel shows for some time. Katherine considered it a point of personal achievement that no one ever called Lali *Coma-mama* or *Coma-girl* again.

✝✝✝

Bob O'Malley watched Katherine's interview with delight. The media coverage would follow its usual pattern. The pattern he had ridden for years, making his way to fame and fortune. First, something interesting happened that would get people riled up and taking sides. Then both sides went to extremes to defend what they believed was right, often by mischaracterizing the other side's position. And then some truth came out which might or might not validate one side or the other, but almost always exposed the unfairness and dishonesty of some argument or other. Which led inevitably to Bob O'Malley's favorite part of all in the cycle of coverage that had made his name a household word and attracted millions of viewers to his show: the media's self-recrimination. What Bob O'Malley liked to call, *The Eating of Crow*. And there would be lots of crow to go around this time!

"The Lali Russo story is in the news again," Bob O'Malley said to his producer with a greedy smirk. "Now, we have a father, a cop who would not allow his daughter to have an abortion when she was in a coma, murdering a Hispanic kid who had raped his daughter, and the daughter saying, 'Yeah, sure I was raped, but my dad was right, I want to keep the kid!' And now, she has the kid, and there she is showing off this beautiful child that most people think should never have been born! This story just keeps on giving."

The producer scoffed, "So, you want to bump the story about the guy who killed the endangered kangaroo rat in his garden?"

"What do you think?" O'Malley beamed with glee. "And I have the added delight of having half my panel on record as saying the father was a fool for thinking his daughter was raped in the first place, and he was nuts to think she would want the child! Tonight, we will have some people eating crow!"

The familiar Bob O'Malley Show theme music concluded with its crescendo to a sudden cymbal crash. The usual commentators gathered once again: Jill Kimberly, Colm Allenby, and Whitney Lesley. Mr. O'Malley exultantly ladled out the heaping servings of crow.

"For our next issue, we have the case of Lali Russo, again. Well, it looks like we owe a man an apology." Bob O'Malley stirred his crow stew with delight.

"Lali, if you will remember, was the girl in a coma who was found to be pregnant and her father insisted she must have been raped, and that his daughter would not want an abortion, even if she had been raped. Well, now Lali has come out of the coma and, what do you know, she says she was raped, and she did not want an abortion even though she was raped! Now, some of us had some harsh words for the father at the time. So, what say you, Jill Kimberly?"

Bob O'Malley handed a heaping bowl of crow stew to Jill Kimberly, saving the best portions for Colm Allenby who would be next.

Jill Kimberly was ready and graciously ate a forkful. "I say this is one crazy family, but I have to apologize. The man knows his daughter and did the right thing by her. I can't say I agree with having a child by a rapist, but the girl has the right to choose and the father really did know what her wishes would be. And, I might add, seeing that baby really makes her case. That child is just a doll."

Colm Allenby did not wait for Bob to ladle out another bowl of crow stew. "I agree. I had it all wrong. I might even apologize to the Catholic Church. Though I still believe their teachings on abortion and contraception are all wrong, they did not lead this girl to despair. Quite the opposite, in this case. I watched the interview with Katherine Kelly. One thing is for sure. This girl was not in despair and did not try to kill herself."

A wave of disappointment slid over Bob O'Malley, as Colm Allenby, jumped into his preemptive grovel, with a full mea culpa, even to the Church. He had the clip of Allenby's commentary queued up and ready, if he had tried to defend his previous statements.

Whitney Lesley, sat tall in her chair, seeming to savor the moment. "Well, I was the one who reserved judgment, so I don't think I owe an apology. I will say that it is refreshing to see a young girl like this living up to her beliefs and that I sincerely wish her all the best. Also, we need to watch this reporter, Katherine Kelly. She was able to scoop all the major networks with exclusive interviews both with the father and the girl and to share a story that was completely against the conventional wisdom and that everybody else missed."

"I have to agree with that last point," Bob O'Malley said. "It really is unusual to find that kind of talent in a small, local market news program."

The crow having been consumed and Leslie having taken her victory lap, without too much gloating, the topic turned now to the murder of the reluctant rapist.

"But the story does not end there," Bob O'Malley said. "The father, once he confirmed that his daughter was raped, chased down the ex-boyfriend and shot him six times in the chest, killing him. But, as it turns out, the boyfriend was forced at gunpoint to participate in the girl's rape and was instrumental in arranging for the girl to be found on the ledge and survive. I tell you, this is the craziest case ever. So, now what do we think happens to the father?"

Colm Allenby was quick to jump in. "He's going to jail! You can't take the law into your own hands like that!"

"Well, I'm not so sure," Jill Kimberly, a former prosecutor herself, interjected. "There is such a thing as jury nullification and all he really needs is one sympathetic juror to hang this thing. The guy is a war hero with PTSD, which may also be a factor. And with all the media on this case, it will be difficult to even get an impartial jury."

"I think he should take a plea deal," Whitney Lesley said. "He could serve a few years and get out. He knows the law, and I bet he figured it was worth the risk. I think he might even have been right if he had gotten the right man. The kid he shot would be considered a juvenile and might not have gotten a just sentence if he were convicted of raping another juvenile. That's what happened with the gang leader who was the real culprit. He served time in juvenile detention for killing a kid, pleading the case down to some illegal gun charge and got out when he was eighteen. If you're a father and think the system will not deliver justice, you might feel you have to do something yourself."

"They probably won't agree to a plea, though," Jill Kimberly said. "The guy's a cop and the kid was an honors student. The Hispanic Community would likely look at it as an injustice if he got a light sentence. It really is a sad case."

"Well, I do join our panel in apologizing to Officer Russo," Bob O'Malley said. "He obviously made the right call for his daughter. And while we can sympathize with his motivations in gunning down the boy who raped his daughter, he is going to have to pay the penalty. But the big winner here will, of course, be the press, who will have endless coverage, discussion panels, opining lawyers, and skyrocketing ratings all through the trial."

Bob O'Malley then turned to the camera to plug tomorrow's show. "Coming tomorrow. To Kill A Rat. A man is arrested for killing an endangered kangaroo rat in his garden. Our panel will discuss, but you make the call: endangered species or destructive vermin."

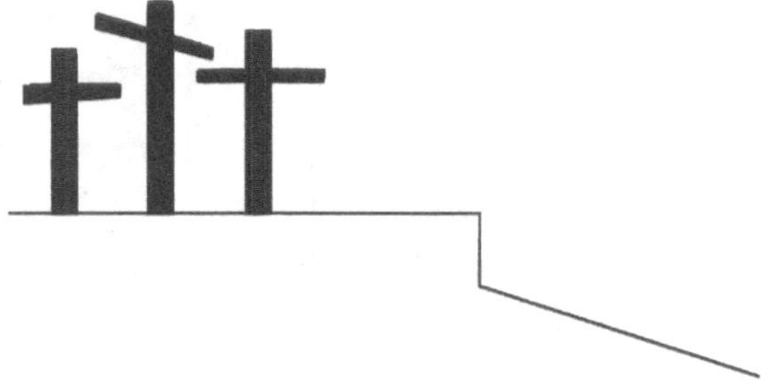

39

Telling Her Story

LALI WAITED HER TURN ON THAT FRIGID Washington day, January 22nd, the anniversary of the Roe vs. Wade decision, the traditional day for the March for Life. She gazed at the child in her arms, so precious, so beautiful, bundled up against the cold, gurgling and smiling up at her. The days ahead would be a struggle. She was still just a young girl with a child, like many other young single girls struggling to care for the children to whom they had had the courage to give life. She noticed the vast crowd gathered for the March, despite the cold. There was life here, and where there was life, there was hope. Her heart swelled with hope and with joy as she listened to the women making speeches talking about abortions they regretted. She realized her own story was something very different and very special, a story of fulfillment, not regret, of the victory of hope and perseverance rather than of loss and redemption. With all the publicity surrounding her story, the March organizers had invited her and a group of others from Santa Inés who had been impacted by her story to speak. Lali anticipated hearing their accounts, as well. She stood up and applauded as Suzie Parks made her way to the microphone.

"Hi, my name is Suzie Parks. I had an abortion when I was just thirteen years old. My mother thought it would be best, and I didn't know enough to object. And I'm not sure if I would have objected even if I were older. I may have made the same decision myself so I'm not blaming my mom. But I had nightmares about that child. I kept having dreams and people kept asking me, 'where's your baby, Suzie?' And I didn't know. I didn't know where my baby was. Then there was this girl in my town who had been raped and was in a coma and her father, God bless him, he wouldn't allow them to do an abortion. And, I was like, she may never even be able to know where her baby is, but her baby will be somewhere. And where was my baby? Gone. I asked the doctor who did the abortion, 'where's my baby,' and he said, 'you never had a baby. The products of conception from your pregnancy were thrown out with the medical waste.'"

The crowd gasped, and Suzie paused. "That's right. That's what he said. I'll never forget that. Products of conception, that's what he called my baby. But I knew. I had a baby and he had killed it. Then when I got pregnant again when I was seventeen, I just could not do it. So, I had the baby, a little baby boy. And this time, a nice couple adopted the baby, and they said I could come see him whenever I want, so I will always know where he is. And you know, I never had that dream again. I know where my baby is, at least this one. Thank you!"

I never knew that story about Suzie. Lali beamed at the child in her own arms as she sat back down. The emcee for the March for Life announced that there would be some special guests who would speak next: former workers from the abortion industry. Lali listened to their stories, some of them talking about harvesting parts of the little bodies for medical research, others talking about how they discovered that they could not continue in the business once they became aware of the reality of what they had been doing. Lali stood again when Mrs. Greene tentatively approached the microphone. Lali tensed as she recalled how Mrs. Greene had threatened to call the police if she did not leave the clinic when she was there with Kim and Ralo. She couldn't believe that she and her husband adopted Suzie's baby.

"Hello, I'm Alice Greene, or…uh…Mrs. Greene, I guess they call me, usually. Well, anyway, I never really cared too much for you people."

The crowd murmured. Mrs. Greene quickly resumed.

"Oh, uh, what I mean is that I'm a feminist, and well, I *was* pro-choice, and we always thought you guys were making us do stuff that we shouldn't be forced to do. Anyway, I was working at an abortion clinic, and I thought I was helping women to exercise their right to choose. But, sometimes, it really wasn't much of a choice. The doctor there, well, he could talk almost anybody into having an abortion. He was very good at it. And, one day, he talked this girl into it, or at least he helped. Really, I think it was that her boyfriend would have literally killed her if she didn't do it. That guy was like a total maniac!"

Mrs. Green stepped back from the mic and took a deep breath, then continued. "Well, anyway, I just started thinking, like that's not what I signed up for. I don't want to help men bully women into having abortions. That's not really a choice. But if you make it so you're never expecting to be pregnant, then you get pregnant, men kind of figure that it's the only choice and they are entitled to it, and that they can force women to do it. Well, this girl, when she signed the consent form, she signed her boyfriend's name, and the doctor didn't even notice it, and just did the abortion anyway. Well, that young lady went home and a day or two later, she…uh…she poisoned her boyfriend, and, well, her boyfriend shot her to death."

Mrs. Greene took another deep breath, trying to compose herself. The crowd murmured in shock. "I'm sorry, it just, well, it gets to me, because that's not what's supposed to happen. We were supposed to be helping women who don't want to be pregnant not to be pregnant. We weren't supposed to be helping men abuse women, and, well, getting people killed. So, I'm like, can I keep doing this?"

Mrs. Greene paused a moment, adjusting her glasses. "And then, there was this girl who would always come to the clinic and pray. And the doctor and I, we thought, well, you know, that's kind of cute because we're atheists. Like, why is she wasting her time? What good is it doing? But she's not really hurting anybody, so, you know, let her pray. But then, this girl ends up pregnant and in the hospital, and she's in a coma and her father says, well, no, uh…sorry, you're not going to terminate her pregnancy, even though he suspects his daughter must have been raped, and I'm like, holy crap, is that for real? Like, it's not just a pregnancy, it's…it's an innocent life to them, even though that has got to be the crappiest way ever to get pregnant! And I'm wondering, you know, maybe that girl was praying for me? But I don't even think I believe in God, so why should it matter, but somehow it does. Now she's in a coma, pregnant, and going to have the child, and maybe she was praying for me? And I'm like, what am I doing here?"

Mrs. Greene stepped back and shook her head. The crowd, seeing her step back began to cheer, then settled down again. "And so, after this, another girl comes in and I can tell, this one wants nothing to do with having an abortion, but I know the doctor, he's going to try to talk her into it. But this girl had one before and she just is not going to go for it, even though she's a teenager and her mom seems to want her to. And she keeps saying, 'I want to be good like that girl in the coma', and I'm thinking, '*I* want to be good!' And then I hear her screaming at the doctor, 'Where's my baby, Where's my baby!' And…uh…well, I guess the doctor couldn't convince her this time because they just hightailed it out of there. And, I'm, like, are we helping people? Or are we causing psychological damage? And is it feminism when we encourage men to abuse women and then pressure them to abort their children? What are we really doing? Are we terminating pregnancies or are we really killing babies?"

Mrs. Greene lowered her head and paused. "So, anyway, I quit my job at the abortion clinic…"

The crowd interrupted Mrs. Greene with loud cheers and applause. She waited until the crowd quieted down then continued. "Well, anyway, I never wanted to have a baby. I'm weird that way. Just the whole idea of it freaks me out. I know, it's weird. That's why I thought, I'd never want to be forced to have one. But I kept thinking, 'I want to be good', you know, I want to help that girl. So, we looked her up, this girl, Suzie, my husband and I, to see if she might be open to adoption and, unlike those adoptions where you never get to see your kid again, we told her she can see him anytime and so she will always know where this baby is. She never has to have bad dreams or any of that about trying to find her baby."

Mrs. Greene turned and found her husband Ray standing behind her holding a baby boy. "Ray, please step forward with me, let them see little Michael, our baby boy. And, Suzie, you too, you're the mom, come on up here."

Ray came forward with the baby, and the crowd started to cheer raucously, then Suzie returned to the stage.

Mrs. Greene continued. "This is little Michael. That means, 'Who is like God?' We thought that would be a great name for him because, you know, who *is* like God? And, like, I didn't even believe in God!"

The crowd erupted in applause as Ray held up the baby for them to see.

And, as she watched, Lali considered all that had happened to her. She reflected on what Jesus had said in her dream, "Sometimes we must suffer if we are to save souls." And she thought about Ralo, and Rodrigo, and Kim, what about their souls? They would now face the most just of judges with terrible sins on their souls, subject to the mercy of God. But who can fathom the depths of God's mercy? Who could know his judgment? Not even God's Church on earth presumed to know when souls were condemned. Her father was in prison, still unrepentant. What about his soul? But then she could see that these people here, they had made something good come from her ordeal. Baby Michael, who is like God, he may not have been here, and Mrs. Greene would likely still be working in the abortion clinic and Suzie, she had changed for the better, so maybe there *were* souls being saved? And even Daniel's suffering had had an impact. Ted Strickland, of all people, had started a club and was raising money for the Cancer Society. And even Jake Turner, though he had not supported Suzie in her pregnancy, visited Daniel and was kind to him in his dying days. Wasn't there some good coming from Danny's suffering? And she wondered about all the people here and how they might remember the stories and tell people in trouble about her, and how, well, one bit of suffering could go a long way! And even Kim's suffering, Kim who had aborted her child and had killed her boyfriend, after suffering terribly, even her suffering, had had a positive impact on Mrs. Greene and Danny, his dying words, a prayer for Kim's unborn child. And she reflected on the Mass dismissal. "Go in peace, glorifying the Lord by your life." *Am I doing it?* Maybe she really was. And she wondered, *Who is like God?*

Lali's mind refocused as the woman ahead of her finished her speech to the cheering crowd. She moved forward, her baby in her arms and peered out over the vast sea of people, all bundled up against the cold but happy and cheering, stretching almost as far as she could see, and there at the end of the reflecting pool, the Washington Memorial, towering over them. So many people! *I don't think you could fit another person on the mall!* Well, here goes…

Lali leaned toward the microphone. "Hi, my name is Lali Russo. We have heard a lot of compelling stories from women who regret their abortions and they are all in my prayers. But I do not regret having an abortion."

The crowd murmured, with people turning to those beside them. Lali gently squeezed her baby and continued. "I do not regret having an abortion because through the grace of God and the faith of my father, I did not have an abortion."

The crowd let out a collective gasp of relief and cheered.

"You see, I was raped by two men, and left for dead with only a small hope that I would survive. I was in a coma for a couple of months before anyone even knew I was pregnant and, even though my father suspected that I had been raped, he knew that I would want to keep this baby."

Lali held up her baby, and the mass of humanity applauded. "And so, my father would not let them perform an abortion. My father knew that this child, however she was conceived, was blameless and innocent just as I was blameless and innocent. You see, I was a virgin when I was raped."

The crowd groaned and hummed. Lali stepped back from the mic and shifted her child to the other arm. She breathed in deeply, then continued. "I was an innocent. And while they could take my virginity by force, they could not take away my innocence. Just as they could have taken the life from this child while I was unable to protect her, but they could never take away her innocence."

The crowd cheered and applauded as Lali held her child up again for everyone to see. "This is my child. I chose to give this child life. I choose to give this child love. I choose to preserve my innocence and to protect and preserve the innocence of my child. And not the men who raped me, nor all the pundits in the media, nor all the demons in hell, no one can take this choice away from me!"

A toddler wandered onto the stage. Lali smiled at the child and at the crowd as the child's mother scrambled to gather him back in. "I'm sure the demons won't get anywhere near that little guy either!" she quipped, and the crowd laughed in thunderous reply. Then Lali became more serious as she continued. "But violence and sin are not weapons that can be wielded to protect the innocent. Rather, only love and faith are fitted for the task. You see, all the people who thought they could protect me through violence or sin, they are all either dead now – may God have mercy on their souls – or, in the case of my father, in jail. And as innocent as I was, who never raised a hand in violence to anyone and kept my trust always in the living God, I am free, and I have friends to help me, and I have this beautiful, innocent, baby girl."

Lali lifted her baby and the crowd erupted in applause. "And I remember in my coma, I dreamed of Jesus carrying the cross, how He met the Daughters of Jerusalem and said to them, 'If these things happen when the wood is green, what will happen when it is dry?' Well, maybe what happened to me is an example of what can happen, though but a small thing compared to His cross. Even so, I know that my suffering was not in vain. I have seen the good coming from these terrible things that I have lived through and I know all too well. These terrible things still haunt me sometimes in the darkness of my sleepless nights. But I have seen the good come from them, nonetheless. The biggest good, this beautiful little girl! Lali held up her baby again, and the crowd cheered wildly. "And I also know that there are great gifts, in this world and the next, for those who keep the faith and persevere and endure the hardships and trials of this life, even in these days, when these things happen, now that the wood is dry."

The crowd cheered and applauded, thunderously. Lali waved and hugged her baby. As the applause began to die down, spinning around with her child, the baby smiled. And, Lali remembered, even when she was just a little girl, how she had always loved to spin.

Author's Notes

WHEN *THE WOOD IS DRY* is entirely fictional, but the reader may be interested in some of the things, real and fictional, that I drew from in its creation. The work was originally envisioned as a screenplay which I had the good fortune to write when I was conveniently between paying jobs in my rather boring but steady work in the data management field. I had recently discovered the works of Graham Greene and had particularly been enamored with his novel *The End of The Affair*. I discovered in this work what I felt may be a kind of literature that was rather uncommon in these days when the wood is dry, so to speak. A work most decidedly written for adults, with very adult themes, but also with very deep religious content that did not openly mock religion, which is how our popular culture often treats religion in adult contexts. I decided that this was the kind of work I would like to attempt; religious, yet not for the whole family, with characters who struggle with faith and evil. At around the same time, I also discovered the Ingmar Bergman film, *Virgin Spring,* which is about a virgin who was brutally raped and murdered and a father taking vengeance. These fictional works clearly influenced *When the Wood Is Dry*. But realities also influenced me in this work. I had been dating a woman, for example, who told me that, as a young girl, she had dreamed of meeting Jesus and tracing her finger over the wound in his hand, much like what occurred in *When the Wood Is Dry*. Also, when on a pilgrimage to Rome, I had heard the account of Saint Agnes, how they had tried to force her into sexual activity before she was martyred, and the more recent saint, Maria Goretti, who was killed when she refused to submit to rape and warned the culprit that he would go to hell, similar to the scene in this current work.

Also of note are certain true testimonies from women who have had abortions telling of dreams where they seek to find their child but cannot, similar to the experience of the Suzie Parks character. And also influencing this work, were the personal stories of women who have been raped, one of whom suggested that she would not let her rapist make her a murderer. This idea impacted my thinking on the Kim character not wishing to become a killer like Ralo, though it is not exactly analogous. There are many true and verifiable stories nearly as compelling as the stories told in this book, though perhaps not so fanciful as a pro-life activist being raped and, in a coma, found to be pregnant. One such story, of a woman adopted as a child and seeking her biological mother, ends with her discovery that her mother had been raped and would have aborted her had abortion been legal at the time. This woman now thanks the pro-life people of her state, who at the time, had passed laws to keep abortion illegal.

I conceived of the town of Santa Inés as an anomaly, and it is so much an anomaly that it likely could not actually exist. The name, Santa Inés, is a bit of a hat-tip to Saint Agnes, which is the English translation. I had written the original screenplay without naming the town, figuring the director would have to find a suitable location, but I don't think there really is one. The idea of a town near the Coastal Trail in Northern California, with full services and a large neo-gothic church, is a complete fiction. I had created a kind of imaginary situation where the characters could walk from their homes to the trail, a trail that would be in a wooded area, with certain locations giving access to see the ocean from a significant elevation. This kind of geography would not be a great location for a town of any significant size to form along the coast. More likely, a town along the coast would be located where the ocean would be accessible, with a breakwater to allow for shipping access. The idea, however, of a place that was an escape for the city folk of Los

Angeles and San Francisco, fleeing the danger and loose morals of such places, and feeling that it was being discovered and infiltrated by drug dealers fits the story well, even if the actual place does not exist. The location problem comes with the idea that a child could fall to a ledge, and be gone when help arrived, as in the story. It is not likely such a place could really exist.

The major difference between a screenplay and a novel is detail. Leaving characters less developed may be required for the sake of fitting the story into a feature length film and is rather common. So, there is a lot more character definition in the current work than in the original screenplay. Since Lali's arc is fairly flat, showing the impact on other characters made sense, given the additional room available in a novel. I expanded many of the characters and included the impact of Lali's suffering on them. For example, the receptionist, Mrs. Greene, is not even named in the original screenplay, and I expanded the characters of Jake Turner, Suzie Parks, and Katherine Kelly a good deal.

Thematically, I played with the idea of the protection of the innocent as a temptation to sin that I encountered in the works of Graham Greene. I haven't read all of Graham Greene's works, but I thought that examining the perspective of the innocent when people are sinning for her protection might be an interesting theme to explore. I also wanted to model a saint-like life on the Lord's passion and be bold and obvious about it. I don't like being subtle when I have something to say. I apologize to anyone who feels a bit clunked over the head by the last chapter, which sledge-hammers home the thematic points by having the characters recapitulate events from their perspectives. I felt it important to show Lali's realization that her suffering was at work in saving souls rather than leaving it to the reader's inference. I thought she deserved explicit validation given all she went through.

I took a bit of dramatic license in the circumstances around Kim's abortion. Large abortion providers would have a separate counselor for the patient who would gain consent and arrange payment before a procedure, so the doctor would not be involved in this task. A large facility would also have a lot more security in place. Also, a normal surgical abortion procedure would likely involve a step to prepare the cervix, which would mean that it is not likely that an abortion would be performed on the first visit to the clinic. This reality could be addressed by changing the circumstances to make this Kim's second visit, but having the event occur on the first visit adds to the dramatic feeling of coldness and alienation. For more information on the technical process of abortions, please see www.abortionprocedures.com.

When I set out to write *When the Wood Is Dry*, I wanted to create a classical tragedy, where most of the main characters die in the end. I added a bit of a joke about that when the Ralo character compares the situation to Shakespeare's Romeo and Juliet and says he likes the ending because everyone dies. I had begun with the working title, *The World, the Flesh, and the Devil,* but I discovered a pretty awful film already in existence with that title. The title would still fit, but *When the Wood Is Dry* seems even more apt, though the original title points to my interest in having the news reports of the incident, the view of the world, be a significant part of the story.

When I described this work to a friend, he suggested that it could be a kind of *Uncle Tom's Cabin* of the Pro-life movement. While any author would be flattered to have his work compared to such an influential classic, there are indeed some similarities. *Uncle Tom,* though our modern world often uses his character as an example of cowardly submission to authority, was a saintly character used as a device to communicate the horrors of slavery to a complacent and tolerant population content to look the other way. The issues of a class of humanity being dehumanized is a parallel, though the dehumanization of the unborn is a degree worse. Dehumanizing a person to property at least maintains a level of value consistent with the value of property. As disturbing as that is, the pre-born human is devalued to the point of being garbage to be thrown out with the medical waste, with no value at all. A more subtle difference, perhaps, is *Uncle Tom's Cabin's* fairly overt appeals to change the state of the laws on slavery. *When the Wood Is Dry,* seldom references the state of the law and does not so overtly make an appeal for its change. While the pro-life perspective is obvious, the focus is on persuasion of the evils of abortion and the damaging effects it has on not only the pre-born child whose life is lost, but on the women who have abortions and on the minds of men in a society where abortion is freely available and actively encouraged as a solution to an unplanned pregnancy. Any law protecting the rights of the pre-born will be difficult to enforce in a society that demands the right to unlimited promiscuity. And, while there may be many voices decrying the evils of abortion, there are far fewer decrying licentious sexuality. Demonstrating that abortion is not a satisfactory solution to the reproductive consequences of sexual activity is but a step in addressing the sickness of a society obsessed with promiscuity as a right, a norm, and almost as a virtue. The root of the problem lies in devaluation of the virtue of chastity where people are convinced of the ability of science to disconnect sexual activity from its reproductive consequences, which science can in fact do, but not without the moral consequences of a degraded society and the dehumanization of the human beings in the womb, a state of being through which all living persons have passed.

My fervent hope is that people will enjoy this work and that the work will have a positive impact on attitudes and beliefs. Perhaps, if we can learn from the suffering of fictional saints, there will be less need for the suffering of actual people. If the world is on a prodigal journey, perhaps a parable will help bring it to its senses? That, at least, is my hope.

Acknowledgments

THE AUTHOR WOULD LIKE TO RECOGNIZE the many people who have supported him in his efforts to make this book a reality. His family, especially the example of his mother, Dolly Cillo, a gentle, prayerful soul who managed to raise seven children, and his father, who provided and cared for his family and provided the proper example of a Catholic man, foremost among them.

Two editors provided indispensable contributions: Heather Flynn who contributed many insights in the developmental stage; and Ellen Page Hrkach for her incredibly thorough copy edit.

Abbey Johnson, of the "And Then There Were None" organization provided some needed feedback on the events occurring within abortion clinics, and the issues facing abortion workers. Her organization may be reached at: abortionworker.com

APPENDIX

Part II Synopsis

I N *WHEN THE WOOD IS DRY, PART II: CRUCIFIXION,* Lali prayed outside the abortion clinic Kim had entered with Ralo. Kim and Ralo came out after the abortion, and Ralo once again threatened her. Lali blames herself for Kim's abortion since she believes that Kim went through with it to protect her. Her father advises that Kim would likely have had the abortion, even if they had never met and may not have thought twice about it.

Dr. Singer, the abortionist, ponders why it had been so difficult to convince Kim to have an abortion, given the circumstances. He discusses with Mrs. Greene that Lali, the girl praying outside the clinic, is trouble for his business.

Lali goes to school the next day, disturbed by the preceding day's events. She tells her father she will once again go to the abortion clinic to pray and then to the unwed mothers' home, thinking it best to maintain her routine, and that the danger from Ralo has passed now that Kim has had the abortion. Lali is moody and sullen and feeling persecuted. She acts out melodramatically in her history class, asserting that she would die rather than sin by telling a lie. Her friend Daniel confronts her over her moodiness, and she tells him about her experience at the abortion clinic. She asks him a third time to go with her to pray at the clinic, but Daniel declines once more.

Lali goes to the abortion clinic and prays. Ralo drives up and in a panic tells her that Kim is suicidal after having the abortion and pleads with her to come help. Lali goes with Ralo to the cabin in the woods, thinking they are going to see Kim. Ralo's ruse works, and he has Lali in his power at the secluded cabin. Ralo rapes Lali, then calls Rodrigo and invites him up to the cabin. Rodrigo comes to the cabin, and while Ralo and Rodrigo are talking at the door, Lali sees a chance to escape through the kitchen window. Outside of the cabin, she runs and hides herself under a bush. Ralo and Rodrigo search for her, and Rodrigo finds her under the bush. She tells Rodrigo that Ralo raped her. Rodrigo tries to keep her hidden from Ralo, but Ralo discovers her under the bush. The three go back into the cabin, with Ralo holding Rodrigo and Lali at gunpoint. As a test of loyalty, Ralo forces Rodrigo to rape Lali.

While Rodrigo is in the bathroom, Ralo hits Lali in the back of the head with a baseball bat. Rodrigo rushes out of the bathroom and advises Ralo that he can't just bury Lali in the backyard with the other bodies, since her father is a police officer, and the police will not stop looking for her if she just disappears. Ralo and Rodrigo take Lali, who is still alive and unconscious, to the cliffs where she likes to walk, planning to stage the scene as if it were a suicide attempt. Rodrigo manages to drop Lali on the ledge where Claire Hennessey was lost, in hopes that Mr. Hennessey will find her there and get help.

Ralo and Rodrigo flee the scene in haste as Mr. Hennessey approaches on the trail. When Mr. Hennessey looks for his daughter on the ledge, he sees Lali, and thinking he has found his long-lost daughter, he runs to Rosie's Dinette to get help. Officer Kincaid investigates the scene with Mr. Hennessey and finds Lali on the ledge. The rescue squad comes and takes Lali to the hospital. Officer Russo, Lali's father, arrives on the scene and asserts that suicide is not likely, and that the scene must be staged, but no one believes him. Officer Russo interviews Rodrigo about the events of the evening, but Rodrigo tells him he has been at home all night and knows nothing about what happened to Lali. Officer Russo goes to the hospital and meets Dr. Okolo, the emergency room doctor, who tells him of Lali's injuries and advises that she is in a coma and may never come out of it.

Ralo and Rodrigo meet at the cabin to discuss the fact that Lali was found on the ledge and alive. Rodrigo tells Ralo that he will keep an eye on her and if she comes out of it, he will finish the job. Ralo goes home to Kim, who he attempts to treat with compassion, given that she has had an abortion. Kim, however, bent on vengeance, poisons Ralo, who in his last breaths, manages to kill Kim.

Officer Kincaid follows the evidence in investigating the crime which leads him to the abortion clinic. He interviews Mrs. Greene about the case and obtains Kim's address. Going to Kim's residence to interview her, he finds Kim and Ralo's bodies and no evidence that would lead to the cabin where the crime was committed.

Dr. Smith, the attending physician on Lali's floor, calls Officer Russo in to discuss Lali's condition. Embarrassed at the oversight, he explains that Lali, still in a coma, is pregnant. Dr. Smith advises that the pregnancy should be terminated. Robert explains that Lali would never want to terminate the pregnancy and refuses to authorize an abortion.

About the Author

J OSEPH C ILLO, J R. WRITES EDGY FICTION in a variety of genres. Whether it's a supernatural thriller like his graphic novel, *Blind Prophet* or a comedy like the 2019 *Illumination Book Award Bronze Medal* winner, *Merry Friggin' Christmas: An Edgy Christmas Comedy*, his work features unexpected plot twists, unique characters, and the highest of stakes.

The added dimension of the supernatural infuses his work with stakes that go beyond life and death, and into the eternal. There is a basic, Catholic moral viewpoint behind his work that gives a solid foundation to what might otherwise be seen as purely fantastical. The reading experience can at times be unnerving, as the reader is drawn to consider whether the mystical nature of his tales is nearer to reality than the plainly material experiences of life. The eternal consequences of choices made by characters and spiritual dimensions of actions made clearly visible are mindbending and thought-provoking.

Joseph Cillo, Jr. classifies his writing as *Edgy Catholic Fiction*. Edgy Catholic Fiction is generally written for adult audiences, at minimum teens and up. The grouping crosses genres and includes a perspective that is generally consistent with the teachings of the Catholic Church, which may include rather dramatic supernatural elements, as in the horror movie, *The Exorcist,* or other less dramatic religious elements, which could be as simple as characters relying on prayer. The religious elements may not be overt and could well lie only in the author's general perspective or a character's perspective that there is a God, and a moral, immutable foundation to the universe.

For more information, please check out www.edgycatholic.com

Examples of Edgy Catholic literature lie strewn throughout genres which no one has grouped together. Literary masters such as *Graham Greene, Flannery O'Connor, J.R.R. Tolkien*, and even, *C.S. Lewis,* who though not Catholic, was consistent with the Catholic perspective in his fiction, wrote works that fall into the Edgy Catholic domain. *Dean Koontz*, whose supernatural and suspense thrillers are written from a Catholic perspective and are quite edgy, is a more contemporary example of an Edgy Catholic author.

Joseph Cillo, Jr. is the fourth of seven children, born within a year of his older sister in a most unplanned and yet welcome way. Having the great blessings of a loving family, however, did not prevent his drift into a sort of foolhardy extended adolescence for many years, broken only by suffering and illness, in a rather miraculous fashion. He now lives a life of quiet prayer and diligent work.

For more on *Blind Prophet*, check out www.blindprophetcomic.com

Resources

I N THE WORDS OF LALI, "No, my sweet girl, I cannot help you do this thing. But if you don't wish to do it, I can help, or I can help you once you have done it."

If you know of anyone who may be distressed by her pregnancy and seeking to explore differing options, or someone struggling with the consequences of having an abortion, here are a few resources to explore:

1) Life Choices - lifechoicesonline.org - Locations in NJ, provides pregnancy counseling, post-abortion counseling, housing and childcare. There are similar organizations in other locations under the Life Choices name, so look them up!

2) Good Counsel Homes - .goodcounselhomes.org - Locations in NY and NJ - "We provide a home and loving care to any pregnant woman in dire need." Also provides post-abortion counseling.

If you know anyone who is working in the abortion industry and would like help transitioning to other work, like Mrs. Greene in our story, check out:

And Then There Were None - abortionworker.com

Also by Joseph Cillo, Jr.

Blind Prophet, Episode 1: A Prophet Is Born

Blind Prophet, Episode 2: Spiritual Warfare

Blind Prophet, Episode 3: The Prophet Goes to Washington

Blind Prophet, Episode 4: The Great Demon of Pride

Blind Prophet, Part I (Includes Episodes 1 thru 4)

Merry Friggin' Christmas: An Edgy Christmas Comedy

Get *Blind Prophet, Episode 1: A Prophet Is Born* for **FREE!**

For details, please visit: **www.edgycatholic.com**